steering wheel repeatedly left and
imprinted tracks in the concrete,
goods vehicles, constantly tried to
As they passed under yet another giant crane, the
occupants were at least thankful that the decrepit car's
heater still worked.

"We need to buy Sammy a bottle of something for this
car," Dave said suddenly.

"For this piece of shit? It smells like an old barn. And I've
got seat springs digging into my arse," replied Gerry
dismissively — a common character trait that grated on
Dave almost daily.

"We almost ended up with the shit-brown minivan that's
been kicking round the motor pool."

"Least I could have had a nap in that thing."

"Not with a busted heater you couldn't."

"This thing blows as much hot air as an asthmatic about
to be admitted to ICU. I'm pretty sure it couldn't be much
worse."

The conversation halted abruptly as Gerry leaned
forward in his seat, straining to see through the
windscreen — a task made harder by the falling snow
reflecting the beams of the headlights in every direction
other than straight ahead.

"I think this is it," he said, though with a hint of
uncertainty. He pointed briefly to his right before once
again trying to fine-tune the direction of the heat coming
from the vents.

Dave didn't reply with words, just a grunt. Driving past
the alley between the two warehouses, he jerked the car to
a halt, shoved the gear selector into reverse, and swung
them into the shadows. It wasn't an ideal location, given
they had just reversed into a bottleneck — a tactically

terrible position if they were to be ambushed. Unfortunately, the instructions had clearly stated where and how they should park. It had taken over six months to set up this meeting, and they weren't about to blow it over something as trivial as a parking spot. Once Dave was sure no part of the car was visible from the dockside, he turned off the ignition — and with it, their only source of heat.

"Why did you do that?" asked Gerry, confused.

"Because if I leave the engine running, the vapour from the exhaust will give away our position," replied Dave. Despite being the junior of the two men, his tone made it clear he didn't appreciate having his judgement questioned.

"I know you're ex-special forces and all that, but who exactly are we hiding from? In case you've forgotten, we're supposed to be here for this meeting. It's not a stakeout or some clandestine hush-hush op."

"Yeah, well, it pays not to take things for granted," said Dave, eyeing his colleague as though expecting him to pull rank.

There was a pause as Gerry held his gaze before allowing a smirk to tug at the corners of his mouth.

"I'm glad to see you've actually been paying attention to my mentoring. Ordinarily, I'd agree, but I'm seeing my lady friend tonight, and I'd really appreciate it — and I'm sure she would too — if my bits were in working order and not ravaged by frostbite. You catch my drift?"

"Okay, okay. Spare me the details," replied Dave as he twisted the key.

The starter motor turned over a few times before the engine finally caught and, somewhat hesitantly, came to life. He jabbed the accelerator pedal a few times to make sure it didn't die on them, and then the two sat in silence.

Baptism by Fire

By

Michael Slater

An Eli Miller story

This is a work of fiction. Names, characters, places, and incidents are products of the author's imagination or are used fictitiously. Any resemblance to actual events, locales, or persons, living or dead, is purely coincidental.

First Edition November 2025

ISBN 9798309784929

To

My wife for letting me indulge my
writing passion

&

AG for pushing me to get this done
and take it to the point that others
get to read it

Prologue

If Gerry and Dave had to choose a day to die, it most likely wouldn't have been this one. Perhaps the sun-drenched spring morning they'd had, but certainly not now. The weather had changed almost without warning, and a cold easterly wind, along with the beginnings of a snowstorm, had quickly made the sunshine a distant memory. Snow swirled around the rusted, faded-yellow legs of the cranes that lined the dockside. Although the cranes were not in use this evening, a row of old, underpowered sodium-vapour security lights fought a losing battle with the elements to illuminate them. As the snow fell, it added to the already eerie atmosphere of the unused machines and the unusually quiet dock.

The warehouses parallel to the waterfront also appeared unused, despite a couple of cargo ships being moored in front of them. Their exteriors were lit only by the lights from the cranes, and the few visible windows showed no signs of life. There were no obvious security patrols or guards, and no evidence of recent activity. For all intents and purposes, the port appeared abandoned — a perfect spot for transactions to take place away from prying eyes.

An old red Camaro gradually made its way along the concrete dock, rocking and creaking as its suspension struggled with the pockmarked surface, better suited to much heavier and newer vehicles. Dave worked the

Dave stared out into the darkness, barely able to see beyond the bonnet, as the snow began to fall more heavily. "If this snow keeps up, we're not going to be making it out of here — never mind back to our normal lives," he muttered. "Do you think these guys are even gonna come out in this weather?"

As Gerry was about to reply, he noticed a flash of light in the distance. His immediate thought was that it must be a boat bobbing on the waves — probably some crazy fisherman heading out early to get a head start on the competition. His ex-wife's family were fishermen up in Maine, and the stories he'd heard from them suggested this was entirely likely. A second flash reinforced the conclusion. What else could it be in this weather?

As he turned to answer Dave, the car suddenly filled with snow, followed by the sensation of warm liquid spraying the left side of his face and neck. The sound of the windscreen cracking and disintegrating seemed to follow a few seconds later. In reality, the events had occurred within a few thousandths of a second.

Almost immediately, his training kicked in as he realised the car was under attack. The flashes weren't from a boat but from a gun, probably a sniper rifle. Two flashes meant two bullets, and one had already ended up in Dave's skull. With his brain about five steps ahead of his body, he knew what he had to do. But before he could go on the defensive, the second bullet struck his right eye, passed through the back of his head, and came to rest somewhere in the rear of the car. His last memory, sight, taste and smell were of the pure, white, crystallised snow as it fell through the space once occupied by the windscreen. His body went limp as he crumpled forward, his head coming to rest with a gentle thud on the dashboard.

Chapter 1

9 8, 99…100. My morning workout was complete. One hundred sit-ups, one hundred push-ups, one hundred burpees. All those YouTube and Instagram body transformation videos had sucked me in. Their results always seemed much better than mine, but it was better than doing nothing. In some ways, it was a good way to start the week, blowing away the Monday cobwebs after a busy weekend.

I quickly checked myself in the bathroom mirror, found a distinct lack of a six-pack despite pulling a few macho poses, and headed for the shower. I'd been doing my workout every morning for the last three months, and while the rest of my body had toned up a bit, my abs seemed oblivious to the daily pain I put them through. After a quick drenching under the rain shower my fiancée had recently installed, I towelled myself off before selecting a royal blue suit and a lightly patterned white shirt from the walk-in wardrobe. Grabbing a pair of cufflinks and my new shoes, I headed to the study where Amelia, my fiancée, was already hard at work. She was the type who liked to get up at first light and make the most of the day — the complete opposite of me. This arrangement worked pretty well, as it meant mornings started with an undisturbed lie-in.

"Morning, honey," I said, leaning in front of the computer screen to give her a peck on the lips before continuing to the sideboard in the corner where I grabbed my wallet and car keys, and began trying to fit the cufflinks.

"Here, let me do that for you," she offered, spinning round on her office chair and beckoning me towards her. Picking up the link I had dropped on the floor, I took the few steps to where she was sitting and dropped them into her open palm.

"Thanks. One of these days, I'll figure out the knack of doing these things on my own."

She sorted out my cufflinks effortlessly as I glanced over her head to see what she was working on.

"Are those two really merging?" I asked. "That seems like a match made in hell — and a whole heap of work for the corporate lawyers. No?"

"Heh, that's confidential," she exclaimed with mock concern.

"But I could make a ton of cash out of that deal. I think I might make a small investment when I get to work," I replied, winking at her.

She gave me her don't-screw-with-me gaze before registering the wink, and her face softened.

"If it goes through, I'll make so much commission you won't need to do any insider trading. But I doubt it'll get past the M&A committee. Anyway, I need to get my head down today. If I don't get some of these reports done, I might not be on this deal much longer — so why don't you stop being a pain in the arse and go play with your cars."

I knew she was joking, but figured I'd play along. My humour was usually sarcastic but subtle, and Amelia often struggled to interpret it correctly.

"And after we've had such a nice weekend, I thought you actually liked having me around. I guess I'll just have to spend extra hours at the office."

"Don't be like that," said Amelia as she followed me out onto the landing and stood at the top of the stairs, leaning against the banister.

"Can't stop. Gotta go play with my cars," I replied with the slightest of smirks.

I saw her shoulders relax as she cottoned on to my joke

"See you later. And don't forget we've got that charity dinner tonight — you know, the one for the art charity," she half-shouted.

"Yep, don't worry. I haven't forgotten. I'll be home by six at the latest," I replied, as I was halfway out the door wishing I had forgotten and double booked.

It was a beautiful late May morning and the air had a pleasant warmth to it, so I paused to enjoy the view before jumping in the car. We were very fortunate to live in a large, imposing old house whose garden stretched all the way to the banks of the Thames. The grass was lush and green thanks to the wet spring we'd had, and the few trees scattered across the lawn were in full leaf, rustling slightly as a light wind blew from the south.

Being a connoisseur of all things mechanical, I, of course, had a boat — a Riva Aquariva, to be precise. I'm not really a boaty kind of guy, but that thing was super cool. Ordinarily, I would have taken the boat to work on a day like today, but even as I gazed out, I could see quite a few rowers out for their morning training session. The rowers and I generally didn't get on. I guess I was one of those selfish arseholes who didn't like slowing down just because they were out in their little plastic tubs. I also wasn't in the mood to faff about with the locks, so it would have to be the car today.

The gravel crunched under my feet as I made my way over to the pearl white Mercedes AMG GT-R. The car auto-unlocked as I approached — a completely unnecessary but neat feature. I dropped myself into the racing seat, neatly folded my suit jacket and placed it on the passenger seat. A quick press of the start button and a deep burble from the twin-turbo V8 almost immediately disturbed the quiet suburban neighbourhood. Don't get me wrong — it's no Ferrari, but I couldn't put up with that high-pitched engine note this early in the morning. I'd always been taught by my dad to treat a cold engine with a healthy dose of mechanical sympathy, so I gently caressed the throttle and headed along the driveway. Gravel crunched under the tyres and pinged off the underside as I timed the gate opening with my arrival so I didn't have to stop. With that mission accomplished, I was about to turn right for the twenty-minute drive to the office when I heard my phone buzz in my jacket pocket and a message popped up on the Mercedes infotainment screen. Two seconds later, I cranked the wheel to the left and headed on a quick detour.

The detour to the deli didn't add much time, and it helped that the owner met me at the kerb.

"Thought you might not be coming this morning, Mr Miller," said Matteo as he leaned through the open passenger window.

"Honestly, I forgot. It's Monday — what can I say?" I replied with a shrug.

True to his Italian roots, he hesitated as he was about to place the food bags on the seat. I caught his eye looking at my jacket, realised how sacrilegious it would be for him to put food on clothing — especially Italian clothing — and quickly whipped it out of the way, draping it over the roll cage behind the seats. A brief smile spread across his face as he placed the food securely on the seat.

"Smells as great as ever, Matteo," I said, as the aroma from the breakfast rolls hit my nostrils.

"Well, I've gone with a new bread recipe this week. Let me know what you think," he beamed.

"For sure," I replied. "I'm pretty confident they won't be disappointed."

He paused at the window for a second or two, as if he was going to say something else, before offering a half-hearted, "Ciao, Mr Miller. See you next week."

As I pulled away from the kerb, I glanced in the rear-view mirror and caught a brief glimpse of a distracted-looking Matteo. Given he was a stereotypically passionate Italian, something was obviously bothering him. I made a mental note to check in with him, then got on with avoiding the mopeds and cyclists as I finally headed towards the office.

I can hardly complain about going to work. In reality, I didn't really work in an office, and the job felt more like a hobby most of the time. I run — or more accurately, I own — a renovated Victorian warehouse that I've turned into a car museum. A museum never made anyone rich, but thankfully, I'd had the vision and good fortune to make it a lot more.

The museum is set over five floors, with half the ground floor allocated to a workshop. The vehicles on display are almost entirely super rare and/or special-edition performance cars from the past sixty years. Whether iconic

Fords, classic Ferraris, modern hypercars or vintage American muscle, we pretty much had them all. There's nowhere else in Europe, possibly the world, that offers the public access to so many rare vehicles in one place.

When I set the place up, I had nothing like the necessary disposable income to fill even one floor. Through a few well-placed contacts, I managed to convince some avid collectors to store their cars in the museum. We quickly garnered a reputation among the rich and famous, and before long we had a full museum_turning away Ferraris and Lamborghinis that most people would rate as exotic.

That would ordinarily have been good enough for me, as we'd already established ourselves as a premium tourist spot in London. This meant our footfall and revenue were good enough to give me a comfortable life. However, about five years ago, a chance encounter developed a new revenue stream that propelled the business in a new direction. A high-profile actor visited the museum and fell in love with a Jaguar XJ220. It just so happened that I was walking back to my office, having popped out for a coffee, when I overheard the film star spouting superlatives about the car to his entourage. I often stop and chat with guests when I sense they have a genuine connection with a car, and this was no different. His celebrity and status didn't matter to me — I'd discovered over the years that those with the most power and money were often innocuous — he was just another petrolhead as far as I was concerned. Before I knew it, we were sitting in the two-seater, listening to the engine tick over and discussing some lesser-known facts about a car that was once the fastest production car in the world.

It wasn't unusual for guests to offer to buy the cars, but this guy was relentless. Eventually, and a little reluctantly, I phoned the owner. Several days later, I brokered the sale of my first car, made a tidy profit, and amazingly got to keep the car in the museum. The exotic car community is small, so word quickly got out, and it wasn't long before we had a reputation for brokering deals for the rarest and most exotic cars ever produced.

About three years ago, we were granted permission to add a modern structure to the roof, allowing us to open a restaurant, and within the last year a coffee shop had been added to the ground floor. This was one of Amelia's ideas, which has added yet another dimension to what we do. The restaurant has developed a fantastic reputation for high-quality bistro-style food, largely thanks to the hard work of Leandro, our head chef, and his team. Our unique location, superb views from every table, and elegant yet comfortable décor impressed most people and made them eager to return. The coffee shop was not a venture I was convinced about, but Leandro reassured me — and I'm pretty sure he and Amelia double-teamed me on that one. They weren't wrong. We get a steady flow of locals, tourists, museum visitors, and clients coming through most days. Bizarrely, given the friction between cyclists and car drivers in London, it has also become very popular with Lycra-clad road cyclists out on their weekend rides. I'd learned that caffeine was a big part of cycling culture, so I guess it meant our coffee must be pretty good.

Pulling onto the premises, I noted that all my employees were already at work and that there were also a few unfamiliar cars, probably belonging to eager museum visitors. You could never predict when we'd be busy, but it wasn't uncommon for Mondays to catch us out. Grabbing the breakfast rolls from the passenger seat, I headed through the front doors and was greeted by the sight of my two favourite cars: a 1968 Shelby Mustang GT500 and a 1998 Mercedes CLK GTR SuperSport. Both were my personal vehicles, and I always looked forward to the diary dates when they went out for their maintenance drive. Pausing briefly to admire their muscular beauty, I dashed up the stairs two at a time and went straight to the meeting room on the third floor.

Chapter 2

The staff of ten were already waiting, and I found my favourite cup filled with coffee, placed in front of my chair. Dropping the food in the centre of the table was like feeding a pack of starving hyenas. The paper bags practically disintegrated as the food was dished out. A quick sip of my coffee had me pausing to inspect it. It wasn't the usual blend we served, and I half wondered if someone was playing a practical joke on me. As I looked up, I saw Leandro watching me quizzically.

"Well?" he asked after a brief pause. "What do you think?"

"Is this it?" I replied slowly, as my brain scrambled to recall the details of our conversation the previous week.

"Yep, direct from Indonesia. Arrived at my place over the weekend."

"Well, it's certainly different. Not sure I'm a huge fan, to be honest — especially since you told me how it's produced," I said, referring to the fact that the coffee was harvested from the droppings of a palm civet and then roasted to bake the flavour in.

"I think it's going to be an acquired taste, but having kopi luwak on the board is definitely going to add to our reputation for the unusual."

I pulled a face that suggested indifference to the idea, eased myself into the chair behind me and got the meeting underway. The weekly meeting didn't last long. It was more of a catch-up after the weekend, a quick briefing about any significant visits or events in the coming week, and a way to keep everyone updated with the different business ventures. I was always most interested in which vehicles would be heading out for their maintenance shakedown, just in case there was something I particularly wanted to have a go in. We'd found that leaving vehicles stationary for prolonged periods did them no good, so a regular outing was part of our storage contract. It also meant we could occasionally offer museum guests a once-in-a-lifetime opportunity to experience a car in all its glory.

With the meeting finished, I headed to my office but first detoured to see my assistant and general organiser of my life.

"Hey, Abi," I said after a gentle knock on the glass partition wall. "How was your date with Dave on Saturday?"

She took a deep breath before replying. Abi had worked for me for close to ten years, and I knew her deep sigh could only mean bad things.

"Not amazing. He fell asleep halfway through. I mean, how do you fall asleep at the Royal Albert Hall, to a live orchestra belting out movie theme tunes? Not only that, he then tried to make out that he'd closed his eyes so he could connect with the music."

"I mean, maybe he did," I offered, fully aware Abi would roll her eyes at me.

"And I suppose the snoring was him making an emotional connection with the drums. It was embarrassing," she shot back, daring me to defend that as well.

I knew this was the point to bow out, and to be fair, I was siding with Abi on this one.

"I guess he's just not a culture guy," I said with a shrug.

"I get it. It's not for everyone. But you've just gotta have the guts to say so. No point pretending you're into something when you're not. That's no way to behave in any relationship," she replied with a huff.

"Gotta be true to yourself at the end of the day."

"How about you? Did Amelia drag you to that fashion show in Bermondsey?" asked Abi, raising an eyebrow.

"She sure did. I caught the Fulham game first, though. I gotta say, the fashion show wasn't so bad. It might even have been better than the football. I mean, how often do us guys get to stare at beautiful women for an hour or so, and the other half doesn't bat an eyelid?" I said, with a glint in my eye and a smirk forming.

"Men!" exclaimed Abi, throwing her arms up in mock horror, knowing full well I was winding her up.

I smiled, grateful that in the current politically correct world, I could still share a little tongue-in-cheek humour.

"Speaking of men, have you spoken with Matteo recently?"

"No," she replied. "Why?"

"He just wasn't his normal self this morning. It looked like he wanted to ask me something but didn't. Can you check with Justin to make sure we're definitely up to date with the account? The restaurant does a lot of business with him, and I don't want him having cash flow issues because of us."

"Will do," Abi said, grabbing a yellow Post-it note and scribbling on it.

"And maybe knock off a bit early today and swing by to see him. What Italian doesn't have a soft spot for a beautiful lady? Maybe he'll confide in you," I teased.

"Whatever," she retorted, waving me out of her office as she got back to work.

Truth be told, Abi is stunning, and it always left me a little bemused as to why she struggled with dating. Amelia and I had talked about it many times. Amelia blamed men for being superficial and flaky. I blamed Abi for being a little too perfect. She was a tall, leggy brunette with an athletic figure many professional athletes would envy. Years of swimming and running had taken care of that, and she maintained an incredibly disciplined approach to her diet — the perfect combo to stay lean and strong. On top of that, she could turn her hand to almost anything and be more than competent. Her interests were wide and varied: music, art, history, languages, travel, politics — you name it, Abi could talk about it for hours. I occasionally wondered why she kept working for me and periodically had a panic attack when she unexpectedly knocked on my office door. Fortunately for me, she and Amelia were very close — though that had been a slow process, as it took Amelia time to accept that we were colleagues and friends, nothing more. I hoped Abi just felt part of the workplace family and that, along with a decent salary, kept her content with organising my sorry self.

I was halfway through the door when I suddenly remembered something.

"Hey, thanks for the text earlier," I said, referring to the message I'd received in the car.

"No worries. As if you were going to remember," she smiled, glancing up from her screen. "I'd been texting

Amelia and she said you'd just left, so I figured the timing was probably perfect."

"Couldn't have been better," I said over my shoulder as I headed next door to my office.

Chapter 3

The morning passed much like most others. I had a few phone calls with prospective buyers and received a couple of requests for storage, both of which I turned down. If you'd asked me a few years ago whether I'd ever refuse the chance to have a Pagani Zonda and a Group B Audi Sport Quattro in the museum, I'd have laughed in your face. As it was, we simply didn't have the room. I always kept a couple of spaces open for something really special, and these just didn't qualify.

I briefly spoke with Amelia about the evening engagement, which I knew nothing about, and figured out where I needed to be and at what time. You've probably gathered by now that I'm not the most organised person, so none of this will come as a surprise. Despite it being a Monday evening — and a pretty random night for a charity event — it looked like there would be a good turnout. At least it was for a good cause. So, despite my reservations (I've been to a lot of these things), it sounded like it might not be a total disaster.

It was just after 2 p.m. when there was a very distinctive tap on my glass door.

"Come on in, Lucas," I called without looking up, waving him in. "Grab a seat," I added, pointing to the brown leather armchair on the other side of my desk.

"Thanks, but I think I'd better not," came the reply as he pointed to his heavily oil-stained overalls.

"Aren't you supposed to be my chief mechanic?" I asked with a smile.

"Yeah, well, we all make mistakes. I mean, you hired me, didn't you?" He paused, then added quickly, "For once, it wasn't actually my fault. The new apprentice from Brooklands isn't quite as switched on as the others have been."

We both smiled for a moment before I remembered that Lucas hardly ever came to see me.

"So, what can I do for you? I'm sure you've not come to tell me you can't handle this one."

"Oh yeah, right. So, I'm down in the car park looking over that 250 GTO we sold a few weeks ago and…"

"Please don't tell me we have a problem. That car has already been too much of a headache. Why couldn't we have sold it overseas, preferably in Japan? Get it as far away from here as possible."

"Long story, but the simple answer is no. For once it isn't the GTO that's at fault. Unless we're going to expand into the brain-transplant business, there's nothing to fix on the car this time."

"Perhaps we should set an exam for potential buyers. Stop the thick people from buying the nice cars," I replied, thinking it actually sounded like a good idea.

It really grated on me when a clueless rich guy (and it was nearly always a man) turned up with absolutely no idea what he was buying.

"Anyway, if you've finished fantasising about ways to crater your business, I'll get to the point. I've got my head under the bonnet when I hear these clicky heels coming towards me — you know, the type the rich girls wear.

Anyway, I come out from under the bonnet and there's this fine-looking lady standing there, dressed up smart, with two big minder types hovering behind her. We look at each other for a few seconds, 'cause I reckon she fancies me a bit..."

"I somehow doubt that, unless she has some kind of fetish for men covered in car oil."

"Hey, I think I look kind of cute like this," he said with a grin. "Look, do you want me to tell you the rest of the story or do you want to keep insulting me?"

I rolled my eyes and waved for him to continue.

"She asks if I'm you. She specifically asked for you by name. So I tell her you'd be so lucky. Not sure she got the joke, 'cause she just stared at me with this kind of unimpressed, bored look on her face. I tell her I'm not too sure where you are, but I'd see if I could find out."

"Mmm," I mused. She didn't sound like one of our typical clients. We often had entourages come through, but the way Lucas described the minders suggested this was something entirely different.

"Sounds intriguing. Guess I should go see what she wants."

"Good idea, boss. I'll come with you just in case," said an eager Lucas, holding the office door for me.

Grabbing my jacket and phone, I said,

"Thanks for the offer, but I can hear that 250 GTO calling your name. Tell you what — I'll put in a good word for you. How about that?"

Replying with only a grumble, Lucas walked with me to the main elevator. It was a large freight lift set in the middle of the building, the type with pull-down wooden doors you usually see in American warehouses. We used it mainly to move the vehicles around, but since Lucas was also heading to the ground floor, we travelled together.

Arriving with a solid clunk, Lucas opened the door and we stepped out. I couldn't see anyone matching his description. Lucas wandered to the doorway of the car park, had a quick look around, and then shook his head at me. Odd. Who requests to see someone in a large office and then goes wandering off?

Maybe she was stupid, or maybe it was some bizarre power-play. Either way, it was odd behaviour and put me slightly on edge. Taking the stairs to the second floor, I caught sight of the mystery guest at the far end. It was almost immediately obvious it was the latter of my two theories.

As I walked towards her, my new shoes echoed on the polished concrete floor. My stride was purposeful and business-like; I was clearly not another car enthusiast shuffling around the museum. Despite the fact I was making a beeline for her — something most people instinctively pick up on — she continued to study the red Saleen S7LM in front of her. She almost pulled it off, but her posture was just a little too rigid, too intense, to be natural. As I got closer, the guy on her right quickly sized me up and then, rather abruptly, walked off in the opposite direction.

"She's a beautiful car," I said without introducing myself.

"She certainly is. A little impractical, though, don't you think, Mr Miller?" replied the woman with a soft American accent as she turned to face me.

I'll give Lucas this: he certainly didn't follow the traditional path when it came to women. Most guys wouldn't describe her as stunning, but there was something angular and unique about her face that made it difficult not to be drawn in.

Some time ago, I'd come up with my own classification system for attractiveness in women (and men, for that matter — so don't get bent out of shape that I'm objectifying women; I'm an equal-opportunities judgemental prick). Basically, there are four categories. Category A is an absolute stunner, plain and simple. Category B is someone not immediately or classically attractive, but the more you look, the more beauty you see. Category C is the opposite — she starts out stunning, but you quickly realise she isn't, usually because she's wearing too much make-up. Category D is simply someone you don't find attractive and never will.

This American lady was most definitely a Category B. Late twenties, average height, shoulder-length blonde hair, and a faint scar on the right side of her neck. Her erect posture and stern face belied the softness in her eyes. Normally, I was good at reading people, but this woman seemed a complete contradiction.

"Well, I agree it's not really a car for the weekly shop. Who needs 1,300 horsepower to go to Tesco?" I replied, giving her my politest smile.

The sarcasm could wait until I knew what she wanted.

"My chief engineer — " I had to at least try to give Lucas some credit " — said you wanted to speak with me, Ms…"

"It's Lawson. Ms Lawson. But you can call me Jessica," she replied, smiling. It looked like an attempt at flirtation, except it was more forced than natural.

If my spidey-senses hadn't already been dialled up to ten, that smile might have softened my attitude. As it was, I ploughed on with being a pain in the arse.

"OK, Ms Lawson, here I am. How can I help you?"

She looked a little surprised her smile hadn't worked, but quickly recovered.

"It's come to our attention that you're a highly competent driver. That you can drive fast, close to the limit, but that you do so safely and in control."

"And no doubt it's also come to your attention that I'm a legitimate businessman with no interest in being someone's wheelman," I said, a little too sharply.

"Mr Miller, do I really look like the type to be involved with crime?"

Before I could respond, she caught herself. "Don't answer that. Your penchant for sarcasm precedes you."

This brought a smile to my face and a look of annoyance to hers. She was already running out of patience after only a couple of minutes. I, on the other hand, was enjoying myself.

"Look, it's simple. You've been highly recommended, and we need someone — specifically you — to spend three months in the States driving for us. We'll cover any costs your business incurs while you're away, all your expenses over there, and pay you one hundred thousand sterling, tax free. It's nothing illegal — quite the opposite, in fact."

"Thanks, but no thanks," I replied, turning towards the stairs. "And don't bother with any more details. I'm not interested. I've got plenty to do here, and I don't need your money."

It was a strange exchange, and I didn't need to hear any more. Still, I had an uneasy feeling. Something wasn't sitting right. Ordinarily, I'd expect those clicky heels to follow, but not this time. Instead, her voice carried after me.

"You know, looking around your museum, I couldn't help noticing several American cars."

That stopped me in my tracks. I slowly turned back.

"What of it? They're all here legally," I said, stepping towards her.

"I'm sure they are. But the people I represent have a lot of power in the U.S. My sources tell me you do quite a bit of business there," she said with a knowing smile.

She was right. While the business was UK-based, I'd built up plenty of contacts in the States, often supplying cars to NFL and NBA stars. Any interruption to those sales would cost me dearly. And then came the kicker.

"It would be a real shame if we had to get the authorities involved," she said, holding my gaze for what felt like an eternity.

She could have meant any number of things, but deep down I sensed she was implying something very specific. Something nobody was supposed to know.

"Let me know by the end of the week," she added, handing me her business card before heading for the customer lift.

My brain was racing, so I wasn't really in the moment as her minders joined her.

By the time the door slid open, I'd regained my composure. I dashed over and thrust a hand between the closing doors. Reaching into my jacket, I pulled out a business card and offered it to her. She looked at it, flipped it over, then handed it to the man on her left.

"Not particularly funny. We have your number anyway," she said with a slight snarl.

"I didn't intend it to be funny. My engineer asked me to put in a word for him. You should give him a call. He's a nice guy when he's not covered in grease."

As I'd hoped, this completely knocked her off guard. She had played her part well, I'll give her that, but it was good to know she wasn't in complete control. While it's always reassuring to see your opponent has weaknesses, it didn't ease the apprehensiveness I had about the whole situation. The door slid closed as she began to say something. I had no interest in hearing anything else, so I walked over to the window overlooking the car park and mulled over everything that had just happened.

I was being a bit childish by handing her Lucas's card like that, but I hate to lose, and I certainly felt that I had. I watched them walk to a dark-blue 5 Series BMW parked next to Lucas's Honda Civic Type R. That gave me an idea. Seeing Lucas just beginning to close the bonnet of the Ferrari, I sprinted down the stairs, taking three or four stairs at a time. Lucas and I reached the main doors almost simultaneously, and I nearly knocked him over as I burst into the parking area.

"Easy, tiger. I know I said she was fine, but no need to chase after her like that. I always find playing hard to get works best," Lucas chuckled.

"Ha ha," I replied, still trying to catch my breath. I really needed to add some cardio to that morning workout.

"Did you see her leave?" I asked quickly — probably a little too seriously.

"Yeah, just now. She turned right, towards the 316."

"Thanks, mate. I need to borrow your car for an hour or so!"

"You mean, 'Lucas, please can I borrow your car?'"

"Whatever, just throw me the keys."

"You alright?" Lucas asked as he dug through his pockets for the keys. "You're acting a bit… well, you know, odd."

"Keys?" I said curtly, holding my hand out.

"You owe me big time for this," he muttered, tossing the keys halfway across the car park.

"I would, but I already repaid you. I'll tell you later," I shouted, dropping into the bucket seat and pulling the door shut.

The car started immediately, and with a little wheel spin I pulled out of the car park and onto the street. Being in the car business, everyone expected me to have points on my licence — especially with the exotic machines we looked after. The reality was I'd never been stopped for speeding nor been involved in any accidents. Unfortunately, there was a good chance that stat was about to change.

A distant memory had been triggered, one I'd tried my best to bury so deep it would never resurface. Yet in the space of two minutes, the mysterious Jessica Lawson had implied she knew all about it. Or maybe I was just reading too much into it. Either way, I couldn't afford to cross my fingers and hope I was wrong. I had to do something — and that meant finding out who she really was.

With my mind sharpened and focused, I drove like a maniac, determined to catch up with her BMW. Numerous times, blaring horns and flashing headlights accompanied oncoming traffic. Eventually, I caught sight of their car as I approached the traffic lights that joined Twickenham High Street. The BMW peeled off left, forcing me to dive into a tiny gap and earning a tirade of horns for my trouble. Sinking lower in my seat in case anyone was watching, I found myself four cars behind them and was relieved to revert to my normal, more sedate driving style.

The rest of my impromptu journey passed without a hitch, and about thirty minutes later the BMW pulled into a long driveway leading up to a Tudor-style mansion in a leafy part of Weybridge. I turned into a side road beyond the house and parked up. I watched as the car disappeared around the back and noted the address, as well as the multitude of security cameras trained on the perimeter wall. Feeling exposed and out of place, I pulled away from the kerb and headed back towards the office.

Chapter 4

B y the time I reached the office, it was just past 4 p.m., which meant I had almost an hour before heading home to prepare myself — both mentally and physically — for the evening's engagement. I opted to spend the time entirely unproductively, staring out of the window and over-analysing every possible scenario from that afternoon. At around five, Lucas came knocking again.

"The way you tore out of the car park, I half expected to get a call from the rozzers telling me my car had been wrapped round a lamppost."

"Yeah, I'm sorry about that. I, err... had to go somewhere," I replied as convincingly as I could.

"Whatever you say, boss."

A pause followed, and I knew Lucas was weighing up whether he should dig a bit deeper.

"Is everything okay? You've seemed distracted since that woman dropped by. Even Abi said you'd been off when I bumped into her earlier."

"Yeah, well, let's just say there's a lot more to that woman than meets the eye."

"Heh, I'd be pretty happy with what meets the eye, if you know what I mean," Lucas said, raising his eyebrows with a grin.

"Well, you've been warned. That's all I'll say."

"Listen, me and a couple of the boys are heading to The Bishop for a few pints. Fancy joining us? You can drown your sorrows in some ale."

"Thanks, but Amelia's already planned my evening. We're hobnobbing at some charity fundraiser in town. Good for our careers — or so she keeps telling me."

"Another time, then. Anyway, I'm off to the pub. Catch you tomorrow."

"Yeah, I'll see you tomorrow. And Lucas — don't come in too hungover."

Closing the door behind him, I watched him head to the lift as I slipped back into my pensive mindset. This was quickly interrupted, though, as Lucas came back into my office.

"I knew there was something else I came in for. My car keys?"

"Oh yeah, sorry," I said, reaching into the inside pocket of my jacket and tossing them to him. Catching them in his left hand, he turned and asked, "By the way, what was that favour you said you'd already done for me?"

"Oh yeah. Let's just say you might get a call from my new friend Jessica — but I wouldn't hold your breath."

"I always said you were a quality guy. I definitely owe you a pint now."

Without waiting for a response, he closed the office door and headed back to the lift. The smile on his face almost stretched around his whole body. If only I felt that happy about Ms Lawson's visit.

I arrived home with plenty of time to change. Amelia was nearly ready but nearly ready and actually ready are very different things. Predictably, the nagging started as soon as I got out of the shower. She was stressed about which shoes best matched her dress. Now wasn't the time to fill her in on my unusual day, so I fobbed her off with the usual: "My day was fine, honey. How about yours?" At that point, I tuned out as she ranted about the trials and tribulations of being a corporate lawyer. We eventually left about five minutes late, which, according to Amelia, wasn't acceptable, and apparently we really needed to work on our timekeeping. I decided it was best not to mention that the shoe debate had caused the delay, and instead just nodded in agreement.

The event turned out to be fairly dull. We had some arty food — the kind where you never quite get enough on your plate — and endured an after-dinner speech from a stuffy politician who tried to amuse us with art-related stories from behind the scenes in the Commons. I've been to plenty of these things. They're a bit formulaic, but not always bad. I genuinely enjoy helping people change their lives and support a lot of charities, but generally it has to be on my terms and not someone else's agenda. It wasn't uncommon for charities to contact the museum asking for donations or items for auction. I figured that was me doing my bit to keep up appearances without getting too personally invested in things that didn't mean much to me.

Tonight's event was about helping the socially deprived gain access to the arts. Not really my scene; a beer with Lucas and the lads sounded far more appealing. But this was the price of being a successful entrepreneur in southwest London — and of having a fiancée who adored anything art-related. It might sound as though Amelia and I weren't particularly well suited, but we actually shared an almost identical world view, as well as appreciating similar personality traits. I've always thought part of being in a relationship is making sacrifices to share in your partner's passions but it's also important to keep your own hobbies and interests — to have the freedom to enjoy what you love without being in each other's pockets all the time. The differences between us kept things interesting, and as they say, opposites attract.

The evening did prove useful in one way: I bumped into a good friend whose ear I bent about my problems earlier in the day. He was the sort of man who knew people — high-up, influential people — and could probably shed some light on exactly what Jessica Lawson was up to. By the end of the night, I felt a little more comfortable about the situation, even though I was still largely in the dark. I decided I would tell Amelia what had happened when we got back home — but not before we enjoyed a bit of personal time together.

Chapter 5

My morning routine was pretty similar every day, except this morning I was greeted by a frosty reception from Amelia. She hadn't taken the news about Jessica Lawson's visit too well and immediately suggested we phone the police. Using my so-called male dominance — realistically just me getting moody and stubborn — I argued it wasn't the best move, and we left it at that. As I grabbed my wallet, Amelia brought it up again. I mentioned the discussion I'd had with Giles, someone she vaguely knew, and we agreed to see where that took me.

The day at the office went smoothly enough, and I was just starting to wind down when the phone rang.

"Hi Eli, it's Giles," came the voice down the line.

"Hey, Giles. I was starting to think you'd forgotten me — or maybe your legendary contacts had failed you," I replied.

"Forget, maybe. Fail, never. Not when it comes to information," he scoffed.

Giles Thistlethwaite is about fifty and speaks with the most stereotypical public schoolboy accent you can imagine. I thought it was put on when we first met, but no — he really was that posh. With his silk cravats and tweed jackets, he looked every inch a duke or an earl, and he played up to the toff image. Underneath it all, though, he was a likeable chap with a touch of the wheeler-dealer about him. He was known across the capital's social scene as the man who could get you anything — like a fixer in prison. If he didn't know something himself, he knew who to ask. Consequently, he had contacts from all walks of life, including plenty in the police and security services.

"Well, my laddie, it appears you have a problem. Fortunately, it's not a major one. It seems your new friend, Ms Lawson, is FBI. I spoke to someone in the service who recognised the address — it belongs to the Americans. Apparently, there's an FBI team visiting the Met. From your description, it sounds like Ms Lawson is one of them."

"The FBI," I repeated, trying to process it. "Are you sure? She can't be more than twenty-seven, twenty-eight. Why send the apprentice to recruit me?"

I know it sounds big-headed, but I like to think I'm valuable enough that they'd at least send someone senior.

"All I know is what I've been told. According to the team bio, she's listed as a junior staff member. My friend in the service might be interested in hearing about their approach, if that's okay with you?"

"Well, I suppose it's give and take," I said, still trying to digest the information. "So, any idea what she wants with me?"

"'Fraid not, buddy. You're on your own with that one. Whatever it is, I doubt it's illegal. The Americans usually leave that to the CIA."

"No probs," I said after a long pause. My brain tends to work in one gear — I can't think and talk at the same time. "Heh, thanks a lot. You've been a big help. I guess all I have to do now is figure out the best way forward."

"Well, there's no harm in finding out what they want. They're offering you a lot of money, after all."

"I guess you're right. Thanks, Giles. Speak soon."

"Any time, Eli. If I hear anything else, I'll let you know. Good luck."

Hanging up, I stared at the desk for several minutes. Something about the conversation felt odd, but I couldn't put my finger on it. Like hearing a song on the radio, knowing the singer but not the title — it was bloody annoying.

The rest of the day passed as usual, and I arrived home to an Amelia-cooked meal, which is never a highlight of any day. It reminded me I needed to book those cookery classes for her birthday. Over dinner, I told her what Giles had found out. Needless to say, she was less keen on me digging deeper.

We spent the evening on the sofa, initially channel surfing, eventually settling on a foreign language film that was surprisingly good despite my hatred of subtitles. But with everything on my mind, sleep didn't come easily. I tossed and turned, pulling the duvet in every direction, my head full of that same restless "name that singer" anxiety. It must have been about 1 a.m. — though I'm probably exaggerating — when it finally clicked.

This is always a dangerous time for me to be making decisions. I have a habit of concocting what I think are brilliant solutions to problems, only to realise in the morning that they'd cause more issues than they'd solve. Despite knowing this, I ignored my better judgement, leapt out of bed — nearly knocking over the bedside cabinet — and dashed into the study, where my wallet was on the sideboard. Digging out the card I'd tucked away, I dropped into the office chair and picked up the phone.

I dialled the number and was startled by the speed of the response.

"Good evening," came a bright, American-accented female voice.

So far, Giles was right. Nobody who wasn't working would sound that alert at this hour.

"Err, hi. Could I speak with Jessica Lawson, please?" I asked, putting on my best copycat tone.

"Certainly, sir. I'll see if she's available. May I ask who's calling?"

"Just tell her it's a friend she met a couple of days ago."

"One moment, please."

The line went silent for about ten seconds, then suddenly began to ring again. It gave me just enough time to come up with one of my childish ideas. I really do need to grow up — I'm thirty-four, after all. I almost didn't manage to hide my amusement when a groggy-sounding Ms Lawson answered.

"Good morning, Ms Lawson. How are you?"

"Pretty tired and pissed off at being woken up in the middle of the night. Who is this, and what do you want?" she asked, her tone sharp.

"Well, Ms Lawson, I'm surprised you don't remember me — especially after our most enjoyable time at the museum the other day."

"Mr Miller, I presume. To what do I owe this pleasure?" she asked, half-bored, half-annoyed.

"Even at this hour, you're still sharp as a tack," I said. I thought a compliment — even if it was tongue firmly in cheek — might help her mood.

"My employer can be very demanding. There are no shift times in my job."

"Ah yes, your employer. We can talk about them next time we meet."

There was a pause as she processed what I'd said.

"So we are to meet again? And when would that be?"

"I thought about coming round to yours, but all those security cameras put me off. How about my office? At least we'll have some privacy."

"Okay, how's tomorrow for you?"

"Tomorrow is just peachy. I was thinking of a spot of lunch — only I can't afford to splash out on your two gentlemen friends. So come alone, okay?"

"Whatever you say. It seems you're running the show this time."

"You got that right. See you tomorrow."

I hung up before she could reply or change the rules. Sitting there for a while, I began to plan how I'd approach our lunch date the next day, before finally returning to bed. Climbing in, I had to literally shove Amelia back to her side. She had a habit of occupying my half of the bed, whether I was in it or not.

Chapter 6

The morning passed with the usual business affairs, but I was only half concentrating as I continued planning how to approach the meeting I'd engineered the previous night. As predicted, I spent the first part of the morning debating the wisdom of that call, but ultimately resigned myself to the path I was now on. I think I've been watching too many films, as I was plotting how to be clever and catch Jessica off guard.

Twelve-thirty came and went. Surely she wasn't going to stand me up — I had given her what she wanted, after all. At 12:45 there was a knock at the door, and to my surprise it was Lucas. Only he wasn't alone; he was accompanied by Jessica Lawson. Opening the door for her, he showed her in and flashed what I assumed was his best smile. They seemed to be hitting it off; maybe there was hope for Lucas yet.

"Sorry I'm late. I got stuck in the line," she said, motioning to the Five Guys doggy bag and cartons of drink, "and then I bumped into your chief engineer. You're right, Lucas really is a nice guy. I might just call him sometime."

I wasn't sure whether that was for my benefit or if she meant it. Either way, I was happy to see the bag of food — I was craving a cheeseburger. She sat down and offered me a drink and a bag of food, which I duly took. We sat in silence for at least five minutes as we tucked into our burgers, and it wasn't until I was halfway through my fries that she finally spoke.

"So, now you have me here. What can I do for you?"

"Well, I was hoping you could tell me a bit more about this job you want me to do," I replied, mouth half full.

"The 'job,' as you call it, is to come to America, help out with some driving duties and do a bit of training. You know, stuff like that. As I said, it's not illegal, and it really is no more complicated than that."

I paused to swallow properly this time — I didn't want her thinking I was a complete slob. I also needed a little time to work through what she'd just said, because it didn't really make much sense.

"Before we go any further, can I just clarify exactly who you represent?"

"The FBI," she replied with a casualness that belied the significance of the answer.

Even though it was what I'd expected, I still paused briefly and did my best to look puzzled.

"So what makes the FBI think I'm a decent driver? For that matter, what makes you think Giles Thistlethwaite knows anything about cars, never mind driving them well?"

To her credit, Ms Lawson hardly flinched. She had the face of a poker player, but her eyes betrayed her surprise at this small revelation.

"Well, Giles did recommend you, you're right about that. But we also asked around a few other people in the industry, and your name came up every time. Plus, you did manage to follow me back to my residence, which is no mean feat."

"I didn't think I'd got away with it. Let me guess — the incident at the traffic lights in Twickenham?"

"Oh no, we didn't spot you. But how else would you know about the security cameras at the house?"

I wasn't sure whether she was telling the truth or just trying to inflate my ego. Either way, it was working.

"So how did you know Giles was working for us?" she asked after a brief pause.

"Oh, he mentioned the money you'd offered me. Thing is, I never told him about it."

"I warned them he might slip up, but they insisted he was the man to go with. Apparently he knows everything and everyone."

He clearly didn't know how much, or little, I value money.

"To be honest, that's the least of your problems. From what you've said, you're looking for a driver to do some pretty routine stuff. I mean, 'driving duties' could mean anything. Why on earth do you want me? There are loads of professional drivers in the States who could meet your needs. I could probably give you ten names right now," I said, reaching for my phone.

"That won't be necessary," she replied, holding up her hand. "Of course we know people. Your reputation isn't that good."

"So...?" I asked, staring straight at her.

"Well, it's been decided we need a fresh face, and that face has to come from outside our borders."

She was about to say more, but I cut in. Once I get the bit between my teeth, I don't like to let go.

"And why exactly do you need someone from outside your borders? That sounds pretty suspicious when all you're asking for is someone to teach your own people."

"It's what I've been tasked to deliver. The decision is above my pay grade," she said, slightly sheepishly, looking away.

I got the distinct feeling that, at the very least, she was withholding information — and most likely flat-out lying.

"The old pay-grade excuse," I replied with an exaggerated shrug. "Well, I hope you've got some backup options, because based on what you've just told me, you'll have to tell your boss I'm not interested."

She didn't immediately respond. Instead, she held my gaze like it was a game of chicken. I wanted to believe that was the end of it, but something told me she had more ammo.

"I really hoped it wouldn't come to this," she said in a steely, businesslike tone. "It would be a shame if you became persona non grata back home. I'd imagine your business would suffer quite badly."

She said it matter-of-factly, with no hint of satisfaction — pure business. It was the same threat she'd used last time, so I was mentally prepared for it. What came next, though, was something else entirely.

"Even more so if the state of Montana decided to take a closer look at you."

My stomach dropped like it had been ripped out, leaving a void in its place. I felt suddenly on edge. Jessica Lawson filled my vision, my peripheral vision gone. My heart picked up speed, and beads of sweat formed on my forehead. I was in full fight-or-flight mode. The mere mention of Montana suggested the FBI knew more than I thought possible. I couldn't deal with that now — I needed time.

"At least I have some idea where I stand," I said, breaking eye contact. "Why don't we go out for a drive and you can judge my skills for yourself? That'll give me time to think things over."

The change of subject was as subtle as a brick to the face, and no doubt told her she'd found leverage. But I didn't care. I wasn't about to tackle the Montana issue head-on right now, and I was happy to concede ground.

"Does that mean you're accepting the job?" she asked, a little surprised.

"No. It means I need to think about the logistics." I didn't add that I also needed to contemplate the fallout from her implied threat.

"We can help with all that if needed," she said almost immediately, sensing an opening. It was the first time she'd shown her inexperience — she should have kept quiet. Silence can be a powerful negotiating weapon.

"I'm pretty sure the FBI doesn't have business managers with expertise in the exotic car world. Let's just go for a drive before you make promises you can't keep," I offered in a conciliatory tone.

She balled up her food wrappers, sank a rimless bin shot, and grabbed her bag from the side of her chair as she stood. I opened the desk drawer and picked up the keys to a Ford GT LM that was sitting in the car park. It was one of the new GTs. The classic GT was tucked away on the third floor and needed a special occasion to make it outside. While not as rare as our usual stock, it was still a unique car with stunning performance for an American vehicle. True, the V6 wasn't what you'd expect, but the way this car handled made it a future classic. I also grabbed my wallet and mobile, and we headed down to the lobby via the freight lift.

I guess I shouldn't have been all that surprised to see Lucas in the lobby, pretending to be busy. Completely ignoring me, he made a beeline for Jessica and struck up a conversation. I left them chatting while I went out to the car to make sure it was properly warmed up and ready to go. After about five minutes I was still sitting in the car park on my own. I began to wonder if Lucas was showing Jessica his workshop, if you know what I mean. I dug my phone out of my pocket, then fished around for her business card. After dialling the number and speaking with the operator, I was quickly connected to her mobile. It rang a few times before she picked up. Without waiting for a hello or identifying myself, I said,

"I know organising your love life is important, but I'm rapidly beginning to change my mind about our discussion."

Without waiting for a reply, I thumbed the end-call button and looked over to the doors. Within about ten seconds, Jessica came through at pace and then stopped as she tried to find me in the car park. I flicked the paddle shifter to select first and crawled up to where she was standing. She hurriedly opened the door — almost caught unawares by the gullwing style — and then hesitated before trying to climb in. This brought a rather large smile to my face, as it always did when someone tried to get into a very low sports car for the first time. Shame she wasn't wearing a skirt; she'd probably have fallen over, which would have added to my entertainment. After a brief struggle, she figured out that the bum-first method was the way to go and unceremoniously dropped into the seat. Swinging her legs in, she pulled the door closed with a firmness that made me cringe.

"You know, I really am sorry about keeping you waiting. I completely lost track of time. It's not entirely my fault — you did sort of introduce the two of us in the first place."

"Yes, I did. Thing is, I was brought up in a house where you own your decisions. So don't try to blame me for getting distracted."

With nothing else to say — and, I assume, feeling slightly admonished — she stopped talking and just sat there as we drove, making a meal of figuring out the four-point harness. It wasn't long before I noticed a car lurking behind us. It's not unusual; the rarity of our cars means we often get followed by petrolheads wanting a glimpse of automotive royalty. On this occasion it was a 5 Series BMW with two familiar-looking gents inside.

"You know something?" I asked in a tone that made it clear I was being rhetorical. "I'm looking in my mirror as I drive along, and guess what I see?"

"I don't know. What?" came a very convincing reply from the passenger seat.

"A blue BMW — very like the one you get chauffeured around in. And I'm pretty sure I recognise the driver and passenger too. I thought I told you to come alone," I said, letting my annoyance show.

"I did, honestly."

The need to be believed sounded genuine and had me thinking she might be telling the truth. Or maybe I just wanted to believe her. Mind games aren't my strong point, so I decided not to dwell on it and instead planned my response.

"They must have decided to follow me... or else they were told to," she added after a pause.

"Either way, I'm not appreciating the lack of trust. You wanted to see how good a driver I am? I suggest you tighten your harness."

I indicated for her to pull on the straps, waited until she was strapped in tightly, then started the getaway. With a car that'll hit sixty in under four seconds from a standstill, I knew I had a huge advantage. Unfortunately, most of that was wiped out by the afternoon traffic. I jabbed the throttle and the car lurched forward, pinning us both into our seats. If she hadn't figured out what was coming, she did now.

"I really hope you're not going to do anything stupid. It's not like they mean any harm."

"The way I see it, we can have a bit of fun and you can judge my driving. Any problems with that?"

Before she could answer, I cut in: "No? Good. Settled."

We reached a set of red lights. While we waited, I kept half an eye on my mirrors in case Jessica's colleagues thought I was abducting her and tried to block us. Given the car I'd chosen, I also needed a route without too many speed humps. The lights turned green and I watched the BMW creep forward impatiently, the driver's anxiety becoming obvious. A slow-moving car coming the other way provided a gap to turn right towards the dual carriageway. A quick swing of the wheel and a firm dab of the throttle saw the rear step out slightly before it found grip and shot away from the junction. I snatched a look in the mirror and saw the BMW trying — and failing — to cut across the oncoming traffic. That's the thing about London traffic: no matter how aggressively you drive, everyone else can match it, or worse.

We reached the roundabout for the carriageway in no time and, after giving way to a few cars, I floored it and sent the car screaming into the junction. Being rear-wheel drive, it naturally oversteered; I soon had the tail out as we slid sideways. I feathered the throttle to keep a balanced slide before taking the third exit. I'm guessing the BMW was only just reaching the roundabout and could probably see the lingering tyre smoke. Either way, with my foot still buried, we were at three-figure speeds in under six seconds. There was no way they were catching up, and I never saw them again.

Easing off, I used the car's race-car-esque handling to weave through traffic. At each roundabout I braked late and carried as much speed through the apex as possible. It sounds nerdy, but over the years I've raced in a few amateur series — still at a decent level. You need a racing licence, not just a pile of cash, so I've a pretty good idea how cars behave on the limit.

So far, Jessica hadn't said a word, which meant one of two things: either she was so impressed she was lost for words, or she was petrified. Judging by how she clung to the seat bolsters, I'd say the latter. I found it rather satisfying; they always say if your passenger isn't scared, you're not driving hard enough. Not being a local girl, she didn't know the back roads I took, and after about half an hour we arrived in Weybridge, stopping in front of her residence. Parking outside the gate, I switched off, pressed the harness release, and turned to face her.

"You can let go of the seat now," I said with a smile, which she clearly didn't appreciate.

"That's not very funny — like your driving. It was irresponsible, immature, and just plain dangerous."

"Does that mean I don't get the job?" I asked, wondering if I'd just created an out for myself.

"I've every right to tell you to forget we ever met, but my superiors are adamant you're the man they want, so you're definitely not off the hook. Have you thought any more about it, or were you too busy trying to scare me?"

I really wanted to ask what she'd meant by mentioning Montana, but ignorance was bliss — for now. She didn't seem in a hurry to speak, so I let the silence fill the car.

"I'll do it," I said at last.

The way I saw it, I didn't really have a choice. The threat to my business was one thing — and I might have found a workaround — but the Montana stuff had to stay buried. As sure as I was that it had been buried forever, I couldn't take the risk.

"But I have a few conditions of my own."

"I'm sure that won't be a problem," Jessica said, visibly relaxing. It concerned me that she'd been so stressed about recruiting me for whatever scheme this was, but I'd have to park that for now.

"I'll be in touch over the next few days with travel arrangements. Give me a list of what you want, and I'll see it gets done. Now I'd better go, or the consulate will be sending out search parties for me — and Delta Force for you."

I couldn't really — nor did I want to — comment on that, so I just nodded. She pulled the handle to open the door but was stopped by the harness. My snort of laughter earned an icy stare. I wouldn't blame her for wishing we weren't going to be working together for the next three months. As she went to close the door, she paused and leaned in.

"Thank you for doing this, Eli," she said, with what sounded like genuine appreciation.

I gave a single nod in acknowledgement.

"Please close the door gently," I said, aiming for a friendly tone.

I watched her speak into the intercom and slip through the gates as they opened. Reconnecting the harness, I started the engine and idled towards the main road. As I reached the junction, the blue BMW that had tried to follow me earlier turned in. I couldn't resist a toot of the horn, a casual wave, and my best fake smile in their direction. I got nothing back. They were probably too worried about the bollocking they were about to get. Speaking of bollockings, I now had to figure out how to tell Amelia I was going back to the States for three months — and that I'd be working for the FBI.

Chapter 7

One week later, I was sitting next to Jessica in Virgin Atlantic's executive lounge, waiting to travel first class to Washington, D.C. They wanted to send me via American Airlines, but I have shares with Virgin, so I figured I'd keep it in the family. The rest of Jessica's team had flown home a few days earlier. She had stayed on to arrange the extra things I'd asked for — and even went on a date or two with Lucas.

"Thanks for sending those flowers to Amelia. They helped calm her down a bit."

"No problem. I figured she'd be pretty pissed. And I know how thoughtless you men can be," she replied with a smile.

"Pissed" was an understatement, but there were things I didn't want to talk about with her. She was far too sharp to accept the simple explanation I'd given, and that hadn't helped. While I hated being untruthful, the fact that I was still hiding from the truth of my past said a lot about my ability to share it with others — even those I wholeheartedly trusted. Despite that cloud hanging over me, I planned to make the most of this trip and enjoy myself as much as possible.

"You know, I think we're going to get on okay. Since you dropped that boss-bitch act, you're all right."

"Gee, thanks. Just as long as I don't have to get in a car with you again, we'll get along just fine."

"What's wrong with my driving?" I said, feigning hurt feelings.

"Oh, nothing, except I almost died. You're the craziest driver I've ever been in a car with."

"You lived to tell the tale, didn't you?"

"Yeah, though I'm not sure how," she replied, a smile forming on her face.

I smiled back to let her know I knew she was joking. We took advantage of the free drinks and snacks before boarding. Surprisingly, the plane left about five minutes early — a first in the world of aviation. The flight was uneventful, the food was good, and the in-flight movies weren't bad either.

We landed at Washington Dulles around 2 p.m., and I was amazed to find our bags already waiting. I wasn't sure if that was part of the first-class experience or simply a perk of travelling with the FBI, but either way, it was a welcome change from the rugby scrum that usually awaited us "normal folk" at baggage claim. I followed Jessica through the terminal and out to the pickup zone, where a black Cadillac CT5-V waited. She tapped a knuckle on the tinted side window, and the driver's door opened. A smartly dressed man stepped out to take our luggage. He was well groomed and looked like he kept himself in shape. I wasn't sure whether all this was meant to make me feel important, but it was certainly helping.

As we got into the car, I almost joked about how unsubtle it was, with "government car" practically written all over it. Then I noticed we already had company in the form of a silver-haired gentleman, so I wisely kept my mouth shut.

Later I learned that the car literally did have "government" stamped on it — on the license plate. My foot-and-mouth problem was alive and well, but for once I'd saved myself some embarrassment.

Jessica, seated next to the older man, broke the silence first.

"Eli, this is Dean Holtzman. He's a deputy director at the Bureau."

"It's good to meet you, Dean."

I deliberately used his first name to see how much of an asshole he was. To be fair, I try not to judge people right off the bat, but something about his body language suggested he might be a sanctimonious prick.

"Likewise, Eli. I've heard a lot about you from various sources. You can rest assured — it's all been good," he said in a surprisingly cheery tone.

"Well, it's always nice to meet a fan of my work," I replied with a genuine smile.

Maybe I'd misjudged him. Maybe he wasn't so bad after all.

"So, I'm not sure how much Jessica has told you, but we've booked you into a nice hotel in the centre of D.C., not too far from our offices. You'll stay there for a few nights until the rest of the team arrives. After a week or two in D.C., we'll move you on to San Francisco for the remainder of your trip."

Things were sounding better already. It's not that I don't like Washington — it's one of my favourite US cities — but being in San Francisco would be great. With its mix of beach and funky city life, it's the place to be, especially in summer.

"Well, you won't hear any complaints from me on that one," I said, smiling. "The heat in D.C. can be a bit much this time of year."

We rode in silence for a while as we left the airport district and merged onto the Dulles Toll Road toward I-95, the beltway around the city. The silence felt uncomfortable, and I could tell Jessica sensed it too — she was sitting a little too rigid in her seat.

"So, what exactly am I going to be doing?"

"Did Ms. Lawson not explain it all to you already? She was briefed to fill you in on what you need to know," Holtzman replied.

"She told me I'd be doing some driving duties, along with a bit of training. I suppose I'm just curious to know more."

"Well…why don't we get you settled at your hotel. When you stop by the offices over the next few days, I'll have someone get you up to speed on the exact details," Holtzman said, shooting Jessica a sharp look.

That was the moment my doubts from back home came flooding back. Things were definitely not as they seemed. I had a distinct feeling I was about to be screwed over, big time. Still, I let it slide — for now, even though my gut was usually pretty accurate in situations like this.

"Well, it'll be nice to be working with Jessica. A friendly face always helps in a strange town."

"I wouldn't get too used to it. Ms. Lawson will be your contact officer, which basically means you won't be seeing a whole lot of her after you leave for San Francisco."

My unease deepened. To be fair, Jessica never said we'd be working together the whole three months — that was an assumption I'd made. Not in the mood for more revelations, I shifted the conversation to sports. As we rumbled along the interstate, I chatted about the Redskins' lineup. I've known them by that name for 20-plus years, and I still can't bring myself to call them the Commanders. Everyone chimed in on the subject, even the driver, who I'd assumed was mute up to this point. Forty-five minutes later, we arrived at my hotel in the heart of the city. Nestled between the White House and Dupont Circle, it gave me easy access to the Metro and the busy shopping streets of Connecticut Avenue — which I planned to explore with my new no-limit credit card, courtesy of J. Edgar and friends.

"Well, Eli, this is you. We have all the details of your room, and the hotel staff have been told to look after your every need. If you need anything, just call this number," Holtzman said, handing me a card from his inner suit pocket. "Someone will put us in contact. Also, Danny" — the driver, as it turned out — "will be close by and at your disposal whenever you need him."

"That's very kind of you, Dean, thank you. I guess I'll see you both later in the week," I said, nodding to Jessica and shaking Holtzman's hand.

I jumped out of the car to find Danny already waiting with my bags.

"I just need to drop Mr. Holtzman and Ms. Lawson back at HQ, and then I'll be waiting in the lobby. If you wouldn't mind staying in the hotel until then, I'd appreciate it," my new babysitter drawled.

He was definitely a Southern boy, though I couldn't guess which state without risking offence. At the door, a bellhop took my luggage and led me up to reception. The feds were clearly on a charm offensive — the receptionist welcomed me like a regular guest.

When I reached my room, I found I'd been given a suite, not just a standard room. Dumping my bags by the bed, I flipped on the TV and skimmed through the 100-plus channels before realising there was nothing worth watching. It was just after four, and while I was hungry, I decided instead to take a jog along the National Mall — the stretch of green in front of the Capitol where all the locals run. Rummaging through my bags, I dug out my running shirt, shorts, and trainers. I figured Danny's "half an hour" would stretch into an hour minimum, since he was no doubt briefed on what I should and shouldn't know. So I decided against leaving a message at the desk for him.

I had just passed the White House, heading toward the Lincoln Memorial, when the black Cadillac pulled up against the curb ahead and Danny jumped out.

"What are you trying to do, get me fired? I thought we had an agreement that you'd stay at the hotel until I got back," he said, blocking my path, clearly eager to get in my face and show his annoyance.

"You actually told me to stay at the hotel, and I simply didn't reply. I'm a grown man. I don't need you to hold my hand. Now, I'm going to finish my run. You can either come with me or get back in the car and do whatever you want, okay?"

"It doesn't sound like I have much choice. I'll see you back at the hotel in about forty minutes."

"Are you telling me or asking me?"

"Asking, of course," he said with a slight smile.

"In that case, I'll see you then."

With that, he stepped aside and I resumed my run while he got back in the car and rejoined traffic. A pang of guilt

53

hit me for being so harsh. He was only doing his job, and he seemed like a decent guy but I hadn't come across the Atlantic to have every moment of my life dictated to me by someone else.

The rest of my run was uneventful, though I noticed my fellow joggers were friendlier than those back in London. By the time I got back to the hotel, I was sweating like a polar bear in the desert — the heat and humidity were brutal. Still, I found the energy to tap my wrist at Danny as I passed him, signalling I was back on time. He returned the gesture with a weak smile and gentle nod of the head.

After a quick shower, I pulled on jeans, a T-shirt, and casual shoes, then phoned the desk to send Danny up.

"Do you want a drink?" I asked after letting him in.

"No thanks, I'm on duty."

"Figured as much. Can I ask you a question?"

"Sure, go for it."

"Am I right in thinking you accompany me everywhere I go?" I asked, smiling.

"Yeeessss," he said slowly, clearly trying to figure out where I was going with this.

"And are you supposed to blend in and not look like a minder?"

"Yes."

"In that case, we're going shopping."

Without waiting for a reply, I grabbed my room card and wallet and headed for the door. Danny hurried after me as we made our way to the lifts. From the look of it, he was a junior agent — still in the phase of following orders to the letter.

"I'm sorry, sir, but I don't understand."

"It's simple. I want to go out for dinner and then grab some drinks at a local bar. I don't have the right clothes, and you might as well be wearing an FBI windbreaker. So, we need to go shopping."

"Okay, but why can't I just go home and change?"

"Because who would supervise me?"

After a brief moment of thought it was clear this was an argument he couldn't win.

"Besides," I said, flashing the Visa card in my hand, "I've got this — courtesy of your boss."

"I can't spend company money on clothes. I'll get fired," he exclaimed, sounding genuinely worried.

"Don't worry, you won't be. I will be. After all, your orders are to look after me and keep me happy, right?"

He clearly hated the plan, but his inexperience left him without a way out. Quietly wrestling with his conscience, he stayed silent until the lift doors slid open.

"All right," he finally said, "but let me choose the bar. I know just the place."

We ended up at Billy Reid in Georgetown and left with outfits suitable for an evening of partying.It transpired through conversation that Danny was single and looking, so I made sure we picked out a suitable outfit that suggested a high-value guy without looking like he was trying too hard.

Danny took me to a nice bar/bistro that, as the evening progressed, also doubled as a club. We both ate a steak dinner preceded by starters and followed by desserts. It seemed Danny was getting used to the idea of the department paying. We stayed out until about 1 am, by which time we were both pretty hammered, knew everyone in the bar by their first names, and collected a few phone numbers that I duly put in Danny's pocket.

We arrived back at the hotel making a considerable amount of noise and found a package waiting for us in the room. Doing his best FBI impression, as it was just that given how much he had drunk, Danny decided it must be a bomb, as neither of us had any recollection of ordering anything. Insisting that we create a cordon and that I should get in the wardrobe for protection, he bent down to inspect the bags. Danny's coordination had clearly seen better days as he staggered over to the bag and tentatively began trying to inspect it. Unsurprisingly, he toppled over onto the bags pretty much as soon as he leant forward, his equilibrium clearly destroyed by the cocktails and shots. Needless to say, the room didn't explode, nor did we suddenly get surrounded by a mysterious gas. On further inspection, it was our clothes from the earlier shopping trip. A very faint and distant memory told me we had asked for them to be sent here, but it was too much effort to summon that memory to my consciousness at this particular moment. I think Danny was asleep before his ass even hit the chair in the other room, so I just flung myself onto the bed. Despite the humming of the air-con unit, I drifted off very soon after.

Chapter 8

It was a close call between who woke up first, but there was no doubt we both felt rough. Still bleary-eyed and not fully aware of my surroundings, I tried to mentally locate the source of the noise that had interrupted my sleep. It turned out that both my mobile, Danny's mobile, and the three hotel phones were all ringing. Lying on the bed, I stretched out and answered the bedside phone.

"Ugh...hello," I groaned in a genuinely ill voice.

"What the hell are you still doing in your room? Don't tell me you're still in bed. It sounds like you've only just woken up."

Jessica sounded both pissed off and stressed. Not being a man of many words when hungover, I simply answered,

"Yes, yes, and yes."

"Look, Holtzman is not very happy with you, never mind the fact that you aren't making a very good impression. I suggest you get your ass down to the E Street entrance — and do it in a hurry. You're already an hour late."

"Yes, dear," I said sarcastically. Probably a grave mistake, but Jessica kept her cool, ignored my response, and continued.

"I don't suppose you know where Danny is? We can't seem to get hold of him either."

As if on cue, Danny stumbled into the room, holding his ringing phone and looking pale. I frantically waved at him not to answer it until I finished my call.

"Err, yeah, he's here with me. He's just making coffee. I'll tell him you called," I said, hanging up before she could ask me anything else.

"What the hell's going on? Anyone would think you're the president, the way the phones are ringing."

"It would appear, Danny, my boy, that we're supposed to be down at headquarters for something or other. Oh, and we were supposed to be there an hour ago."

It was like I'd flicked the "look of horror" switch inside Danny as his brain quickly caught up with where he was supposed to be.

"Oh shit. We — and by that, I really mean you — are supposed to be downtown going through the welcome-to-the-FBI paperwork and completing a shitload of legal forms. I was supposed to have you there at 9 a.m. sharp. I am so dead. Holtzman is going to transfer my ass to Louisiana or some hick town in the middle of nowhere."

I took that last comment to mean it was open season for dumb Southern jokes, but I decided they could wait until later in the day.

"Heh, don't sweat it. Leave it to me. I'll straighten things out with the boss. Dean and I are best buds."

"You don't know Dean Holtzman. He comes across nice when he wants something, but he's a major hard-ass. Everyone in the Bureau is scared shitless of him — even the director."

"What's the worst he can do, shout at me? I'm too valuable for him to piss off."

As the words left my mouth I wanted to punch myself in the face ⏹ I could be a pretentious prick at times.

"Don't believe all your own press," Danny said with the sternest look I'd ever seen on a fellow human.

Deciding we could continue the discussion on the way to the Hoover Building, I jumped out of bed and headed for the bathroom. After a quick shower, I dressed in a blue-checked shirt and my only suit. By the time I finished, Danny had also showered and was back in his previous day's black suit and white shirt, although the creases made him look decidedly less suave. Ten minutes and a roller-coaster car ride later, we were being waved into the secure underground parking of the Hoover Building.

Even though I was accompanied by Danny, the security guard insisted on searching me. Following protocol, he also phoned someone to confirm I was expected. In many ways it was reassuring that they took security so seriously — especially since the Western world had gone security-crazy after 9/11 and the multitude of other terror attacks that had plagued Western European cities. Once my clearance came through, we drove down a few levels until we found a parking spot. I figured it would only be a couple of minutes before we made it upstairs to be welcomed by the impending wrath of Dean Holtzman.

However, despite our arrival being announced, I was searched another three times before we finally made it up to the sixth floor, where Dean, Jessica, and some guys I hadn't met were waiting in an office.

"Good of you to join us, Mr. Miller."

He completely ignored Danny's presence.

"Yeah, sorry about that. Danny came to wake me up, and I must have dozed off. I guess he thought I was in the shower or something."

The least I could do was cover for him. It was my fault, after all, that we were almost two hours late for my first day. Shooting me an angry stare, Holtzman slowly turned to my chaperone and issued a stern warning.

"I want you to wait outside my office until I'm finished. I don't care if you have to wait there till midnight, take a leak, or the end of the world comes. I want you to make like a tree and grow some roots, you got me?"

"Yes, sir," came the regimental reply.

With an about-turn a soldier would have been proud of, Danny left the room. Headstrong idiot that I am, I was ready to jump up and defend him, but a subtle cough from Jessica told me to rethink that plan. Apparently she knew exactly how I was about to react. I made a mental note to thank her later.

"Well, Eli, Ms. Lawson has done a good job briefing us on your abilities and temperament, and I can only say that so far you've managed to make her look good. We're going to put this down to transatlantic teething problems. So how about we start afresh?"

"That's fine by me. Just tell me where and when you want me. Leave the rest to me. Oh, and you can forget the minders. I know my way around D.C. and I can take care of myself, all right?"

I figured the pleasantries were over, so there was no need to keep playing at being cordial.

"Fine. You'll spend the rest of the day here while Ms. Lawson and these gentlemen take you through the necessary legal stuff. Tomorrow, I expect you here at 9 a.m. sharp for a full medical and physical examination. Any questions so far? Shall I write this down for you?"

Normally I'm the first to appreciate sarcasm, but in this case, it pissed me off. I gave him a forced smile meant to be interpreted as: fuck off you tosser.

"Then, as of Monday, we'll move you to an apartment overlooking the Potomac River. There, you'll link up with the rest of your team. From that point on, you'll attend training courses and briefings at Quantico."

My cool, relaxed attitude was starting to wane. During his entire sermon-like speech, he never took his eyes off me. It's not that they were particularly scary eyes, but they gave me the feeling that if I looked away, he'd won. And I wasn't one to turn from a challenge — especially not from a prick like this.

He rambled on some more, but I'd tuned out after the first few minutes so had to hope it wasn't anything important. The next thing I heard was him asking for questions. Unsurprisingly, there were none. Chairs scraped back, which I took as my signal to get the hell out of Dodge.

Unfortunately, still not grasping how thin the ice was beneath my feet, I decided to leave a few parting words.

"Well, Dean, it's been a pleasure as always. We should do it again sometime — maybe same time tomorrow."

Giving my best smile, I extended my hand but was left hanging. Two seconds of eye contact — an unspoken Come on, take a swing — were interrupted by Jessica gently touching my arm and ushering me out. I finally understood what Danny meant about him. I wasn't going to last long if our paths crossed again.

Out in the corridor, I stopped to speak to Danny.

"Heh, man, I'm really sorry you got dragged into this."

"It's not your fault. I've only got myself to blame. Shouldn't have gotten so smashed last night."

Jessica, clearly impatient, practically dragged me down the corridor and into a large conference room.

"I'm not sure what you're playing at, but this isn't a game. This is our careers — our lives — you're fucking with."

Being a man of the world, I'd had plenty of experience with women hurling abuse at me. I'd come to the opinion that the best thing was to let them finish before defending yourself. The key, however, was not tuning out — because you had to be ready before they hit you with the classic: Well, don't you have anything to say?

"You know that Danny is probably going to be sent off to the remotest field office we've got."

Breaking my own cardinal rule — I just couldn't help myself — I interrupted her mid-flow.

"Well, I hear New Mexico is really quite nice this time of year."

"See what I mean? You're not even taking this seriously. You really are a prick, you know that?"

I'm sure if she'd been close enough, she would've slapped me. To be fair, I probably deserved it.

"Look, I'm sorry, okay? What happened with Danny was mostly my fault, and if I thought it would help, I'd go tell Mr. Anally Retentive back there what happened. The fact is, he simply doesn't like me."

"You couldn't be more wrong. He's the one who sent me to England to bring you back. He's the one who thinks you're the right man for the job. He just demands more respect than a homeless guy, which is how you've been acting toward us all. You won't be surprised to hear that Dean Holtzman has a reputation for busting people's balls, but he's a committed and hard-working member of this organisation who demands the very best from his team."

I hadn't felt so put in my place since my first day at school, when I got bollocked for speaking out of turn. It reminded me of a joke I'd heard a few years back, but now wasn't the time to share it. Grovelling was not one of my strong points, so I opted to engage my brain and put my mouth in neutral.

As we wandered through the corridors to where my first mountain of paperwork awaited, I replayed what Jessica had said. From the moment I'd met her, I'd caused trouble at every opportunity. Maybe it was genetic — when in doubt, blame the parents was another of my favourite phrases. I concluded I was going to make an effort to get through the rest of the week — all two days of it — without being rude, sarcastic, costing someone their job, or getting myself deported.

The rest of the day went by quickly. Even though I was filling out form after form with the same details, I suppose it was the novelty of being in a new place surrounded by new people. Half the time I wasn't even sure what I was signing — so much small print, which I guess is what you'd expect from a government organisation. By the time 5 p.m. rolled around I was done with the day, I was exhausted and relieved to see the American personnel promptly pack up and head home.

As I sat at the conference table considering my evening options, I felt a hand on my shoulder. I turned to see Jessica, who had somehow slipped into the room almost silently.

"Well, I'm glad to see you've behaved yourself after this morning's mishaps."

"I took on board what you said, and you were right. I wasn't behaving professionally. I'm sorry."

"It's not me you need to apologise to. Anyway, it's time for you to go home — or to the hotel, at least."

"Great, a night in front of the TV. Just what I was looking forward to on my second night in a new city."

"I think you saw enough of the city last night. Why not hit the gym, the pool, or maybe just the sauna? Get some room service, catch a film. Just stay out of trouble — and don't forget to be here at nine in the morning."

"Yeah, yeah, I know."

It was like being home with Amelia again.

"So, how do I get out of this place?"

"Just follow the crowd to the elevators, ride down to the basement, and there'll be a driver waiting for you."

"I think I'll walk, if that's ok?" I said as I got out of the chair and headed toward the open door, noticing a steady stream of people heading left.

"You know how to get back, right?" she asked.

"Yeah, yeah, I know the way," I half-lied, giving a flippant wave over my shoulder.

While I had a good sense of direction, it wasn't true that I actually knew the way to the hotel. It was going to have to be an educated guess. Still, I fancied the fresh air and the freedom, so it seemed getting lost was worth the risk.

As I reached the bank of lifts in the sixth-floor lobby, I caught a glimpse of Danny still waiting outside Holtzman's office. I threw him a wave, which he returned with a nod, and then gave him the universal "call me" signal with my thumb and pinkie finger. Two minutes later, I was outside on E Street, turning left toward Lafayette Square.

Danny's predicament was still on my mind. I felt guilty, but I told myself I hadn't forced the drinks down his throat. Still, I got the distinct sense — from everyone —

64

that it was unlikely Danny and I would cross paths again, which was a shame, because he was a fun guy to hang out with. Hopefully the guys I'd be living with would be half as much fun.

After stopping with the tourists at the White House gates, I reached the junction of Pennsylvania Avenue and Connecticut Avenue and turned right toward my hotel. It had been easier than I'd thought — the grid pattern of roads and alphabet rise of the east-to-west streets made it simple to correct any mistakes.

I arrived at the hotel about twenty minutes later and decided to hit the gym and pool as Jessica had suggested. After an hour and a half of exercise, I was ready for dinner and chose the sociable option of dining at the bar. At least that way I might meet some interesting people to help pass the time.

I was halfway through my mushroom cannelloni when I struck up a conversation with a fellow guest. A short while later two others joined us, and we spent the rest of the night drinking scotch on the rocks and swapping stories. It was just after midnight when I left the three of them and headed up to bed. I'd laughed so much there'd be no need for sit-ups in the morning.

Tired — a combination of jet lag and the workout — I quickly stripped and practically launched myself into bed.

Chapter 9

For reasons unbeknownst to me, I woke up at 7:58 a.m.. This was fortunate, as in my semi-drunken state the night before, I had forgotten to arrange a wake-up call. I guess my screw-ups from the previous day were weighing on my subconscious more than I knew. I went through my morning routine and left for the walk to E Street at about 8:40 a.m..

As soon as I stepped out of the hotel entrance, a wall of humidity instantly hit me. The hotel's air conditioning had created a false sense of comfort compared to the reality of the outside weather. Not wanting to arrive at the office with sweat marks on my shirt, I jumped in the nearest taxi and travelled in air-conditioned luxury. Despite this, by the time I arrived in the lobby of the Hoover Building, I was only five minutes early.

As I rode up in the lift, I wondered where I should go once I reached my floor. Thankfully, I had a reception party. Jessica, accompanied by two different gentlemen from the day before, was waiting in the lift lobby.

"Good morning," I said in an upbeat voice.

"Good morning, Eli. I'm glad to see you made it on time today."

I gave her a little smile to let her know that her sarcasm was both recognised and appreciated.

"These are Doctors Frazier and Kapowski," she said, gesturing to the two men who had positioned themselves slightly behind her. "They'll be taking care of you today. Try to do as they tell you."

"Yes, ma'am."

I resisted the temptation to salute, deciding I'd take a day off from playing the fool. With nothing more to say, I followed the two doctors back to the lifts. We travelled up to what I assumed was the top floor — which wasn't that high, as I'd recently learned that no building could be taller than the Capitol. Pierre Charles L'Enfant, the city's 19th-century planner, had made it D.C. law.

We stepped out into a glass-partitioned room full of laboratory equipment. The rest of the morning was taken up with the first of two medicals. Three hours later, feeling like the FBI must now have a map of both my insides and outsides, I was finally set free for lunch.

I had until 2 p.m., so I headed to a burger bar on D Street before shopping for some athletic gear I'd need for the afternoon's tests. That afternoon was a pretty unpleasant affair. I spent most of it getting on and off treadmills, being pricked with needles in my earlobes and fingertips, and having tubes stuck in my mouth. I wasn't really sure why all this was necessary for me to drive a car — probably something to do with avoiding a lawsuit in case I dropped dead.

Glad the day was over, I was heading toward the exit when the security team at the front desk stopped me and handed me an envelope. Opening it, I found details about my next residence, along with contact information in case of any problems.

I had just stepped out onto the street when a black Cadillac CT6 came out of the underground parking garage and sped past me. While I was sure the FBI owned plenty of these cars, I was very surprised to recognise the driver. Maybe Jessica had been a bit over-eager in her predictions about Danny's future, but one thing was clear: he definitely wasn't in New Mexico.

Chapter 10

After two nights of moderately heavy drinking, I decided tonight was going to be a chilled one. I took the opportunity to make some calls back home, first to Amelia and then to Lucas, who I had promoted to caretaker CEO. I was a little disappointed to hear that everything was running smoothly at the office and there hadn't been a crisis yet. I think most business owners feel their businesses will collapse as soon as they step away from the desk. My ego was clearly a little bruised, but in some ways it was a good sign that the business was running as normal. At the very least, it was proof that I had a very competent team working for me.

The second call, to Amelia, was a little less easygoing. She was clearly tired and stressed from her work and wasn't very easy to talk to. After twenty minutes of a disjointed conversation, I gave up and said I would call on Sunday, after she'd had a weekend away from her job.

The rest of the evening involved room service and cable TV, until I got the welcome interruption of a phone call. Surprising me for the second time today, I was greeted by Danny's voice.

"Hey, Danny, how are you doing?"

"Yeah, not too bad. I got a bit of a bollocking from Holtzman, but I'll survive."

"Well, I didn't think I was going to hear from you again, never mind see you again."

"Oh, well, actually, that isn't going to happen for a while. I've been warned off you."

"I meant that I saw you driving away from the office today. But why aren't we allowed to hang out?"

"I believe his words were 'bad influence, irresponsible, and reckless.'"

"I didn't think he knew me so well. I'm touched," I said, which was accompanied by a chuckle — and met with one.

"Yeah, well, I just thought I'd call to see how you are."

"I'm doing pretty well, thanks. I've been through all the paperwork and medicals and I'm off to meet my team on Monday. If I'm honest, I'm really looking forward to getting my teeth stuck into something that doesn't involve sitting in an office."

"Yeah, I know what you mean. Listen, if you need anything once you start your assignment — or just someone to talk to — then call me, okay?"

He gave me his mobile number before hanging up, just in case I misplaced my phone. At least I had some comfort in knowing that Danny still had a job and that I had another friend to call on if — or should I say when — I got myself into trouble.

My weekend passed with very little drama. I visited a few of the Smithsonian museums, took a trip over the Potomac to Alexandria — the site of a World War II torpedo factory — and stopped by a few neighbourhood bars and bistros to feel less like a tourist.

I didn't have to check out until 1 p.m., so I took the opportunity to use the gym again. On returning to my room, I noticed the red light flashing on the phone, indicating a message at the lobby desk.

"Hello, Mr. Miller. How may we assist you this morning?" asked the duty concierge.

"I think you have a message for me?"

"Ah, yes, you had a package delivered about an hour ago. Would you like it sent up to your room?"

"Yes, thank you. That would be great."

About two minutes later, there was a knock at the door, and the bellhop was waiting with two A4-sized white envelopes. After palming him a five-dollar bill as I thanked him, I wandered over to the settee and began tearing the top off the envelope. To my disappointment, it was the results of my paperwork exercise from two days ago. I was now in possession of a legal driver's license, social security card, and some other photo IDs I didn't immediately recognise. I also came across a firearms license and, to my surprise, the ownership details of a car.

In the second envelope were the keys to my new car, detailed directions to my new apartment, as well as an itinerary for the upcoming week.

Looking at the itinerary, it appeared we had a busy week ahead, but thankfully most of it wouldn't be spent sitting in an office. Instead, we'd be doing practical, outside-based activities. There were a lot of gaps in the schedule — probably for breaks and bonding sessions. As for the car I was now the owner of, I knew what I'd requested, but I was a little hesitant that it wouldn't be quite what I'd asked for.

After my shower, I quickly repacked my bag and added the new IDs to my now overflowing wallet. After checking the room one last time, I headed down to the lobby for the perfunctory "my stay was great, no, there was nothing I needed, it was excellent, thank you" checkout process. It was nice, for a change, not to have to pay at the end of this stay. Sometimes it's the little things in life.

As I reached the front door, I saw the doorman, Rocco, and beckoned him over.

"You're checking out, Mr. Miller? Can I get you a taxi?"

"Thanks, but I believe you've a car waiting for me in the garage."

"Yeah, right, I saw it earlier but didn't realise it was yours. I'll go get it for you, sir."

"Thanks," I shouted as he scurried off around the back of the building.

Two minutes later, my new chariot appeared from the service road that I assumed led to the hotel car park. So far, my request for a BMW M5 CS in frozen deep green had been met. While not the typical exotic car I'm used to, there's no doubt this thing is an absolute monster. True, I could have gone for something from a domestic manufacturer, but ultimately I liked driver's cars — a tag rarely given to the likes of a Dodge Charger.

This thing was a proper sleeper. A sleeper is a car that looks like an everyday vehicle but hides a high-performance engine under its "plain" exterior — subtly styled to belie the monster twin-turbocharged V8 under the hood. Coupled with physics defying handling, some wizard-level electronics, and a premium interior, the M5 is hard to argue with. The CS was a limited edition that added a little extra je ne sais quoi. The gold detailing against the deep green paint, coupled with red accents and plenty of carbon fibre, means this M5 was almost certainly destined to be a classic. Given this was likely to be the last non-hybrid M5, it already had a reserved spot back home — probably in my personal garage.

Swinging it into the spot reserved for hotel guests, Rocco jumped out of the driver's seat, leaving the door ajar for me.

"That's a very nice car — brand new as well. You can smell the fresh leather in there. The rental company is really looking after you with this one."

"Sure looks like it," I said as I handed him five dollars while heading for the driver's door.

I didn't see the need to tell him it wasn't a rental. I'm pretty sure he wouldn't know what to make of the fact that his tax dollars, via the FBI, had bought it for me.

Once inside, I took a few minutes to familiarise myself with the switches and buttons. It never ceases to amaze me how complicated some manufacturers make it to access basic functions in a car. Thankfully, BMW has been fairly consistent over the years, so this was straightforward enough. The nature of my day job meant I occasionally drove abroad, so being on the other side of the road wasn't too strange either. My main concern was the notoriously aggressive American drivers and the sometimes inflexible police officers when it came to the road rules.

Feeling as comfortable as possible in a completely new car, I joined the flow of traffic and headed north up Connecticut Avenue. I used the filter lane to access Dupont Circle and then headed back southbound on Connecticut Avenue. Stopping at a red light, I punched the zip code of the apartments into the Sat Nav system and continued my journey, focusing on the roads rather than my direction.

Chapter 11

I headed south down Route 1 and, after crossing over the Potomac River, drove for 20 minutes to North Alexandria, the site of the waterfront apartment I'd been told to report to. With the property not being in the centre of town, there was plenty of parking. However, it appeared that the apartments had underground parking. With no security barrier, I drove straight in, stopped in the nearest spot, and headed up to the apartment with my bags.

With no door key or security swipe included in the welcome pack, I opted for the doorbell as opposed to knocking. I waited for about thirty seconds with no reply and was about to ring the bell again when I heard the distinct sound of a lock turning. Much to my surprise, I was greeted by a woman in her late twenties. I stereotypically decided that her olive skin tone made her Spanish. She was about 5'10" and quite slender, with faded blonde highlights in her mid-brown, wavy, softly permed shoulder-length hair. Dressed casually in blue denim jeans and a close-fitting Hilfiger white tee, it was apparent she had a very athletic physique. This lady was 100% Category A — a woman who looked this good dressed this casually was a lock. First Jessica, and now her. I had to give it to the FBI: they certainly employed some nice-looking women.

"Hi, I'm Eli Miller. I believe I am your new roommate."

"Eva Fuentes," she said in a pleasant, though not overly friendly tone, while extending her hand. "Come on in. We've been expecting you."

We. I guess it was a bit optimistic to think I'd just be living with her. Leaving my bags at the door, I followed her — while trying not to look at her ass — down to the last doorway. This opened into a large open-plan kitchen cum lounge. The glass-lined space offered fantastic views over the river and the Washington skyline, while letting in enough natural light to need few fixtures. At the far end was a large TV surrounded by an equally large L-shaped brown leather sofa. My first impressions were good: the place was well-decorated, well-equipped, and looked very comfortable.

After the initial five seconds of taking everything in, I noticed two guys sitting on the sofa. As I wandered over to introduce myself, I also noticed several pictures of me on the dining table. Not wanting to make it too obvious that I'd seen them, I continued, but I couldn't ignore that the pictures looked like they'd been taken in front of the hotel that morning. That meant I had been watched.

I walked to the back of the sofa, noticed the baseball game on TV, and said,

"So, how … "

I was cut off before I could finish, as one of the guys raised his hand to shut me up.

"Don't mind them. They're too engrossed in their stupid stick-and-ball game. It'll be over in a few minutes. You can do your introduction then," came Eva's voice from the kitchen.

I was about to reply when I was cut off again, this time by a deep voice.

"Nah, it's already over. The Mets can't win."

Turning back to the sofa, I saw the guy who'd raised his hand get up and make his way around. He was a black guy who looked like he spent at least eight hours a day in the gym. If I had to guess, I'd say he weighed about 250 pounds and stood 6'4" — the kind of guy you never wanted as an enemy. With his hair closely cropped, it was difficult to put an age on him, but I'd guess late thirties. With an outstretched hand, he introduced himself.

"Hi, I'm Isaiah Johnson."

"Hey, Eli Miller."

"I'm your team leader for the next few months. If you have any questions or problems, then come and see me. Okay?"

"Sure thing, sir." I wasn't too sure whether to call him sir, but I didn't want to get on the wrong side of this guy. This brought a chuckle from him.

"There's no need for the sir. In fact, get out of that habit right now. The last thing we need is for you calling me sir at the wrong moment."

That confused me a little. I had no idea what he meant by the wrong moment, but I let it pass. Funny thing — my usual sarcastic and abrasive manner was nowhere to be found in front of this guy.

"That's a funny accent you've got. You're not from around here, are you?"

"No. I, err... flew in from London last Wednesday."

The look of surprise on his face was obvious, and it was a differently accented voice that vocalised the thought.

"Oh jeez, the final part of the team arrives, and not only does he not live over here, but he isn't even American..."

By this stage, Eva had come over and perched herself on the arm of the sofa. All eyes were now on me, and I could see the concern in them. Isaiah spoke first.

"You'll have to ignore Steve. He's still quite new to the company, and we're working on removing those personality traits that make him say whatever's on his mind. By the way, that" — he pointed with his thumb to the guy on the couch — "is Steve Weinhart. Steve is the final member of the team and is the resident electronics and surveillance expert."

"So, English," came the distinctive Midwestern accent, "what's your specialty then? I'm sure you've not been brought in for a bit of cultural flavour."

"I believe I'm here as a consultant for the driving bit of our time together. I think I'm also going to be chauffeuring you all around."

"Well, that's encouraging," said Eva. "So who do you work for back home? The Flying Squad, SO17, or are you a regular James Bond with MI5?"

"Bond is MI6, but I'm not quite sure I follow. I sell cars for a living."

I think that was the last answer any of them expected, and not even Steve seemed to have anything to say. He was, however, the first to break the uncomfortable silence.

"So let me get this right. Not only do you have no idea about this country, but you have no formal training and you sell cars for a living."

Turning to Isaiah and Eva, he continued,

"This is bullshit. I was told this was a crucial mission, yet Holtzman decided to send some foreigner to join us. When this goes south, I'm going to make damn sure everyone knows how screwed up this situation is."

"Heh, listen," I said in an unusually unyielding tone. "I didn't ask for this job. Your bosses approached me with threats that if I didn't get on board, they'd sabotage my business. I didn't really have a choice."

"So you're here just for the driving, hey? Well, I have a licence, and I'm pretty handy behind the wheel, so problem solved. Thanks for coming, but you've been replaced," said Steve offhandedly.

I began to dig into my trouser pockets for the car keys when Isaiah spoke up.

"Listen up, Steve, and this goes for you too," he said, pointing at me. "Eli is not going anywhere. I don't know why Holtzman invited him to this little party, but he did. It's not our job to question it or try to change the outcome. We will be at Quantico tomorrow. Any questions can be asked, and hopefully answered, then. Until then, Eli is a part of the team, and we will all make him so. Got it?"

"Fine by me," said Eva, heading back to the kitchen to finish her coffee.

"Steve, you got it?"

"Whatever you say, big man," came the nonchalant reply.

"Okay then, welcome to the team. Eva will show you to your room. Treat the place like home, and don't mind Steve. I think he's got a bit of PMT."

"Thanks," I said with a chuckle.

I walked back to the hallway, grabbed my bags, and turned to find Eva waiting at one of the doorways.

"In here," she said, opening the door and then disappearing inside.

The room was a good size, with an en suite as well. The double bed was set in the centre of the room, with a desk to the left and a large oak wardrobe to the right of the main door. Putting my bag next to the bed, I decided to take the opportunity to try to understand what the hell was going on. Since Eva seemed the most receptive to me being here, now seemed like as good a time as any.

"Look, I'm really confused. What exactly is going on?"

"Yeah, you aren't the only one. I think we've all been thrown off balance by your arrival. From what we've been told — and that isn't very much — we're working on a very important mission with long-term consequences for crime in this country."

"Whoa, whoa, hold up a minute."

All of a sudden, that feeling of being screwed over had returned yet again. Only this time I had a better idea of exactly whose fault it was.

"What's all this about a mission and crime? I was told I was consulting on driver training and doing some chauffeuring. Are you telling me something different?"

"I'm not telling you anything," she said, heading for the door. A previously undetected tension had suddenly appeared between us. "Maybe that's why you've been brought in. I don't know. You'll have been told what you need to know, and if there's anything else, you'll find out tomorrow along with the rest of us."

Things seemed to be moving in a direction I had no control over, and before I could probe further, Eva left the room and pulled the door shut. I wasn't in a state of shock — complete confusion was a better description. Had I been lied to about this whole trip? Was my being here going to prove to be a huge mistake?

I sat on the bed, pondering this, along with a few other worrying questions, for about 15 to 20 minutes. I came up with no answers, a whole heap more questions, and a new level of anxiety about this whole situation. They say secrets never stay secret forever and eventually come back to bite you in the ass. That certainly rang true for my current predicament. I didn't really have much of an option apart from waiting for the following day, as it was clear none of my housemates could help me out on this one.

Chapter 12

Finally, bored with my own company, I decided I needed to clear my head. I grabbed my running gear from my bag and headed back to the main lounge area.

"Heh, guys, I'm heading out for a jog. I'll be back in about an hour or so."

As I was about to leave, Isaiah said,

"Mind if I join you? I could do with some fresh air."

"Help yourself. I just hope you can keep up, because I won't be waiting for you," I said with a smile.

"Sounds like a challenge to me. Give me five minutes to change, and I'll be with you. Steve, Eva, you coming?"

"Mr. Car Dealer thinks he can outrun us. I wouldn't miss it for the world," replied Steve as he jumped off the sofa and headed down the hall.

It looked like this was going to get quite competitive, not exactly what I had planned but it might at least help me feel less like an outsider. I reckoned I could handle Isaiah, but Steve might be a different matter. We were both around 6'1", give or take, but Steve looked a little leaner and certainly more built up in the upper body. With his black hair cut quite short all over, he was not someone you'd voluntarily pick a fight with. He reminded me of Edward Norton in American History X, except he probably didn't have a swastika tattooed on his chest.

"I think I'll pass," said Eva from the comfort of the sofa. "Seems like there's a bit too much testosterone involved for it to be fun."

Isaiah disappeared to his room to get changed, so I sat on the sofa and watched a bit of telly. I ended up just chit-chatting with Eva about the news and weather. My first impression told me she was a nice person and very easy to talk to. At the same time, I was aware that she worked for the FBI, so there was likely a lot more to her than my brief chat was ever going to tell me.

Almost to the second, both of my running partners appeared, and the heckling began.

"You sure you're up for this?" asked Steve.

"I mean, you look really comfortable on the sofa," said Isaiah as they continued their double act.

"You do realise that you'll have to wash your hair when we get back," said Steve, earning a high five from Isaiah.

"Well, I just hope there's more to you two than words. It would be a real shame to mess up those egos."

That got a laugh from Eva, and as I got up to go, she said,

"I'm relying on you to win. I don't know if I can cope with their egos otherwise."

"I'll do my best," I said, smiling.

We set off along the riverbank, going north back toward the city centre, and it wasn't long before we were crossing the Arlington Memorial Bridge and running along the mall. The sun was still pretty strong, and all of us were sweating despite the leisurely pace. We chatted about general things like sport, politics, and cars for a while until we made it to the top of the mall and were in front of the Capitol building.

"I reckon the last one back cooks dinner," said Steve, who had been eager to increase the pace since we left.

"Sounds fair to me," said Isaiah. "Eli, any objections?"

"No, as long as you promise to make something nice," I replied with a smile, wiping my forehead on my shirt.

Without another word, Steve accelerated and started to open up a gap, and within a minute or two Isaiah was also beginning to pull away. It was obvious that my mouth was bigger than my ability on this occasion, and I was resigned to defeat — until I came up with a wonderful idea. While jumping in a taxi was obviously cheating, and that wasn't my style, the route back to the apartment hadn't been specified. Having visited Washington a number of times — and the previous few days had helped me re-familiarise myself with the area — I had a pretty good picture of its road layout in my head.

Leaving the other two to head down the mall and back the way we'd come, I took a left turn and headed for the 14th Street Bridge. Fortunately, my memory served me well, and I ended up on the riverside path I was aiming for. This shortcut probably saved me about five minutes, but at the pace the other two were running, the difference could easily be wiped out. I ran as hard as I could, to the point where I was almost sick a couple of times.

I finally reached the apartment block to find that I was the first one back. Less than a minute later, I saw the bulk of Isaiah sprinting down the path with Steve very close behind. When they saw me sitting on the steps, they both looked surprised but were too out of breath to comment. After a few minutes of heavy breathing, Steve challenged,

"How... the... hell did you get here before us? There was no way you came past me."

"Nor me," said Isaiah. "I know we didn't stipulate no taxis, but you must have cheated."

"I never thought you guys would be sore losers," I said, smiling. "Can't you just accept that you were beaten by a car dealer? I'd get used to it if I were you."

"There's no way you beat us both fairly."

"Well, I didn't swim across the Potomac," I said, indicating my sweat-drenched T-shirt. "I just took a slightly different route, that's all."

"I knew it. There was no way you could have won without cheating," said Steve.

"Cheating? Nah, I don't think so. I just played by the rules — which, on this occasion, didn't exist. So I took the 14th Street Bridge."

"I knew it. I told you he cheated," said Steve, appealing to Isaiah.

"Yeah, well, I suppose you could look at it that way, but I prefer to think Eli used his initiative to outwit us both. In which case, it looks like you're cooking dinner, Stevie."

"Ah, man, that's no way fair."

"That was the deal, and you did finish behind me."

Seeing an opportunity to get on Steve's good side — since he had been the most vocal about me being part of the team — I decided to interrupt with what I hoped was an olive branch of sorts.

"I'll tell you what, how about I give you a hand with the cooking."

"I'd take that offer if I were you. If I remember correctly, your cooking isn't the best."

"Yeah, okay," said Steve reluctantly. "Thanks."

We headed up to the apartment to give Eva the good news. After both Steve and I had showered, we made a quick shopping list, got the drink orders from the other two, and headed to the local supermarket in the car.

The evening went smoothly, considering the reception I'd gotten on arriving. The dinner of spaghetti bolognese went down well — though I have to claim credit, as Steve managed to limit his involvement to chopping and stirring. Washed down with a few bottles of French red, the evening passed in a jovial manner, with no mention of the following day. We all eventually hit the sack sometime after midnight.

I struggled to get to sleep straightaway despite all the alcohol I'd consumed. I lay in bed thinking about what the immediate future held. Despite my concerns about tomorrow, I felt a lot more comfortable around my new flatmates and marginally more accepted by the team for who I was.

Chapter 13

Despite setting off for Quantico at around 8 a.m. the next morning, we were still cutting it fine by the time we turned off I-95 and headed for the training centre. If it hadn't been for the bridge works at the Franconia/Springfield interchange, we would have been pulling up to the security gate twenty minutes early. Instead, we had five to spare. Flashing our passes at the guards on duty, it quickly became clear my passengers had been here before, and I was directed by Steve to a set of buildings behind the main complex.

There were already a few cars in the parking area, one of which was a black Cadillac that I guessed belonged to Dean Holtzman. We were inside within a minute and directed to a boardroom at the end of the corridor. Walking in as a group of four, I finally felt part of the team — albeit with me bringing up the rear. The room was well-lit, very plush, with lots of wood and metal, and had a long glass table in the centre. On either side were four leather chairs, with an additional one at the end. Five of the nine seats were occupied. Some were familiar faces, though there were two I didn't recognise.

"It's good to see you all. I had begun to think you had corrupted more of my agents, Mr. Miller," said Dean Holtzman, predictably sitting at the head of the table.

"Well, I tried my best, but to no avail," I replied in an equally sarcastic tone as Steve and Isaiah shot me a surprised look at how I was talking to their boss.

We sat down at the near end of the table. I ended up next to Eva, with Isaiah and Steve opposite. Looking around, I saw Jessica on the other side next to Steve, and then Danny next to her. On my side were two guys who couldn't look more different if they tried. The one nearest me looked like one of the desk jockeys from E Street. The other could have easily passed as a crackhead who'd just been pulled off the street.

I gave both Jessica and Danny a friendly wave, which they returned with subtle smiles. The table was otherwise empty apart from the standard jugs of water, glasses, and some bound paperwork in front of us new arrivals.

"Before we get started, I want you four," said Holtzman, pointing towards our end of the table, "to read the information in front of you. You know the drill, but for Eli's sake, no notes — and you can't take any of the documents away with you."

I noticed that Danny now had a laptop in front of him and was tapping away at the keyboard. I guessed he was the nominated note taker. Opening the binder, I was surprised to see a picture of Steve, followed by a detailed account of his life and career.

A computer software developer since high school, Steve attended USC, where he studied IT and various other tech courses. He was an all-star track athlete before a knee injury cut short that career. After working in Silicon Valley for a number of years, he got caught up in an internet scam. Although the full details weren't there, I got the impression that he'd been a computer guy mixed in with the wrong crowd. Either way, he was headed for prison until the FBI stepped in — more than likely Dean Holtzman — and recruited him to the Bureau. Details of his work since then were omitted, which I assumed meant they were classified. All in all, he seemed like a very capable person with a few years' experience. The backstory certainly didn't fit with the impression I'd formed of him yesterday. Maybe the Bureau had made him a new man — not necessarily for the better.

Next up was Isaiah Johnson. Having joined West Point Military Academy at the age of twenty, he'd been a career soldier for most of his adult life. It was no surprise to see he had been a member of the Army football team, playing tight end and running back. Having been part of various international task forces, as well as seeing action in Afghanistan, he had risen to lieutenant colonel before opting for an easier life in the private sector. After a six-month period of not working — during which his wife passed away — he joined the agency and had been with them in various capacities ever since. The last five years had seen him rise to some level of seniority within the organisation; however, his most recent history was also absent.

Eva's biography was considerably less complicated. Aged twenty-eight, she had been a cop with San Francisco's finest for three years before applying to the FBI and being accepted in the first draft. She had been top of her class throughout training and graduated as one of those earmarked as high-potential. Various stints within the Alcohol, Firearms, and Tobacco (ATF) units and other field-based assignments had earned her a reputation as a highly skilled and competent operative. She had spent the last year and a half at the Hoover Building working on office-based projects centred around major crime outfits.

All in all, my three teammates seemed like very well-rounded individuals, and when put together as a team, they would undoubtedly complement each other.

The final pages were about me, Eli Miller. This should be interesting. The dossier said I'd been a student at a private school since I was eleven and had finished with mediocre GCSEs and A levels. From there, I went to university in Manchester, where I studied both business and economics. Finishing my degree with a 2:2 and with no immediate prospects, I travelled to both North and South America for a year.

On returning to the UK, I set up a business involving the import, export, and domestic sales of exotic and rare cars. Well, at least they didn't know everything. They hadn't managed to find out where the money had come from. For the past few years, the business had grown, and I had become a well-known amateur race car driver, competing in several different UK series. To be fair, this was a pretty accurate life story. The summary suggested, and correctly so, I had never been through any hardship; both my parents were still alive, and I had a reasonable relationship with the rest of my family.

Two things struck me when reading my own bio. Firstly, it made me look like a bit of a chump compared to the other three. True, I didn't have the same skills or background, but the bio did me no favours in helping me fit in. Given that it most likely came from Holtzman's office, I had to wonder what his game was.

Secondly, while it mentioned my travelling, there was very little detail. While that wasn't a bad thing, the fact that Jessica had dropped the Montana threats confused me. If they knew, then why was it omitted? If they didn't know, then why had it been brought up at all? I was going to need more time to get my head around exactly what they knew.

It took about ten to fifteen minutes to read all the info, and I even reread it to make sure I remembered the important bits. At the other end of the table, I noticed the other five were engrossed in conversation. It wasn't until Isaiah coughed that they, and I, realised the other three had also finished.

"Well, I trust that was an interesting read," said Holtzman. "Now that you all know each other's backgrounds and strengths, there'll be no need to risk asking questions at inopportune moments."

"That may be so," replied Isaiah, assuming the leader's role. "But we, as a team, have a little issue with the personnel choice. No offence, Eli," he said, turning to me.

"Heh man, none taken. You say what you gotta say," I replied.

"I had a feeling this was going to come up," said Holtzman. "Please continue." He gave a dismissive wave of the hand and leaned back in his reclining chair.

"Well, we've all been told how important this assignment is. So, you can understand our confusion when we found out that one of the team is a car dealer from England with absolutely no experience in this sort of thing."

The other two nodded in agreement, and I almost did the same until I realised that I had no idea what it was I was talking myself out of.

"Mr. Miller brings two things that this team doesn't have. Firstly, he is more skilled behind the wheel of a car than I've seen in a long time — certainly more so than any of you three. Secondly, he is the only one of you who knows what it is really like to have money — by which I mean millions, not thousands. We feel that this will be a hugely beneficial aspect of his personality and hence his addition to the team. The buck stops above you, so it really isn't anything to be concerned about."

"It's our concern if he gets us killed," said Steve.

It was obvious from the look on Holtzman's face that he didn't like being challenged. It felt good to know I wasn't the only one he might be taking a dislike to. It was also obvious Holtzman had no intention of responding to what seemed like a reasonable objection from Steve.

"Well, as long as our concerns have been noted," said Isaiah, looking in Danny's direction.

"Don't worry, sir," said Danny. "They have."

"You needn't be concerned. You're all going through intensive training over the next week, and I have a feeling Eli might surprise you," replied Holtzman as he sat upright again and drew himself to the table's edge.

Well, it was nice to know that he had confidence in me, even if he didn't seem to like me.

"So now that we've got that out of the way, we'll continue," said Holtzman. "You all know why you're here."

I couldn't stop myself from interrupting — and to be fair it was justified, as I still didn't have a clue why I was sitting at a boardroom table in the heart of the FBI's training centre. I was, however, beginning to believe my gut: there was no way this was going to be a three month holiday.

"Well, actually, I have no idea what I'm doing here. I mean, I know what I've been told, but I have no doubt there's more to it."

"All in good time, Mr Miller. We'll get to all that shortly."

"Okay," I replied slowly, not really sure what else to say. I clearly wasn't getting anything more helpful.

"So, Brad," said Holtzman, pointing to the suited-and-booted man, "is going to run through the history of this assignment, and then Gene," who, up until this point, we all took to be the homeless-looking crack addict, "will give you all the lowdown on the target and what the whole aim is."

As if on cue, the room lights dimmed, and we sat in the dark as a large screen almost silently dropped behind the far end of the table. Inexplicably, Brad was now standing at the head of the table, as the projector burst into life and the room was again illuminated, albeit not as brightly. The first photo was a bit of a shocker. It showed two men sitting in a car covered with snow, with some strange marks on their heads.

"These pictures are of David Arther and Gerry Brooke. They were both FBI agents who had been working undercover, trying to infiltrate a drug and gun-smuggling ring. As far as we knew, they had been making steady progress. Last March they had a meeting at one of the Seattle dockyards, a meeting that was supposed to get them a significant step closer to the upper echelons of the organisation they were investigating."

It was at this point that I realised both had bullet wounds. One in the forehead; the other in the eye. As the pictures moved on to various images of the same subject, Brad continued to talk.

"Looks like they got set up," I said, a moment before my brain kicked in with the realisation that such a comment wouldn't go down well with this crowd.

Literally everyone turned to look at me, but nobody spoke. Sometimes words are simply not necessary. This was one of those moments. I shrank back into my chair and Brad carried on.

"It wasn't until their bodies turned up that we realised their identities weren't as secure as we believed. Both were experienced undercover agents, and despite our best efforts, we've been unable to find out exactly what went wrong. Based on the ballistics from the local PD, we have determined that it was a rifle bullet that did the damage — more specifically, a Steyr HS .460. The working theory is it came from a building across the docks. They'd been undercover for several months and this was the first time they'd got a sniff of whoever is in charge."

"So, put simply," said Steve, "these two got killed while undercover, and now you're wanting to send us four in their place to finish the job they started?"

"That's about the size of it," said Holtzman.

"Well, that's fine by me," replied Steve, who went back to reclining in his chair.

"It's a pretty unusual bullet," offered Eva. "Not sure I even came across one of those during my time with ATF."

Eva and I were clearly on the same wavelength. Despite my non-military past, I know a thing or two about guns, and the Steyr HS .460 is certainly not an everyday weapon. It also made no sense that such a weapon had been used from a couple of hundred yards away. It's a big, cumbersome rifle that would comfortably kill at up to a mile. An AR-15 would have been just as effective at the range Brad had suggested, and a whole lot more difficult to trace. I figured I'd keep that to myself for now, as I had more important things to get off my chest.

"It's not okay with me. If I remember correctly, Ms Lawson told me I'd be doing some chauffeuring and consulting."

"And that is exactly what you will be doing. Driving your colleagues around and helping with the planning,

92

journeys, etc.," replied Holtzman, almost as if he had pre-scripted this little interlude.

"That may be so, but you forgot to mention the bit about dodging snipers and what sounds like a very real risk to my health."

"Yeah, well, I'm sorry if we forgot to mention it, but you're here now, so we'll make a note to try harder next time," he replied, in what I can only assume was his best 'I don't give a shit' tone.

"Forgot to mention it?" I almost exploded. "It's not the sort of thing that just slips your mind."

"Well, it was Ms Lawson who recruited you. Don't blame me," replied Holtzman, as he looked in Jessica's direction and put his hands up as if to show he was innocent.

"Heh," I shouted. "Don't try and pass the buck you slimy little bastard. She works for you, so the buck stops with the ass that's sitting in your chair."

With no reply from him, I decided to continue.

"So I'll tell you what's going to happen from here. Firstly, I am going back to the apartment. Then I am going to pack my bags, and after that I am going to Dulles Airport and booking myself on the first flight out of here."

Without waiting for a reply, I got out of my chair and headed for the door. I was just about to push the stainless-steel handle down when Holtzman spoke in a very calm voice. He was supposed to be irate and about to plead with me. Instead I got that sinking feeling again, although as far as I could see there was nothing he could do to make me stay.

"Actually, Mr Miller, what is going to happen is this. Firstly, you will sit back in your chair. After that, you're going to sit through the rest of this briefing. And finally, you are going to see out the rest of your contract."

"Okay, so how about you tell me why exactly I would want to do any of those things?"

Before replying, he slowly rose out of his chair and walked over to me. He placed an arm over my shoulder and gently turned me so that both our backs were facing the rest of the room.

"Well, basically, I own you," he said softly, but with enough malice that it was clear he wasn't happy. "You can issue all the threats you want, but remember all that paperwork you were signing? Well, one of those was a contract that stipulates the only way you can get out is when you end up dead or the mission is complete to MY satisfaction."

Note to self: always read the small print in future.

"So basically, what you're saying is that if I walk out, you're going to sue me."

"Or just throw you in some godforsaken jail in the middle of nowhere," replied Holtzman, smiling as he sensed victory.

"So I walk out, and we spend years in court going through appeal after appeal, and eventually one of us wins, which I would like to think would be me, as there are bound to be a few judges out there who will agree with me that you are a complete asshole."

"You make a good point, except you have overlooked one thing. You see, everything you've said is very true. However, in case you have forgotten, we're the FBI," he said as he indicated towards the others present in the room, "and we can do pretty much anything we want. That means an APB at all ports of entry and exit for your immediate arrest. After that, who knows? Nobody will know where you are or that you're really missing."

It was pretty clear what he was saying and also pretty smart to be doing it out of earshot of the others. I got the feeling this had all been anticipated a long time ago, and consequently it was a pointless battle. I stood in the corner, Holtzman by my side, for what felt like two or three minutes, mulling over my predicament. There really wasn't a choice at this point, or at least as far as I could see. I slowly turned to face the rest of the room, took a step forward, and then said loudly,

"You are a grade-A prick, you know that?"

"Now now, Mr Miller. Calling me names isn't going to do anything for our working relationship. And if you need any further motivation to stop you from thinking you can wriggle out of this situation, we can always sit down a bit later and have a chat about your visit to Montana ten years ago."

That threat was starting to get old, although no less real. It also meant it didn't take me by surprise this time.

"Yeah, how about we don't do that," I shot back, aware that he had purposely said that for the rest of the room to hear. He was playing a pretty advanced game of psychological warfare; I'll give him that. I looked around the room as I headed back to my seat. It was time to start employing my own strategies, and that started with a quick bit of body-language analysis. Times of heightened tension always bring out people's true character, so now was as good a time as any to learn a bit about my colleagues. Isaiah was leaning back in his seat, playing with his phone and seemingly paying no attention to my plight. That certainly wasn't very encouraging. Steve was watching me intently, twirling a pen around his thumb in what I translated as a nervous tick. He was trying to look relaxed, but there was a tautness to him that meant he

95

didn't quite pull it off. Eva had a look of mild concern on her face as her eyes flicked from me to Holtzman and then on to Jessica. Jessica was nervously sipping at a glass of water, probably praying I didn't look at her, and Danny was rigid as a board, sitting bolt upright, staring at the laptop screen with such intensity you'd have thought he'd been hypnotised. His fingers rested gently on the keys, motionless, as if he had decided my interaction with Holtzman wasn't going to be documented.

"Tell me," I said, addressing the others in the room, "are you going to let this happen? If I walk out, will none of you help me? Please don't tell me you are all too scared of this bully?"

I waited for someone to say something. I suppose I was relying on Jessica to speak up in my defence. Instead, the silence told me everything I needed to know.

"You see, Mr Miller, you are making the mistake of thinking the people you have met are your friends. The reality is they all work for me, and when it comes down to it, their loyalties are with the FBI."

Now no one would meet my eyes. Perhaps the glass table and the carpet really were more interesting. In reality, I had got what I wanted. Although I knew my hands were tied, I had shown contempt for Holtzman, and in return had learned that despite their reservations, most people in the room had some kind of sympathy for me. That was something I could definitely work with. As I sat back down, I turned to Danny and said,

"Given that it looks like I am staying, I would like it noted that I have grave concerns about my inclusion in this project."

Not really knowing what to do, he turned to Holtzman for direction who, with the slightest nod of the head, indicated that it was okay. I assumed it would get deleted the second the meeting was over, but that wasn't the point. I now had witnesses.

"I've got to get to the course for a 5 p.m. tee-off, so if there is nothing else, shall we get on with it? Gene," he said, motioning his hands in a circle to suggest things should start moving forwards.

Chapter 14

A little hesitantly, Gene stood up and moved towards the head of the table. Dressed in dirty jeans, ripped in several places, a stained Iron Maiden T-shirt and with hair as long as most women's — probably halfway down his back — he was the last person you would ever expect to be an FBI agent. I suppose that's what makes him a successful undercover guy. The lights dimmed again, but fortunately this time we were presented with a picture of a suave-looking man instead of a dead one. Not only that, but it was a face I knew — not well, but he was certainly no stranger. I struggled to think of what deal I'd done with him and promptly gave up, as Gene began talking.

"This is Edwin Jameson. He operates out of the Bay Area on the West Coast and is believed to be the main importer and distributor of illegal arms and drugs into this country and Canada. The only problem is that we've never been able to put anything on him. As far as the SFPD and the mayor's office are concerned, he is a pillar of society, an untouchable in some sense. Don't get me wrong, I'm not saying they're corrupt, just that they are wary when it comes to investigating Mr Jameson. This is the primary reason we are sending you four in," he said, making eye contact with me.

I guess standing next to Holtzman had given him an extra boost of confidence.

"And exactly what is our story?" interrupted Eva.

"We'll come to that in a minute," replied Gene. "Due to the overly cautious attitude of the city cops, they will not know of your presence. So if you get into any trouble, you'll be on your own."

The last part was accompanied by more eye contact with me. He must have had a pre-meeting briefing from Holtzman. It was at this point that I switched off. I hated being talked at when I wasn't pissed off, so right now my interest in the current topic couldn't have been any less. He rambled on for another ten minutes about this Jameson bloke, about what he had been doing undercover, and some other stuff that I neither understood nor cared about. I tuned back in for the parts that had some relevance to me: the group's history.

"While I've been in the city, I've been trying to create a history for the four of you. Being from Philly, I have been spreading the word about a four-man crew from the east that has been hitting some major heists, and generally causing the local cops a real headache. As I'm sure you have already guessed, I am not exactly mixing it with the most notorious West Coast criminals, but the word on the street is that you are a quartet of badasses and you are heading their way. Lots of people are aware of your existence, but only a select few know of your personalities. By now the Chinese whispers have you as living legends. They are expecting a con lady, a computer wiz, a badass black dude and an expert wheelman with a funny accent. The rest of your legends will be for you to make up. With so much bullshit flying around, no one will know what to believe anyway, so you can afford to get creative."

"So what you're saying is that we basically have carte blanche to do as we please?" asked Isaiah.

"To some extent, yes. But bear in mind that Jameson will probably have some checks done on you, so if you are going to claim a job, make sure nobody — and I mean nobody — knows who did it, or else you will end up joining the last two," he said, indicating over his shoulder to where the two dead agents' pictures had been.

"Okay," said Eva. "What I'm hearing is that we have some scope to be imaginative, but we'll need to establish ourselves once in Cisco. Sounds like we're going to need to carry out a job."

"Hang on a minute," jumped in Brad, while Holtzman pondered Eva's suggestion, "we are the FBI. We are supposed to be preventing and reducing crime, not sending our agents to commit it."

"You know, Brad, your problem has always been that you're a stickler for the rules."

I guess Holtzman didn't genuinely like anyone. It must be difficult not having any friends.

"I like the idea. Thinking outside the box — good job, Eva. I'll speak with the field office in the city and organise something. You have to realise that the local PD won't be in on it."

"That's not a problem. We're a quartet of badasses," said Steve, chuckling along with Isaiah.

Things appeared to be going from bad to worse. Not only was I going to be dodging bullets from an expert sniper, but in the space of five minutes I'd been signed up for a bank job. Just great. This would have been the ideal time to point out my prior involvement with this Jameson bloke, but I figured — admittedly irrationally after my run-in with Holtzman — I was going to play that particular card close to my chest for a little while longer as no doubt he would have a pre planned reason why it didn't matter.

"I suggest we take a break, get some coffee and something to eat. There are pastries and doughnuts in the adjoining room," said Holtzman.

With nothing further said, the eight other chairs rolled away from the table and everyone made their way through the doors behind me. I stayed seated for about a minute and was surprised to feel a hand on my right shoulder.

"No hard feelings, Eli," said Holtzman in a tone similar to that on my first day in Washington. "You know, I'm positive you can be a really important asset to the team, and I really want you to stay."

I wasn't sure whether I should punch him in the face or just pass it off as him being a two-faced dick. I opted for the latter; the punch in the face could wait until I was on the plane home.

"Absolutely, Dean," I replied with absolutely no sincerity, "apology accepted."

I got up from my chair to find that he had his right hand extended. Unfortunately for Dean, I wasn't about to shake it, although I made a show of looking at the hand and then walking straight past him. Since coming on this trip I'd found a new sense of freedom. At the end of the day, I no longer wanted to be here, and the worst they could do was send me home. I guessed they were just going to have to put up with some rudeness and sarcasm. I headed over to the coffee percolator and got myself a cup of strong black, then made a beeline for the cake table. With a good selection to choose from, I was debating which looked best when Jessica appeared at my side.

"Heh."

"Heh yourself," I replied.

"You know, I'm sorry about back there."

"Back there, why? What happened?"

"Don't be like that, Eli. You know we're friends, but where Holtzman's involved, well, you've seen what he's like."

"Yes, I have, but I still would have liked some support. You left me hanging."

"Okay, okay, I'm sorry. It's different for you. It's not your job. The Bureau is my life."

"And as for you," I said, as I saw Danny approaching.

"Hey buddy. Look, I'm sorry. I'm on thin ice as it is."

"I know, I'm just kidding. Just make sure my objections are in the minutes, all right."

"I'll do what I can, but no promises."

I slapped him on the shoulder and gave him a smile to show that I understood. I had just picked my pastry — a coconut and cinnamon Danish — when Holtzman waved for us to reconvene in the boardroom. I hung around to slow things up a bit and just generally annoy him, but I decided not to push my luck too far in case he genuinely was bipolar.

Once I sat down, we went through some more details of what was expected in terms of evidence and then covered the more mundane matters such as accommodation. It appeared that thanks to our high-flying criminal legends, we were to get a place in the heart of the city. Although the site hadn't been determined, there were two to choose from: either in the marina part of the city or on Hyde Street, a five-minute walk from Pier 39. The following hour was spent going over the week's training schedule, which looked like it was going to be a lot of fun, if a little intense. There would be some firearms training, surveillance training and general physical stuff. I got the impression from the body language of the others that this was quite basic stuff and more of a refresher than anything else. All the same, it would be interesting to see just how good my partners were; they were the professionals, after all. At around 1 p.m. we broke for lunch, and as soon as I saw the buffet of salad and cold meats, I felt depressed. Realising that I had the car keys, I announced to the group that I was going out for something less healthy. It obviously came as a surprise, as nobody knew what to say, but it was Isaiah who spoke up and said he'd join me.

"You know, it's a really shitty thing that Holtzman did," said Isaiah as we pulled into a parking spot outside In-N-Out Burger.

"Tell me about it," I said as I pressed the alarm button as we walked in.

It was only after we had ordered and sat down that he spoke again.

"You know the rest of the team feels for you, but there's no turning back. You're in now, and we need you to commit to the team. We'll help you out where we can, but if you fuck up, then it could get us all killed."

"I'm guessing that was Steve's issue when we first met?"

"Pretty much. We were all concerned, but Steve's brainless enough to let his thoughts become words. At the end of the day, this is some serious shit. This isn't James Bond. In our world, the punches hurt and the bullets kill."

It was at this point that I began to fully understand the gravity of my situation and how serious this whole thing was. The logic side of my brain told me Holtzman and his superiors wouldn't have recruited me if I wasn't up to the job. At least if I told myself that, I could try to park my fears somewhere in the recesses of my brain.

"I hear what you're saying. I guess I am just getting used to it, that's all. But you have my word that I'll do my best by all of you."

And that was the truth. It had suddenly dawned on me that I am partly responsible for the lives of three other people, and that now weighed heavily on my conscience. I guess this meant I would have to start paying attention during Holtzman's lectures — oh, what fun. We ate the rest of our meal in silence and then just chatted about general stuff on the drive back. We walked back in to find the rest of the group ready to start, although I checked my watch and saw we weren't late. I noticed Holtzman was primed to have another go at me until he too realised that we were early and restrained himself. The afternoon promptly flew by with discussions about Jameson's setup and the crew he had working for him. There were pictures of some of his bodyguards — some of whom made Isaiah look like a matchstick — as well as a few pictures of women he employed.

I had drifted off at this point, and my mind had gone to a joke Giles, of all people, had emailed me a few days ago. I was obviously sitting there with a smile on my face as Brad stopped his presentation.

"Is there something funny, Mr Miller?" he asked.

"Apart from your tie, not really," I replied, almost under my breath.

I'd seen Eva and Steve laughing about it earlier and felt it was my right as their team-mate to try and stitch them up. Mission successful, as they both burst out laughing like a couple of naughty schoolkids.

"Would you like to explain what is so funny?" asked Holtzman, looking directly at Eva and Steve.

Realising they were about to cop an earful from him, I jumped in before either could comment. "Actually, I think they were laughing at a joke I told them earlier," I said in the most convincing tone possible.

Although they had stopped laughing, neither commented and just nodded in agreement.

"Well, seeing as it is so funny, perhaps you would like to share?" he asked, in my direction.

Oh shit. I was really not very good at jokes, especially when put on the spot.

"I'd really rather not. This is a professional setting after all. Perhaps another time," I said, feeling my cheeks turn crimson.

"In that case, please keep your jokes to yourself."

With me firmly put in my place once again, Holtzman turned to Brad and urged him to continue. I'd be glad when this week was over and I wouldn't have to see Holtzman again. That way I wouldn't have to watch my mouth all the time. Brad continued to bore us all in his monotonous tone about some crap that flew right over my head. The final half-hour was more of Brad telling us about the financial aspects of our operation and the reserves we had at our disposal. Although this was obviously important, the rest of the team were giving him their undivided attention. I had the knowledge that in my jacket pocket was all the money we were going to need, in the form of my FBI-issued credit card.

With the day's meeting over, my new team and I wasted no time getting out of the meeting room and heading back towards Alexandria. Just as we were turning off the interstate, my mobile rang. I'd not got round to setting up the Bluetooth connection, so I got Eva to answer it. After a brief conversation, she covered the mouthpiece and said,

"It's Jessica. She wants to know if you fancy going out for dinner tonight?"

I was a bit surprised that, firstly, she had called, and secondly, that she still wanted to be around me. I couldn't work her out. One minute she was berating me, the next she was friendly and flirty. She either had an unnaturally forgiving nature or early onset dementia. My thoughts were interrupted by Steve and Isaiah.

"Ooh. Is there something you're not telling us?" asked Isaiah.

"No wonder Holtzman is pissed at you. Everyone knows he has his eye on her," said Steve, laughing.

I tried to ignore them, but I couldn't help smiling.

"For your information, I have a fiancée. Tell Jessica I'll meet her on E Street at 8 p.m."

"It appears that we have a player in our midst," said Eva after she had hung up.

"Ha ha. I owe her, that's all."

"Right, whatever you say," said Steve. "Owe her what is what I want to know?"

We all started laughing. I took the piss-taking as a sign that they were beginning to accept me as one of the team.

"That reminds me," said Eva. "Thanks for covering for us back there, but exactly what were you smiling at in the first place?"

"Oh right, yeah, I was thinking about a joke a friend sent me the other day," I replied.

"So?"

"So what?" I asked, knowing exactly what she meant.

"Stop being a dick and tell us already."

I paused for a few seconds, contemplating how well my sense of humour would go down, before deciding not to overthink it any further.

"A middle-aged man bought a new sports car and was out for a nice evening drive. The top was down, the breeze was blowing through his hair and he decided to see what the new car could do. As he was about to hit three figures he suddenly saw flashing red and blue lights behind him.

"'There's no way a cop car can keep up with my new car,' he thought to himself, and opened her up further. As the needle hit 110, reality finally struck and he knew he shouldn't run from the police, so he slowed down and pulled over. The cop came up to him, took his licence without a word and examined it and the car.

"'It's been a long day, this is the end of my shift and it's Friday the 13th. I really can't be bothered with any more paperwork, so I'll do you a deal. Give me an excuse for your driving — one that I haven't heard before — and you're free to go.'

"The guy thinks for a second and says, 'Last week my wife ran off with a cop. I was afraid you were chasing me down to try and give her back.'

"'Have a nice weekend,' said the officer, and he walked away."

Isaiah and Steve let out a spluttering laugh that I'm sure would have been more raucous if Eva hadn't been in the car. Although I was keeping my eyes on the road, I could tell she was giving me a long, hard stare.

"Holtzman would have loved that one," said Steve, still smiling. "You 100% should have told him."

Eva was still silent, and I was beginning to think I'd managed to offend her, until she finally broke the silence.

"Why are sexist jokes so short? So men can remember them."

I've got to be honest, it made me smile. It was the perfect comeback.

"Touché," I responded, as I put my right hand out in her direction and received a low five.

The rest of the journey was spent telling jokes, most of which I found deeply unfunny, given they were full of American humour and mine borders on the arid side of dry.

Once home, we all went for a non-competitive jog, although the last mile was spiced up by last-one-home forfeits. Unfortunately, that was me, although I managed to rope Steve in after pointing out that I did most of the previous night's cooking. With me having my date with Jessica, I headed for the shower while the other three relaxed in front of the telly.

Showered, shaved and smelling good — at least in my opinion — I reached E Street fifteen minutes early, only to find Jessica already waiting. On the drive up, it had been on my mind what Steve had said about Holtzman having his eye on Jessica. That was another piece of information to store for future use. The dinner seemed to go well. We chatted about England — she was born in Manchester — and just general things that friends talk about. By the end of the evening, she was a little worse for wear and I ended up almost pushing her into her apartment complex. Although strictly a social engagement, I left her feeling I had another ally, as if she was back on my side. Maybe that was the idea of the whole meal/night out business — who knows.

Chapter 15

We spent the next few days back at Quantico, beginning an intensive five-day training session. It was finally my time to show everyone what was so special about me and my inclusion in this little circus. Unfortunately, it wasn't five days of thrashing a car around a track.

The first day had us learning surveillance and, more importantly, counter-surveillance. It was just the four of us and our instructors. It was a steep learning curve for me and a refresher for the others. Day two was the practical version of the first day. By the end of a long and exhausting day, I was getting the hang of it and felt confident — most likely misplaced — that I could function as a member of the team.

Day three couldn't have come at a better time. I was on a semi-high from the previous day's activities and it was finally time to do some driving. At last, I wasn't the student anymore. It felt good for the shoe to be on the other foot. I'd received plenty of stick from the others, both over breakfast and on the hour-and-a-half drive to Summit Point Raceway. As we arrived at the track, the realisation that I needed to perform began to weigh on my shoulders ever so slightly. While it was true that I was looking forward to the day, it was also a big opportunity to show everyone I wasn't a spare part. Unfortunately, that came with a certain amount of self-inflicted pressure.

The morning was spent going over the theory of driving — cornering speeds, general car physics etc. We also spent some time on a skid pan as well as learning and practising high-speed evasive manoeuvres, like the J-turn and bootlegger turn. After a more appetising lunch than day one (I'm guessing the caterers had been forewarned), we headed out to the pit lane to find three very sporty cars waiting for us: a Corvette C8 Z06, a Ford Mustang Mach 1, and a Jaguar F-Type SVR. I'm guessing the Jag was for my benefit, being British and all.

"Damn," said Steve. "That Jag is all mine."

"Sorry, Steve, but that car is for our guest from out of town," said the instructor who had been with us all morning, tossing the keys my way.

"That's bullshit," he began to exclaim, just as I launched the F-Type keys towards him.

"It's all good. You take her. I don't want you whining that I only beat you because you think I had the better car," I responded with a sarcastic smile.

"Nooo way, I'm not taking your hand-me-downs," Steve shot back. "Give me the keys to the Vette. Nothing is better than American-made anyway," he added, once again lobbing the keys back to the instructor.

The instructor gave Steve what he wanted, then took a step towards me, hand outstretched, dangling the Jag keys.

"Thanks, but I'm going to take the M5," I said, pushing his hand away.

I heard a snigger from Steve, who had taken half a step back since he'd started complaining.

"Hope you like humble pie," I said with a wink as I turned and headed to the car park for the BMW.

The reality was this was never going to be a fair fight. Not only was I pretty sure I could outdrive Steve, but I also knew that the M5 wasn't the executive saloon most people thought it was. In my hands, it was more than a match for the American muscle cars it would be up against.

A short walk later, and I was buckled into some of the best seats on the market. Stiff and ultra-supportive, they certainly weren't made for anyone carrying excess body weight. I blipped the throttle a few times, out of habit more than necessity, and set about making adjustments to the car's settings. From previous experience, I knew I wanted this thing in track mode: super sharp gear changes, sensitive throttle response, and the suspension and chassis as stiff as possible. The only change I made was to set it to semi-4WD. Having most of the power to the rear wheels was ideal, but a little to the front helped with acceleration. From memory, the computer wasn't very intrusive, so it should allow me to get tail-happy when I wanted.

As I confirmed the override of the "safe" settings, the passenger door opened and Isaiah levered himself into the seat.

"If you don't mind, I'll come along for the ride. I'm keen to see exactly what you can do."

"Be my guest, but I'd recommend holding on tight. We ain't going to be hanging around."

He pulled the door closed and immediately wound the window down. The car had been sitting in the sun all morning and now felt like a sauna. I looked over to my right and saw that Steve and the instructor had got into the Corvette while Eva had taken the Mach 1. I let the other two pull away first. It was go time. At this point there were no excuses left on the table.

With the smell of a challenge in the air, Steve blasted off down the straight, soon putting up tyre smoke as he stamped on the brakes for the deceptively sharp first corner that opened into turn two. It took me a few laps to learn the nuances of the track — where the off-camber sections were and where the subtle dips lurked, waiting to unsettle an unsuspecting driver. It was also a good chance to feel how the car behaved when pushed harder.

"Is this the best you've got?" asked Isaiah, glancing over his shoulder. "Steve's going to be on your tail in about ten seconds if you don't hurry up."

I checked my mirror. The red Corvette was quickly bearing down on us and came past with the engine screaming. He was giving it everything. Deciding it was time to stop cruising, I pressed the throttle and caught up with him as he wrestled the car around the sweeping hairpin at the northern end of the track. I carried way more speed into the corner and, as we hit the straight towards the final turn, we eased past. I fought the urge to give him a cheery wave, focusing instead on nailing the right-hander ahead.

"How's this for you?" I asked, just before stamping on the brakes, flicking the paddles twice and smoothly turning the wheel.

"More like it. I knew I'd chosen the right car," came the reply as he braced against the door and the seatbelt to counteract the G-forces.

We powered down the straight and over the start/finish line. I could see the Corvette slowly making ground as Steve benefitted from his car's lighter weight. As we approached the corner I quickly glanced in my mirror to make sure he wasn't making a Max Verstappen-esque last minute dive up the inside. Instead I saw the nose of his car dip as Steve jumped on his brakes way too early. I decided to leave my braking for another 50 metres. Once again I pressed the brakes as hard as I could and at the last minute turned into the corner while simultaneously coming off the brake pedal. A small amount of tire squeal meant we were right on the edge of the available grip. As we hit the apex, I buried the throttle and let the rear end slide out just a little as the corner began to slowly open up.

"Holy shit," shouted Isaiah. "We should never have made it round that corner in a month of Sundays."

Despite hearing him, I didn't reply. I was in the zone. For the next twenty minutes we hurtled round the two-mile circuit, passing both Eva and Steve. Isaiah was permanently gripping the seat bolsters now, his knuckles pale. I pulled into the pits just as the marshal waved the chequered flag for the end of the session. A sharp yank on the wheel and a bootful of throttle spun us in a near-perfect pirouette around the stationary Jaguar.

Getting out was refreshing. The breeze felt good against my damp sweatstained shirt. A small crowd had gathered, chatting animatedly as we walked over to the instructors.

"Damn, man, that's the most scared I've ever been in a car. You're one crazy dude behind the wheel," Isaiah said.

"Thanks," I replied, patting his shoulder. "I'm just glad you didn't vomit — we've got to drive home in that thing."

One of the marshals ambled over. "Dude, that was some of the best driving I've seen at this track," he said, offering a high five.

"Thanks, man, I was just trying to keep it together."

"You were flowing out there. Effortless. A real thing of beauty. Made the others look like they were out for a Sunday drive."

"Make sure you tell the guy in the Corvette that," I said, nodding at the red car pulling in.

The marshal wandered off to speak with Steve and the instructor, still glancing my way. Meanwhile Eva joined us, with Steve and the instructor trailing a moment later. It was a relief to get the monkey off my back and prove I had something to offer. I just hoped Steve's pride wasn't too dented.

"You've got to go in a car with this guy," said Isaiah.

"I wouldn't say no," replied Eva, "but maybe take it easier than you did just now."

"Anytime, just say the word."

I looked at Steve. "Well?"

"Well, I thought you were a little dangerous, actually. You almost crashed a few times."

"Always the bad loser, huh Steve," said Isaiah.

With no comeback, Steve stayed quiet, letting the instructor step in with advice. With half an hour left, Isaiah jumped into the F-Type and headed back out, Steve and Eva following. To be fair, all three of them were decent drivers. Not naturals, but solid, with a good grasp of the physics of speed. I let the M5 cool down after the hammering I'd just given her. I needed to be sure the tyres were still road-legal for the drive back.

The rest of the day passed uneventfully, apart from Steve going off and requiring a new front bumper — and a plaster for his bruised ego. We rolled back into Alexandria around 5:45 p.m.. Not having spoken to Amelia in days, I decided to risk waking her. To my surprise, she was still

114

up and worrying about my silence. I didn't mention my life-and-death situation, but I did say I'd soon be heading to San Francisco and would try to call again soon.

Oddly, I wasn't missing her much, or more accurately I wasn't missing my mundane London lifes. I'd worked solidly for ten years, and the freedom I had now was an eye-opener — what life could be like without expectations and responsibilities. Maybe I wasn't ready for marriage and settling down after all. More likely, I just needed a little more time having fun, and to plan a way to step back from the intensity of full time work.

Chapter 16

Day four delivered more of the same, as we headed off to a multi-acre cityscape that was to be our firearms training centre. This place was the real deal — multiple pistol ranges, a mile-long rifle range, and streets' worth of buildings to rush, breach, and generally just shoot up. Many years ago, I'd gotten myself fairly familiar with guns, but it had been a while since I'd handled one. There were experts on hand to guide and correct where needed, and by the end of the day I'd got my eye back in — though I was careful not to raise too many questions about why I was better than I probably should have been.

The final day acted as a sort of end-of-course exam. We were sent out to run a covert mission designed to test all our skills and training. I decided to just follow the others' lead, do as I was told, and generally try to be a team player. It seemed to go well; I managed to spot a tail and shake off a half-hearted pursuit. Nobody had anything particularly critical to say about my performance, so I took that as a win.

By Friday evening, we were all mentally worn out. Fortunately, it meant our heads were now crammed with contacts, scenarios, names, and all the other details we might need. My final evening with the team, before heading to the West Coast on Monday, was spent on the phone arranging for the BMW to be transported, and reaching out to a long-time friend who lived in Berkeley, across the Bay from San Francisco.

Several years earlier, while travelling down the West Coast, I'd met Jonathon Rosean. We'd become good mates and gotten ourselves into, and out of, all kinds of mischief. Luckily, we'd never been caught. Jonny had decided to stay in the US after his visa expired. As a Brit, he stood out like a cowboy at the ballet among the predominantly Mexican migrant community, and sensing his deportation was inevitable if he carried on working in the vineyards and orchards, he set up his own horticulture business. To his surprise, it flourished, and he was soon employing others. A natural wheeler-dealer, he kept his hand in a number of scams and knew people who could provide all sorts of services. In short, a very handy man to know. A year ago, having entered the immigration lottery, he'd been lucky enough to win citizenship. That gave him the chance to go straight, though he still kept his network of useful contacts.

The phone was ringing and I was about to hang up when he answered.

"Hello."

"Hey Jonny, how are you doing?"

"Pretty good, thanks. Who's this?"

"You mean you don't remember your travelling buddy?" I asked jokingly.

"My God, Eli, you little shit! How the hell are you?"

"Yeah, pretty good, thanks. Yourself?"

"Well, you know — getting by the legal way," he replied with a cackle.

"I bet you are," I chuckled.

"So, what do I owe the pleasure? Haven't heard from you in a while."

"Well, I'm going to be in the area and was wondering if I could come round. I need to make use of your famous contact book."

"For sure. Are you here for business or pleasure?"

"Not sure what you'd call it, really. I'll fill you in when I get there."

"You're staying with me, right?"

"'Fraid not. I've got accommodation on Hyde Street. Appreciate the offer, though."

"Hyde Street? Doesn't sound like your usual style. How long are you in the city for?"

"About three months."

"Three months?" he exclaimed. "Is everything okay between you and Amelia?"

"Oh yes, everything's fine. I'll tell you all about it on Monday or Tuesday."

"That soon? I'll have to get the wife cleaning now."

"I can believe that," I laughed. "I'll see you in a few days."

"For sure. Take it easy, stay out of trouble."

"Yeah, you too. See you later."

I thumbed the off button and lay back on the bed. It was good to have a proper friend, someone I knew could help if I got into trouble. I also knew Jessica and Gene were both going to be in the city, so the more friendly faces around, the better.

The weekend at the apartment was fairly quiet. Isaiah and Steve had left late Friday evening to spend time with their families, leaving just Eva and me. Turns out we had quite a bit in common. As I'd arranged for the car to be transported to LAX, we were without wheels, so we just hung out at a few local spots. She left on Sunday to visit her parents in California, leaving me alone again. Deciding this was no way to spend a Sunday evening, I grabbed my wallet, dug out Jessica's and Danny's cards, and called them, inviting them round for a party. I told them to bring friends but not to worry about beer or food. I — or rather the FBI — had that covered.

We partied late into the night, though Jessica seemed a lot more restrained than she had on our semi-date the other evening. She was proving to be unnecessarily hard to read.

Chapter 17

I woke up to find it was 9:30 a.m., and I was 40,000 feet in the air. I only had the faintest recollection of boarding the plane, and the headache I now had was a sharp reminder of the unnecessarily heavy drinking from the night before. After a bad experience involving whisky, several air stewardesses, and a flight back from Ibiza, I had vowed never to fly drunk or hungover again — well, definitely not again after this flight. I spent most of the journey curled up under the in-flight blanket, with earplugs firmly embedded and a sleeping mask pulled over my eyes. Predictably, I didn't manage to sleep, but it was still considerably less painful than dealing with the bright lights and the noise of screaming children.

I've no idea what time the plane landed, but with only carry-on luggage, I was through the terminal and outside in ten minutes. The first thing that hit me wasn't the smog — that came second — but the sheer heat. The sun was blazing, without a cloud or breeze in sight, and I was already regretting leaving the terminal. Although I felt slightly better than I had on the flight, the heat and humidity knocked me back a bit. The rest of the team were flying directly to San Francisco Airport, while I'd had to come via LA because, for reasons the transport agent failed to explain, the car could only be delivered here, not in San Fran until Thursday.

The car was waiting in the parking structure as requested. After a brief chat with the valet and signing some paperwork, I jumped in, started the engine, and cranked the AC to full blast. Five minutes later, considerably cooler, I was heading along Highway 1 to Santa Monica. Driving along the Venice Beach promenade, I found it typically packed with sun worshippers, fitness buffs, and new-age stalls. Just another day in SoCal. Before long I reached my first stop, pulling into a space behind a row of shops. Fifteen minutes later, I walked out with a brand-new, top-of-the-range Transition Spur mountain bike, all the kit to go with it, and the FBI $14,000 lighter.

The car hadn't been designed for lugging bikes and other bulky gear, so I stuck it on the roof with a Seasucker mount and got back on the road, heading for the I-5. Two hours later, I was approaching the outskirts of the Golden Gate City. Instead of taking the interstate straight into Hayes Valley, I decided to explore some of the older neighbourhoods near Golden Gate Park and the beach districts. After cruising around for forty-five minutes, I stopped for fuel — which still amazed me was roughly a quarter of UK prices. Finally, after wrestling with San Francisco's maze of one-way streets, I reached Hyde Street, which doubles as a cable car route. Doing my best to avoid the tracks, I made it to the corner of Hyde and Chestnut. Checking my phone, I saw our house was on Chestnut, in the 1000 block.

As I pulled up, I was relieved to see a dropped kerb and an open garage to park in. The place looked modern from the outside, the numbering suggesting it may once have been a block of flats. Being on an east–west street also meant I wasn't dealing with one of San Francisco's infamous inclines — just a simple reverse park, handbrake on and grab my bags. I headed for the front door, deciding to risk leaving the bike on the car for now. The house looked large and comfortable enough, though not exactly the kind of place you'd picture hardened criminals using. I'd been given a key back in Washington, so I let myself in to find a wide hallway, decorated in a sleek, modern style. Wooden floors, soft wall colours, and splashes of chrome and steel gave it a classy feel.

As with many American homes, it was symmetrical: a room on either side at the front, a bathroom at the end of the hall, and then the kitchen and sitting room, where all three of my housemates were lounging.

"Hey guys," I said with a nod.

"Yo, what's up, Eli?" replied Isaiah.

"This is a nice place. The FBI really looks after you guys."

"I wish," said Steve. "We reckon this is for your benefit. The usual undercover houses are total shit holes."

"Well, I reckon this place makes up for it."

I headed back out to grab my bags and then upstairs in search of the last empty bedroom. Sure enough, I found it — the smallest room in the house. No surprise there; no one else was going to pick it. With the West Coast being four hours behind the East, and an eight-hour gap with the UK, I decided on a quick nap before calling Amelia. It might even help kill off the last of the lingering headache.

Chapter 18

For reasons unknown — though I'm guessing it had something to do with the Sunday party I'd thrown — I didn't see Monday again, only surfacing at 7:30 a.m. on Tuesday morning. I had planned to see Jonny that day, but figured it best to call first rather than just showing up on his doorstep unannounced. I was about to pick up the phone when I remembered he was a heavy sleeper. That brought back memories of hostels where everyone but Jonny would be kept awake by the one person snoring — that was usually him. He always denied it, insisting some obscure anatomical quirk made it impossible.

After my morning exercises, I pulled on running gear and headed to the kitchen. To my surprise, Steve was already up — and even more surprisingly, he was blending some kind of fruit-and-veg smoothie.

"Well, if it isn't Sleeping Beauty," he said with a grin. "What happened to you yesterday? We thought you'd gone out."

"I've no idea. I just lay down for a few minutes, and the next thing I know, it's Tuesday."

"You fancy a shake? It'll set you up for the day — and no offence, but you look like you could use it."

"Thanks, but I'm heading out for a run."

"Mind if I join you? Could do with blowing a few cobwebs away."

"Be my guest, but are you sure you want to on a full stomach?" I asked, nodding at the blender.

"I'll be fine. You'll see. Give me five minutes."

He was back in less than three. We ran straight downhill to the water's edge — and I immediately regretted it, knowing we'd have to climb back up at the end. We followed the Embarcadero as far as Pacific Bell Park, then cut through the neighbourhoods, circling back to retrace our route. San Francisco's cool air made the run easier than it would have been in Washington, but the slog back up Hyde Street was every bit as punishing as expected. Credit where it's due: Steve managed to keep his smoothie down.

By eleven I was boarding the ferry near Pier 39. I'd rung Jonny at half ten and arranged to meet him at the terminal on the far side of the bay. The trip caused friction back at the house: Isaiah had planned out the day's schedule, and to be fair, he wasn't wrong that it was important. But seeing Jonny mattered to me in a way the others couldn't understand.

It had been six years since we'd last met, and I almost didn't recognise him. The Jonny I remembered had been short, stocky, tattooed, with a dark ponytail. The Jonny waiting for me looked softer round the middle — at least two stone heavier — with cropped, styled hair and laser scars where the tattoos had been.

"Hey, buddy," I said as I walked up.

"Hey, if it isn't my favourite English Jew," he shot back, grinning.

It was an old joke between us. He knew perfectly well I wasn't Jewish, but people often assumed I was because of my name. I'd moaned about it so often on our travels that he'd started using it just to wind me up. We shared something like a hug — awkward shoulder pats instead of a proper embrace — before heading to the car park.

"You're looking well," I said as I slid into the passenger seat, "though a little… different."

"Yeah, well, now that I'm a legit citizen, I figured I should conform a bit more."

"You fit right in. Keep eating red meat and you'll have the arteries to prove it."

"Heh, I've worked hard for this physique," he said, patting his belly proudly. "Cost me a lot of beers."

The drive from the ferry took about twenty minutes and took us up into the hills overlooking the bay. A far cry from his old flat in a housing block.

"I guess the garden services business is going well?"

"Hell yes. Never better. I've got fifty people on the books and we're nudging a mil a year."

"Those are good numbers, but this place looks above that league. What is it — five beds?"

"Seven, actually. Three receptions, four bathrooms, a couple of acres and a pool," he said with a smug smile.

"How the hell do you afford it?"

"Let's just say I've got a wallet full of IOUs."

"Your famous connections. That's one of the reasons I'm here."

"You mean you didn't just miss your old pal?" he asked, mock-offended.

"Friendship first. But yeah, I need some help too."

"For sure. Just say the word. You know I've got your back."

"Thanks. But let's leave business till later. We've got some catching up to do."

We spent hours by the pool, drinking cocktails and beer. I was starting to get some colour — a definite improvement on my usual pasty white. It was earlier than I'd normally start drinking, but it's not every day you reunite with one of your best mates. His latest wife — he was on number three — brought us club sandwiches, and while he was busy stuffing his face, I told him everything. Against my better judgement, I laid out the whole situation: the target, the operation, all of it. I needed someone outside the Bureau to know, just in case.

"Well, you've really landed yourself in the shit this time. I've heard of Jameson, and you're right — he's got a status above the law. Want me to see what I can find out?"

"Thanks, but I don't want you getting dragged in. What I need is something else."

"Okay, shoot. Surprise me."

"Well, three things, actually. First, I need someone who knows their way around a car. I've got a BMW M5 that needs looking over."

"That I can do. I know a guy in Castro. Expensive, but he knows his shit. Mention my name, he'll treat you right." He tapped his phone, and a second later mine pinged with a message.

"Perfect. Money's not a problem. I've got government plastic for that."

"I'll let him know to expect you."

"Thanks."

"So, what else?"

"As bizarre as it sounds, the Feds won't give me any protection."

"You mean they won't give you a gun?"

"Yep."

"For real? With your experience?" he asked, eyebrows raised.

"Oh yeah. They don't know about that. Figured it was best to keep some things to myself. They already know too much."

"Smart. So — you after a concealed carry permit?"

"If it's possible?"

"I can put you in touch with someone who can sort you out. You'll need cash for that kind of thing though."

"Any chance I can give you a list of what I need? I'll make sure you're not out of pocket."

"You sure? I know what you're like about guns."

"Yeah, well, it's getting harder to sneak off from the others. I don't want to end up in the middle of a sting — that'd go down really badly with pretty much everybody."

Jonny nodded in understanding. I'd almost forgotten the third thing, and it was only on the ride back to the ferry terminal that I remembered.

"You still riding?"

"Nah, not really," he said, glancing at his belly. "Though I probably should start again. Why?"

"I'd rather keep your name off the radar. I was thinking we could leave messages out on the old trails, in case I need something."

"Jeez, Eli, you're really getting into this undercover business. What did you have in mind?"

We had reached the terminal entrance, but I stayed in the car and laid out my idea. We worked through the details before I finally got out, bought a ticket, and waited for my ferry.

I arrived back at the house late afternoon and, to my surprise, found Jessica sitting in the lounge with the others. Dressed far more conservatively than when we'd first met, she gave me a warm smile — which was more than I got from Isaiah.

"The wanderer returns. Pleasant day sightseeing?" he asked, still clearly annoyed I'd derailed his plans.

"Yep, pretty good, thanks for asking. Give me a mo and I'll show you my holiday snaps." The sarcasm was probably unnecessary — most likely the beer talking_so I quickly moved on. "Looks like something important is going on. Maybe I should be involved?"

"This is for team members only. Maybe you can go see Alcatraz or something," Isaiah shot back, just as sarcastically — and, I thought, a bit childish for the supposed leader of the group.

"Look, man, I had something I needed to do, all right? Sorry if it clashed with your schedule, but it's not like you told me I'd be busy today."

"Boys, boys," Jessica said, trying to ease the tension. "Let's put this down to teething problems. In future, Eli, you check with the team before making plans. And Isaiah, you keep Eli in the loop. He's part of this, whether you like it or not."

"Fine by me," I said, looking straight at Isaiah.

"Whatever," he muttered, turning away. "Let's just get on with this."

I ducked into the kitchen, grabbed snacks and drinks for everyone, and pulled up a chair. At first, I wasn't sure what the conversation was about, but it quickly became clear: our reputation-building heist. Jessica was leading the briefing, so she'd obviously come round to deliver the details.

"Holtzman — and people way above my head — have been arranging it. The target's a jewellery store on the other side of the hill, near Market Street. It's set for Sunday afternoon, just before closing."

"Market Street on a Sunday?" said Eva. "Bad idea, by which I mean terrible idea. I grew up around there and worked those streets for years. Which shop?"

"Sachmann's Jewellers. Don't blame me for the timing — that's down to Holtzman."

"I know the place. It's upmarket, like Cartier and Bvlgari. They'll have serious security."

"According to the brief," Jessica continued, "there'll be two armed guards inside, and a panic button linked to the PD. If pressed, you'll have about two minutes to get out before the cops arrive. The secure room's time-locked, so you're only after what's on display. Holtzman's exact words were: 'free rein, within reason.'"

In hindsight, this would have been the perfect time to come clean about my history with Jameson. But given the mess I'd already caused, I decided this wasn't the moment to drop that little bombshell.

"Sounds good," Isaiah said. "We've got five days to scope it out and build a plan. We'll each visit the area separately. Steve, check the alarms and cameras, see if you can buy us extra time. Eva, you and Eli go in as customers. He's supposed to be a rich guy, so that's his scene." He turned to me. "And Eli, I want you to pick up a street map and start learning the city."

"Done," said Steve. "What about you?"

"Don't worry about me. I'll be busy."

"I'm just saying upfront — I've got something I need to do tomorrow morning."

Isaiah gave me a look I couldn't read — somewhere between simmering irritation and homicidal intent. He slowly stood from his chair before stalking into the kitchen without uttering a word.

"I have a feeling this is important," Jessica said, stepping in before things escalated.

"So is this — and it's for Sunday. I only need a few hours in the morning, then Eva and I can do our thing at the jewellers."

"Well, don't fuck it up," Isaiah called from the kitchen, clearly still pissed.

As far as I was concerned, that was the end of it. The others didn't agree so we spent another half-hour rehashing details and nitpicking the alternative angles. Jessica stayed the rest of the evening, leaving me her number in case I wanted to talk.

My situation with her was starting to mess with my head. One minute she was offering her shoulder to cry on, the next she was all business and pushing my buttons. And then there was Lucas — clearly smitten with her. Why can't women just be straightforward, instead of playing games?

Chapter 19

Wednesday morning kicked off with a quick breakfast meeting before we all split up. Eva stayed behind to change into something smart while I jumped in the car and headed for Castro and the tuning garage. After battling the morning traffic, I finally turned down the alleyway Jonny's text had directed me to. I was looking for Sense Tuning and its owner, Chris Parks — apparently a well-known tuner and car exhibitor.

From the outside, the workshop looked like a derelict building, and I was more than a little dubious about driving under the half-open metal shutters.

Inside, though, it was a completely different story. From my years of dealing with garages and high-performance service centres, I could tell this place was top-notch. The concrete floor was painted high-gloss grey and it was spotless, not the usual oil-stained chaos you'd expect. Along the far wall were rows of red tool chests that probably held every car-related tool known to man. Several lifts held exotic machines that looked like they belonged to the street racing scene. That was one corner of the car world I didn't know much about.

I parked in front of what I guessed was the office and stepped inside, where I was met by a plump Hispanic woman who greeted me with a smile.

"How you doin' today, honey?" she asked in a thick Mexican accent.

"Pretty good, thanks. You?" I replied, noticing her brow furrow slightly at my accent. I half-expected her to ask me to repeat myself.

"Good, thanks. What can I do for you?"

"I'm here to see Chris Parks. He should be expecting me."

Without another word, she leaned through a service window and bellowed for Chris. A couple of minutes later, a ginger-haired guy in grease-stained red overalls appeared. I almost stuck out a hand to shake before remembering that mechanics don't do handshakes on the basis that their hands are normally covered in oil.

"You must be Eli, right?"

"You got it."

"Yeah, Jonny said you'd be coming by. Told me to look after you. So what can I do for you?"

"Well, I was given this car," I said, pointing my thumb at the BMW. "The guys who gave it to me are a bit… particular about the law. Can you check the electrics, see if anything looks off?"

"Yeah, Jonny mentioned a BMW. Not exactly my usual line of work, but I owe him, so I'll see what I can do."

"Great. And if you spot anything you can tune, feel free."

"When he called, I did some homework. There are a few tweaks we can make, though bear in mind this thing's already pretty high-spec from the factory."

"That's fine. Reliability's my main concern. When can you have it ready?"

"Early next week. And that's only because you're a friend of Jonny's."

"Any chance of Saturday?"

"We're swamped right now man. Next week's the best I can do."

I paused. I needed the car for Sunday, but more importantly, I needed it with proper power. There was really only one option.

"I'll be back Saturday lunchtime. Have it ready, and I'll pay double," I said as casually as I could. He swallowed hard, trying to mask his reaction, but he nearly choked on the air. I tossed him the keys and turned for the door.

"If you run into any real problems, my number's in the car. Call me — and I'll let Jonny know you couldn't help."

The thought of disappointing Jonny, plus a hefty payday, seemed to settle it. He nodded slowly.

Within minutes I was back on the main road. After a five-minute wait, I flagged a taxi and headed back to the house to collect Eva.

I got back in time for an early lunch with her. The other two were already out, so it was just us two, chatting about family and me trying to get a feel for what growing up in San Fran had been like. To my surprise, Eva was ready almost as soon as we'd finished eating. Why can't all women get ready that quickly? It was refreshingly different — and, I'll admit, it earned her a little extra respect in my book.

Unfortunately, her idea of rich and wealthy hadn't translated into an appropriate choice of outfit, and it didn't really go with the smart casual shirt and pants I'd chosen. I sent her back upstairs for a quick costume change, and she returned in a much more appropriate jeans, shirt and boot combo. I took the time to find a luxury car service and ordered a car for immediate pickup.

"You know we are still a few blocks from the jeweller's," said Eva as we pulled over to the kerb.

"Yeah, I know. We are taking a minor detour first," I replied, smiling at her.

"Don't you think you should have run it by Isaiah first?"

"Maybe, but we need a little latitude to do our own thing. And it's really for your benefit."

I asked the driver to keep the car nearby, and we walked along the pavement for a minute before I gently took hold of her right elbow and steered her into the Armani store. We spent the next forty-five minutes nipping into the boutique shops and picking up various outfits for the both of us. I suggested Eva do a quick change before we headed to the target. Coming out of the changing room, she looked like a different woman — most definitely the sort to be shopping in Sachmann's and certainly the type I liked to be seen with. I left Eva with some of the bags — I guessed it made her look more the part — and suggested she walk into Sachmann's alone, with me following a few minutes later.

This was the first time I had seen the shop, and I have to say it was very impressive. Situated down a very exclusive side street, the front had several small windows displaying huge rocks of various colours. I sent a text to our driver to park in the only customer space, which I figured would come in useful if someone decided to rob the place, and headed for the door. The door was solid glass, no doubt heavily reinforced, with huge polished gold handles, and I could see that Eva was already inside, having a good look around. A doorman held the door for me and welcomed me to the premises. I approached Eva from behind, wrapped my arms around her waist, and proceeded to give her a kiss on the cheek. I decided not to press the loving husband/boyfriend routine too far, even though I figured we were friends by this point. I wasn't a huge fan of public displays of affection — probably a British thing — and, given we wanted our visit to be forgettable, the subtle approach seemed the best hand to play. Eva tried on various bits of bling while I did my best to seem interested. Given that I had my bombshell to drop, I decided not to put too much effort into assessing the security setup. In all honesty, I didn't bother; I wasn't one for wasting time on unnecessary enterprises.

Despite seeming to have the time of her life, Eva had been multitasking, a fact I found out on the drive home as she offloaded all her observations on to me. She might have been on a high after our recon mission, or, more likely, she'd figured I was useless, so she was letting me know she'd done my job for me. At least I could try and sound like I'd done something when Isaiah undoubtedly quizzed me later.

We arrived back at the house before the others, and it wasn't until later that evening that Isaiah and Steve returned separately.

"So how was the lovebirds' day out?" asked Steve, grinning mischievously.

"Pretty good, thanks," replied Eva. "I got to go shopping for expensive clothes and stones. You aren't going to hear any girl complaining about that. Oh, and we did a bit of work too."

"Well, I'm glad to hear it wasn't all fun," said Isaiah from the kitchen area.

"How about you two?" I asked, figuring showing interest might help build a bond with Isaiah.

"Well, I have got us a safe house sorted and some equipment for Sunday," replied Isaiah. "I also went to see Gene and Jessica just to clarify some details about the next few days."

"I've been checking into the comms system at Sachmann's, and it comes as no surprise that it's state-of-the-art," offered Steve.

"I think we all knew that would be the case," said Isaiah, "but can you do anything about it?"

"Yes and no. Basically, they have a programme that I can hack to some extent and probably buy ourselves an extra minute or two, but at this short notice, that's the best I can do."

"Not ideal, but I guess it's better than nothing," said Eva, "considering what the state of play is like inside. There are two obvious guards in uniform, and I think I spotted one posing as a customer, as well as four or five counter assistants. There is no telling if there is further support behind the scenes, but either way, it is a tall order, and I think we should aim to be out within two minutes."

"I'm glad you said that, 'cause that was my gut feeling in the first place," said Isaiah as he joined us on the sofas. "How about you, Eli? How's the map-learning coming along?"

"Yeah, not too bad. I'm going to spend the next few days driving the streets; it helps me remember things better."

"Well, it sounds like we are all up to speed. Steve, Eva, I want you both with me tomorrow. Eli, I'd have you along, but the road layouts are more important."

"Sure thing," I replied. I preferred doing my own thing, and I was glad to be given the freedom to do so.

"Right, I'll see you both in the morning," said Steve, as he headed toward the hallway and stairs.

It wasn't long before the other two had left me on my own with the TV remote and a bottle of Jack Daniels. Finding nothing of any real interest on the cable TV, I decided to turn in for the night and try to get some sleep. As I headed to my room, I noticed that Eva's light was still on. I had wanted to speak with her earlier about the hug and kiss in the jeweller's but hadn't found the right opportunity. I gave her door a gentle knock and was greeted by an invitation to come in. She was sitting on her bed wearing a pair of cotton hot pants and a cleavage-revealing vest. Up until this very moment, I'd have bet the house that women going to bed dressed like Eva was pure movie fiction. I couldn't help but take in the view before I remembered to speak.

"Listen, I er… want to apologise for the kiss and hug thing earlier today. I didn't want you to get the wrong idea."

"What would the wrong idea be?"

This was almost immediately more awkward than I had imagined, and I began to wish I'd left it alone.

"You know… that I am getting too friendly. It was purely professional."

"Sure it was, but feel free to be purely professional again," she replied with a look that seemed to offer an illicit liaison.

I had no idea what to say or do at this point. Understanding the games that women played had never been my strong point. It was a good job I was engaged, or else I might have made a silly choice, so I just nodded my head and turned to go to my room. This could be getting a little tricky, and the last thing I needed was to cause friction with a fellow team member. My early night's sleep didn't materialise as I lay in bed tossing and turning, keeping one eye on the door, half expecting — or was it half wanting — her to sneak in. I mean, show me a guy who doesn't like the ego boost of a super-hot girl giving him the come-on.

The next couple of days went by without much happening. Eva seemed to be her normal self, and nothing was said about our little bedroom chat, although I struggled to keep it out of my mind for long periods. Bizarrely, none of the others had even noticed, or maybe more accurately hadn't bothered to ask me, that the BMW wasn't around. In need of a backup car for Sunday, I came up with what seemed like a good plan. Grabbing a regular yellow cab, I headed over to the airport to put my plan into action. I got dropped off at the main departures, and after a quick look at the various signposts, I headed to my destination. It wasn't a long walk, and I was soon at the long-stay multi-storey car park. I wandered around several levels before finally finding what I wanted. By my logic, a car in long-stay was going to be there for at least three days, most likely more. Any car with a layer of dust on the windscreen had already been there for a few days, so I scouted around looking for cars that looked obviously clean. My theory was this gave me the best chance of the owner not finding it stolen for a good few days, which was plenty for my requirements.

While the idea of stealing a car was far from perfect, I needed a vehicle that was going to be untraceable. That meant rental cars were out of the question. I could have purchased a used car, but that came with paperwork, and if not, the car was likely already dodgy as shit and couldn't be trusted legally or mechanically. Theft was my only option at this point, but I had a plan that made it more justifiable, in my head at least. I quickly snapped a few photos of the Tesla Model Y I had settled on and headed back to the terminal to find a coffee shop where I could work. It probably took thirty minutes of internet searching before I landed where I needed to be. I recall reading an article in a trade journal that talked about the vulnerability of "connected" cars being hacked. I'd managed to find my way to a very dodgy website that appeared to sell what I needed.

Using the café's Wi-Fi, I downloaded the various programmes that I apparently needed and then headed back to the car. Following the instructions I'd had sent to a fake email account, I slowly made my way through the steps. Getting to the end, I patiently waited for the indicators to flash to no avail. I'd probably been ripped off. I had my doubts it could be that easy. As I looked at the screen, I realised I hadn't pressed the confirm icon. Thumbing the button with blind hope that this was going to work, I was relieved to see that the lights flashed and the driver's door handle popped out. With no charging cable attached, it was simply a case of jumping in and quickly leaving the airport complex in the direction of the city.

After about thirty minutes, I parked up at a shopping complex and went to grab some food and a drink. I wasn't entirely trusting that the software I'd used to access the car had definitely disabled the functions that would notify the driver their car was moving. I gave it an hour, and thankfully nothing happened. I returned to the car, feeling pretty happy with the morning's activities. I spent a good few hours driving through the streets and figured that by

Friday night I would be getting myself around without a map or Sat Nav. Even so, Eva was a local girl, so if things got really bad, I always had her to help me out.

Things were also pretty quiet on the car front, so I assumed that Chris was getting on just fine, but I texted him anyway to let him know I wouldn't be needing the BMW back quite so soon. I smiled to myself, thinking about my exchange with Chris. It was nice to know that the old adage that everybody has a price was just as true on this side of the Atlantic as it is back home. The skill was just finding what it was. Despite the Tesla still having a decent amount of charge, I parked it a few blocks from the house and hooked it up to a slow overnight charger. It was handy to not have the car too close to the house, just in case SFPD suddenly got interested in it.

Chapter 20

It was Friday evening and all four of us were working our way through several pizzas when the doorbell chimed. We all looked at each other. It was obvious none of us had any plans to get up, so we just sat there. It wasn't until the bell chimed a second time that I decided to answer it. I snapped on the hallway light and tentatively headed for the door — after all, nobody really knew we were there. I opened it and was so surprised I lost all my manners.

"You have to be shitting me. What the fuck are you doing here?"

"Nice to see you too, Eli. Don't mind if I come in, do you?"

I guess I was still in shock, otherwise I'd have told him to get lost, but by the time my brain caught up with what was happening, Holtzman was already halfway down the hallway.

"Hey Eli, good to see you, pal," said Danny as he hung back with me.

"Yeah, you too. What the hell is going on? Why is he here?"

"I think he's just concerned about the success of the mission."

"Please don't tell me he's staying in the city?"

"Well, he told me to book us into a hotel for the next

month."

"Oh, that's just great. I figured I'd seen the last of him when we left the East Coast."

"Don't worry about it too much. I don't think you'll see a lot of him once you get going on the assignment."

"In that case, let's get things moving," I said, smiling as we joined the others in the sitting-room area.

The look on their faces spoke volumes about our late-night visitor. None of them looked particularly happy to see him, but being professionals, they sat there like good employees as the boss shared his wisdom. Holtzman was sitting in my chair, and while I was tempted to make a comment about it, I decided it best not to cause unnecessary friction. It felt a little like the geeky kid from class trying to hang out with the cool kids — not that I was ever one of the in-crowd.

About an hour later, with the door finally closed behind him and Danny, I returned to find JD and Bacardi being liberally splashed into the four tumblers that had appeared on the coffee table.

"Well, that was a turn-up for the books," I said, sitting down.

"I guess so," said Isaiah. "I've worked with him a few times before and he's never done that. Strikes me as a little odd, to say the least. I guess he really does have a lot riding on this producing a result."

"You can say that again," said Eva. "From what I've heard, if we come back with Jameson in cuffs, Holtzman's up for promotion to director or some shit like that."

"That sounds about right," added Steve. "He never does anything unless there's something in it for him."

We continued chatting about the visit for a while longer

before heading to bed. I had the impression Holtzman was acting a little out of character, but it seemed he had a genuine motive for it. I still wasn't sure I trusted him, but that was probably because I simply didn't like him.

Chapter 21

Chris finally replied the next morning with a slightly cryptic message, so after my morning workout and a spot of breakfast, I caught a cab round to his garage. The place was surprisingly busy, with cars queued up in the alleyway and people stood in groups chatting away. It looked like a local car club judging by the number of Toyota Supras, 350Zs and even a Lexus LFA. I figured I'd be hanging around for Chris, so I began checking out some of the cars. Thankfully, it wasn't more than two minutes before I felt a tap on my shoulder and turned to find Chris standing there.

"Some pretty sweet rides here," I said, indicating the surrounding cars. "They all your handiwork?"

"Most of them," he replied with a nod. "I prefer to work on slightly more exotic things than imports, but these guys pay well and loyalty is only ever a good thing, right?"

"For sure," I replied with a knowing nod. "Gotta pay the bills."

Chris smiled and beckoned me to follow him to a slightly less busy part of the garage. He pulled the cover off a car to reveal my M5, looking exactly as I'd left it. At least he hadn't fitted some crazy body kit to it.

"Ya know, when Jonny vouches for a guy, that's good enough for me. I don't know what you're into, and I don't want to know, but nobody will hear about it from me."

"Okay," I responded slowly. "What exactly did you find?"

"The car is legit, a real work of art, but someone's installed all kinds of extra electronics on it. Extra tracking devices, remote engine-management gizmos, and, if I've understood it correctly, they can even take control of the car remotely."

I wasn't really sure what to say. I kind of expected some of the stuff, but the remote-access functions were a real surprise. Why would anyone want that?

"There are also internal and external cameras that aren't factory, as well as audio recording. It's all set up so they can be viewed as a live stream or uploaded to the cloud whenever the car is near a Wi-Fi point. Someone wants to keep a very close eye — and ear — on what you're up to."

It could only be Holtzman. What I couldn't figure out was why. What on earth did he have to be so paranoid about that he'd had all that installed?

"So..." I began after a momentary pause.

"So I left the cameras alone, muffled the microphone and completely disabled the remote functions. Whoever 'they' are can still watch, but they can no longer fuck with your driving."

"Knew I could trust Jonny to send me to the right guy," I said, smiling.

"As for the performance stuff, I threw on some new tyres as the others looked like they'd been tortured at some point. We also tweaked the ECU, uprated the fuel pump, changed the exhaust and fitted a larger intercooler. Nothing that's going to set the world on fire, but you're going to need to use super or premium from now on. The engine's mapped for only the best fuel, so do yourself a favour and spend the extra."

"Gotcha," I said, dapping him in appreciation. "Send me your details and I'll have the cash wired ASAP. And one last thing: I was never here, you've never seen my face before and you definitely have no idea what a BMW M5 CS is."

"I got your back, bro," he replied, smiling, hands up in mock surrender as he took half a step back.

I gave him a nod of respect as I stepped towards the driver's door and began to get in.

"Yo Chris. Whatcha doin' with that euro shit-heap in the shop?"

I turned to see a tall, muscular blond-haired guy heading over with several friends in tow. If I were the type to stereotype — and, let's face it, I am — I'd have pegged him as the high-school jock still living in the past. I'd met too many like him over the years of travelling around the States and was pretty sure how this was going to play out.

"Just doing a favour for a friend, Jed. Job is a job and I gotta keep the lights on," replied Chris, obviously all too familiar with this douche-canoe (a word I'd only recently found on Urban Dictionary but had probably made my list of favourite words this year).

I started the engine, blipped the throttle a few times, dropped the driver's window and slowly rolled towards Chris and the group who had now come together.

"You're going to need more than a muffler to make that piece of shit any good," offered Jed, referring to the pops and crackles coming from the exhaust.

"And you're going to need a lot less juice before your IQ reaches fifty," I replied with a smile.

"The fuck you say?" he asked, taking a step closer to my window. "Anytime, Anywh — "

I could see he was still talking, but my right foot was gently bouncing on the accelerator, drowning out whatever nonsense he was spouting.

"Sorry, old boy, I didn't quite catch that," I said in the most proper English accent I could manage. "Damn accelerator's just too sensitive."

"Whatever you faggot. Let's go, right now, me and you outside."

I couldn't help but laugh. It was clearly not what he was expecting; a confused look spread over his face.

"Faggot, is that the best you've got?" I mocked. "I mean, that's a throwback to the '90s and not very politically correct these days. I'd have thought even a man of your intelligence could come up with something more on-trend. Maybe try asshat, twat waffle or fucknugget next time."

He opened his mouth, then closed it again as he tried to work out what to say. I took the moment to leave: I hung a fist out of the window, caught a bump from Chris — who was also smiling — and rolled out of the garage and back towards the house.

The remainder of the day was spent going over the plans, the potential problems and our planned solutions. Despite the repetitive nature of the topic, the others were still throwing up eventualities I wouldn't have thought of in a million years. Thoroughly briefed and ready for anything, I went to bed early because I had a morning bike ride to get on with — else Jonny would probably call in the West Coast Mafia to come and raid the house in search of me.

Chapter 22

Not wanting to cause an argument on a pretty important day in the grand scheme of things, I opted to not even leave a note on the table. I just grabbed my bike, and gear, and headed straight out. I was going to the Golden Gate Recreation Park, just over the famed bridge of the same name. It's a mecca for city cyclists, so it wouldn't look too out of place if I stopped and chatted with someone I met — someone who just happened to be a longtime friend as well. With my training in counter-surveillance, I had come up with what I considered a foolproof way of passing information. Being a keen mountain biker years ago, I figured that if I arranged for a drop to be made on a particular section of a trail, there was no way it could be seen and next to impossible to track. I had agreed with Jonny, who used to ride competitively, that we would meet on the trail and pick a drop point that either of us could use.

I rode through the car park and noticed Jonny's Audi was already there, so I decided to head straight for the trail. Halfway round, I recognised Jonny's bulk heading towards me, so I pulled to the side and waited for him to reach me.

"I'm not too sure why I agreed to this, but I must have been out of my mind. Not only are my legs about to fall off, but my lungs feel like they want to burst out of my ribcage."

"Well, look at it this way. You're going to get fit and help me out at the same time."

"Yeah, well, you owe me. And this one I won't forget in a hurry."

"So, have you found any decent spots we can use for a drop?"

"Yeah, about two miles back that way there's a section with a jump, some bomb holes, and some pretty nasty tree roots. It's the sort of place a lot of people would come off. I figured the odd water bottle on the ground wouldn't look too out of place."

"Sounds like a good idea. I'll check it out and, I guess, see you around sometime. I'll be coming up again next Sunday, so if you have any messages, you know what to do."

"Sure thing, buddy. I'm heading back to the car. Give me your keys, will you? I've got something to leave in your boot."

Catching on to what he meant, I dug the keys out of my backpack and threw them over to him.

"Any problems?"

"Nope, as you requested. Brand new spare mags, spare ammo. I've had them oiled, so they're ready to shoot."

"Perfect, thanks mate. I'll find a bit of time to put a few rounds through them. Send me the bill, all right?"

"I'll put the keys under the front wheel," he said, nodding.

I gave him a thumbs up, nodded my head, and with that we both remounted our bikes and headed off in opposite directions. Things had worked out well. In the five minutes we'd chatted, no other rider had come past. I actually felt proud of myself for such a well-devised plan. Perhaps I had learned more than I thought during the week of training in Quantico.

I arrived back at the house just before noon, a three-and-a-half-hour ride in total. I breezed into the kitchen like everything was normal, and to my surprise Isaiah didn't say a thing. I liked to think I hadn't been missed, but I figured he was just keeping the harmony until after the day's main event. Fed, showered and dressed, I was ready to go by two o'clock and passed some time flicking through the cable channels. I had just started an episode of Quincy when Isaiah entered, carrying a large black holdall, followed by both Eva and Steve.

"We all know what this is about, so I'm not going to bore you with the details. Remember, this is the real deal. Things will be unpredictable and highly likely to go wrong. Make sensible decisions, be safe, and don't forget we are all in this together — so let's watch each other's backs."

Rather than offering any reply, the three of us just nodded in agreement.

"I got some hardware from the bureau. We're packing light-loaded rubber bullets, and the shotgun Eli will be in charge of is full of beanbags."

This basically meant I wouldn't be able to kill anyone unless I put the gun to their head. The beanbags would be enough to knock someone over but ultimately only cause bad bruising. Rubber bullets can technically penetrate the body, but with the light load — meaning less gunpowder than a normal round and hence less terminal velocity — the damage that could be inflicted would be minimal. It was obvious Isaiah didn't want to risk the loss of life, which was fine by me as I had no desire to kill anyone. Well... perhaps if Holtzman was there, I might have been tempted to change my mind. It was all rather academic anyway, as I still had to drop my little bombshell. I'd decided to wait until we were all in the car. That way, I had a captive audience and plenty of witnesses. I grabbed my keys from the sideboard and we all headed out the front door. The other three walked over to the BMW, Steve pulling impatiently at the offside rear door handle.

"We ain't taking that car," I said as I closed the door to the house.

"Eli, now isn't the time for surprises," said a slightly exasperated Eva.

"Look, there can't be more than five of these cars in the city, if that. It would take the local feds five minutes to track us down, and I ain't dumping her."

"Makes sense," responded Isaiah with a nod, which I took as appreciation for my forethought, especially given it was something they had overlooked.

"Well, we sure ain't taking a taxi," said Steve, gesticulating towards a passing cab.

"Don't worry," I smiled. "I've got this. Walk two blocks or wait here and I'll collect you in five? Scratch that," I quickly added before anyone responded. "I think the four of us walking down the street dressed like Reservoir Dogs will probably get us more attention than we need."

I headed off at a brisk pace to collect the Tesla and arrived back almost exactly five minutes later. I could tell they were all curious about the car but said nothing. I think they were getting in the zone and didn't need any of my nonsense to distract them. The guns were handed out as I drove downtown, and I was half expecting a mask of some sort to be thrust my way until I remembered Steve had our back where that was concerned. He had spent the last few days hacking into phone lines and other technical stuff to ensure the security cameras in the shop and streets were set on a loop and hence wouldn't record us. That obviously did nothing about eyewitnesses, but it was better than nothing.

We'd left a little early, and traffic had been kind, so as we were ahead of schedule, I decided to drive around for a bit. As I rolled past the shop, I immediately noticed we had a problem: the valet parking spot had been coned off. Not only was it a problem, but it was also a very unusual thing for a business to do. We carried on and I decided to keep the observation to myself.

I looked out of the window and saw exactly why Eva had said Sunday afternoon was a bad idea. There were people and cars everywhere, street performers on the corner gathering a crowd, and just general hustle and bustle. The area around Market Street was notorious for panhandlers and the homeless, which added up to a large police presence on weekends — another factor going against us. Having said that, the SFPD weren't as prominent as I'd expected, and despite the general busyness of the area, something felt off. I couldn't place it, but I'd learned over the years to trust my gut. I steered the car into the next street and looped back to the end of the street with the jewellery store on it. There was a row of parked cars to my right, and despite there not being a free space, I perched the Tesla on the end, technically in a no-parking zone. This had to be the moment of my big reveal. I stared out of the window as I summoned up the courage to start the conversation. Just as I was about to break the silence, my attention was drawn to a man standing in a doorway. He was looking up and down the street — not particularly at us, but definitely scanning for someone. Almost as soon as I registered what he was up to, I noticed a couple walking on the opposite side of the street, clearly doing the same thing. To the casual observer, neither looked out of place. I guess that training at Quantico hadn't been a total waste, because I knew they were professionals on the lookout. I quickly clocked at least two other groups that just didn't seem a natural fit for the environment. I was pretty sure I knew what was going on, but rather than do the obvious and leave, I decided on the less predictable approach. If they were there for us, then at least I'd have them guessing slightly.

"I'll be right back," I said, grabbing my phone and wallet and practically jumping out of the car.

Once there was a break in the traffic I quickly jogged across the road and into a store specialising in watches — a store Eva and I had visited during our shopping trip a few days before. Nobody seemed to pay me the least bit of attention, which was promising, and I didn't notice any glances from those I'd earmarked as suspicious. I didn't need to look back at the car to know how apoplectic Isaiah was going. That was a problem for the future. Right now, I needed to shop. I'd seen a beautiful IWC the other day and made a beeline for the counter where it was on display. This was more of an investment than for day-to-day use, so I wasn't too bothered how it looked, but tried it on all the same. Feeling generous — and also hoping a little gift might marginally reduce the ball-busting waiting for me in the car — I picked up an Omega and a Hamilton for Steve and Isaiah. Eva could go without; she'd done pretty well out of our shopping trip earlier in the week. As I headed back out to the car, I saw that an SFPD buggy had pulled up next to the Tesla. I hustled over just as the female officer was getting out of the driver's seat.

"I'm really sorry, Miss," I said apologetically as I approached. "I know I shouldn't park there. I just needed to collect some presents for my wife before I fly home."

She paused momentarily — I'm guessing thrown either by my accent or my honesty.

"I'm literally about to leave, but if you need to give me a ticket, I'm not going to argue," I offered meekly.

"Well, you better be getting on with it then," she smiled, before turning back to her buggy and rejoining the traffic.

That was a close call. It could have been awkward. I was about to get in the car when I heard it off in the distance. There was now no doubt in my mind about what was about to go down. I popped the door open and dropped myself into the driver's seat. The others had clearly been chatting while I was gone, as neither Steve nor Eva uttered a peep, and Isaiah didn't even look at me. After about five seconds of silence, Isaiah very softly said,

"Eli, you are an absolute prick, you know that?"

I realised that what I did next was akin to kicking a hornet's nest but I felt I had a point to prove, so I simply put my right index finger up — the universal sign for "hold that thought" — while simultaneously pressing the button to lower my window. The street noise increased in volume, but it was the high-pitched engine notes I was really interested in. Two bikes came past the car at speed. I'm not a bike guy, but I know a Ducati when I see one, and the characteristic rumble was unmistakable. The other bike could have been any number of brands, but it was liveried up in orange, blue, red and white — the unique colours of the Repsol Honda motor racing team. Both bikes had pillion passengers, all riders dressed in leathers with mirrored lenses on their helmets. The passengers had empty black bags slung over their shoulders. I wasn't surprised to see the bikes slow and swing into the coned-off parking bay. As this happened, I noticed the various characters I'd spotted earlier suddenly come to life, moving purposely towards the two bikes. By the time they were within thirty metres, the bikers had dismounted, and the last of them was heading into the store.

As if on cue, several SFPD cruisers pulled up and started placing a cordon around the street. I could no longer see what was happening, but a sudden flurry of activity was followed by shouting and multiple gunshots. Chaos erupted as shoppers ran in all directions, screaming and pushing as they fled. What sounded like automatic gunfire broke out as more police arrived, closely followed by several ambulances and finally the high-pitched scream of motorbike engines. The car was completely quiet, everyone just watching things unfold. I'm pretty sure everyone was more in shock than anything, struggling to believe that the very heist we had been planning had just gone down at the hands of another crew. I tossed the bag containing the Omega into Steve's lap, handed the Hamilton to Isaiah, and brought the window back up.

"You are welcome," I said, locking my seatbelt into place and pulling the car back into traffic.

The last thing we needed was for the SFPD to drop a cordon on the area and leave us — and our stolen car — trapped with no good answers to some very awkward questions.

Chapter 23

Nobody spoke on the drive back to the house. I was itching to have my ego stroked and throw it in their faces, but I decided humility was the best way forward. We had been home less than two minutes before Steve let loose with his thoughts, otherwise known as losing his shit.

"What the actual fuck just happened?"

"Your guess is as good as mine," replied Isaiah with a shrug, seemingly still a little lost for words.

"Whatever it is, something is very fucked up about this whole situation," responded Steve as he paced up and down the living room. "We got screwed over, and there is only one person I can think of who might be responsible."

"Hold up one minute," interrupted Eva. "Let's not jump to any conclusions just yet. I think we all need a bit of time to think things over. Things are never quite as simple as they seem."

"Whatever," replied Steve, clearly getting more irate as the conversation continued. "If it wasn't for Eli, at best we'd be in custody right now."

I decided silence was still my approach, so I just looked between the three of them as impassively as possible.

"Well, I need to clear my head, so I'm heading to the gym around the corner if anyone wants to join me," stated Eva as she looked in my direction.

"I'll come," replied Steve after a momentary pause.

"I've got to run an errand with the car," I replied, avoiding eye contact with her.

With that, Eva and Steve headed out of the room. As she passed me, she gently laid a hand on my arm and said softly,

"Thanks for today, Eli; I genuinely mean it."

I briefly met her gaze, nodded in appreciation, and gave her a smile. Isaiah had made his way over to the fridge. As he turned, holding the orange juice, he stared straight at me and paused briefly.

"You know you did well today. We almost ended up in a whole heap of shit. It's only thanks to you that we're all still breathing. I'm sorry for the way I've been treating you."

I held up my hand to interrupt him before he could continue.

"Let's be honest, I've deserved it. I've hardly been a committed member of the team — you know, doing my own thing half the time and all that."

"I ain't going to argue with that, but I think you've proven today that you don't have your entire head up your arse."

"Well, maybe not all the time," I responded with a smile.

"So, how did you know? I mean, I had no clue."

"It was the parking space. A shop like that would only close off its parking space for a VIP, and they don't tend to shop at the time us mere mortals do. After that, things just didn't feel right, so I guess I was looking for anything out of the ordinary. I quickly noticed a few people that seemed out of place and then came the bike engines in the distance. I just somehow knew what was going to happen."

"Some pretty impressive intuition for a rookie," he said, with what I took as genuine appreciation.

"You'll be surprised to know I wasn't asleep the whole time we were at Quantico."

He chuckled at that one. Maybe I was finally making a friend out of him.

"Given we aren't on the run and now have the afternoon free, I'm going to need a favour from you."

"It's the least I can do. What do you need?"

"I need to get rid of the Tesla. Can you follow me to the airport in the BMW?"

"The airport, really? Do I need to take your passport off you?" he asked, a look of concern spreading over his face.

"As if," I replied with a smile. "I'm just starting to get the hang of this undercover shizzle. Just drive the car — you'll understand when we get there."

He grabbed a can of Coke and a sub from the fridge and headed out to the car. As I passed him on the way to the Tesla, I threw him the BMW keys.

"No crumbs in the car," I said, indicating the food he was munching on, "or else you will have a whole set of new problems."

I didn't wait for a response and a few minutes later was on my way to the airport.

The drive was uneventful, and, just as I'd hoped, I dropped the car off back in the exact spot it had come from. Being the considerate petrolhead I am — ironic, given it was an electric car — I put it back on charge. I let Isaiah drive the BMW back, given the smile he had on his face when he picked me up. He had all kinds of questions about the Tesla, and I think my creativity even helped push my stock up a little further, which is never a bad thing.

Chapter 24

Monday morning didn't really start as I had hoped. Half asleep, I heard someone repeatedly ringing the doorbell. Obviously, nobody else was up, and with my room being at the front of the house, albeit several storeys up, I decided to try and sneak a peek to see who it was. Fearing the police were coming to arrest me, I did my best to move the curtains as little as possible. The smallest of cracks enabled me to see Dean Holtzman standing on the pavement, looking up at my window. It must have been Danny leaning on the bell, as Holtzman spotted my eyes peering through the curtains. He impatiently beckoned for me to come and open the front door.

"You know, perhaps I should get a key," he said as I opened the door and Holtzman walked straight past me.

"Yeez, Eli, you're looking rough. Out celebrating last night, were you?" asked Danny.

"Celebrating what? Keeping us all out of body bags?"

Danny looked slightly puzzled by this comment but didn't say anything. Holtzman slapped the morning editions of the San Francisco Chronicle and the Bay Times on the table, the headlines leading with the downtown shootout.

"Thanks, but I've got the internet on my phone. Printed media is literally yesterday's news."

"I was actually going to congratulate you on a job well done, but I guess you'll have to be satisfied with the group's regular debrief. Danny, you may as well go and wake the other three. Let's get this over with so I can get out of here."

"Another game of golf?" I asked sarcastically.

"No, a meeting with the serious crimes unit about a certain jewellery heist, so I would watch my mouth if I were you."

Five minutes later, the other three walked into the sitting room. None had bothered to change out of their bedclothes, which made me feel less awkward. Both Steve and Isaiah were wearing shorts and grey T-shirts emblazoned with FBI. Eva looked considerably more classy in short-sleeved silk pyjamas and a robe, a very different look from the other night. It was enough to make Holtzman look away from the morning news show. With Danny instructed to sort out the coffee, we moved to one of the front reception rooms, as yet unused by anyone. It seemed a strange thing to do, but I guessed Holtzman wanted a slightly more formal atmosphere.

"So, how do you think it went yesterday?"

We all looked at each other, a little unsure what to say, although I was pretty confident Steve would deal with the awkward silence. As if on cue, he turned to Holtzman and said,

"A complete shit show, plain and simple."

"Shit show or not, you are still supposed to follow the plans. We got the safe house for a reason. Would one of you like to explain why you aren't there? Danny and I have been round there looking for you already this morning."

"Why would we go there? Why wouldn't we be safe here?" asked Eva.

Holtzman reached over to the papers and again dropped them on the table. The four of us just looked at each other. None of us needed to say anything; our eyes said it all.

"What the fuck are you on about?" exclaimed Steve. "Do you have any idea what happened? Did you even bother to read the papers?"

Holtzman first looked at Danny, who resembled a third grader being asked a question about quantum physics, and then slowly at each of us, pausing for several seconds while he locked eyes with each in turn. None of us shied away from his stare.

"So?" he finally asked. "Does someone want to tell me what is going on here? Because I have no clue what any of you are talking about."

Steve snorted in disbelief and was about to launch into it when Isaiah began to speak. He recounted all the events from the previous day, leaving no details out. I've got to give it to him, he played it really well. He laid it on thick when it came to how organised the police were, how suspicious it was that our "job" had been done by another crew that resembled our setup, and how it all happened on the exact same day. He also did me a solid, making sure to underline my role in everything, although he conveniently forgot to mention the free watch he'd got. I never took my eyes off Holtzman the whole time. He was listening to Isaiah but also scanning the room. I wasn't sure if he was nervous or not, and I sure couldn't tell if he knew about anything Isaiah was recounting. Looking at Steve and Eva, I saw two very different responses. Steve was clearly itching to launch himself across the table and tear Holtzman apart. Eva, on the other hand, was statuesque, her face displaying no emotion at all. Only her eyes betrayed the fire burning inside. Isaiah finished recounting the previous day's events, and the room was deathly silent for quite a long time.

"So, to summarise, the months of planning myself and Gene have put into this are in the crapper, and it's only because of him that this didn't go completely bent," stated Holtzman as he indicated toward me with his thumb, all while avoiding eye contact.

"Yep, it's a real bummer for you. I feel sorry for your golf game. Imagine what your handicap could have been," shot Steve, in a tone that even a deaf person couldn't have missed.

"I, for one, am pretty concerned about your lack of concern for the bigger picture here," started Eva in a surprisingly even tone, clearly wanting to offload her thoughts while trying to remain professional. "SFPD clearly knew something was going down. They were prepared in a big way. Then there's the question of who was on those bikes and what are the odds of the same jewellers getting hit on the same day, at the same time as we were supposed to be doing it?"

"I hope you aren't implying what I think you are?" replied Holtzman, eyebrow raised.

"You tell us. What are we supposed to think? As far as we know, only two other people, who aren't in this room, knew about yesterday. If you're trying to tell us this is just one great big fucking coincidence, then you clearly think a lot less of us than I hoped," responded Eva, frustration and anger beginning to creep into her voice.

Holtzman didn't say anything for at least thirty seconds. He just slowly looked at all four of us. His face still gave nothing away. Then, completely out of the blue, he sprang out of the chair like a man with a rocket up his arse and took some very purposeful strides toward the door.

"I'll be back in a few hours," he muttered over his shoulder as he left the room.

Danny had clearly been caught off guard as he suddenly snapped his laptop closed, grabbed his pen, pad of paper and coffee cup off the table before hurrying after his boss.

"Well, that says it all," started Steve almost immediately. "Guilty as charged, no doubt in my mind."

"He sure didn't seem surprised," I offered.

I wasn't quite as convinced as Steve, but I also didn't see any other obvious explanation.

"Steady on, guys," interjected Eva. "He may be a bit of a prick, but I just don't see it. He's a career agent and, as far as I know, he's completely by the book. It just doesn't make sense. Why would he sabotage our plans like that? I mean, why sabotage them at all, never mind in such a random way? I'm willing to give him the benefit of the doubt for now, at least until he comes back."

"IF he comes back," muttered Steve under his breath.

"Look, guys, let's see how this plays out," said Isaiah, exerting a little control over the situation. "We're all in this together. There's nothing lost in giving him a chance. If he doesn't come back, then we have our answer and the pleasure of a kick-arse manhunt. Maybe he comes back with a plausible story we can work with. Or we call it what it is and arrest his arse."

The other two nodded slowly after a short period of contemplation and then headed back toward the kitchen for coffee and breakfast. They ate and then went back upstairs for showers, etc. I opted for my sit-up/press-up/pull-up routine and then grabbed the bathroom once Eva had finally finished.

I spent the rest of the day just chilling around the house. Eva had gone to see some friends, which left the three of us to have a typical lads' day at home. Pizza and beer were ordered while we watched replays of classic NFL games before deciding to catch the afternoon Giants game at Pacific Bell Park. With the Giants victorious, we arrived home slightly more sober than when we'd left to find Eva back early. With Holtzman nowhere to be seen, and no message from Danny, we decided to take the cable car to Market Street and, not long after, found ourselves sitting down to the opening credits of a Tom Cruise film.

Unfortunately, I didn't get to enjoy the film as much as I'd have liked, mainly because of Eva constantly brushing her leg against mine, her advances becoming more frequent and less subtle. On the journey back, she held onto my arm. She said it was for support, but my ego was convinced there were ulterior motives. She knew I was engaged to Amelia, but that didn't seem to be stopping her. My ego was loving it, even though my brain was telling me to be careful, so I wasn't about to stop the advances of perhaps the most beautiful woman I had ever met. I justified to myself that it was harmless at the moment; there had been no sexual contact of any form, and that was how I'd make sure it stayed. I just hoped we would remain friends, as beyond her beauty I simply enjoyed her company.

Unfortunately, things took a small step in the wrong direction later that night, as Eva decided to pay me a visit in the early hours. A little freaked out, and not wanting to hurt her feelings, I pretended to be asleep. The reality was I just didn't know how to deal with the situation, so I took the coward's way out. She either suddenly developed a conscience or thought I needed my beauty sleep, as I sensed she was no longer there. I was a bit hesitant to move in case she was sitting in the corner, so I fell asleep contemplating the grief my less than moral friends would give me for turning down sex with such an attractive woman.

Chapter 25

The next morning, I woke early with the intention of going out for a run. I picked up my phone to find a message from Danny. Short and sweet, it simply said: 10 a.m. I guessed we might be getting some answers after all. As I headed out onto the landing to use the bathroom, Eva was coming out of her room.

"Sleep well?" she asked.

"Pretty good, all things considered," I replied, contemplating just how loaded that question was and if she understood the double meaning of my answer.

"Did you get the message from Danny?" she responded with what I took to be a teasing smile.

"Yep. Figured I'd head out for a run beforehand."

"Give me five minutes and I'll join you, if that's okay?"

"Sure, see you downstairs in five," I replied, caught a little off guard and not too sure what else to say.

True to her word, Eva arrived downstairs five minutes later. She wore her hair in a ponytail, a crop-top vest showing off her toned abs, and proper running shorts revealing her tanned, athletic legs. She looked like she meant business and could definitely make a living on social media with that look. It was going to be a tough run. I wasn't one for ponytail rage — that common affliction for sporty men being beaten by women — I just didn't like being beaten by anyone and would push myself hard not to get dropped.

It turned out to be a great run. We mixed up running intervals with circuit-type exercises. After about an hour, we turned the intensity down and slow-jogged back to the house, both dripping in sweat. With just enough time for a shower and some breakfast, we met the others downstairs about ten minutes before our visitors were due.

"So, what's the word, guys?" asked Isaiah.

"Like Eva said yesterday, we just have to hear him out. Let's see what he's got to say," I replied quickly, as Eva nodded in agreement.

"'What Eva said,'" Steve mimicked in a slightly childish accent. "Whatever, man. Let's just get this over with."

I wasn't really sure what Steve was implying or why he was acting the way he was, but before I could give it any more thought, the doorbell rang and he headed off to the front door. Two minutes later, he beckoned us with a shout from the hallway:

"Conference room, now. The cavalry's here."

As we filtered into the front room, not only did we find Danny and Holtzman, but Gene and Jessica were also sitting at the table. I nodded to Danny, who smiled back, gently patted Gene on the shoulder as I walked past, and smiled at Jessica, who returned it with concern but also with what seemed like genuine warmth in her eyes. We all sat down and nobody spoke. We simply fixed our gaze on Holtzman. Getting the message that this was his show, he started.

"First up, I'm sorry about yesterday. I was completely caught off guard; I hadn't heard anything about what had happened."

Steve was already huffing and puffing but let Holtzman continue uninterrupted.

"Of course, I am concerned about what happened, and I agree it doesn't look good. I can assure you nobody has sold you guys out. One of the reasons I walked out yesterday was the impact this is likely to have on the assignment we're here to complete. It's been years of work for both myself and the Bureau. The idea of it going down the drain was difficult to take."

"And we were about five minutes away from ending up dead," replied Steve aggressively. "I know what's more important to me."

"What can I say? I'm sorry that almost happened, and I'm grateful to Eli for having the awareness to notice things weren't right." He made a purposeful turn to me as he said this. I surprisingly found myself taking him at his word, despite my dislike of the man. This humble, humane side of him was completely unexpected, and I wasn't too sure what to make of it.

"I, or rather we," he said, indicating Danny, Jessica, and Gene, "spent most of yesterday doing our best to find out what happened. I've had multiple conversations with the scene commander from the jewellery heist, as well as the commissioner and the head of the serious crimes division. The basics of it are that two of the four you saw are dead, the other two are on the run with a few million in gems. SFPD got a tip-off two days beforehand. I couldn't get to the bottom of where it came from or why they believed it to be true, so I can only assume it was from a CI."

"That's a confidential informant," Eva whispered from my left side.

"I know," I whispered back, rolling my eyes to suggest I wasn't a complete dumbass.

"What we didn't know was that the shop was owned by one Edwin Jameson. Not direct ownership, but ultimately the buck stops with him," offered Gene.

"I'm eager to hear what you've got on the bikers," asked Isaiah.

"Nothing so far," replied Holtzman quickly. "Not yet, anyway."

"How can that be? Two of them are dead, for heaven's sake," said a slightly exasperated Eva.

"They're unknowns. No DNA match, no fingerprint match, no facial recognition," replied Jessica.

"Also doesn't help that one of them was shot in the face," added Holtzman.

"How is that possible?" asked Isaiah. "We've all done this job long enough to know that Joe Public doesn't just one day decide to pull an armed robbery. There is no chance in hell they're strangers to the law. Someone either isn't talking, or else something fishy is going on."

"I can't explain it. All I can say is that we've spoken to every contact, source and official we can find, and it's the same story, no deviation whatsoever. At the moment, it's both the official and unofficial story," said Holtzman, as he looked at the other three for support.

"It's true," said Jessica. I could see out of the corner of my eye that Danny was also nodding. "I spoke with at least a dozen people yesterday, and it's the same story. No way someone has got a conspiracy this well organised in such a short time frame."

"So, where does that leave us?" asked Isaiah.

"Well, we've lost our way in with Jameson, and given it was one of his businesses, he's going to be on high alert," replied Gene, somewhat dejectedly. It was clear that seeing months of his work go down the drain had hit him hard.

"I think Gene is right," said Holtzman. "There is no way we can realistically send you guys in now. It would be far too obvious. I think we need to pack up and head back to the East Coast and get you reassigned to your old units."

"Maybe, maybe not," I replied, barely aware I'd even spoken.

Everyone turned to look at me, a mixture of intrigue and confusion on their faces. After a short pause, Holtzman broke the silence.

"Well, are you going to keep us in suspense all day, or would you like to tell us what's on your mind?"

I considered my options for a moment. I hadn't really thought my plan through in any great detail, so I realised I was likely to get shot down. That wouldn't be the end of the world; I could head back home to my normal life and put all this behind me. If I'm honest, I'd rather enjoyed this career break and wasn't quite ready for it to end, especially now the life and death stuff was pretty much done with. I also wasn't sure who I could trust, or at least I had doubts about some of those sitting around the table. I definitely needed more time to decide how wise and plausible my idea was.

"No," I finally said. "I don't think I will right now. Maybe later."

At that, I got up from the table and headed toward the kitchen for some coffee. It was going to be interesting to see who approached me first. After a brief period of silence, I heard the conversations start up, and to my surprise, nobody came to join me. I tossed up what to do with myself and, despite not having arranged to see Jonny, opted for a trip out on the mountain bike. Ten minutes later, I was changed, the bike was on the roof of the car, and I was heading out of the city towards Lake Tahoe and the national forest.

It was a solid drive there and back. It gave me just what I needed: some quiet time to myself to reflect on the morning and work out what to do next. I'd made a purposeful effort to watch everyone round the table as closely as possible. Other than Danny drifting off and looking bored several times, which given his usual attentiveness was very odd, nobody else had done, or said, anything remotely out of character. As far as I could tell we were all still on the same team, despite what had happened on Sunday. That left the unanswered question of who was pulling the strings behind the scenes.

The drive there flew by, and it didn't take long before I was cruising down some flowy trails, enjoying the peaceful surroundings and generally just loving life. Cycling had always been a means to escape stress, especially in my younger years, and this was a reminder that once I got back home, I needed to make more time to do things like this. London isn't known for its off-road trails, but there's riding close enough that makes it possible to still have a good time.

The drive back was a little more of a drag, but I stopped at an In-N-Out Burger in Sacramento to fuel myself up. The cycling had definitely eaten into my reserves, and it wasn't until I downed a chocolate milkshake that I felt I could think clearly again. By the time I reached the outskirts of San Francisco, I was pretty sure I knew what I was going to do. I decided to finish the journey with a call to Amelia. Not because I wanted to run things by her — I knew she'd tell me to do the opposite of what I'd decided

— I just wanted to hear her voice and chat with someone I knew was 100% on my side.

It was just past 7 p.m. when I finally walked into the house. I wasn't expecting to find the others patiently awaiting my arrival, but I was pleased to see that Isaiah, Eva, and Steve were all milling around the kitchen. The other four were nowhere in sight.

"Evening, all," I said as I dumped my bags in the corner.

"Hey, Eli," Eva smiled in response. "We were just talking about you. We were beginning to wonder if you'd jumped on a plane back home."

"Tempting," I said with a wry smile.

"So, where have you been, man?" asked Steve in a slightly less friendly tone.

"Needed some time alone with my thoughts, so I took the bike and hit the trails around Lake Tahoe."

"And did it have the desired effect?"

"Sure did. I had a great time."

"I think you know that's not what I meant," Steve shot back.

"Look, guys," I said, holding up my hands and making sure I was addressing all of them. "I know you have questions after how I left things this morning. Can we discuss it in the morning? It's been a long day for us all, and if you'd be gracious enough to let me sleep on my thoughts, I'd appreciate it."

"Sounds fair to me," responded Isaiah.

"Want a beer and some pizza?" asked Eva without missing a beat as she handed an opened bottle in my direction.

"Let me grab a shower and I'll definitely take you up on that," I replied, taking the bottle and swigging at least half of it in one go.

"By the smell of you, I'd say that's a pretty good idea," offered Steve, as he grabbed a bottle of beer for himself and dropped down onto the sofa.

Twenty minutes later, I was back downstairs, and despite my earlier meal, I quickly devoured several slices of whatever pizza they'd ordered. To their credit, none of them even attempted to tease any info out of me. I've got a lot of time for people who respect boundaries in that way, so it was nice to just sit around the telly, half-watch the basketball, and chat shit with what felt like a group of mates. As the night wore on, Eva slowly crept closer towards me and finished the night basically leaning against me. I caught Isaiah shooting a few glances in my direction that clearly suggested he wasn't fully happy with what he saw.

Chapter 26

S lightly foolishly, we had agreed the night before to get
up early and head out for another run/workout.
Despite us all looking slightly bleary-eyed, it didn't take
long for us to push each other to our limits, and in my case
beyond them. It wasn't like it had been in D.C.; there was
no longer an atmosphere of having to prove myself or beat
the others. It was friendly, good-hearted motivation that
we all seemed to benefit from. There was, of course, a
penalty for last place — one that I took with pride on this
occasion. Having had to jump into the Bay as my
aforementioned penalty, I was allowed to hit the shower
first once we got back. It also meant I was first in the
kitchen, so I set about organising coffee and breakfast for
when the others came down. Unsurprisingly, Eva was last
down and came to join the rest of us sitting at the kitchen
table. I figured I'd drawn this out long enough and my
mind hadn't changed since my journey home from Lake
Tahoe. It was now or never — time to get the ball rolling.

"Look, guys, I know what I'm about to say is going to
cause some raised eyebrows, but please just bear with me,
okay?"

I could see Steve shift slightly in his chair on hearing this.
The other two remained impassive, so I continued.

"I had been planning to tell you all this before things
went down on Sunday, but hopefully my cowardice might

work out in our favour. The thing is, I've met Edwin Jameson before."

Unsurprisingly, Steve looked ready to attack, but Eva was ready and placed a restraining arm on him.

"Go on," said a surprisingly calm Isaiah.

"Several years ago, he came to London and we ended up selling him a car. Completely legit business deal. I only knew him as a rich American looking to get hold of a vintage Ferrari. I think it's pretty unlikely that he wouldn't remember me, but obviously I was aware of the issues this might cause when it was revealed he was to be the target."

"Why on earth didn't you say anything at the time?" asked a slightly irritated Isaiah.

"I don't really have a good answer to that. I can only say that I realised it would completely ruin the plan as it was, and I hoped that something would materialise that meant I didn't have to say anything. I realise it's a pretty lame excuse, but it's the only one I've got."

"You aren't doing yourself any favours with that explanation," responded Steve quickly. "I mean, what if those biker clowns hadn't shown up? What if we'd bumped into this Jameson character? Either of those could have ended really badly for all of us."

"Well, I was going to tell you before the job, so I figured that wasn't an issue. As for bumping into him, it's a big city. What are the chances?" I responded a little too flippantly.

"Well, I'm glad you're so carefree about it," responded Steve dismissively.

I appreciated that Steve and I had never really seen eye to eye, but he was clearly taking a proper dislike to me over this. To be honest, I knew I had been a bit reckless and my attitude could be better, but I really felt he was laying it on a little thick and I couldn't really understand why. He certainly wasn't at the top of my 'trusted list', mainly due to his overly emotional reaction to everything, so I'd have to keep an eye on him. For now, that could wait. I needed to hope that my concocted plan could get me back in everyone's good books.

"At the end of the day, we are where we are. No point analysing my screw-ups. We need to look at what we can do to change our current situation, and I think we can use my previous relationship with Jameson to our advantage."

Steve seemed to settle at hearing this, and Eva sat forward in her chair — just a little, but enough for me to notice. Isaiah, on the other hand, was playing it super cool; he just remained in a slouched and relaxed position, looking in my direction but not avoiding direct eye contact.

"The way I figure it, I can go to him with a business idea. I've got some thoughts, but we can discuss that a bit later. I have some contacts back home that can add some credibility to things if need be. After that, we can play it by ear, but it would be a way into his organisation. I can then bring you guys in as part of my Stateside operation, and before you know it, we'll have this thing sewn up and put to bed."

"Just like that," retorted Steve, not trying to hide his sarcasm. "And how exactly are you going to get to see him? Just knock on his door?"

"Actually, Holtzman gave me an idea on that one. He mentioned that the jewellers belonged to him, and I'm guessing he has other businesses that he uses as fronts. We just need to research what and where, and then go pay one a visit."

"And then?" asked Isaiah as he sat forward, this time meeting my gaze straight on.

"Well, I remember from chatting with him: he liked to have parties on his yacht. I reckon I can swing us an invite once he hears I'm in town."

Nobody spoke for thirty seconds or so as they mulled things over. Although I was no expert in the field of undercover investigations, I felt confident my plan had some merit.

"It's not the most convincing plan I've ever heard, but I think it could work — even better that it basically needs very little pre-work," said Isaiah. "We probably need to run things past the boss and get some support from the tech team..."

"Not this time," I interrupted, a hand held up. "This stays between us four, or else I'm out. I don't mean to be dramatic, but there is someone involved in all this, so it's either between us or not at all."

"First sensible thing I've heard from you in a while," said Steve with a nod of appreciation.

"Cool with me," said Isaiah. "As long as you know what you're doing. It sounds like we're heading into your world on this one. It's way above our pay grade, so it's going to be on your shoulders."

"Yep, I think I've got it. Eva?"

"Seems rough around the edges, but we've got a bit of time to sort that out. I'm game if the rest of you are."

"So, boss, what's first?" asked Steve.

"Let's just be clear: Isaiah is still the boss, so everything still goes through him," I quickly replied. There was no need to make an enemy if I didn't need to. "But as you're asking, I think we need to get out on the streets and find out where we need to show our faces."

"Eva, this is your neck of the woods. Know anyone that can help?" asked Isaiah.

"I sure do," she replied with a smile. "Let me make some calls and I'll get back to you a bit later."

At that, she excused herself from the table, snatching up her phone as she went, and disappeared upstairs. A few minutes later, we could all hear her on the phone, and not long after that, she was out of the door and off to who knows where.

"So, what about us?" asked Steve.

"You two need to go update your wardrobe," I replied curtly. "There's no way anyone will believe we're business partners the way you dress. Get yourselves over to a mall, find a proper men's clothing shop, and pick up some decent outfits. And make sure you ask for some help. No jeans, no trainers — just simple, smart attire without looking like you're going to work in an office."

"And how do we afford this makeover? Do you know what an FBI agent gets paid?" asked Steve with concern.

"Work expenses," I suggested, "and if you aren't comfortable with that, then use this," I said, flicking my personal credit card in Steve's direction.

Steve snatched it up and pocketed it in one smooth motion.

"Big mistake," he said with a laugh. "Come on then, boss. We've got our orders," he added, beckoning Isaiah as he got up and headed toward the stairs.

"And take the car too," I said to Isaiah as I fished the keys out of my pocket.

He looked at me with slightly closed eyes, as if querying my motives.

"And what are you going to do with the day?"

"Oh, I've got a little errand to run," I said with a smile and a wink.

Realising he wasn't going to get anything else from me at this point, he jokingly shook his head as he walked off toward the stairs, leaving me contemplating the wisdom of what I'd just put in motion.

Chapter 27

A bout an hour later I was standing on a street corner trying to hail a cab. I'd come to the realisation that I had quite a bit of work to do if my plan was going to play out as I imagined. First things first: I needed to sort out some transport that hadn't been tampered with by the Bureau. I'd left a message with Abi to send me the details of our West Coast contacts, so it hadn't taken long to find someone who could provide what I needed at short notice. My next task was to lean on Giles for a very big favour, although I reasoned that he owed me for my current predicament. I was about to phone him when my phone began to buzz; I was surprised to see it was Matteo.

"Hey, Matteo. How are you doing?"

"I'm good, Mr Miller," he replied cheerfully.

"Glad to hear it. What can I do for you?"

"I just wanted to check if everything was okay. I haven't seen you for a few weeks…and I wanted to say thanks for sending Abi around. How did you know?"

I'd completely forgotten to ask Abi how things had gone when she visited him. Now that I thought about it, she'd been unusually quiet about the whole situation.

"Err…you're welcome," I said, partially stalling as I tried to work out exactly what I'd done. "I'm guessing you two had a chance to chat?"

"We sure did. It was everything I hoped it would be. I think we might have something."

"That's great," I said slowly, catching on that I'd unwittingly played Cupid.

"You and Ms Russell will have to come round for dinner, you know, a double date."

"Easy, tiger," I laughed. "Can I offer you some advice about Abi. You've got to play it cool — don't come on too strong. Just let things progress slowly; don't push it. She's not that kind of girl."

"It was her idea, Mr Miller."

"In which case, ignore me. What do I know?" I chuckled.

"Will you be around on Monday? Perhaps we could grab a coffee? Abi speaks so highly of you; I'd like to hear your thoughts about her."

"I'm afraid not. I'm out in San Francisco for a little while. I'm not sure when I'll be back."

"Lovely part of the world. I've got a cousin out there. If you get a craving for some proper Italian food, go see him. I'll send you his details."

"Thanks, mate. Listen, Matteo, I've got to go — I've got an appointment and we're just about to pull up."

"Sure thing, Mr Miller. Thanks again, and let me know if there's ever anything you need from me."

"Thanks, I'll keep it in mind."

I ended the call and immediately opened my messaging app, finding my chat with Abi. Quickly searching the GIF library on my phone, I sent her a soppy romantic message with an Italian flag on it. Her reply landed as I was about to get out of the taxi: a simple 'up yours' emoji followed by a smiling one. The car I'd come to see was parked outside the showroom, and I gave it a cursory glance as I headed for the main doors. I couldn't help wondering why Amelia hadn't told me about Abi and Matteo.

I was treated like an old friend at the dealership. Over the years we had done a lot of business with them, but this was the first time I'd visited personally. Although I was only really interested in the car outside, I was given a tour. It was a really nice setup and, despite not having a lot of inventory, what they had was right up my street: classic American muscle with a smattering of unusual European cars like a Lancia Integrale Evo 2 and an Audi Quattro. It turned out the owner was a massive WRC fan. I promised I would help him get an RS200, the pinnacle of the group B generation. I decided not to mention that we had one back home in the museum — no point in getting his hopes up. After a quick test drive, it didn't take long to conclude our business. I'm not usually so quick to close a sale, especially for a classic, but given our history I decided it was highly unlikely he would try to screw me over. The impact on his reputation would be significant, so it wasn't worth the risk. To be fair, he was very open about a few small issues with the car, but none of them were deal breakers, so I put him in contact with Abi, who would sort out the finances, and left as the proud owner of a beautifully restored and modernised Ford Mustang GT500E Super Snake.

The drive back to the house was fantastic. I never tire of driving these cars, and to do it on the streets of one of America's hippest cities felt even more iconic. The supercharged 427 V8 rumbled and whined away sweetly; the vibrations when stopped at the lights seemed to permeate every part of the car. And then there was that unmistakable supercharger whine that hinted at the power available. Painted in metallic pepper grey with two central black stripes, the car looked like a perfect copy of the car it was modelled on — the car known as Eleanor from the film Gone in Sixty Seconds (the Nicolas Cage version, obviously). Unsurprisingly, it drew quite a bit of attention; most people looked around as they heard it coming. One thing the car didn't have was hands-free calling, so I held off contacting Giles until I got back to the house.

Although there was nobody home, I fancied someone else making me lunch, so I headed out to Tartine Bakery on Guerrero Street. It was predictably busy, but after a short wait they seated me outside. I watched the world go by, waited for my food and contemplated how to approach the conversation with Giles. I polished off an excellent pastrami-pressed sandwich and a piece of quiche, then sat nursing a macchiato while I picked at a hazelnut tart. I finally popped my earbuds in and dialled Giles. It took a few rings before he answered; he was probably trying to figure out why I'd be calling him.

"Eli, my dear chap. How the devil are you? You are the last person I expected to be calling me."

"You know me, Giles. Always trying to be unpredictable. How are you?"

"I'm halfway through a great pinot noir, puffing on a Partagas and enjoying the company of a delightful lady from UNESCO. I'd say I'm having a pretty good evening. How are things in the good old US of A?"

"Yeah, ticking along. Listen, any chance you could excuse yourself from your company for a little while? We need to chat."

"Err…sure, Eli. Give me a few minutes and call me back."

I hung up, downed the macchiato and took a giant bite of the tart. I then wedged some bills under the coffee glass and headed off through the neighbourhood towards Mission Bay. Five minutes later I popped my earbuds back in and flicked through the menus to redial Giles. A slightly less jovial Giles answered within three rings.

"Eli."

"Giles," I replied equally formally.

"So, out with it then — what can I do for you?" he inquired, slightly impatiently.

"First things first: I feel the need to remind you that you helped me get into this mess, so you better think carefully before you say no. The way I figure it, you owe me one."

"Eli, Eli, let's not get carried away. From what I recall, you didn't exactly run away from your current situation."

"And if it wasn't for you, they probably wouldn't have even looked in my direction, so yes, you owe me, and there ain't no way you're weaselling your way out of it."

"Well, let's hear it, then I'll decide just how much I owe you," he responded in a resigned tone.

The beauty of Giles, and what he did, was that he worked in a world of 'you scratch my back, I'll scratch yours'. Favours were asked for, granted and traded, but once you acquired an IOU it was good forever — or at least it was when you dealt with a man of integrity like Giles. I filled him in on nearly everything that had happened while I'd been stateside.

"Sounds like there's a rat on your ship," he commented ponderously, "but I'm not sure how you think I'm going to help you from over here. I know people over there, but not the kind of people you need."

"Don't worry, that's not what I'm looking for. I've got a plan that will hopefully see me out the other side and with the FBI off my back for good."

"And let me guess — that's where I come in," he offered as a statement rather than a question. "So what exactly do you need from me?"

I was momentarily distracted by a commotion off to my left on the opposite street corner. Two teenagers were hassling a smaller kid, pushing him around and grabbing at his backpack. As I watched, they started rummaging through his pockets, eventually fishing out his phone as the smaller child tried to resist, despite it being obviously futile. Seemingly satisfied, they were about to walk away when they saw me watching. Pausing briefly and staring straight at me, one of them moved back towards the young lad. I thought they were going to give the phone back, but instead he reached up to the victim's ears and slowly, deliberately removed his headphones. The act was a pure challenge to me, and the look in their eyes said they were ready to defend themselves if I was stupid enough to intervene. Wisely, I stayed put but held their gaze, keeping an eye on their hands just in case. The bigger youths began to back away up the street, smiling at me while chatting to each other. The one with the headphones said something to his pal, flipped me the bird and turned away, laughing as they strode off. The young kid had sat himself on the pavement, looking pale and with a bloody nose. I turned to head in his direction but had to wait at the crosswalk.

"Eli, are you still there?" I suddenly heard in my ear.

"Oh, sorry, Giles — just got distracted by something happening on the street."

"I was kind of hoping you'd had a change of heart," he joked.

"Unfortunately for you, that won't be happening this time," I teased.

I was keen to get across the road and check on the boy, who was still sitting on the pavement. I quickly laid out exactly what I was hoping to do and how I needed Giles to help me.

"That's a huge ask, Eli. I'm not sure I can deliver on that," he responded after considering it for a moment.

"Don't give me that, Giles. If anyone can make it happen, it's you," I replied, hoping a little flattery might help.

"And do you have some ideas on how exactly I'm supposed to achieve what you need?"

"If I had all the answers, I wouldn't need you, would I?"

He just grunted in response, so I continued.

"I'm counting on your Giles. I don't think I need to remind you that I'm working for the FBI, if you catch my drift. I'm going to work on the assumption that you're going to deliver. Any issues, let me know; otherwise I'll take your silence to mean 'mission accomplished'".

The lights changed, and I made my way across the road. The young lad was still sitting on the pavement, but he seemed to be getting himself together as the adrenaline began to wear off.

"I think you're going to owe me big time for this one," Giles said as I reached the other side.

"Maybe, maybe not. We can talk about that over a glass of Malbec sometime," I said, hoping the friendly olive branch would keep him onside. "Any questions?"

"I mean, I have about 5,000, but I'm pretty sure I won't be getting any answers."

"Reading the situation as well as ever," I chuckled. "Listen, mate, I've got something I need to do. You know the deal — no news is good news, but don't screw me on this one, Giles."

"Roger that, Eli," he said as he disconnected the call.

Chapter 28

It was perfectly timed, as I'd just arrived at the spot where the boy was sitting on the pavement. He was probably about thirteen, with scruffy mid-length brown hair, dressed in jeans, a T-shirt and white Converse trainers. If I were to stereotype him, I'd call him a skater kid, although the lack of a board made me doubt that was accurate. His jeans were scuffed, there were a few drops of blood on his T-shirt, and I could hear him sniffling as he tried to fight back the tears. He didn't look up as I approached, so I knelt down beside him.

"Hey, kid, you all right?" I asked, slipping my earbuds back into their charging case.

He didn't reply straight away, just looked up at me for a moment, probably trying to figure out what my angle was.

"What's it to you?" he asked, his tone overly aggressive, clearly trying to hide his vulnerability.

"I just wanted to check on you, that's all," I said gently, holding both hands up to show I wasn't a threat. "I was on the other side of the street and saw what happened. The same thing happened to me when I was about your age, so I wanted to make sure you were okay."

This wasn't entirely true. Mobile phones were barely a thing when I was thirteen, but I had been mugged once. I was big for my age, so I only got pushed around a little and lost a few quid, but it was still a shock to my otherwise sheltered upbringing.

"It was just the neighbourhood losers throwing their weight around. I'm okay," he said, his face softening as he wiped his bloody nose with his forearm.

"You hurt?" I asked, nodding at the smear of blood.

"Nah. It's nothing compared to what I'm going to get from my mum when I get home," he said, realising this was just the beginning of his troubles.

"Did they take something important?" I asked, knowing what it was like to have a strict, money-conscious parent.

"Just my phone and headphones. They were a Christmas present from Mum — she had to do five overtime shifts to afford them. She's going to go screwy, and I won't get a new one for five years."

Normally I'd have thrown out a sarcastic line about surviving without Snapchat or Instagram, but I figured a thirteen-year-old wouldn't see the point.

"That really sucks. I'm sure your mum won't be that pissed once you tell her what happened," I said, trying to offer a little hope.

"Dude, you ain't met my mum. This is only going one way," he said, resigned.

"Okay. Well, are you sure you're all right? Anything I can do for you?"

"Nah, man, I'm good," he replied. "Unless you've got a spare phone lying around?"

We both chuckled, though he clearly wasn't expecting an answer.

"Thanks for coming over to check on me. Not many people round here would bother. I'm guessing you're not from around here."

It was more of a statement than a question, but I decided to humour him.

"I don't know what you mean," I said with a smile.

"Australian?"

"Why do you Americans always think I'm Australian? Haven't you seen enough James Bond films to recognise a British accent?"

"Yeah, but you don't exactly have that James Bond thing going on."

"Ouch," I grinned. "Should've just kept walking."

"No offence. You're not exactly Daniel Craig."

It was kind of ironic, given that the very reason I was in town was for some kind of spy work. I guess I should take it as a compliment that I looked like an ordinary guy, albeit to a 13-year-old kid.

"Fair point," I said, laughing. "Listen, I gotta get going. You sure you don't need anything?"

"Nah, man, I'm good," he replied, a smile forming on his face.

I nodded my head in respect for his decision to manage this on his own and turned to head towards the seafront. Making my way back to the crossroads, I looked up and down the street to make sure it was safe to cross, and had my attention drawn by a flashing sign half a block away. I paused briefly as an idea popped into my head. I turned back to retrace my steps and found the kid just picking himself up off the pavement and bending over to get his bag.

"So," I said, catching him off guard, "what's your name?"

"Err...Brian," he replied cautiously. "Why?"

"Nice to meet you," I said, offering my hand. He shook it tentatively. "I'm Eli."

He nodded, then just stared, still trying to figure me out.

"Listen, I'd like to help you out. Got five minutes?"

"Help me out? How exactly?" he asked warily. "And what do you want from me?"

"No strings. Just offering to do you a favour," I said, trying not to sound suspicious. "Look, I noticed a phone repair shop down the block. Thought we could see if they've got anything for you."

"For real?" Brian asked, torn between wanting a phone and mistrusting a stranger. "Why would you do that?"

"Because I can. And just so you know, I don't want anything in return. No strings. Just promise me that one day you'll pay it forward."

He thought about it — or at least pretended to — but he'd already made up his mind. Dusting off his trousers, wiping his nose again, he slung his backpack over his right shoulder and we walked to the shop.

We chatted about school, family, sports, and of course, cars. Turns out my gut instinct about him was pretty good. He was the youngest of three brothers; his parents both worked as many hours as they could to make ends meet. The way he spoke of his parents made me think he'd been brought up with good morals and values, respected them, and admired their work ethic. He loved the outdoors and most sports, and hated computer games and movies — especially the comic book-based ones. I almost stopped in my tracks when he told me his favourite car was a Honda NSX. I thought at first that he meant the recent hybrid version, but lo and behold, this 13-year-old kid knew his stuff when it came to one of the greatest cars to come from Japan in the 90s — some would argue ever. We talked about the NSX for a couple of minutes, and it was clear the kid had a love for Japanese cars. I got the sense he really wanted to pursue a career designing cars.

We weren't in the phone shop long before he quickly zeroed in on a Samsung Galaxy S21, and after giving it the once-over, a deal was done. I opted not to buy him replacement headphones; he needed to fix part of this situation for himself. However, I did get him a new SIM card with a few dollars on it to keep him online until he got home and sorted his old one out. We walked out of the shop and stopped on the sidewalk. Brian looked at me awkwardly.

"I'm going this way," I said, pointing to the waterfront.

"I'm that way," he said, pointing the opposite way.

"Take care of yourself — and stay away from pricks like those two. I'm not buying you a new phone every week."

"I'll do my best," he said ruefully. "Not sure how I'll explain this to Mum," he added, patting the phone in his pocket.

"Just tell her you met a generous stranger. Wouldn't be a lie."

"As I said, you don't know my mum. She'll think I've been up to no good."

I thought for a second, then pulled out my wallet. His face fell when I handed him not money but a black metal card. One side bore my company logo, the other my name and contact details.

"I don't hand those out to just anyone," I said.

"I bet you don't. It's not like any business card I've ever seen. What did you say you did again?"

"I didn't," I said with a smile. "You never asked."

"Well, I'm asking now," he said, mock attitude creeping in.

"Doesn't work like that. Quick life lesson: be interested in people, ask questions, listen. Assume they know something you don't — until they prove otherwise. People like to talk; not many listen. Be different. Not just to stand out, but because being you matters more than fitting in."

"Any other pearls of wisdom? You do know I'm fifteen, right?" he said after a pause.

"Lecture over," I laughed, keeping to myself that I'd thought he was thirteen.

He turned the card in his hand, clearly appreciating its weight and etched finish.

"If you've any issues with Mum or Dad, get them to call me," I said, nodding at the card. "Anyway, I've got to go. Been good meeting you. Keep in touch — you never know when you might need a friend across the pond."

I held out my hand for a shake, but he slapped me a high five instead.

"Thanks, man," Brian said humbly. "I really appreciate everything — the lecture included."

I nodded, turned and carried on my wander, leaving him watching after me.

The walk back was uneventful. I browsed a few shops, watched the activity in the bay and as late afternoon edged into evening I finally walked into the kitchen to find the others lounging around. Steve had already cracked open a beer, while Isaiah and Eva were watching something on TV.

"Thought we were going to have to send out a search party for you," Steve quipped, clearly amused with himself.

"It was either that or start dredging the bay," added Eva with a disarming smile.

"What can I say? Went for a walk, made some calls, made some friends…and maybe one or two enemies," I said.

"Enemies?" Isaiah turned, suspicious.

"Nothing serious. I'll tell you another time," I said with what I hoped was a reassuring smile.

Isaiah still looked doubtful, but I didn't give him a chance to push it.

"How about you, Eva? How did you get on?"

"You mean you don't want to know about our day of shopping first?" Steve interjected sarcastically.

Eva ignored his comment and grabbed the TV remote, thumbing the standby button. The screen quickly went black, and the noise in the room reduced to the hum of the dishwasher.

"Hopefully, pretty successfully. I've called in a few favours and twisted a few arms, but the gist of it is that I've got a good insight into which pies Edwin Jameson has his fingers in."

She proceeded to fill us in on all the different businesses Jameson was involved in. It was quite a list. He was definitely an influential man in this town and no doubt commanded the ear of many politicians. Given that he was suspected of being involved in drugs, it wasn't surprising to find he had 'interests' in the San Francisco nightlife scene.

"So, you know any of these clubs?" I asked when she was done.

"Most. Standard stuff — average music, overpriced drinks. But one of them's different. Exclusive, upmarket. No trouble — at least none the SFPD deal with."

"Could be promising," I mused. "Where is it?"

"Chinatown. I can find the address. It's not the kind of place you just walk into."

"Leave that to me," I said confidently.

I'd had plenty of experience getting onto guest lists. It always came down to who you knew, or money — or both.

"Saturday night?"

All three nodded.

"And what about you?" asked Eva. "Got anything to share?"

I briefly filled them in on my conversation with Giles. There was some scepticism about whether this would play out the way we needed it to. The way I figured it, and sold it to them, was that either Giles would come through and things would fall into place, or we'd go to a couple of high-class parties and call it a day. Nothing to lose, everything to gain.

"And the car?" asked Isaiah. "I assume that beast on the driveway is yours and not some random parking in our space?"

"That old thing?" I smiled. "I figured we needed some wheels that were more befitting of my normal style. If my being here is to be believable, at the very least I need a nice car."

"Whatever you say, man," said Isaiah with a shrug. "It's a beautiful machine. Do I get to borrow it sometime?"

"We'll see," I grinned.

Chapter 29

S aturday arrived quickly, despite our spending the last couple of days lounging around the house. I had ventured out a few times, but San Francisco's temperamental weather cut those trips short. The forecast promised a warm, dry Saturday, so Isaiah suggested — though it felt more like a command — that we stroll down to Chinatown, where Jameson's nightclub was located. One thing I loved about the city's weather was the lack of humidity. In most other American cities, a twenty-minute summer walk would have drenched us in sweat, but fortunately not this time.

With only an address for the club, we were surprised to find it at the junction of Broadway and Mason. Feeling out of place as we stood on the street corner, staring at a nondescript building, Isaiah led us into a diner-cum-sports bar. We settled into a window booth with a view of the building in question. Fulfilling the American stereotype, Isaiah took the opportunity to order breakfast, even though he'd already eaten earlier that morning. When the biggest fry-up I'd ever seen arrived, my taste buds kicked into overdrive, and soon all four of us were tucking into various fat-drenched foods and syrup-covered pancakes. With the plates now empty — save for pools of congealing grease — our conversation turned to the club across the street and how we'd approach it later that night.

"I vote for the all-guns-blazing approach, personally," said Steve.

"Why doesn't that surprise me?" replied Isaiah. "Quick in and out, just like with the ladies, eh, Steve?"

Embarrassed in front of Eva, Steve didn't reply, which helped quell the chuckles and prevented further heckling from distracting us from the job at hand.

"Do either of you two have any thoughts?" Isaiah asked, looking directly at me.

"From Eva's description, it's not that kind of place. There'll be some rich pricks showing off, plenty of people partying, but none of them will need roughing up. They come here to stay away from the average Joe. It's about exclusivity, privacy and luxury. There might be some muscle around, but they won't bother us. We just need to get noticed — make a few waves with generosity and extravagance. If we can draw the eye of the bar staff, the maître d' and the regulars, I'm sure I can talk us into a meeting with Jameson."

"So what are we supposed to do?" asked Eva.

"Make an impact, plain and simple. I'm pretty sure you won't have a problem doing that."

I almost immediately regretted the comment as I saw the twinkle in Eva's eyes. Out of the corner of my eye I could see Isaiah staring at me, his gaze boring into the side of my head. I quickly continued, hoping to end the awkwardness I'd created for myself.

"We need to make sure everyone remembers the four of us, and it has to be as a group, not as individuals. 'Life and soul of the party' is perhaps the best way to think about it. It might ruffle a few feathers, but we should be able to deal with that. Any thoughts, objections or other ideas?"

Nobody spoke; they all just shook their heads. Nothing further was said, so we finished our coffee before settling the bill and heading back out into the hustle and bustle of a typical Chinatown morning. One of the things I loved about the States was just leaving a wad of notes on a table to settle the bill. The Brits were always less trusting and liked to see the money before you left; the American way gave you a feeling of confidence and trust. I was still lost in thought as Isaiah began to talk again, and as I tuned back into the conversation he finished and headed off in the opposite direction. Opting to save face, I didn't ask where he was going; it probably wasn't all that important however he did seem to have a habit of going off to do his own thing. I guess it was a bit rich for me to say that but I knew I wasn't the one undermining our plans.

Once back home, it was decided a jog would help blow away the cobwebs from the last few days of idleness and prepare us for the evening's events. After protests from both me and Steve, we headed into the city and towards the park rather than down Hyde Street. While the gradient changes were nowhere near as severe, we were all breathing hard and sweating profusely as we arrived home fifty-five minutes later. In an act of generosity, Eva let us boys use the bathroom first; otherwise there's every chance we wouldn't have made it to the club that night. We'd all noticed she spent quite a while in there, but to be fair it was no longer than Amelia ever did.

With a makeshift dinner of chicken salad eaten, I decided to share a little fashion advice with the boys. To be honest, it was mainly for Steve, as Isaiah had a look that worked well. I also didn't know much about African American fashion, so figured I'd leave that well alone. Steve disappeared back upstairs for 10–15 minutes before returning looking quite the part. Eva finally came down looking what can only be described as stunning. She wore an emerald-green dress that looked like it had been made for her, and a pair of dark scarlet high heels. The dress showed off her athletic figure without being remotely slutty. It gave the briefest glimpse of her long, toned legs via the mid-thigh slit, while the tight-fitting upper section revealed her slightly muscular arms and shoulders, while suitably covering her breasts so that only minimal cleavage was on view. Pretty much every man would not only notice her but want to see more than the dress revealed — a lot more. Her make-up was subtle but used to accentuate her beauty. Her hair was the only disappointment: pulled back tight into a bun of some kind. She looked stunning, but given I had a soft spot for her curls, her hair was the only thing I'd change. Either way, she'd nailed the brief: she would be the centre of attention tonight.

"Damn, girl," said Steve from behind me, followed by a soft wolf whistle.

"Up yours," she retorted, giving him a "fuck you" smile before flashing him the finger.

I realised I hadn't taken my eyes off her since she'd walked in and quickly diverted my gaze anywhere that wasn't her. Isaiah saw this and shot me a quick smile and a look that shouted "you are in some serious trouble". He was partially right, but I was old enough to know that nothing was going to happen. My relationship with Amelia was more than skin deep; as beautiful as Eva was, at the end of the day she couldn't compete. As if reading my mind, Eva broke into my thoughts.

"You look nice, Eli," she said, with a subtly coy tone.

"Thanks," I replied, slightly embarrassed to be doing this in front of the others. I'd opted for a fitted black shirt and silvery-grey trousers and jacket, complemented by the IWC on my wrist.

After a brief, uncomfortable silence, Isaiah brought us back to reality.

"So, shall we do this?"

"Yeah, let's get this night underway," said Steve. "Can I drive?"

"Sure," I said, tossing him the keys to the BMW. "I was thinking it might be better if we arrived separately rather than all together. You and Isaiah go in the BMW. I'll take Eva in the Mustang."

This elicited an eye-roll from Steve and a nearly imperceptible shake of the head from Isaiah.

"We'll go first," I continued. "You guys give it fifteen and follow on."

"And what if we can't get in?" Isaiah asked. "Surely it's better if we all go together?"

"Separate is definitely better. It looks more natural."

I reached inside my jacket and retrieved my wallet. Pulling out another of my business cards, I handed it to Steve.

"Give this to the doorman. I'll make sure he's expecting you. You won't have any problems."

Steve examined the card much as Brian had earlier, flexing it between his fingers before pocketing it.

"All right then, we'll see you there," he said at last, clearly unable to find a way to use the card to belittle me.

I quickly grabbed something I'd forgotten, and two minutes later Eva and I were reversing off the driveway, heading for downtown. When we were about five minutes from the venue, I pulled over and turned to face her.

"You do look stunning tonight, Eva," I said, aware I was treading on potentially dangerous ground. "Exactly what we need."

"Thanks," she said, with a serious expression I couldn't quite read.

"If you don't mind, I'd like to make a small addition." She looked puzzled, clearly not expecting this. I reached into the door pocket on my side and pulled out a small jewellery box. Handing it to her, I turned away, not wanting to see her reaction.

"Eva, please don't get the wrong idea. It's just a gift from a colleague."

In the reflection in the windscreen, I watched her open the box to reveal a delicate silver necklace with a diamond pendant. She held it up to her neck, then extended it towards me, turning away slightly.

"Are you going to put it on or not?" she asked, slightly impatient.

I quickly fastened the clasp, and she turned back with a beaming smile, adjusting how the necklace rested on her chest.

"Thank you, colleague," she said mischievously. "It looks great. Shall we go?" she asked, saving me from overthinking the situation yet again.

I shifted into first, waited for a gap in traffic, and let the rear wheels spin a little as we pulled away.

Arriving at the club, I was surprised to see a queue outside — not what I'd expected for the type of place Eva had described. A Ferrari had just pulled up ahead of us and, as its occupants got out, a valet appeared to take the car. Figuring that was the routine, I pulled in behind the Ferrari just as it moved away. Eva's door popped open and a hand reached in to help her out. I, on the other hand, had to handle it myself. As I straightened my shirt and put my jacket back on, a valet appeared in front of me. He handed me a ticket, and I handed him a $100 bill.

"Keep it close," I said gently.

"Yes, sir," he replied eagerly as he clocked the numbers on the note.

He couldn't have been more than eighteen and had clearly landed a good gig for his age. The way he carefully closed the door and eased away with the car suggested the tip had the desired effect.

Chapter 30

Eva was waiting for me on the pavement. As I joined her, she threaded her arm through mine and we headed towards the doors. I glanced to my right and noticed the queue was about 100–150 people deep. Reading my mind, Eva said,

"People queue for hours to get in here. Most nights they let a few 'normal' people in. I think they watch and decide who's worthy, or something like that."

I nodded, thinking it was a clever business model. As we approached the doors, I quickly assessed the situation. Two very tall, muscular security guards flanked the entrance. The doormen were clearly the main gatekeepers. Neither looked particularly friendly, so it was hard to decide which one to approach. I needn't have worried: the guy on the right stepped towards us.

"There's the queue. Use it," he said, his deep voice reminiscent of Barry White.

"We're on the guest list, courtesy of Mr Jameson."

"Oh, right. Which ones are you?" asked the other bouncer. "Let me get the list… Oh, wait a minute; there is no list tonight, and I sure as shit don't recognise you. Nice try, but the queue is to the east, so I suggest you get to walking."

Realising we were about to be shut down at the first hurdle, I went with straight-up bribery.

"How about you start a list, then," I suggested, as I slipped five $100 bills from a fat roll of cash.

Eyeing the money, Barry White's verbal doppelgänger reached out and took the bills. A long pause followed; I was about to object when I realised he was thinking it over. It was immediately apparent this was a rare experience for him.

"Now that you mention it, I seem to remember Mr Jameson saying a Mr Franklin was coming by, bringing four friends with him. Now your party's a bit short, but your ID says Franklin all over it," he said, flicking the notes. Then I understood: Ben Franklin's on the hundred. Maybe he was sharper than I'd given him credit for. A gap appeared between the doormen, and I took a step forward.

"If I have to throw you out later, you ain't gonna like the other side of me," he warned.

"Understood," I replied, holding his gaze. "You won't have any issues from me. Listen, I've got a couple of friends joining me later. I'll vouch for them."

He was about to object when I extended my hand again, this time with another $500. He passed it to his partner, and I handed him my business card, explaining that they'd be arriving in a green BMW with an identical card.

"All right, Mr Miller, I'll see they get in."

"Eli is fine," I said with a smile, tapping him on the shoulder as I stepped toward the door. Eva squeezed my arm and whispered, "Where the hell did all that money come from?"

"Expenses," I replied with a grin.

It never hurt to be on the good side of a club's employees, so I left another sizeable tip with the lady at the welcome desk once we had 'purchased' a table in a secluded corner. I again made a point of mentioning

Jameson's name, hinting that we were hoping to see him. As we entered the main club area, it lived up to its billing. The décor was opulent: low lighting, lots of glass and gold fixtures, and a central dance floor surrounded by tables and seating areas. The bar, off to the right, was the most populated area, with patrons three deep at the counter. The staff were efficiently mixing cocktails of all colours. Despite the music from the DJ booth, the volume was just right, allowing conversations to flow over the hum of activity. The dance floor was empty for now, as our fellow club-goers prioritised cocktails and champagne at this point in the evening.

"It's not too busy. I expected it to be heaving," I said, leaning close to Eva's left ear.

"Give it time. I hear this place keeps going deep into the morning."

I nodded and we made our way to our table. Eva's dress was having the desired effect; nearly every man — and plenty of women — followed us with their eyes as we wove between tables. We sat down and Eva got comfortable. A waitress came by to take our drinks order, but I waved her off.

"Don't tell me I've got to be dry all night," Eva teased.

"Nah," I laughed. "I want to go to the bar and have a chat with one of the barmen. What do you want?"

"Surprise me."

She began to scan the room as I headed for the bar, which also gave me the chance to check out the other guests. The clientele were as expected — well-heeled and clearly with money. I was confident there were a few pretenders in the mix; there always were. The women were predictably varied: some clearly belonged, others seemed to be on the hunt for a rich husband. They were easier to spot by their outfits; it's often more challenging for women to create the 'wealthy' look compared to men, who can usually pull it off with a well-fitted suit.

At the bar, a slightly raucous laugh caught my attention. Off to the left, five guys and three women were drinking champagne. They looked like regulars, though two of the men seemed more serious — potentially a problem if my plan played out as intended. I waited a short while before getting to the front, listening to the conversations around me. Three hip-looking barmen and a slightly harried woman, all seemingly in their early twenties, were working the bar. They looked highly competent, seamlessly serving drink after drink.

"What can I get you?" one of the barmen asked.

"What bottles of beer do you have?"

"The usual — Bud, Michelob, Corona. A few imports if that's your thing."

"Give me three imports; I don't mind which. And an Espresso Martini, please."

He nodded and returned a few minutes later with three bottles of Staropramen and a beautifully balanced Espresso Martini.

"Thanks," I said, handing over a $100 bill, knowing it would more than cover the drinks. "Can I set up a tab?"

"Not my call, pal. You'd have to ask the boss," he said, nodding towards a slender, dark-haired man standing near the DJ booth.

"Perhaps you could ask him to come over and see me?" I suggested, indicating where Eva was sitting — unsurprisingly no longer alone.

I slid another $50 across the bar, which he smoothly pocketed.

"I reckon that could be arranged."

"If you could mention that I'm a friend of Edwin Jameson, that would be great," I added with a smile.

"Don't know who that is, but I'll mention it all the same," he replied a bit too quickly.

I hooked my fingers through the bottle tops, picked up Eva's drink with my other hand and headed back. Two guys were now sitting with her, clearly trying to get better acquainted. They had their backs to me and didn't see me until I set the bottles firmly on the table. I slid Eva's drink toward her and stood there. The guy to my right turned, clearly annoyed.

"Help you?" he asked, eyeing me up and down as if assessing my social standing — and finding it lacking.

"If you wouldn't mind moving, I'd like to sit next to the lady. I did just buy her a drink."

"Push off, will you, and wait your turn. We were here first," he said with a smirk, barely masking a hint of aggression.

"You obviously didn't see us arrive together," I replied calmly. "I'll let you off, but now you know, I reckon it's time you moved on."

"She came with you?" he sneered. "I doubt that. Anyway, I'm sure she'd rather be drinking Cristal than bottles of beer."

I glanced at Eva and caught the smirk on her face. She was clearly enjoying the macho posturing.

"That may be so…" I began, but he turned his back on me, as if the conversation was over.

I was momentarily at a loss. I didn't want a fight, but I wasn't about to back down either. I was about to grab his arm when a voice over my shoulder stopped me.

"Hey, dickhead," came Steve's instantly recognisable voice. "I don't think you heard my friend. Grab your

drinks — and your boyfriend over there — and fuck…
off."

The elongated "fuck off" carried a distinct, direct threat.
The guy on Eva's left turned first and almost immediately
sank back into his chair, processing the sight of me flanked
by Isaiah and Steve as an imminent threat. The other
turned slowly, ready to mouth off again, but paused as he
took in the new scenario. His brain was a bit slow to catch
up he just stared for a few seconds before realising this
wasn't a fight he wanted. He grabbed his glass and the
champagne bottle, muttered something under his breath
and slid out from behind the table. As he passed me, he
deliberately bumped my shoulder, muttering something
that sounded like "prick".

"Perfect timing, guys," I said, handing the beers around.

"Anytime," Steve smiled, clinking bottles before taking a
long swig.

We sat, enjoying some chill-out time as I surveyed the
room. It wasn't long before the man I took to be the
manager headed our way. Phase one of tonight's plan was
almost complete.

"Hi, I'm Andrew Collins, the floor manager tonight. Jeff
said you wanted to speak with me?" he said, nodding
towards the bar.

His focus was on me, so I gestured to the empty seat and
extended my hand.

"Thanks for taking the time. I was hoping we could start
a tab. I'm visiting the city, as you can probably tell, and I
was hoping my friends and I could party the night away
here. Settle up in the morning."

"I'm sorry, Mr…?"

"Miller."

"I'm sorry, Mr Miller, but we only offer that service to regulars approved by management."

"If it's a liquidity issue, you do have my car in your garage. I'd imagine that's enough to cover our expenses."

"Even then, I'm sorry, but this is above my head. The rules are the rules for a reason."

"Oh… that's a shame," I said, having expected as much. "I told Edwin a couple of years ago I'd visit this place next time I was in the city. I guess things have changed."

"Edwin?" he asked, slightly suspicious.

"Yes, Edwin Jameson. We've done business a couple of times. He always said he'd look after me when I was in town. Insisted, actually."

This wasn't entirely true, but a little flexibility with the facts wouldn't hurt.

"That may be so, but there isn't anyone by that name on the staff here."

"Oh… that's odd. Maybe I've got the wrong place."

"Must be," he said quickly. "I'm sorry, but I need to get back to the other guests. I can only apologise that I couldn't assist you, but if you need anything else, please speak to Jeff at the bar. And allow me to have a bottle sent to your table — on me, of course."

Without waiting for a response, he nodded subtly towards Jeff and walked off.

"Well, that didn't go well," Eva said almost immediately. "I swear I was told this was the place."

"Don't worry," I said. "Give it time."

The other three looked at me, slightly confused.

"For now, we play our roles. Let's make some noise," I said, finishing my beer and heading towards a group of twenty-somethings by the bar. I kept an eye on the others as I mingled and quickly made friends with some generous drink purchases. It didn't take long before Steve and Isaiah were doing their thing, and Eva made her way towards me. After maybe an hour of being excessively extroverted, I saw Jeff beckon me over.

"Mr Collins asked me to let you know there's been a change in the arrangements. Just tell me what you need and I'll sort it out for you," the barman said with a smile.

"Thanks, dude," I said — uncharacteristically — slapping him on the back. I probably needed to cut back on the alcohol before I did something seriously embarrassing.

Quite a few people had gravitated towards me in the last hour, and I noticed the same had happened with Steve and Isaiah. It seemed we'd mastered the art of drawing attention to ourselves. I wandered over to the DJ, had a quick word, and the next minute the bass was pumping and all three groups were mingling on the dance floor. It's safe to say the club was now rocking, as even those not in our groups were enticed onto the floor by the energy we'd created.

We partied hard into the night and decided to wrap things up around 3 a.m. The club was still pretty lively as all four of us made our way to the exit, everyone seemingly disappointed to see us go. As we reached the main doors, Andrew Collins appeared from a side room.

"Mr Miller."

"Hey there," I said, trying to remember his name through my alcohol-fuelled brain fog.

"Did you all have a good night?"

"It was going off in there tonight," slurred Steve, clearly a little worse for wear.

"I'm glad to hear it," he said with a slightly forced smile. "Mr Miller, I've been asked to give you this. If you call that number tomorrow, I think you'll be able to make arrangements to speak with your friend."

He handed me a cream business card embossed with gold lettering and numbers.

"Thanks," I said, placing the card in my inside pocket.

He turned and went back into the side room without another word, leaving us to continue through the front doors and onto the pavement.

To my surprise, there were still a few hopefuls queuing, even at this hour. The two security guys were still there, bright-eyed and bushy-tailed despite the sun being only a few hours away. The valet saw us coming and was about to retrieve the car when he paused and approached.

"Perhaps a taxi is a better choice?"

"Mmm... not sure I can be bothered coming back to get the car tomorrow. How about you take us home?"

"I'm not sure I'm allowed," he said, slightly disappointed. "Perhaps if I ask inside?"

I nodded, watching him dash in, probably to ask Mr Collins for permission. Eva had hooked her arm into mine and I could feel her shivering slightly. I draped my jacket over her shoulders just as I heard the doors behind me open and close. I turned, expecting to see the valet, but instead found myself face to face with the goon who'd declined my earlier invitation to leave our table — this time with two wingmen. He was clearly much worse for wear than earlier, which probably fuelled his idea that he could take us on.

"Well, if it isn't the English prick and his little whore," he snarled, spraying enough saliva in my direction that it felt like I was taking a shower in alcohol gel.

I felt Eva tense beside me, so I locked her arm into mine, just in case. I wasn't sure why — I knew she could probably take care of them better than I could — but my traditional upbringing was obviously kicking in.

"Look, man, we've all had a lot to drink, and it's the end of a good night. You go your way; we'll go ours. No harm, no foul."

"Chicken-shit as well," he sneered, squaring up to me. "Come on, do something. I just called your girl a whore and you want to walk away?"

"I just want to save you a whole lot of money in medical bills," I replied, doing my best to look bored.

"Tough talk from a pissant like you."

He brought up both hands and shoved me in the chest. Most people don't want to take the first swing so I'd seen the shove coming and had set my feet in a staggered stance. He was clearly expecting me to stumble back, but I let my rearward leg absorb the push. I swayed slightly, but otherwise barely moved. What I hadn't expected was the follow up, no doubt due to the alcohol I'd had slowing down my brain. I hadn't disengaged Eva's arm, leaving me in no position to defend myself. I saw his right shoulder draw back and braced for the incoming punch — hoping to pivot and at worst get a glancing blow — except he was yanked backwards and dumped on the ground. Standing over him was the doorman, his mate holding the other two by their collars and dragging them away from us.

"Don't worry, Mr Miller, we'll take care of these idiots," he said with a smile, nodding respectfully as he bundled them through the doors and back into the club.

I was about to call after them when the deep burble of a V8 caught my attention. Turning, I saw the Mustang and BMW parked in a line, both with drivers inside, ready to take us home. It looked like contact had well and truly been made.

Chapter 31

I woke up feeling worse than I had in a long time — yes, even worse than on that recent flight to LA. The house was completely silent, so I headed to the bathroom for what felt like the world's longest pee — one of the joys of too much alcohol. When I returned to my room, I was surprised to see it was already 11:30. Even more surprising was that my drinking buddies were still dead to the world.

Deciding there was only one option to ease my crushing headache, I started getting ready to head out to the local café. As if on cue, the others began to stir and decided to tag along. We must have looked a right group of misfits — me still in my creased suit from the night before, Eva in joggers and a vest with her hair tied up in a messy ponytail, and Steve in jeans, a threadbare T-shirt and half-laced boots. Isaiah was the only one who looked halfway presentable in chinos and a shirt

Coffee and a semi-healthy brunch later, none of us felt much better. Unsurprisingly, the rest of the day was a complete write-off as we all suffered the effects of the previous night's overindulgence. While I knew I needed to make contact with someone, I decided to leave it for another day. I rationalised that it was best not to appear too eager. While partially true, the reality was I just couldn't face engaging at that level while feeling the way I did.

Sunday was therefore a chilled affair, but Isaiah quickly got us back on track early Monday morning, dragging us out of bed for a run. Over breakfast, I decided it was time to make that call. I gathered the others around the dining table, set my phone to speaker mode, and keyed in the number. It barely rang twice before a female voice answered.

"Good morning, Mr Miller."

I was taken aback to be greeted by name, causing me to stumble over my words.

"It is Mr Miller, isn't it?" the voice prompted again.

"Err, yes," I replied, glancing around at the others with puzzlement etched on my face.

"Oh, good. My name is Sandra Twoi. I'm Mr Jameson's PA. He told me you'd be calling, although I had expected your call yesterday."

This was definitely a question disguised as a statement.

"Yes, sorry about that. I, err, wasn't feeling too well."

"No worries. I hope you're feeling better now?" she said with a hint of humour, clearly aware I'd been nursing a hangover.

"Yes, much better, thank you. I was hoping to speak with Mr Jameson, if possible?"

"Unfortunately, Mr Jameson is tied up with some business arrangements. However, he left some details for me to relay to you. Do you have a pen?"

I didn't, but both Eva and Isaiah were already taking notes, so I carried on.

"Go ahead, I've got a good memory."

"There's a function on Mr Jameson's boat this Friday. He would very much like you to join him. Your friends are also welcome if they don't have other plans. However, due to the short notice, you'll need to arrange your own transportation to the boat."

"Okay, that sounds great. We'd be delighted to accept. Is there a dress code?"

"It's black tie for the men and cocktail dresses for the ladies."

"Got it, thanks."

Eva was scribbling furiously, aggressively underlining something before thrusting her note towards me. I glanced at it, shook my head, and refocused on the call.

"And Mr Miller," she added, "Mr Jameson would like to remind you that this is a more formal occasion than your last night out. He would appreciate it if you could keep that in mind."

"Yes, of course, Ms. Twoi. Consider it done," I replied, feeling slightly admonished.

"I'll make sure Mr Jameson knows you will be coming."

The line went dead before I could say thanks. Without even looking up, I could sense Eva was about to berate me, so I spoke first.

"Looks like it's game on," I said with a smile.

I leaned back in my chair, feeling a sense of satisfaction.

"Don't start believing your own hype just yet," Eva said icily. "I don't suppose you've given any thought to where and when this party is?"

"Friday," I replied, knowing that would wind her up since she already knew it on Friday.

"Don't be a dick. You know exactly what I mean."

"Well, I know it's Friday, and I'm pretty sure it's at 19:00..."

"How can you possibly know that?" Isaiah asked, challenging me.

"Formal party, Friday night. They're always at 19:00. It's an unwritten rule."

"And what's the unwritten rule about the location? The third boat on the left, after the first bar showing the football?" Eva asked sarcastically.

"Err, no, that would be ridiculous, but I bet it won't be hard to find out."

"Why didn't you just ask when Eva suggested it?" Isaiah pressed, siding with her.

"In my experience, if someone doesn't give you the details, there's usually a reason. Either they don't really want us there — which seems unlikely, given the reminder to behave — or it's some sort of game or test. Either way, it's not proper etiquette to ask."

"So what's the play?" Isaiah asked.

"I don't know," I shrugged, "but I'm sure between the four of us we can figure it out by Friday."

The others shrugged in resigned agreement.

"There's a marina just down the street. I bet someone there can help," Steve suggested. "And if all else fails, I can hack some databases."

"Sounds like a plan," I concluded. "How about we head over there for lunch and see what we can find out?"

We ate at one of the seafront diners, giving ourselves a chance to scope things out. For a weekday, the crowds were big, and the marina was full of boats. There were several good-sized vessels, but none that stood out.

"So which one is it?" Steve asked.

"If we knew how big this party was going to be, we could narrow it down," Eva offered.

"That would help, but there has to be some sort of register," I suggested.

"If only," Isaiah said. "The harbourmaster keeps the records, and he's behind that gate."

The gate in question was keypad-activated and ringed with barbed wire. Climbing over was out, and swimming round wasn't an option either.

"Leave it to me," Eva said, setting off before anyone could reply. She waited at the gate until a deckhand arrived. With a flick of her hair and a sway of her hips, the young man was instantly captivated. Less than thirty seconds later, he was pointing out into the bay, towards the boats moored there. Blowing him a kiss, she returned with a satisfied smile.

"Mission accomplished. It's the boat moored out in the bay, near Alcatraz."

Almost in unison, we all looked towards the abandoned prison island.

"Holy shit, it's a cruise ship," I exclaimed.

"It's certainly big," Steve added.

"Well, there's no chance of missing it. Now we just need to find a way to get out there," Eva said.

"Leave that to me," I said, mimicking her jokingly.

The others eyed me suspiciously but didn't comment. They seemed to be getting used to my resourcefulness, though I had a few more surprises in store.

"The guy also confirmed there's a party on Friday, so it's definitely not a trap," Eva added.

Isaiah gave her a puzzled look.

"The guy's running the shuttle service for the guests."

"Did you offer to give him a blow job or something?" Steve asked, half-joking.

"No, I gave him a phone number."

"Yours?" Isaiah asked, surprised.

"No — Holtzman's," she replied with a grin.

"Damn, girl. Remind me not to get on your bad side," Steve chuckled.

Back home, the others discussed FBI matters before heading to a pistol range for extra practice. I declined, using the excuse that I didn't have a gun, though I could have borrowed one. It reminded me I needed to test fire the weapons Jonny had left me, but that could wait. Instead, I decided to call Amelia.

"Hi, honey, it's me."

"Hi, darling. Good to hear from you. I was beginning to think you'd forgotten about me."

"Nah, just been really busy, that's all."

"Where are you? The airport?"

"No, why?"

"The line's really clear, like you're in the next room."

"The wonders of modern technology, I guess."

"So, how are things? Are you keeping out of trouble?"

"Yeah, not too bad. Things are pretty quiet, really." I couldn't tell her about the other night's events; she'd be upset. She didn't like me drinking heavily, and the near-fight wouldn't have gone down well.

"Are you making friends with our American cousins?"

"Yeah, they're nice. A few have mistaken me for an Aussie, but otherwise fine."

We chatted for ten or fifteen minutes, but it quickly became hard to keep the conversation going. Not only could Amelia always tell when I wasn't telling the whole truth, but I found it difficult to engage, knowing it was only for this fleeting call. I'd always been like this. I guess it was a way of protecting myself emotionally — or at least that's what I'd convinced myself over the years. I wrapped it up before I got into trouble; managing her emotions over the phone was hard enough without being thousands of miles away.

"Honey, I have to go. We're about to start work again."

"Oh, okay. It was good talking to you. Call me again soon, okay?"

"Yeah, sure. When I get a chance. Love you."

"Love you too. Bye."

I considered calling Lucas but didn't feel like answering questions about Jessica, so I opted against it. Besides, he had my number and hadn't called, so I figured both his love life and the business were running smoothly. Despite the brief and sweet call with Amelia, it was all I could handle. It was nice to hear her familiar voice, but I needed to compartmentalise that part of my life from what was happening now. I decided to let Jonny know how things were going and arranged to meet him the next day on the trails, hoping to leave my first proper message.

The trails were unusually busy, and I had to pass the drop point two or three times before I could leave my message. Further along I came across a red-faced Jonny puffing and panting as he dragged himself and his bike up a hill. Neither of us spoke — Jonny likely didn't have the air to manage words — but we tipped our helmets like any other riders would. My message contained a request for several things for Friday. Since we wouldn't meet again, I just hoped he'd deliver and save me the embarrassment of letting everyone down.

The next couple of days were spent trying to plan for Friday, but it quickly became clear there was no way to plan for this one. We'd be on a boat in the middle of the bay, with one way on and one way off. There'd be no backup; we were on our own and would have to make our own luck. With a spare afternoon, I chose to mix business with pleasure and took a trip to Alcatraz. Before setting off, I borrowed a surveillance camera from Steve, just in case I could snap some shots of the boat. The ferry was packed with tourists, but I found a spot offering a vantage point of Jameson's vessel. I probably took thirty or so pictures during the ten-minute trip — a mix of general shots and close-ups of the living quarters. I hoped the others would be impressed; no one else had suggested it.

The Alcatraz tour was fascinating. The audio guide had won some kind of award and added to the eerie atmosphere of the deserted prison. Even with the crowds, you could still feel what the place must have been like. The wind howling off the Pacific must have been enough to send a chill through even the most hardened criminal. The few open cells, most undergoing restoration after years of salty air, were ridiculously small. Measuring about six feet by four, they felt claustrophobic. I'm not one to fear small spaces, but standing there — even with the door open — gave me a shiver. I was glad to get back onto the gangway and board the ferry. I could understand why several men had tried escaping, despite the odds.

Returning to the pier, I joined the throng of tourists and headed down towards the Ferry Building at the base of the Bay Bridge. By early evening I was back home and, finding no one there, I settled in for a night of nostalgic sports TV, watching Playmakers, a gritty NFL drama from 2003. I also took the chance to text Giles to check if everything was in order. Surprisingly, given the late hour in the UK, I got a prompt thumbs-up emoji in reply.

Chapter 32

By 4 p.m. on Saturday I decided a walk was in order — mainly to check on Jonny's arrangements for me, rather than just to get some fresh air. After spending the day indoors poring over boat photos, a change of scenery would do me good. I felt pretty good about myself; all three of them — especially Isaiah — were impressed with my ingenuity and my photographic abilities.

"Where are you going?" Isaiah asked, his tone a bit too sharp for my liking.

"Just popping out to check on something," I replied as diplomatically as possible.

"Yeah, well, make sure you're back by seven. We have an appointment, remember?"

"We do? Why didn't someone tell me?" I responded sarcastically.

"Very funny," Isaiah shot back with a forced smile. "Just make sure you're back, all right?"

"No probs, boss."

Fisherman's Wharf was predictably busy. I almost drew a crowd as I stopped at the gate to the marina; several passers-by paused to watch as I headed towards what I hoped would be a waiting boat. The random curiosity of the general public never ceased to surprise me. The marina wasn't large — about thirty-five boats, give or take — so I quickly spotted that Jonny hadn't let me down. In Bay 16 — he knew 16 was my number — sat the boat for us to use. It wasn't as classy as my Riva back home, but Jonny had at least managed to find us a sleek, dark-blue vessel with several biscuit-coloured chairs near the rear. About thirty feet long, smart-looking, and capable of making short work of the trip across the bay.

The key was predictably left in the ignition, and after a quick inspection I untied the lines and started the engine. Whatever was running under the body sounded good as I carefully manoeuvred out of the marina. Treating it like a car, I let the engine temperature and oil pressure settle before opening the throttle. It wasn't quite Ferrari-like in acceleration, but it definitely moved. With the water calm, I quickly got used to the handling, which was surprisingly responsive for such a big boat. It was a fantastic feeling, zipping across open water with the wind rushing through my hair. Soon after passing under the Golden Gate Bridge I swung the boat round in a large arc and headed back for the marina, making sure I stayed clear of Jameson's yacht. Parking the boat was more challenging than it looked, but I managed it without appearing a complete novice.

When I got back to the house, I received a few enquiring looks at my windswept appearance but nobody commented. After a quick shower and a change into outfit for the evening — again opting for an open collar — I found myself downstairs waiting for the others. It wasn't until 6:55 p.m. that they appeared, and while I wanted to make a comment, I sensed tension in the air and opted to keep quiet.

"So, what's the deal, Eli?" Steve asked as we headed down the hill towards the marina. "Did you get us a boat?"

Suddenly all eyes were on me. I was glad I'd checked the boat earlier.

"Oh yeah, the boat. I think I managed to organise us a little dinghy of sorts."

"You think?" Isaiah asked incredulously.

I just flashed him a smile, and we continued in silence. Parked in front of the marina entrance were several limos and a few expensive cars — one of which was a Ferrari 250 GTO, one of the most expensive cars in the world. I've sold one or two in my time, and I'm pretty sure I sold this one to Edwin Jameson — but I could be wrong. A noticeable reduction in stress occurred as I punched in the code to gain access to the marina. I hopped aboard our waiting boat while the others paused.

"Are you taking the piss?" Steve asked.

"Is this really our ride?" Eva said, disbelief edging her voice. "Who are you exactly, Elon Musk's cousin?"

"Just a regular guy."

"Regular guy my ass," said Steve as he untied the lines.

He jumped in, high-fived me, and dropped into one of the sumptuous leather chairs. After clearing the marina wall, I pointed the boat towards the Bay Bridge — the opposite direction to Jameson's floating palace.

"You know the party is the other way?" Eva said, tapping me on the shoulder.

"Yeah, I know. I figured if we came from the other direction, it wouldn't allow Jameson to pinpoint our base location."

"Good idea," she replied, leaning over to speak with Isaiah. "Oh, and try to keep the speed down — you're messing up my hair, and Isaiah gets a little seasick."

I laughed and nodded. So the boss man had a weakness. We passed Treasure Island before swinging round the other side, making it look like we'd come from Alameda. We arrived at the boat around 7:30 p.m., just as the sun began to set on the far side of the Golden Gate Bridge. The sky was a brilliant mix of pink and bright orange, the city surrounded by a golden haze. I brought the throttles to an idle as we cruised up to the side of the yacht, giving Eva a chance to fix her slightly windswept hair. As our lines were thrown to the waiting deckhands, I cut the engines and we were pulled alongside the suspended stairway. Tossing the keys to the nearest deckhand, we disembarked, taking our first steps towards the lion's den. I followed Eva up the stairs, unable to stop myself noticing how fantastic she looked in her black-and-white Versace dress.

"Good evening, gentlemen — and lady," said the concierge, eyeing Eva. "Do you have an invitation?"

"We were invited at the last minute by Mr Jameson," Isaiah replied, as usual taking the lead.

They looked unsure. Jameson's parties were obviously highly organised affairs where everyone either had invitations or was so well known they didn't need one. Clearly, we fell into neither category.

"If you could just wait a few minutes, I'll have to check."

"Sure thing. It's Eli Miller and his three associates," Isaiah said, casually leaning on the railings and looking back at the city.

The concierge barely took two steps before stopping, putting a hand to his ear, then nodding slowly. Someone was obviously watching our arrival, although no cameras were immediately visible.

"Ah, Mr Miller, I was told about your attendance. Please forgive me; I wasn't expecting you quite so promptly. This way, please."

We were escorted towards the front of the boat and through a set of large wooden doors into the main reception room. It wasn't crowded, but there were a healthy number of guests, all deep in conversation. Although I'd had to send Steve and Isaiah out again for tuxedos, I have to say we fitted in perfectly. They looked like they really belonged. I, on the other hand, had gone a little more rogue with my outfit: a crushed-velvet burgundy jacket with matte black lapels, a black shirt and black dress trousers. It was an acceptable look and one I favoured for these kinds of events back home — not classic, but definitely me.

No one paid much attention to our entrance, so we started to mingle, doing our best to grab champagne as it passed by on silver trays. We kept together as a group, exploring the different rooms and learning the layout of the boat before settling in a forward room on some perimeter chairs. One by one, the others went off to mingle and simultaneously try to locate Jameson. I simply studied the wealth on display. There might have been some former and future clients here, but that wasn't occupying my thoughts. I was rehearsing my speech to Jameson when I suddenly saw a face I recognised — not a friendly face, but a woman I'd seen at the club last Saturday. She was chatting with a silver-haired guy, maybe in his fifties. Grabbing my glass, I got up and headed over. As I approached, our eyes met and she flashed me a welcoming smile. However, my attention was captured by the man with her. He looked familiar now I was closer, but I couldn't place him.

"Hi," I said. "I'm Eli Miller." I directed it mostly towards the lady, but couldn't help looking at the man.

"Bill. Bill Sipowitz," he said, extending his right hand.

Shaking it firmly, I replied, "Good to meet you, Bill. I guess this must be your lovely wife?"

Both of them chuckled.

"I wish," he said, giving me a playful punch on the arm. "My wife is over there chatting with the host," he added, jerking a thumb. I looked over to see a woman in her mid-thirties in a small group surrounding Jameson. A vivacious redhead; I was pretty sure Bill's wife was more into his money than him. I nodded. I'm not entirely sure how I'd missed Jameson, but there he was. My stomach tied in a knot. Watching him for a few seconds, I turned back to the pair in front of me.

"And who, may I ask, are you?"

"I'm Isabella."

It struck me as odd that she left out her surname. I assumed it was an American privacy thing — women withholding personal details to maintain a little anonymity.

"So, Eli, where are you from?"

Before I could respond he decided to try to be clever — maybe to impress Isabella.

"Australia, right? Sydney?"

"No, actually I'm from England."

"Oh right, nice place. I've been a few times. I actually bought a car there a few years back."

And with that, the penny dropped. The Ferrari back at the marina wasn't Jameson's but belonged to this Bill guy. With my memory jogged, I remembered his face from the museum. From memory I wasn't involved in selling him the car, but I'm pretty sure I met him once while he was finalising arrangements to have it shipped home. I really didn't want to get into a car conversation; that wasn't why I was there, and I didn't need him suddenly remembering me. I could only hope he kept drinking like a fish; that would further impair his memory. Thankfully, we moved on quickly.

"So, how did a young fella like you end up here?" he asked, indicating the higher-than-average age of the guests.

"I'm here with my colleagues," I said, pointing to the other three, who had regrouped and were watching me with curiosity.

"Business, huh? What industry are you in?"

"We're in, uh... acquisitions and distribution."

"A perfect match with Mr Jameson."

"I know it's not really the done thing, but we were hoping to have a quick business chat with our host at some point."

"Well, good luck with that. You'll need it," he said with a smile that said "been there, done that".

"Thanks," I said, noticing Jameson heading towards the other three.

"Hey, I need to get back. Maybe I'll see you both later."

As I turned, I felt a hand on my arm.

"Don't forget," Isabella said, with a smile that was impossible to forget. I didn't know what it was about this trip to America, but it seemed every attractive woman I met was hitting on me. I wouldn't consider myself ugly, but I was definitely punching above my weight. Nodding slightly, not really sure how to respond, I spun on my heels and returned to the others.

"Making new friends, are we? I guess I'm not good enough for you," Eva teased — though I was no longer sure how serious she was.

"Far from it. I recognised her from the club and wanted to find out who she was. And the other guy actually knows me, though he doesn't realise it."

"Oh?" Isaiah said, clearly listening in.

"I'll fill you in later. Jameson is coming over."

We all looked in his direction, watching as he greeted people on his way. He was everything I remembered. Somewhere in his early fifties, he fit the stereotype of a classic American man — tall, athletic, a healthy tan, very well groomed. His salt-and-pepper hair was the only indication he wasn't still in his late thirties. If Abercrombie & Fitch ever ran a campaign aimed at the midlife-crisis generation, Edwin Jameson could have been the poster child.

"Good evening, Mr Miller. Thank you for coming. I'm glad to see you found your way here," he smiled.

"I think it's I who should be thanking you for the invite."

"Not at all. I seem to recall asking you to look me up if you were ever in town. And after your lavish night out on Saturday, the least I can do is host you here for the evening."

It appeared he'd been fully briefed — beyond just the fact I'd been asking about him.

"Well, all the same, we're grateful for the thought."

"And who is 'we'?" he asked, looking at Eva, Steve and Isaiah.

"These are my associates: Eva, Steve and Isaiah."

"Associates, you say? I don't recall meeting them when we last did business — and I'm very good with faces."

"Well, that was a few years ago. Personnel changes, as does the direction of a business. Adapt to survive."

"Very true, although I'm not entirely sure what adaptations you need to make to a classic and exotic car business to stay relevant."

There was no doubt Edwin Jameson was a shrewd businessman, so I didn't take the comment at face value. There was an underlying meaning.

"You'd be surprised," I said with a polite smile. "I was hoping we might have a few minutes of your time to discuss some business."

"Yes, Sandy did mention you wanted to talk. The thing is, I really don't need any more cars at the moment, so I'm not sure we have anything to discuss."

"It's not cars this time; it's something else. Something I'm sure you'd be interested in."

I figured being vague might be enough to entice him into a conversation.

"I think that's very unlikely, but… I was always told to give people an opportunity — that's how I ended up here, after all," he said, indicating our surroundings. "I need to attend to my guests, but maybe we can get together a little later, somewhere quieter, and I'll listen to your proposal."

"Sounds good to me. Thank you, Mr Jameson," I said, offering my hand to seal the agreement.

He shook it limply — a pet peeve of mine — nodded to the others, and turned back to a group of guests who seemed to be waiting for him. I turned to the others, conscious there might be electronic eyes and ears on us.

"Game on. Let's talk a bit later," I said.

"Time to party?" Steve asked, eager.

"Mingle, not party," I cautioned. "Let's not get ourselves thrown off the boat now we've got this far."

Chapter 33

Without a word, Isaiah peeled away from the group and headed to the buffet, quickly striking up a conversation with some other guests. The other two slipped off, leaving me to ponder the next step. A thought that had crossed my mind some days ago was now back at the forefront, but I wasn't sure how great an idea it was — or if I could bring myself to do it. I wandered out to the bow of the boat, partly for some quiet to think, but also to enjoy the unique view of the city at night from the water. Despite the light pollution from the city, hundreds of stars still glinted in the clear night sky. Although a gentle wind was blowing over my right shoulder, I could hear the water lapping against the hull and the distant drone of diesel engines chugging across the bay. Given the size of the boat, the swell barely moved her, so I was surprised when a hand suddenly grasped my forearm. I turned, expecting to see a doddery old lady — or perhaps Eva. Instead, I found myself looking at Bill's lady friend, Isabella.

"I'm so sorry," she said with a laugh. "Dad always told me not to wear these heels on a boat. I guess he was right after all."

"It's all right — I think I was more surprised that I didn't hear you approaching."

"You looked lost in thought, to be honest. I was in two minds about disturbing you."

"Just enjoying the view," I said defensively.

She stood for a minute, looking out into the night.

"It is beautiful. You know, it's funny — I've spent so many days and nights on this boat, but I've never come out here and just taken a moment to appreciate it. Thank you, Eli."

"You're welcome," I said with a smile, realising at the same time that she hadn't yet let go of my arm. "So, how come you've spent so much time on the boat? Is your dad in business with Mr Jameson?"

"Something like that," she replied — vague enough that I noticed.

I hadn't really had a chance to get a good look at her until now. I'd seen her at the club, but hadn't paid much attention, and Bill's history with me had been a distraction earlier. I'd guess she was mid-twenties, with blonde hair falling to mid-back, clearly cut by a skilled hand. It wasn't conventional — multiple layers and angles made it striking and hard to categorise. Unsurprisingly for California, she was tall and athletic, but not extreme. There was a softness to her physique that suggested she wasn't obsessed with her body shape. Her features were soft, and her green-blue eyes had a vitality about them.

"That's a fairly cryptic reply. What do you mean?"

"Honestly, I try to avoid that question — it never plays out well."

I think she thought that would be the end of it, but I just stood there, holding her gaze and saying nothing.

"You aren't going to make it easy, are you?" she said, with a smile that showed she was slightly uncomfortable.

"It's never been my strong point," I said, smiling back in a way that admitted I knew exactly the game I was playing.

With a small huff of resignation, she replied, "Because the boat belongs to my dad."

I hadn't seen that coming, and my face clearly showed it. How the fuck had the FBI missed this one? I don't even remember being told Jameson had a daughter. Given that I zoned out of a few briefings, I could have missed it — but there's no way I'd have missed it if they'd shown me a picture of this woman.

"And that's why I don't tell people. The look on your face — and the way your body moved imperceptibly away from me — is the same reaction I always get. It would be nice if people didn't judge me by my surname."

I hadn't even realised I'd reacted, but her senses were obviously well tuned. An apology seemed the only way forward.

"Look, I'm sorry. I didn't mean anything by it. I just didn't know your dad even had a daughter. When I did business with him a few years back, he didn't mention you."

She seemed surprised by that, but also somewhat comforted that I already knew her dad.

"He tells me he likes to keep the family out of his business. He gets me doing the accounts and such, but I rarely meet clients or go to his meetings."

She shrugged — equal parts not understanding and resignation. I didn't really know what to say, so I said nothing. She eventually broke the silence.

"Would you like to dance with me?"

"Err… I'm not sure I'd call what I do dancing, but why not? Best I can offer is I'll try not to step on your toes."

At that, she moved her hand from my forearm to my hand and led me back inside, where a band was playing a jazz number.

"It looks like I have some competition," Isabella whispered as we danced. Correction: she danced; I shuffled in a mostly uncoordinated wiggle.

"Oh? In what way?" I asked, genuinely confused.

"The woman you were with the other night — she's shooting daggers at me as we speak."

"Oh," I almost laughed, "she's just protective, that's all."

I should have moved to San Francisco years ago — two stunning women fighting over me. The possibilities were endless. How much fun I could have had in this city as a single man.

"Strictly platonic, huh? If you say so," she said, not entirely convinced.

We danced a few more minutes before the conversation continued. Having her whisper in my ear had shifted from sensual to slightly annoying. The things we men put up with.

"You know, I don't normally mingle with my dad's business associates like this, but you interest me."

"Really? Why is that?"

"I was watching you the other night at the club. I couldn't quite get a read on you. It looked like you fitted right in, but I've been around enough genuinely rich people to see things were a bit forced with you. And then there are your friends — they're a really odd mix. You don't look like four people who'd naturally end up together. It's almost as if an HR department went through the personnel records and tried to select a quartet of the most ethnically and socially diverse people they could find."

I didn't know what to say. I hadn't prepared an answer to that, and she had a point. Thankfully, she dug me out of the awkward hole — only to throw me into a deeper one.

"Either that, or some kind of government agency that should know better, but is clearly incapable of spotting the simple stuff," she laughed.

At "government agency", my internal organs tried to exit via the nearest orifice. If we hadn't been so close, she'd have seen my pupils dilate to the size of quarters. She'd probably have noticed the beads of sweat forming, too. I wasn't sure what to say, so I tried to play it cool and ignore the line.

"So, my mysterious past interests you. In that case, I'll keep it that way. It never hurts to keep a few secrets in your pocket."

I smiled, hoping that was enough to defuse her interest.

"Seriously, though?" she asked, with a little more intensity.

I couldn't be sure, but I suddenly felt this was more than a friendly, flirtatious question. Maybe Isabella had been sent to flutter her eyelids at me and coax out the truth. A stark reminder of the game I was playing. I'd learned a long time ago that being on the defensive is usually a weak position.

"I get the feeling you might know more than you're letting on. How about you tell me what you know, and I'll fill in the blanks? I'd hate to bore you with stuff you already know."

It felt like a good plan: I wouldn't give away anything she (or they) didn't already have, and I'd avoid putting my foot in it. She looked a little put out — annoyed she might have been rumbled.

"Well, not too much, really. Obviously I know about the museum and the driving stuff. I also know about your fiancée."

The mention of Amelia tugged at my heart. I'd have preferred to keep her out of this. Still, it was nice to know the damsel-in-distress act was just that.

"Yeah, that's right. The museum is my passion. The driving's a hobby. Only amateur stuff, really, but I do all right."

"Maybe — but still important enough to get some press coverage."

She was right, so I nodded. They'd dug out some obscure race results from a local paper. It felt familiar somehow, though I wasn't sure why.

"But there was a period where we couldn't find anything."

A leading question — a proper fishing expedition. Ten out of ten for effort; considerably less for subtlety. The FBI had hinted at knowledge of my past; weird that Jameson's outfit also had access to something. Coincidence? It seemed unlikely. My stance didn't change: admit nothing and play dumb. I hoped my faith in my own ability to hide the truth wasn't misplaced — and that she was just testing me.

"Yeah, well, that's how I like it. See my earlier comment — it pays to keep a few secrets," I said with a slight smirk. "What about you? You seem a lot more clued in than you hinted at."

Her answer gave me a brief glimpse of the real Isabella Jameson.

"I help my dad with the business. I'm a chartered accountant — and a damn good one — so I know exactly what's going on."

The emphasis on exactly was a message: she was influential and powerful. It also departed from her earlier description. Pride or truth? Time would tell.

And that's where we left it. We danced a little longer; she slipped back into the flirty woman I'd met on the bow; and we mingled, playing at being a couple among the other guests, before I made my excuses and rejoined the team — who'd managed to entertain themselves while I was dancing.

Chapter 34

"Did you have a good time?" Eva asked as soon as their new acquaintances had moved on. The sarcasm that accompanied this would have been difficult for a five-year-old to miss.

"It was very pleasant," I replied, deliberately trying to be provocative. I then filled them in on my brief conversation with Isabella. Turns out I wasn't the only one surprised by the whole daughter revelation.

"What is it with you and attractive women? You need to share your secrets with the rest of us," said Steve.

"Honestly, mate, I'm as clueless about it as you are. But I'm not too sure Isabella was really that into me. I think she was sent on an information-gathering mission, using her charms to get what she wanted."

"From where we were standing, I'm pretty sure you read that one wrong," Steve said, raising an eyebrow as he chuckled.

I gave him a sceptical look.

"So, just to summarise," Isaiah began, "Jameson agreed to a further meeting. His daughter — who is also his accountant, and possibly his business partner — has a crush on you and is digging around for info. And we have no clue what they do or don't know about us."

"Pretty much sums it up," I said, deciding not to waste my breath on the whole flirting thing.

"Well, all I can say is I'm glad I don't have to report in on this one," Isaiah replied, shaking his head.

"A bit of investigative autonomy never hurt anyone," I offered, trying to put a positive spin on things.

Thankfully, our conversation was cut short by the approach of a stocky, muscular man dressed all in black. "Your presence has been requested in Mr Jameson's quarters below deck."

I placed my glass on the table beside us, as did the others, and prepared to follow him.

"Just him," he said, pointing at me.

Eva looked ready to protest, but I shot her a quick glance to let her know it was okay.

"Lead the way," I said in a faux-jolly tone. "Don't get up to anything I wouldn't do," I called over my shoulder as they watched me walk away.

The private quarters of the boat were as luxurious as I'd imagined. I've been on my fair share of boats over the years — mostly at the Monaco Formula 1 Grand Prix — and there's no doubt this one would fit right in. I was shown into a large living space where I found Edwin Jameson, Isabella Jameson and another man I hadn't yet met. I was directed to a comfortable single-seater, with the other three sitting in similar chairs arranged in a rough semicircle in front of me.

"Drink?" Jameson offered.

"I'll take a rum if you have a nice one."

Jameson just nodded, and I heard the faint sound of someone moving away behind me.

"Make that two," said the unfamiliar face.

"Three," followed Isabella.

I smiled at them both and turned to the mystery guest. "I don't think we've been introduced."

"My name is Jurgen. I'm an associate of Mr Jameson."
He didn't offer any more details, so I left it.

"Well, it's nice to meet you. I'm Eli — "

He cut me off. "It's okay, Mr Miller, I know plenty about you already. Edwin tells me I might have to make a visit to see you in London sometime."

"Of course," I replied politely. "Any friend of Edwin's is a friend of mine."

The drinks arrived and were placed on the tables next to our chairs by the man who'd summoned me earlier. I noticed that Jameson had a whisky on the rocks and was expertly preparing a cigar. His lighter sparked to life and soon he was puffing away on what was undoubtedly an expensive stogie. The other two didn't speak, so I decided to follow suit and waited.

"So, Mr Miller," Jameson began — the formality of my surname no doubt intentional — "what exactly is it that you want to discuss with me? And before you start, let me be clear: I don't like having my time wasted, and I don't like being treated like a fool. Be concise and transparent."

I took a deep breath, realising this was the last moment to back out. I took a quick swig of my rum and started to speak, aware that three pairs of eyes were fixed on me.

"As I think you all know, I have a successful car business in London. Based on my conversation with Isabella earlier, I believe I've managed to keep how I ended up with it pretty well hidden. Let's be honest, it's not the kind of business you can set up with minimal cash flow."

All three looked on impassively, though I imagined Jameson was processing what I was saying. I've always been told that if you're going to lie, stick as close to the truth as possible. So far, I'd been completely honest. Unfortunately, the lies were about to start.

"Obviously, the big banks weren't about to lend a twenty-something with no business experience a few million. And although I pursued various venture capitalists and angel investors, nobody shared my vision, so I had to look into other sources of funding. That meant dealing with what you might call some unsavoury characters. In the end, I got my money, but there were certain conditions attached to it. Due to the nature of my business, and its location on the river, I was in a prime position to help my backers with their own business issues."

"And what line of business are they in exactly?" Jameson asked.

"Import, export and distribution."

"Of what?" was his next question.

"Mm… recreational substances."

Jameson nodded slowly at my slightly cryptic answer. I noticed Jurgen taking notes while Isabella pressed her fingers to either side of her nose, her gaze fixed on me.

"So, as I went about my business, my partners piggybacked on my transportation arrangements to move their stock around Europe. It went surprisingly well, and the business grew a lot quicker than I could have imagined."

"That's a lovely story," Jameson interjected, "but I don't see what that has to do with me."

"My business partners have run into some trouble recently. They've been having issues maintaining their stock levels, primarily due to some overzealous customs personnel. I don't know all the details, but they asked me to come over here and talk to you — to see if you might be able to help. Hopefully we can create a new business arrangement."

"Just so I'm clear, and to make sure I've read between the lines correctly: for some reason you think we can help you smuggle drugs into the UK?" Jurgen asked.

"Whoa, whoa... I never mentioned the D-word," I said in a slightly hushed tone.

Jameson smiled. "It's okay, Mr Miller. You're among friends here. And there definitely aren't any flies on the walls out here. The beauty of being on a boat."

If only he knew there were three FBI agents just above their heads — I doubt he'd be so relaxed. Speaking of relaxed, Isabella appeared anything but. The mention of drugs had caused her to momentarily freeze before she turned her attention to the other two, as if looking for answers.

"Besides, we have people in the right places," Jurgen added.

"Okay," I said, after a short pause. "Yes, I'm talking about drugs mainly, but also other contraband."

"So why are you coming to us?" Jameson asked. "Why do your 'business partners' think we're involved in that line of business?"

"I can't answer that directly — you'd have to ask them yourself. What I do know is that, at the level I've been dealing with, it's a small world. If they say 'go to San Francisco and speak to Edwin Jameson about our problems,' I take that to mean they know you're in the loop, if you catch my drift. I don't know for sure, but if they know you, then it's safe to say that, at a minimum, you at least know of them."

"So tell us something — why you? Why didn't your business partners visit us personally? Then we wouldn't have all this... vagueness," Jurgen pressed.

"There probably isn't a better person. I've done business with Edwin before; I travel to the States a lot for clients; and the police back home — and here, for that matter — have no interest in me whatsoever. When my colleagues fly anywhere, they pretty much immediately set off all kinds of domestic and international alerts. So really, who better than me?"

I'm sure a bright person with more time and less alcohol could poke holes in my logic, but it was the best I could do. I prayed the vagueness would at least pique their interest. The fact the room sat in silence for a while was a good sign I hadn't blown it. Jurgen broke the silence.

"So what do you want from us? What's the deal you're proposing? And just so we're all clear, this is not an agreement. We need to know what's in it for us."

"Well, as I said, we're having issues with importation, and the rumour is you guys haven't lost a shipment in some time. We're also struggling with quality. You clearly have a successful operation, so it would be helpful to understand what you're doing."

"And what do we get for sharing our secrets with your people?" asked Jurgen, who, surprisingly, seemed to be taking the lead.

"A business partner. A regular income stream. Access to a whole new market."

"Seems like you're coming from a position of weakness. Given everything you've said, why don't we just come over and take over the whole thing?" Jameson asked, surprising me.

"And start a war?" I said, surprised he'd propose such a thing.

"I hardly think that would be a problem for us," he replied confidently.

"You clearly have no idea what you'd be getting into. You're not just going to fly over there, throw some money around and everyone will fall into line. In case you forgot, the British don't take kindly to invasions. But by all means, give it a go. I've got no loyalties here — if anything, you'd be doing me a favour."

Jurgen smiled, knowing I was right and recognising the foolishness of the idea. Hopefully he also saw I was potentially a lot more shrewd than they'd given me credit for.

"I think I can offer something a lot more attractive. On the basis of you sharing some of your business practices — and those practices proving to be as successful as we believe — we could offer you a shipment fee: something in the region of ten per cent."

"Go on," Isabella said, intrigued.

I'd been surprised by how quiet she'd been up to this point. I know she's supposed to be the accountant, but it was almost as if she'd been caught off guard by the conversation so far.

"The way we figure it, you get ten per cent of the value of each successful shipment — like a consulting fee. You basically get money for doing absolutely nothing other than the initial input."

I could see Isabella and Edwin working it over in their minds. Jurgen was ahead of the curve — already nodding.

"Twenty per cent," Jameson said suddenly, exhaling a large plume of cigar smoke into the room.

I pretended to consider it, though I'd expected a counter-offer. Negotiation's the same whatever the industry. Even though this was an entirely fictitious deal — perhaps why I felt more relaxed — I suddenly felt very comfortable. The negotiation was a positive sign they were buying my story. I relaxed my posture, subtly signalling I wasn't about to be played.

"No, I think ten per cent is fair. You basically have no exposure. As I said, it's money for nothing. Given we'll be using your product too — which, no doubt, won't be at wholesale price — I'd say you'll do very well out of our arrangement."

"Okay, then fifteen," Jameson replied, a little too quickly.

I was surprised that a man in his position wasn't better at this. I guessed he was used to getting his own way. This was good for me; I knew I had them. I decided to go with a slightly risky strategy, which I believed would work in my favour.

"With all due respect, the offer is a good one, and I think you know it. You obviously know you aren't our only option — you were just at the top of the list."

My stomach knotted as I said it, hoping the ultimatum wasn't a red rag to a bull. Whenever a client suggested they could go somewhere else for a car, I almost immediately began to shut down the deal — primarily because I knew no one else had what I was offering, but also to maintain the power dynamic in my favour. Over the years it had only let me down once, with a ridiculously stubborn Middle Eastern chap I was glad not to do business with. In this case, there was no doubt other people could provide this service, and they had to know that too.

"Ten per cent is fine," Isabella interjected quickly, sensing that her dad might be about to dig his heels in and ruin a potentially sweet deal. ".

I nodded and raised my glass to Jurgen and Isabella in agreement before turning to Jameson, who was looking directly at me, his eyes intense.

"There's one other matter to deal with," Jurgen said. "While all this sounds lovely, how do we know you are who you say you are? Obviously, we know Eli Miller the car guy, but who's to say the rest of your story is kosher? I mean, for all we know, you could be here under the guidance of our federal friends. It wouldn't be the first time."

I had expected this to come up, but even so it made my heart beat faster. I figured that if they were genuinely suspicious, they wouldn't have mentioned it — they'd have just thrown me overboard with a chain round my neck. I did my best to maintain a relaxed attitude as I tried to allay their concerns.

"You wouldn't have got to where you are without being cautious. Obviously, I can't prove it directly. So how about I give you a few days to make some enquiries. Speak to your people in the UK — I'm sure they're well connected enough to confirm everything I've said."

"That sounds fair," Jurgen replied. "Give us some time to check out your associates upstairs too."

It was inevitable that they would be dragged into the conversation; I'd hoped to bring it up myself. Thankfully, I'd had the foresight to plan for this. My plan wasn't going to go down well with the other three, but now my hand had been forced I didn't feel as guilty about what I was about to do.

"On that…" I began slowly, choosing my words carefully, "let me save you some trouble. They're all FBI agents."

I paused to see their reactions. To their credit, there was barely a flicker from any of them, so I continued — before someone did something rash. It was inevitable they'd find out. Given the connections they'd hinted at — and the connections I assumed they had — it was only a matter of time. At least this way, I could try to spin it to our advantage.

"The FBI has been investigating you for some time, as I'm sure you already know. You're considered high priority. The guys upstairs are high-level operatives skilled at infiltration and exposure. Eva and Isaiah are one hundred per cent taken care of — I will personally vouch for them. They've been engineering their careers to undermine and protect our contacts in the US. They also purposefully got themselves attached to their current assignment — essentially to protect your operations for my, and your, benefit. Unfortunately, Steve is an outsider. His skill set and background meant his inclusion was unavoidable. Ultimately, he represents a potential hiccup — but also a potential patsy if things fail to progress."

The look from all three was stern and concerned. I opted to plough on, knowing the flaw in my story was obvious.

"I became involved in this through fortuitous timing. We had word the investigation was progressing to the infiltration stage, and a suggestion that you'd previously dealt with such an investigation in a terminal way. Doing so again would likely have resulted in all-out war with the FBI, and that would only have ended one way. We needed to keep you in the game, so our guys hatched this plan to involve me, sold it to their superiors, and — lo and behold — they went for it."

"That all sounds pretty far-fetched. Do you really expect us to allow three FBI agents into our organisation?" Jameson asked.

"No. I don't. Because I'm not asking you to let them in. I'm telling you who they are so you don't let them in. Eva and Isaiah will work for you as much as for me — they're an asset for you to use, or not. They will continue to

245

protect you. If you want to feed them some misinformation, so be it — I'll leave that up to you. They will also make sure Steve is kept off your back without raising any suspicions back at the Hoover Building. They're the ultimate insurance policy."

"And what if I said we already have insurance?" Jameson asked, his tone factual rather than theoretical.

"Whoever complained about having too much insurance? Especially when you're not paying for it."

"Valid point," he said.

Wanting to bring this to an end before I had to get even more creative with the truth, I decided to shut the conversation down.

"Look, how about you check out what I've been saying? Speak to your people in the UK; speak to your contacts here. Judge me on what you find. If you think I've not been on the level, then we can shake hands and go our separate ways. Otherwise, hopefully, this is the start of something lucrative for us all."

I gave that a few seconds to sink in, threw back the last of my rum, and rose from my seat. I shook hands with each of them, receiving three firm and convincing shakes in return, then turned on my heels and headed for the stairs to the upper deck.

There was an expectant look from all three upstairs, but I decided to play it cool for now. I knew I had to tell them everything, and even though I'd half planned dropping Steve in it, I wasn't quite ready to have that discussion. The crowd slowly thinned just after midnight, and it wasn't long before we were back aboard our motorboat, heading for shore.

Chapter 35

None of us were up before noon the next day, and it was only the doorbell that woke me from my slumber. We hadn't seen or heard anything from 'the management' since the debacle with the heist a week earlier, so I was surprised to see Jessica sitting at the breakfast bar, sharing a coffee with Eva. Pausing her conversation, she flashed me a friendly smile as I walked in. We'd come a long way since our first meetings, although I still wasn't entirely confident everything was good between us.

"As cute as you look with your just-out-of-bed look, you could at least have put some pants on. We do have a guest," said Eva, who looked at Jessica and shook her head in mock disgust.

Looking down, I realised I was still in my boxers and, rubbing my face, found that my night's stubble could be marketed as an alternative to the coarsest sandpaper. With a quick about-turn, I returned ten minutes later looking considerably more presentable — and feeling it too.

"This any better?" I asked playfully.

"Much," came the almost simultaneous reply from both ladies.

"So, to what do we owe this pleasure?" I asked as I poured myself some coffee, catching sight of Steve as he walked in, frantically miming for a drink.

"Just wanted to see how things were going. I've heard off the record that you guys are running your own op. I am supposed to be your case agent, remember?"

"So basically, Holtzman sent you to do a bit of snooping?" I asked directly.

"Kind of, yes. I'm genuinely interested in what you've got planned. But I'd be lying if I said I hadn't been ordered to get a report."

"Figured as much. Thanks for the honesty at least," I responded in a friendly tone.

"So," she asked after a slight pause, turning to face Isaiah, who had just wandered in, "what are you guys up to?"

"You're asking the wrong person," he replied, pointing at me.

Jessica looked surprised and suspicious, as though she expected to be the butt of some joke we were all in on.

"Eli?"

"At least you don't sound disappointed," I said with a smirk.

I gave her a brief rundown of what we'd been up to. I was purposely vague with the specifics, but did mention that we'd successfully made contact the night before. Given I hadn't spoken to the others about the details of my conversation with Jameson, I left all of that out.

"I'm not sure I understand what your angle is exactly," she said once I'd finished.

"That's the idea. After what happened with the initial plan, this is strictly need-to-know — and only four people fall into that category."

"So what am I supposed to report?" she asked, slightly frustrated.

"Whatever you like, but you won't be getting anything else from me."

"You do realise they could just pull the plug on this whole thing? Holtzman has been very close to doing that already."

"He can do whatever he likes," I said dismissively.

My irritation must have shown, as Isaiah glanced at me with a look of restraint on his face.

"If he wants to shut us down, then so be it — but that would be both foolish and potentially incriminating, given the way this whole thing has gone wrong."

"All right, all right," she said, holding up her hands. "Have it your way."

Jessica lingered for another ten minutes, catching up with us and organising anything the others needed. Once she'd left, I decided it was time to brief the team on my conversation from the previous night. I did my best to recount everything verbatim, including my exchange with Isabella on the bow of the boat. I tried to keep my own interpretations out of it, but shared what I felt were pertinent observations. Predictably, my revelation at the end wasn't well received.

"You fucking did what?" Steve roared, taking a step towards me.

I was fairly convinced he was going to take a swing for me, so I stepped left, putting the breakfast bar between us.

"Jeez, Eli, what the fuck were you thinking?" Eva asked, the most serious look I'd seen etched across her face. "Even for you, THIS has to be the most brainless thing you've done. You've basically fucked every single one of us, including yourself. What do you think is going to happen when he calls his people in England? We won't be able to protect you because we'll be too busy protecting ourselves."

Steve still looked ready to kill me, but at least he'd stopped moving in my direction.

"What was I supposed to do? They were always going to look into us — all of us. I've got my guy back home covering that angle, but there was no way to hide you three. I needed it to come out in front of them. If they'd found out from anyone else, this whole thing would be in the shitter. I had to give them as much truth as possible — stuff I knew they'd find out regardless."

"Why didn't you tell us?" Eva asked.

"Because I needed it to be believable. I needed you guys not to know."

"Bullshit," Steve spat. "I've had your number from day one. You've always been about you, and this is no different. I don't know what your game is, but I'm beginning to think all these screw ups aren't accidental."

He took another step forward, but Isaiah stepped in front of him.

"Sorry, Steve, but you need to stand down this time. As surprised as I am to say it, Eli is right on this one."

"Like fuck he is," Steve shot back, squaring up to Isaiah. "You ain't the one that's been screwed over."

"I'm not going to argue with you on that. All the same, Eli read the situation and took the right action. We need to thank him. If his guy comes through, then we're still in the game."

"I'm not thanking him for shit," said Steve, though calmer now.

"We're going to need eyes in the back of our heads for a while," Eva added, seemingly coming round to what I'd done now Isaiah had condoned it.

"I'd say that's not a bad idea," Isaiah said, slipping back into his leadership role. "If we're going out, I want us in pairs. We need rotating sentries watching the streets during the day. Steve, see if you can get some kind of security system set up discreetly."

Having a job seemed to settle Steve down, or maybe it was just having a senior colleague telling him what to do. He nodded in understanding and was heading out of the kitchen when he turned back to me.

"Why me?"

I paused before answering, weighing up how honest to be. In the end, I went with straightforward truth.

"Simple — racial profiling," I said with a shrug.

The other two turned to look at me, clearly not expecting that answer. Steve smiled, sensing I was about to piss off my two allies.

"Look, what's more believable? Who's more likely to be corrupt? A black guy from a working-class neighbourhood in Baltimore, a Mexican woman from a first-generation immigrant family, or a white guy from an Ohio farming family? Even I can tell you who kisses the flag and who's chasing the dollars."

Steve paused, then grinned.

"If I'm not wrong, I think the English expression is 'wanker'," he said, before disappearing upstairs.

I turned to see both Isaiah and Eva shaking their heads, smiling at each other as they poured another coffee.

"So what's your take?" Isaiah asked after a while.

"I think he's got himself another lady friend," said Eva with a knowing smile. "Although I think this one is pure trouble. The daughter of a gangster is not a wise choice."

"Might work in our favour," Isaiah offered. "Let's see where it goes."

251

I wasn't thrilled they were considering me a pawn in this situation, but I wasn't in much of a position to complain. Opting to ignore the nonsense about Isabella, I tried to contribute something constructive.

"I reckon we've got a good chance of this working out. I'm most concerned that Jameson suggested he has someone on the inside at the FBI. That could completely screw us. We've no idea how high that goes, and that worries me."

"I think we knew that was likely," Eva said. "I'm more interested to know how his operation works."

"Yep. If we could figure that out, we'd be able to shut him down for sure."

"No idea, but I'd bet it has something to do with that boat. Can't tell you how exactly, but there was just something off about it," I said. Not exactly helpful, but at least it felt like a contribution.

"We've had a big crackdown on the ports for a while — never come up with anything," Eva replied. "Anyway, talking of boats, where did you get that little beauty from last night?"

"Just from a guy I know."

"Remind me to get an introduction. Who couldn't use friends like that?" she said with a smile.

"You know, I'm curious about you, man," Isaiah said. "Contacts everywhere, capital to just buy a car at a moment's notice, lending your credit card out like it's nothing. There's more to you than just a rich Englishman who sells fast cars."

"Maybe there is, and maybe I'll tell you about it sometime. But now's not the time. It's too long, complicated, and not something you need to bother with at the moment."

They were getting more interested in my past — which was understandable; they were law enforcement officers trained to dig. I didn't like talking about it, which was why it remained a mystery. Only a few people in the world knew the truth, and that was how I intended to keep it. I decided to change the subject with all the tact of a sledgehammer.

"Do you think there's a bigger fish in this? The Mayor was there last night, as was the Police Commissioner — and no doubt some other important city people."

"I think it's very likely," Eva said. "And it wouldn't be a massive surprise if there's another link in the chain. There nearly always is."

Before the conversation continued, Steve came thundering back into the kitchen.

"Heads up!" he shouted, launching an American football into the air.

The ball smacked the ceiling with a heavy thud, followed immediately by a crash as the fire alarm dislodged. Luckily for the alarm, it landed directly on one of the sofas; otherwise, I'm guessing there'd have been bits of white plastic flying everywhere. Being naturally practical, I volunteered to fix it while Steve and Isaiah sheepishly tried to ignore the accident. With the alarm mostly intact, I clipped it back into place and promptly forgot all about it.

Chapter 36

Two uneventful days passed with no word from Jameson about when, or even if, the next meeting would take place. It slightly concerned me, and the others were becoming noticeably nervous, which, in turn, concerned me even more given the fate of the previous agents. I was the third to arrive for breakfast, Eva was the only one not present. My arse hadn't been in the chair for five seconds when the previously broken fire alarm made a noisy and impromptu return to ground level. Someone had obviously moved the sofa, because this time it landed on the armrest before bouncing onto the hardwood floor. We all looked at each other and burst out laughing.

"If you're trying to knock one of us off, there are easier and more accurate ways," joked Isaiah.

I just nodded, still chuckling.

"Well, since your DIY skills are obviously a bit shit, I guess I'll show you how it's done," said Steve, getting up.

"Knock yourself out," I replied.

I watched as he stooped to pick up the alarm. His movements visibly slowed for a few seconds before he straightened up and began clipping it back in place. Something in Steve's body language had shifted subtly from thirty seconds ago, but I couldn't quite put my finger on it.

"Heh, Isaiah. You wanna grab some fresh air?" Steve asked suddenly.

"Nah, I'm good."

"I think you should. You're looking a bit pale."

Obviously getting the message, Isaiah levered himself off the sofa and followed Steve down the hall. Left alone, I flicked on the TV to catch the morning news.

"Morning, Eli," said Eva as she entered the kitchen and started making breakfast.

"Oh hey, Eva, how you doing?"

"Yeah, not too bad. Feeling quite refreshed, actually. Where are the other two?"

"They just popped out for some fresh air. Needed a bit of private time, I think."

Before Eva could make a sarcastic innuendo, both Steve and Isaiah reappeared. Steve had his index finger over his mouth in the universal signal for silence. Grabbing a pen and paper, he scribbled a note and handed it to Eva, who was now by my side. Five seconds later, she passed it to me and headed straight for the front door. I looked at the scrawl and began to decipher it:

Don't speak, we need to talk outside. Now.

Ordinarily I'd have thought it a joke, but the body language of both Steve and Isaiah told me otherwise. Whatever was bothering Steve was deadly serious. Grabbing my glass of orange juice, I followed them out onto the veranda.

"What's up, Steve?" asked Eva, noticing how harrowed he looked.

"Trouble, that's what. You know how we knocked the fire alarm off the other day?"

"Yeah."

"Well, it fell off again."

"Heh, I'm sure the FBI will still get their deposit back," I joked.

"Shut up, you idiot," Steve snapped — restrained but aggressive.

"Go on," Eva said, flashing me a warning glance.

"Well, I went to put it back up and found a listening device implanted in the circuitry."

That explained his sudden mood shift.

"Are you sure?" asked a stunned Eva.

"Yeah, I'm sure. I've used enough of them in my time to know this baby is top-of-the-line gear."

"Shit," Eva muttered.

Being a bit slow on the uptake, I didn't immediately grasp the implications.

"So, what does it all mean?"

"It means someone — most likely Jameson — has been listening to our conversations. Depending on when it was planted, they may know everything we've discussed since we arrived," Isaiah said.

The gravity of the situation sank in, and I was instantly reminded of the photos of the two dead agents I'd been shown a few weeks earlier. I decided to add my two cents.

"Oh, that's fucked up."

I realised then that I hadn't told them about the surveillance devices in the BMW. While arguably relevant, bringing it up now would only muddy the waters — it was practically impossible Jameson had planted those. It didn't mean Jameson hadn't been listening in on us, but did suggest that it could equally be the FBI. Which meant our secret plans might not be all that secret.

"You got that right," Steve said, dragging me back to the moment. "So what are we going to do about it?"

"First off, we need to get out of the house — go our separate ways for a while. I suggest we regroup later and hash out a plan," Isaiah replied. "I'll go in and speak with Jessica, and Holtzman if he's around. Either way, we have to stay low. Let's say we meet at around four at the coffee shop."

The coffee shop was a predefined meeting point we'd picked out when we first arrived — a fallback in case things went to shit.

We all nodded in agreement before heading back inside for essentials: phones, wallets and, in my case, a set of car keys.

Chapter 37

I almost backed the BMW off the drive but opted for the Mustang at the last minute. It wasn't until I was already driving, carefully ensuring I wasn't being followed, that it occurred to me that if the house had been bugged, there was no reason they hadn't got to this car too. It wasn't worth the risk, so I pulled a quick U-turn and headed for Chris's garage. He was clearly busy, but when I told him to name a price, my car was up on one of his lifts within two minutes.

"So, what am I looking for again, bro?"

"Something like last time. You know, electronic shit with flashing lights. Something that doesn't belong."

I know it was a little lame, but it's not like I knew what I was talking about. About thirty minutes later, he tossed a hand-sized box onto the desk where I was sitting.

"Looks like someone with some serious wedge really wants to keep an eye on you. Not quite as sophisticated as what I found on the BMW, but it's top-level GPS stuff."

"What do you mean?" I asked, turning the box in my hands.

"This is proper next-generation kit. The sort of thing you read about on web forums but nobody ever sees. Connects to every satellite ever sent up, most likely. I only found it by accident, hidden deep among the pipes in the engine bay."

"Thanks, man, I owe you one," I said, offering over a few grand in notes.

"Don't sweat it. Whatever you're into, it's some deep stuff. Watch your back, dude. Forget the cash — I'll be able to sell that thing for a small fortune. There's always someone in this country wanting to buy next-gen tech like this."

Never one to waste money, I slipped the wad into my back pocket and left it at that. With the worry of the tracking device behind me, although the mystery of more next gen tech rearing its head now occupying my thoughts, I headed for the beach and watched the tourists and locals going about their business without a care in the world. I hoped the other three were making some progress with the issue of the day, as so far I had nothing. A few coffees and pastries later and I'd come up with a grand total of fuck all. I was officially out of my depth once again.

By 3:30 p.m., slightly sunburnt, I hopped back into the car and headed for the house. During my afternoon of people-watching, I realised I'd need a car with four proper seats, so I had to switch back to the BMW. After performing a few textbook counter-surveillance manoeuvres, I headed in the direction of the city centre for my 4 p.m. rendezvous. I was about four blocks away — and a few minutes late — when I first heard it: the unmistakable sound of gunfire. A mix of semi-automatic, full-automatic and shotgun blasts shattered the relative quiet of the Saturday afternoon. It could have been paranoia, but I knew immediately that my friends were in trouble. We weren't in gang territory, to my knowledge, and the only thing that could rival the cacophony I was hearing would be a full-on SWAT assault, which would have resulted in the roads being shut down.

With the car already in attack mode, I flicked the paddle shifter to downshift and buried the throttle. The rear squatted and then launched forward along the thankfully empty road. On a slight downhill section, I jumped on the brakes and yanked the wheel to the right as I flew round the corner. With the rear stepping out, I fed in a little throttle to keep the drift before lifting and bringing the car to a stop, straddling both lanes. I looked out of my open window to see what could only be described as an urban battlefield. About fifty metres away was the café where we were supposed to meet. Instead, overturned tables and chairs were strewn across the pavement. Thankfully, there were a few cars parked on that side of the road, and I could see several people huddled behind them. It's safe to say those cars would be needing a visit to the body shop when this was over; there were multiple bullet holes all over their offside panels. Despite this, I could make out small pools of blood forming in the gutter, although there weren't any obvious bodies. Random pistol shots came from behind several of the upturned tables — a good sign that at least someone was still alive. These were followed by rapid shotgun blasts, most likely from a semi-auto. Unlike in the movies, where guns seem to have unlimited ammunition, the assailants had to stop and reload. They clearly weren't professionals; there were plenty of moments when covering fire should have been provided. Instead, their lack of professionalism allowed return fire from the café area.

I scanned across the road and spotted a black Chevy Tahoe on the opposite side, roughly twenty-five metres away — plenty close enough for their weapons to be effective. Given my angle, I couldn't see the gunmen well, but it was clear that three or four people were using the car as cover for the attack. Pistol shots and bursts of automatic fire started up again, and I could hear screams from the café as glass shattered and the upturned tables took a beating. Unusually, the tables were heavy, solid-wood things, so they provided decent protection. Despite my less-than-subtle arrival, my presence seemed to have gone unnoticed by the bad guys. I swiftly exited the car, popped the boot and, almost without thinking, grabbed the bag Jonny had put there. Good thing I'd switched cars after all; otherwise I'd be walking into a gunfight with my bare hands. I'd typically be cursing myself at this point for not having been true to my word and testing the weapons I was now about to use in anger. As it was, the mixture of fear and the desire to help my friends meant the thought didn't even cross my mind as I threw on my body armour. At least I'd taken the time to set it up to hold my two SIG Sauer P220s and some spare ammo. Next, I grabbed the APC10 Pro, slotted in a full 30-round magazine and crouched out of sight. The final thing was to extend the telescopic stock, lock it in place and bring the gun up to a ready position as I looped the strap over my head. I took a deep breath, thumbed the selector to full automatic, grabbed the foregrip and began moving quickly towards the Tahoe in a crouching zigzag, intently watching the red-dot sight for a target.

As I passed the front of the BMW I opened fire with a couple of bursts aimed at the car rather than at a person — I still couldn't see anyone. The APC10 was suppressed, so I didn't immediately draw attention to myself, and I hoped this would cause some mild confusion among the attackers. I was surprised to see the Tahoe showed little impact from my rounds; clearly it had some sort of armour, typically reserved for the security services. I let off another quick burst and then ducked behind a parked car. I'd made it to within twenty-five metres of the SUV and, as far as I could tell, was still undetected. I looked over to the café, where I could see Eva and Isaiah frantically reloading while Steve — visibly relieved to see me with guns — wiped blood off his head. I did my best to indicate I was going to try to flank the SUV when another volley of gunfire hit the tables. I was about to return fire when I saw Eva slump backwards. Steve and Isaiah immediately turned to her, leaving themselves vulnerable, but she didn't move.

Anger welled up inside me at seeing her lifeless body — I was in full red-mist mode now. I was faintly aware that the surrounding noise of gunshots and screams was no longer so apparent, and as I focused on the target my peripheral vision had all but vanished. In the same crouch, but moving slower, I came out from behind the car and into the road, keeping the Tahoe to my left to stay out of view until the last moment. I hadn't taken more than two steps — now fully exposed, with no cars between me and the target — when a masked man with a shotgun appeared from the rear nearside of the Tahoe. His gun was facing forward, his attention on the café. He clearly wasn't expecting to see me, which was fortunate because, although I had the APC10 up and ready, I wasn't mentally prepared to use it in anger. It's the kind of pause that can cost you your life. As his brain recognised the threat, mine processed that his shotgun was turning towards me. Pulling the trigger was never a conscious thought, but it must have happened — the gun kicked three times and my masked attacker hit the road in considerable pain.

It didn't occur to me to kill him, despite his screaming

undoubtedly drawing attention — perhaps a professional wouldn't have thought twice. I advanced to the side of the car from which he'd emerged. The driver's door was wide open, cartridge casings everywhere. I saw a pair of feet on the other side of the door; I assumed the person was leaning on the bonnet for support as they fired. This time I didn't hesitate and fired another three-shot burst under the door and into the target's lower legs. Another masked man collapsed in agony. Again I advanced and was surprised to see no one else there, despite still hearing gunfire. As I kicked the gun away from my latest victim I saw why. In the middle of the road a third man was advancing towards the café in a combat-ready posture, an assault rifle aimed forward and firing single shots. I rounded the front of the car, dropped to one knee and fired into his back. He stumbled but didn't go down. He began to turn towards me, not understanding what was happening, so I put out a second quick volley — more deliberately at his head. This time he hit the road and didn't move. The silence that followed was a stark contrast to the earlier cacophony. There was barely a sound — no screaming, no shouting, almost nothing. What couldn't be ignored was the gun smoke hanging in the air and the stench of nitroglycerin from all the discharged weapons. I was still kneeling when Steve and Isaiah slowly stood from behind their tables and began to walk towards me. Both were smeared in blood, clothing torn, faces streaked with debris. I stood, felt myself relax as I lowered the gun to my side and took a step forward — then suddenly remembered Eva. My stomach knotted and I began to run towards the other two. I'd barely taken two steps when I saw Isaiah screaming as he and Steve brought their guns up. I didn't understand why I couldn't hear Isaiah until I realised the tinnitus from

all the gunfire had left me temporarily deaf. For a split
second I thought Steve was going to shoot me — his gun
had come up and seemed to be pointed right at me. He
made a slight correction to my right and I saw the slide of
his gun cycle, a casing flick out to his right and — swear to
God — felt the bullet fizz past my head. I swivelled and
simultaneously brought the APC10 up. To my amazement
it wasn't one of the men I'd already shot, but a completely
new guy still in the car, sitting at the rear passenger
window with some kind of sub-machine gun poking out.
My subconscious told me there was something familiar
about the silhouette but before I could think further, flames
burst from his muzzle — also aimed at me. For the second
time in five seconds I felt rounds pass by. My finger was
already on the trigger; I pulled it… and nothing. No recoil.
No bullets. No spent casings.

I'd made two rookie errors. In my adrenaline-filled state
I'd forgotten to clear the car, assuming the only targets
were out and attacking. The second mistake was losing
count of my ammunition, compounded by assuming there
were no more targets after dropping the last guy. I
instinctively pushed the APC10 back and let it swing on its
strap into the small of my back, grabbed for the SIG in the
chest holster and brought it up as the target's gun tracked
towards me. Before I could fire, two shots cracked from
behind. The masked face and gun snapped back inside; I
let off two shots of my own. I glanced over my shoulder:
Steve was face down in the road, a pool of blood spreading
beneath him. Isaiah stood with his gun still trained on the
Tahoe, the slide locked back — empty. I tossed him the
pistol in my hand, reached for the second on the rear of my
vest and moved to him, keeping my eyes on the rear
window.

"We need to get out of here," he shouted as I reached him, his gun and gaze fixed on the target.

"What about Eva?"

"We need to go right now," he replied, seemingly ignoring my question.

Sirens wailed in the distance — surprisingly late, all things considered. I nodded at Isaiah and we shifted into a back-to-back stance, edging towards the BMW. Our foe seemed more tactically aware than his comrades; he stayed hidden until we reached the car. We had to split up to get in, but we were coordinated enough to provide suppressing fire when he tried to show his face. I'd left the engine ticking over, so I dropped into the driver's seat, selected first and lit up the rear tyres, hoping the blue-white smoke would give us a little cover. As Isaiah fell into the passenger seat, I let off a few rounds towards the Tahoe, swung the wheel right and took off in the opposite direction. I didn't hear the gunfire over the engine, but I did hear the unmistakable ping and thud of bullets hitting the rear of the car as we made our escape.

Chapter 38

Powering through the streets, it soon became clear that whoever was left wasn't going to give chase — the imminent police arrival likely put them off. I took this as a sign to trim a little speed, although with such a recognisable car I had to be careful. The last thing we needed was to get involved with the local PD. With the action apparently over, I found myself gripping the wheel harder by the second in the hope it would stop my hands from shaking. It wasn't long before I felt my whole body trembling as it became starved of adrenaline. I had to pull over before the car became intimately involved with a truck. My face was running with sweat, and the uncontrollable tapping of my foot disturbed the otherwise silent car. It took a few minutes of deep breathing and mentally telling myself to get a grip before the adrenaline withdrawal symptoms began to recede.

I looked across at Isaiah, who was staring motionlessly out of the windscreen, and got a shock. His once white T-shirt was now covered with a mix of blood spatter and road grime. His jeans were equally messy, but it was his face that caused me the most distress. Covered in blood and what I guessed was human tissue, he looked like an extra from Hacksaw Ridge. I immediately wanted to retch, but somehow kept it in.

"Jesus," I said eventually, "we need to get you to a hospital."

"It's cool," he replied solemnly.

"But — "

He was so relaxed I thought he was about to burst into a rendition of Shaft.

"It's not mine."

"But how did you not get shot?" I asked. As usual, my brain was a couple of seconds behind my mouth as it slowly dawned on me that I was looking at the remnants of what, ten minutes ago, had been two good friends. This time I did puke. Luckily the window was open — otherwise it probably would have ricocheted back into my face.

"Yeah, well, I was wearing a vest. The shots hit me square on the metal plate."

He turned and showed me the holes in his shirt. The three shots were closely grouped — a sign of an expert marksman — and sure enough, as I reached out, I could feel both the vest and metal plate, now sporting inwardly concave dents. We sat in silence for a while before I became so uncomfortable I had to speak.

"So what now?"

"We have to get out of town. Like, right now."

"You ain't gonna hear any arguments from me on that one, but why not go in? I mean, Holtzman and the rest of the Bureau will protect us."

"Things are just too busy at the moment. We've just lost two agents, and things are about to go apeshit. Don't forget, you just left a body count to rival Jesse James. There'll be too many people in on this — people we don't know if we can trust. The best thing for us is to drop off the radar for a while. You have somewhere to go?"

"Not really, but I can find somewhere," I said, thinking of Jonny — and also Matteo's cousin.

"Look, drop me in Sausalito. I'll be in contact in a week or so. Don't use your credit cards and try to stay in places that don't require ID. Keep your cell off — they can track you by it."

Nodding, I pulled away from the kerb, and we travelled the next five minutes in silence. Several times, police cars going in the opposite direction had us checking mirrors, but none turned to follow. As I pulled off the Golden Gate Bridge — thankfully, the toll payment was for those going into the city — Isaiah turned to me and offered his hand.

"Stay out of trouble, okay?"

"Sure thing. You don't want your stuff from the house?"

"No, and neither do you. They know where we were living, so there's a good chance they'll be expecting us to return. Whatever it is you want, replace it. Do not go back."

With that, he began to open the door, then pulled it shut again.

"I'm curious — where exactly did those guns come from, and who the hell taught you to shoot like that?"

Looking straight ahead, I smirked before answering.

"You really don't want to know about the guns. As for the shooting lessons, I was taught by an old, dear friend. You know that part of my past you were all so interested in the other day? Well, once we get through this I'll tell you all about it."

Getting the message, he brushed himself down a little, then finally got out and walked away without any suggestion he knew me.

I think we both knew I was going back to the house. I was funny like that. Although I could afford to buy new stuff I also didn't like to waste money, and I sure wasn't about to leave my bike there. I parked a couple of blocks away and watched the house for a few minutes until I was satisfied no one was hanging around outside. It made sense, to my amateur logic at least. We'd just had a gun battle in the middle of the city, and if they knew we were FBI, they wouldn't risk coming to a house that would most likely be full of agents out for blood.

With my bike quickly dismantled and bundled into the back of the Mustang, I decided my luck must be in and headed into the main part of the house to get my clothes. It felt strange walking through a house that earlier the same day had been full of life and laughter. Now I found myself staring at where Eva used to sit, and at the dishes Steve had promised to wash earlier. I dashed upstairs and quickly stuffed my two holdalls with clothes, which turned out to be a challenge as I was loathed to leave my suits. In the end I rationalised that one suit was an acceptable compromise. Although it was of no use where I was going, you never knew when a suit might come in handy. I slung my bags over my shoulder and headed downstairs. It was at this point that I heard hushed voices and the downstairs floorboards creaking. I carefully set the bags down and automatically reached behind my back for my SIG Sauer.

Nothing.

Isaiah had kept one, and I'd tossed the other into the back seat along with the APC10.

Fuck.

I should have listened to Isaiah. I should have known that escaping one gunfight was good going — I'd practically gone looking for a second. I suddenly had a brainwave that might just save me. Thanks to my midnight trips to the toilet — where I'd made a point of learning where all the creaky floorboards were so as not to wake everyone — I made it back to my bedroom in relative silence. Reaching under the bed, my hands found what I was looking for: a Walther PDP strapped to the bed slats, a gun I'd snuck into the house one day when the others were out. I checked the magazine — making that error once in a day was enough — and racked the slide to chamber a round. I stepped back onto the landing and slowly headed down the stairs.

I could hear voices from the kitchen, and, strangely, they sounded familiar. As I reached the hallway I found the two doormen from the club examining the smoke alarm. They'd obviously come to remove the evidence before the FBI took the house apart.

"Hey, guys — bye, guys," I said, gently squeezing the trigger.

Nothing happened, and I glanced at the gun in confusion before realising it had a safety built into the trigger — I just needed to pull harder. I took deliberate aim at the bigger of the two, but that tiny pause let my conscience step in. I couldn't murder them in such a non-threatening situation.

"Look, man, J-J-Jameson just sent us round to check things out. We're not looking for trouble — take it up with him," he stammered.

"Check things out? You mean check if we're all dead. I'm not stupid — you're here to finish the job. Only you seem a little under-gunned," I said, waving the pistol.

They looked at me and then at each other, bemused, before the shorter one replied.

"Look, buddy, we've got no idea what you're on about, so don't do anything stupid, OK."

Both sets of eyes tracked the gun as I waved it. They probably thought I was in an irrational mood which, to be fair, I was.

"You think I'm stupid? 'Just checking things out'? What's that?" I snapped, pointing at the smoke alarm.

"Last time I went shopping, they were called fire alarms," came the sarcastic reply — unwise, given their predicament.

They either didn't know — which I considered unlikely — or were trying to buy time. Since I couldn't bring myself to kill them, I needed an alternative.

"Take off your clothes."

"You what?" the smaller one asked, glancing at his friend, concern written across his face.

"You've seen Pulp Fiction, right? Down to your underwear, please."

A look of fear spread across their faces, which, I admit, was pleasing in a sadistic way. Once they were down to their boxers, I wrapped them in cling film, then dashed upstairs for the handcuffs I'd seen in Eva's room. Slotting the cuffs through a gap at the hinge of the door, I laid them head-to-toe on either side and cuffed one's hand to the other's foot. There was little chance of escape — and even if they did, they wouldn't get far in just their boxers.

"Well, guys. I'm off now. Say hello to your boss for me."

I dumped my bags by the Mustang and jogged back to the BMW to park it on the driveway. By my reckoning, if I left it nose-out, it would go unnoticed for a few days at least, and if anyone came looking, they might assume I was still in the city. I'd thought about taking the BMW, but with all the electronics and GPS, I chose the low-tech Mustang. I bundled the bags into the rear seats and took a quick look at the maps to plan my route. Before leaving, I fired off a text to Matteo with some urgent instructions and then turned the phone off. I pointed the car back towards the Golden Gate Bridge — and hopefully somewhere I wasn't constantly looking over my shoulder for someone with a gun.

Chapter 39

I woke up wishing I'd at least tried to get a room at the Holiday Inn I'd passed a few junctions earlier. Instead, I was lying on a lumpy, spring-riddled bed in a dark, musty motel room on the outskirts of Fort Bragg — the city in California, not the military base in North Carolina. My night had been terrible; if the dreams — or more accurately nightmares — of the shootings hadn't been enough, I kept seeing Eva shouting for my help. I swear I was awake more than I was asleep, not helped by my constant debate over whether my actions on the boat had caused the ambush. To add to my misery, both neighbouring rooms seemed to be occupied by local hookers, and business was apparently good. The shower was a pathetic dribble, and consequently I didn't feel much better as I checked out. Opting to skip the free continental breakfast — no doubt a stale doughnut and a Styrofoam cup of old coffee — I headed to Denny's, America's trusty diner chain.

Eating was difficult: I couldn't shake the images of the previous day's events, nor the nausea sitting in my stomach. Knowing I needed to eat, I forced down a plate of grits, bacon, eggs and a side of French toast. While eating I leafed through the morning paper. Several pages in I found a short column reporting a recent hit-and-run involving two motorbikes. Both riders had died. Ordinarily I would have moved on without a second thought; however, on this occasion I was completely focused on the accompanying picture. The image was of a recovery truck. Loaded on the back were two bikes: a red Ducati and another with the distinctive Repsol livery. To every other reader it would mean nothing — and maybe that's exactly what it was. To me, it took me back to the Market Street heist where I'd seen two identical bikes. What were the chances? They had to be slim — so slim that I was immediately suspicious the hit-and-run hadn't been an accident. With Holtzman reporting that two had been killed at the scene, this had all the hallmarks of someone cleaning up loose ends. I needed to look into this a little more, as it had to be entwined with my current predicament. For now, though, that would have to wait. I had other, more important things to investigate.

I soon got back on the road, welcoming the drive as a distraction from my thoughts, and headed for the coast. It was a one-lane road, which meant it was considerably slower than the interstate, but the lack of traffic helped ease my paranoia a little. That said, every time a car came up behind me, I spent more time looking in the mirror than at the road ahead. Every now and then I pulled into a lay-by, primarily to check the skies but also to try to enjoy the views.

After eight hours of driving the twisty coast roads, I arrived at Oregon Dunes National Recreation Area, my home for the next week. Starting just north of a town called North Bend, the dunes ran for about forty miles up the coast and, in parts, were as much as two miles wide. Littered with state-run campgrounds, I opted for Jessie M. Honeyman Memorial Park. The northernmost of the parks is a few miles south of Florence, one of the major towns on this stretch of the coast. Much as I enjoyed the Mustang, I was left wishing I'd opted for the BMW — I reckon I'd have been a lot less stiff and achy when I finally got out to pay for my stay. With the weather nice, the campsite was very busy, and I was lucky to find a spare site — more fortunate still that it was tucked away in a corner, surrounded by tall pines. With a week paid for upfront in cash, I headed into town to pick up some essentials.

First stop was the outdoor store: I needed a tent, sleeping bag and various other camping necessities. Second was the food mart, despite knowing from previous visits that my palate wasn't exactly catered for in American food stores. Even so, I managed to accumulate a sizeable collection of fresh fruit and tinned foods. Picking up a few books from the library, I caught sight of a phone box on my way back to camp. Jonny would have returned from his ride and was probably concerned about my lack of appearance or message. The mobile number I called was answered immediately.

"Hello."

" Jonny, it's me."

"Hey, man, I missed you today."

"Yeah, I had to leave town suddenly."

"Where are you?"

"Just went up north for a while. I just wanted to let you know I'm okay."

"Are you okay? The news is saying you lost it. Just went on a rampage."

"I'm fine, and that's not what happened. My friends were ambushed — I should have been there too, probably dead."

"Whatever you say, man."

"Listen, I gotta go but I just wanted you to know I was ok. You don't need to be involved in any of this. I'll speak with you soon, okay?"

"Sure, Eli. Take care, mate. If you need anything, call me, OK."

"Thanks, mate."

It felt good to hear a friendly voice — someone I knew I could rely on. Back at my campsite, I pitched the tent, which was surprisingly complicated given it was advertised as quick assembly. To be fair, it was probably my own fault; I'm the sort not to bother with instructions, believing I've enough intelligence to cope without them. I had to scrap my plan for an early night when a passer-by — who happened to be staying at the site next to mine — interrupted my open-fire dinner.

"Nice car."

"Thanks," I said with a mouthful of potato.

"A '67, right?"

"Yep." At least he knew his cars.

I'm a little surprised my monosyllabic answers didn't make him keep walking. To my surprise, he carried on.

"Fine-looking beast. Listen, my mates and I couldn't help noticing you're here on your own. Wondered if you might want to join us for a drink?"

"Thanks, I may just do that," I replied, pondering the motive for his generosity.

I'd forgotten to buy any alcohol earlier, and the idea of a couple of drinks sounded appealing, despite the risk of being recognised. I finished my dinner and, about ten minutes later, ambled over to their RV. I'd already had enough of reminiscing over the previous day's events, and a few cold ones coupled with the lively chat of a group of twenty-somethings temporarily distracted my overburdened conscience.

It transpired my neighbours were keen mountain bikers and recommended some trails immediately inland from the park for me to explore the next morning. I was finding that every time I sat down to have some alone time, my mind drifted back to the shootings and what I could have done differently — whether I could have saved them all. The short answer is, of course, I could have. If I'd been earlier, if I'd stuck with them rather than going off on my own, if I'd cleared the car... and on and on it went. I was still having the same dreams about Eva that I'd had at the motel. I decided the concentration needed for single-track forest riding would be an adequate distraction. After a bowl of cereal and a cup of coffee I could only describe as rocket fuel, I donned my various pads and helmet and headed out in search of the trails I'd been told about the night before.

Two crashes — neither more serious than denting my pride — and three hours later, I rode back into camp with the blood beginning to dry on my arms and shins. Sweating, dirty and bloody, I headed for the empty shower block and a welcome chance to clean myself up. As I stood under the pleasantly warm water, I suddenly had a flashback. I could see Steve and Eva's bodies lying in the road, then the image of Isaiah sitting in the car, all bloody with holes in his shirt. I could hear the bullets whizzing past my head. Then I became a spectator of the whole event, as if watching myself on a TV screen. As I rejoined reality, I once again pondered my involvement in the whole affair, but this time I tried to find some positives. If I hadn't turned up when I did, Isaiah would now be dead — and if I hadn't known how to shoot, no doubt I would be too. Bizarrely enough, it was Uncle Sam himself — or more accurately one of his GIs — I had to thank for that blessing.

Chapter 40

I took myself back about ten years, to when I was travelling around the USA as a backpacker. I was in Montana at the time, just passing through on my way to Seattle, when my not-so-trusty steed — a 1980s Buick Century — decided enough was enough and died a sudden, spectacular death. Parked on a sun-scorched grass bank, I waited for the next car or truck to pass, hoping to thumb a ride to the nearest town, as steam seeped from under the bonnet. Half an hour later I was still waiting — albeit with considerably less patience — so I threw a few essentials into a rucksack and started walking. My map suggested there should be a town about five miles away. I just had to hope it wasn't much further, as I didn't have much drinking water and there was no shade in sight. Leaving most of my belongings in the car, I headed west — towards a meeting that would eventually change my life.

I'm not sure how long I walked, but my shirt was dripping with sweat and I was wishing I hadn't started. As I reached a crossroads, a pickup came flying past out of nowhere and almost ran me over. Shouting profanities and flipping the driver the finger, I started to dust myself off — a thankless task given the dust clung to my wet t-shirt. It was then that I caught a whiff of smoke. Having travelled through my fair share of forests — and being a closet pyromaniac — I knew the devastation rural fires could cause. Although the area was more prairie than dense forest, I could see a small wooded area in the distance and what looked like smoke. Deciding it was my civic duty, as a temporary resident of the country, I somehow found the energy to jog down the gravel track the pickup had come from.

I reached a coppice of trees — bigger and denser than I'd expected — and eventually came to a clearing. Thick, acrid smoke hung in the air, and I could hear the unmistakable roar of a raging fire. As the woods thinned, it became clear what the truck had been running from. An old farmhouse stood with several wooden outhouses. One of them, a stable block, was ablaze, with what appeared to be animals still inside. As I got closer, I saw an old man staggering around in the yard between the stables and the house. Congealed blood in his hair and a swollen right eye, he was frantically trying to steady himself but kept falling.

To this day, I still don't know what possessed me — perhaps my love of animals — but I dropped my rucksack and started freeing the livestock. The bewildered guy didn't know what to make of me at first and started shouting angrily. That soon abated as the spooked horses bolted the moment their stable doors opened. By the time they'd all escaped, I'd sustained some second-degree burns to my hands and face. Although second-degree burns typically heal, I still carry faint scars — a constant reminder of that day and that phase of my life. The old guy had found his balance — I assumed he had a concussion — located a hosepipe and set about dousing the flames. Seeing I came a distant second to the stable block, I dove into the nearest water trough. It made me smell like a horse, but I could live with that for the relief it gave my burns. The fire raged beyond the control of a garden hose, and it wasn't long before the barn was a heap of smouldering ruins — perfect for a BBQ but not much else.

After ten minutes of splashing around in the water, I walked over to the now collapsed, dejected old timer.

"Hey, man, I'm really sorry about the barn. At least your horses got out."

"Yeah," he sighed. "Thanks, kid. I owe you. Where the heck did you come from?"

"My car broke down. I was walking along the road back there when I almost got taken out by a pickup. By the time I'd dusted myself down, I could smell smoke and figured I should try to do something in case it was a wildfire."

"I appreciate it. Not sure many other folks would've bothered. If I can do anything for you, just let me know. I like to make sure I pay my debts."

I felt a little bad asking for a favour at this moment, but I was in a tricky situation without a car.

"Well, I could do with a tow to the local garage and a place to stay tonight."

"Sure thing, the least I can do," he said with convincing cheer.

After another half-hour of drenching the ashes, we jumped in his pickup and headed back to my crappy Buick. Thankfully it was still there; unfortunately it still wouldn't run. He towed the car back to his place — the local garage was shut until after the weekend — and offered to put me up for a few days. It wasn't until we sat down to stew with cornbread that the conversation got back to the fire.

"So what happened? I saw those guys come tearing down the road — I couldn't miss them. I assume they had something to do with that?" I said, jerking a thumb towards the pile of ash in the yard.

"That was Bill and Mark Cartwright. Local bullies. They've somehow got it into their heads that my land is worth a fortune, and they want it."

"Is it? I mean, is there oil or something?"

"Nah, just some weird metals I never heard of. Either way, I'm not selling, and that's the end of it. Especially to those jerks."

"But why burn down the stables? Why not just threaten your family or something?"

"'Cause I have no family — and in case you missed it, they did beat me up," he said, pointing to his scalp. "My horses are the love of my life — there's nothing like a ride on the range — and my babies, they're competition thoroughbreds. They know that; that's why they targeted the stables."

"Can't you go to the local sheriff? Surely they'd protect you and your horses."

"Why didn't I think of that?" he replied, the sarcasm not even slightly hidden. "You obviously aren't from a small town, are you? Small town means everybody knows everybody else's business — including their debts. Take a guess who the sheriff owes?"

"The Cartwrights," I said, as the pieces fell into place. "So where does that leave you?"

"Mano a mano. Me versus them."

The ambiguity left me contemplating exactly what he meant — probably how he intended it. Not knowing what to say, I changed the subject.

"At least you'll get insurance for the barn, right?"

"'Fraid not, kiddo," he said, slurping his drink, followed by a chunk of cornbread. "Built it with my own hands, so no professional certificate. The money-grabbing fuckers at the insurance agency set the premium so high it wasn't worth it."

I was astonished. Fred looked well on his way to seventy. His heavily tanned skin looked like a pair of my dad's leather walking shoes, minus the mud. Thinning silver hair, bags under his eyes, broken veins from too much booze, and stubble to rival Popeye. That said, he was still a big guy — about 6'1" — and, belly aside, quite lean.

"So you're just going to rebuild?"

"Yep. Chop down a few trees, run 'em through the shop, and hey presto — a few weeks later I have my stables back."

As he talked, a thought began to take shape.

"I've got a proposition for you," I said.

"This should be funny."

"Well, you've a stable block to build and I've a dead car. What d'you say to me hanging around and helping? I'll earn my keep, but maybe a small stipend to cover the repair costs?"

I'd expected him to bite my hand off, but his face stayed passive. After several minutes' silence, he countered.

"You stick around, help out round here, and I'll fix your car up like new."

Sounded like a damn good deal — better than the one I'd offered — so I accepted.

"You've got a deal," I said, extending my hand.

The handshake was quickly followed by what would become nightly drinks and tales of conquests won and lost.

Over the next month, I became a regular all-American boy. We slowly rebuilt the stable block — which turned out to be more work than advertised. After a few weeks of trips into town with Fred, I was entrusted to go on my own. The town was small, so everyone knew me as that foreign kid helping old man Fred. I was on a first-name basis with the grocery clerk, the hardware-store owner and — much to the annoyance of some local lads — semi-dating the doctor's daughter. It was stereotypical small-town America — the exact experience I'd come looking for. Being welcomed as I was genuinely heart-warming. I'll always remember it only happened because I allowed myself to be blessed with their friendship and kindness — a life lesson I try never to forget.

When Fred wasn't pushing me to finish the barn, we spent hours on horseback, heading into the Montana wilderness. I wasn't a bad horseman, but Fred's seventy years' experience meant he was always offering advice — mostly via mockery. I think I improved quickly; or maybe he gave up on me. After a few weeks of saddle sores and aching thighs, we often rode in silence, simply enjoying the freedom and tranquillity of being the only humans as far as the eye could see.

During these rides, Fred started teaching me to shoot. He'd been a gunnery sergeant in the army years ago, with service in several conflicts. While I picked up close-range pistol shooting easily enough, it was the long-range work where I excelled. Using Fred's bolt-action rifle, he taught me the intricacies of long-distance marksmanship, and soon I was regularly hitting targets at 800 metres.

Life settled into a routine and, with no sign of the Cartwrights, Fred introduced me to his next project. I hadn't kept up with the car repairs — I was trusting Fred to tell me when it was time to go. I wasn't complaining; I couldn't have been enjoying myself more.

About fifteen minutes from his ranch was a rundown shooting range Fred had bought a few years earlier. He wanted me to revamp it, open it to the public and even run it for him. I wasn't convinced. In a state with so much open space, there wasn't exactly a shortage of places to fire a gun. But Fred was willing to pay me, and as a backpacker I'd be stupid to look a gift horse in the mouth. Only one problem: my visa.

"You know I'd love to, but my visa won't let me. I only have six months, and I've already been here for four. And it says strictly no work."

"Oh, don't worry about that. It's just a bit of paperwork," Fred said.

As much as I loved the country folk, they were a bit behind the times and didn't quite grasp the consequences in today's society.

"I don't think you get it, Fred. If I stay too long, I'll be an illegal immigrant. People will start calling me Manuel or José. I'll get deported, maybe jailed, and I'll definitely never be allowed back."

"You surprise me, Eli. How long have you been here now, two months?" He didn't wait for an answer. "Round here, we have our own rules. Money and law aren't always the answer to every problem. It's more about who you know and what they can do."

"I get that, but we're talking about federal laws — maybe international ones."

"Yeah, and I'll sort it."

Fred hadn't let me down so far — the Buick was already back gracing America's roads. I'd trusted him on that; he'd been true to his word. So what the hell, I thought. And that was that. The next day I went to check out my new place of work. Set in a small wooded area just off a main road, it was at least well located. "Run-down" didn't cover it — "dilapidated" was more accurate. The main building was barely standing and the roof non-existent. Both the pistol and close-quarters ranges were severely overgrown, while the 1,000-yard rifle range looked like a field of weeds. The bones of a business were there, and with a few weeks' graft the place could be ready.

I headed into town to place orders for the kit I'd need. I was chatting with Bert, the hardware-shop clerk, when a chilly atmosphere descended as two scruffy guys walked in. Normally I'd look away, but I felt confident enough to follow them with my eyes as Bert did the same. They were about my height but carried a lot more weight. I'd never seen them before and assumed they were passing through — probably bikers.

Oddly, they put down a few bills instead of letting Bert ring up the prices. As they brushed past me, they both gave me a hard stare. I was tempted to say something, but felt Bert's hand on my shoulder.

"We've got our eye on you, kid," one of them said, pointing at me.

"Leave it," Bert whispered.

As the door slammed behind them, I thought the glass might fall out.

"Who the hell are they?" I asked, already fairly sure.

"That, Eli, was your first — and hopefully last — meeting with the Cartwright brothers. I'm surprised you've avoided them this long."

"Oh — those are the guys who burned down the stables."

"One and the same."

"You always let them walk all over you like that?"

286

"We don't have a choice. They move from town to town, bullying their way around. The law's either scared of them or in their pockets. You can file complaints till the cows come home, but nothing ever happens."

"Yeah, Fred mentioned something similar."

"You'll have to watch your back. Not only are any friends of Fred's automatically their enemy, but they're grade-A gun nuts. You'll see a lot more of them once you open."

Great, I thought. Just what I needed. With that weighing on my mind, I headed home to get ready for my date with the doctor's daughter.

We'd just left the cinema after A Streetcar Named Desire. Not my typical film, but when the other option is The SpongeBob SquarePants Movie, it was the only choice. We were strolling down Main Street when the roar of a V8 pickup broke the quiet. The truck pulled up beside us, and a worse-for-wear Bill Cartwright stuck his head out, slurring.

"Hey, Lotte, why don't you hop in? We'll show you a good time."

"Yeah, we'll show you what a real man is," his brother added from the driver's seat.

I hadn't yet reached the "I'm not scared of anything" phase of my life, so I replied as politely as possible.

"Thanks, guys, but I've got this one covered."

They looked at me and laughed.

"Why settle for rump steak when you can have fillet? That's what I always say," Bill retorted, grabbing his crotch.

Bravery, stupidity, or both — my next sentence came out before I could stop it.

"You know, I seem to remember your mum saying something different."

In hindsight, it didn't make much sense, but the meaning was clear. As quickly as their faces changed, I found myself staring down two gun barrels. They obviously didn't appreciate the insinuation that both of them — and I — had slept with their mum.

"We know you're new to town," one snarled, "so we'll give you a break this time. But don't try to play the big man with us again."

I decided silence was my best option and just nodded. Fortunately, a police cruiser appeared round the corner and crawled towards us. The guns vanished. Reassuring that some laws still applied to them.

"Everything all right here?" the officer asked, blocking the pickup and joining us on the pavement.

"Just saying hello to the neighbours," the brothers said with a sarcastic smile.

"Charlotte? Eli?"

"Everything's good," I said.

"Okay then, you two should be getting home — it's late. Doc and Fred'll be wondering where you've got to."

We nodded and began walking again.

"See you soon. Very soon," one brother shouted.

Looking back, I saw the cop — who turned out to be the sheriff — staying to chat, giving us a chance to put some distance between us and almost certain trouble.

Chapter 41

A fter our late-night meeting, I saw them nearly every day from then on. Sometimes they were in town, but more often than not they were crawling past the shooting range or Fred's place. My biggest fear was that they'd trash the house and then burn down the range once it was finished. I needn't have worried. They never got the chance.

About a week later, a pickup truck pulled into the yard at the front of the house. It was around 2 a.m. when I stumbled onto the veranda to find the horses loose and drunken laughter echoing from the open stable block. There was no surprise to see the Cartwright brothers emerging. They paused when they saw me. A smile formed on Mark's face as he turned and flicked his cigarette deep into the darkness of Stable No. 3. Within ten seconds the darkness erupted into a ball of orange flame. The sudden glare left me temporarily blinded as my eyes struggled to adjust. Several seconds later, through squinted eyes, I began to process the scene. Several horses galloped off, spooked by the fireball. The barn was fully alight, obviously aided by an accelerant.

The Cartwright brothers had moved to the middle of the yard and, on a double take, I saw they had Ellen. Ellen was Fred's favourite horse: a chocolate-brown mustang with white patches, a truly beautiful animal. Unfortunately, she was being whipped and beaten by two skilled ranch hands who blocked her every attempt to escape. Few things in life pull at my heartstrings; cruelty to animals is one of them. With every crack of the whip came a heart-wrenching whine from the animal. If it had just been the barn on fire, I might have let it go, but this was too much.

Knowing I stood little chance against the alcohol-fuelled brothers, I dashed inside for Mary Jane. Mary Jane was Fred's nickname for his semi-automatic 12-bore Beretta A400 shotgun that he kept propped up just inside the front door. Knowing she was always fully loaded — in case an overzealous mountain lion or wolf needed reminding the farm was off limits — I grabbed her and hit the veranda for a second time. Giving my eyes a few seconds to reacclimatise, I thumbed the safety off, tucked the weapon into my armpit and pulled the trigger without really thinking where I was aiming. My plan was to fire over their heads, scare them, and hope they jumped in the truck and drove off.

The shot rang out, and the crack of the whips was replaced by a man's screams. The horse's movement obscured my view but, as I turned back to the noise, I saw Bill Cartwright on the ground clutching his abdomen, his brother standing over him.

"You fucking shot him, you cunt. You are a dead man," he screamed.

I just stood there in disbelief. I'd shot another human being. An ugly, cruel, heartless bastard — but a man all the same. My life was over; I'd go to jail; for all I knew Montana still had the death penalty. Mark Cartwright was shouting something at me, but I couldn't process it. My whole body was shutting down; my vision was tunnelling; my limbs trembled uncontrollably. Somewhere in my brain it registered that Mark was walking to his truck. It meant nothing until I heard Fred's voice.

"Shoot him," he said, stepping out from behind me and to my left.

"What? You can't be serious?" I replied as I slowly re-entered the real world. "I just shot one of them. Don't you think I'm in enough trouble as it is?"

"Well, if you don't, you'll be too dead to go to the pen," he said, pointing at the pickup.

I followed his finger to see Mark reaching into the cab and snatching a shotgun from the bulkhead. Working the forend to load a cartridge, he didn't even bother to shoulder the weapon. The shot thundered into the wooden cladding of the house about two feet from me. As he worked the action a second time, he took several angry steps towards me before bringing the weapon to his shoulder for accuracy. Self-preservation kicked in and my gun discharged — still without my making any effort to aim. Almost simultaneously came the distinct crack of a high-powered pistol. No return shot followed. Mark Cartwright stumbled forward, fell to his knees and then toppled forward, landing face down in the dirt. Looking left, I saw Fred holding a large-barrelled revolver, a faint wisp of acrid smoke drifting from the barrel. He slowly, deliberately, tucked the gun into his waistband and walked over to Bill, who lay silently clutching his stomach. I followed at a distance, still shell-shocked at what I'd just witnessed. Standing a few steps away, I watched as Fred loomed over him. I strained to hear over the roar of the burning barn.

"You know, for all the years you've been terrorising the town and me, I really don't feel sorry for you."

"Fuck you, and your faggot friend," he spat between spasms of pain. "Don't forget your soap on a rope."

The laugh that followed, that had all the hallmarks of a hyena's cackle, soon stopped as the pain overwhelmed him. Then it stopped forever. Without a second thought, Fred drew his revolver and put a round in his forehead. I stumbled back as the shot reverberated around the yard, despite the fire's noise. Dropping my gun, I had no idea what to do with myself. Two men — bullies and thugs though they were — were now dead, and I was mostly responsible for one. It might have been self-defense, but America wasn't known for its leniency, and this would be the biggest thing the town had ever seen. I flopped onto the ground and was shortly joined by Fred. Neither of us spoke for several minutes. Still in a trance, I finally broke the silence.

"Why did you kill him? We could have got him to a hospital."

"Let's get one thing straight. You started this by shooting him."

"It was an accident," I muttered, trying to block the memory. "I was just trying to scare them off."

"Either way, he was dead. A shotgun blast to the stomach is a slow death. The nearest doctor is fifteen minutes away; the nearest hospital's at least an hour on top. He'd never have made it. I did him a favour — put him out of his misery. And if he'd got to town, we'd be in a whole heap of shit and he'd still be dead."

Fred was thinking far more clearly than I was. He was surprisingly calm; I was a nervous, twitchy mess. Every time my eyes fell on the bodies my stomach threatened to empty from both ends. Several minutes passed before Fred suddenly got up, collected both guns and headed to the house.

"What's going on?" I asked, feebly.

"I'm calling the sheriff."

"You what?" I said, jumping up and chasing after him.

"I can hardly leave two bodies in the yard. You've seen CSI — there's no point trying to cover it up."

"So what, you're going to confess and send us both to prison? You're an old man; I've got the rest of my life ahead of me."

"Eli, go get the horses back. Let me deal with the sheriff."

I was about to protest until Fred squared up to me, glaring into my eyes with an intensity I'd never seen in him. I knew this wasn't the time to argue. I turned and jogged into the pitch black as embers drifted skyward.

I rounded up most of the horses, including Ellen. They'd headed to a favourite spot where the grass was green and sweet. The remaining two would have to wait for sunrise. I came back expecting the yard to be lit with blue and red, cops everywhere, a set of cuffs with my name on them. Unbelievably, the yard was empty — apart from Fred wandering round with a hosepipe. It was no longer lit by the barn, now a pile of smoking timbers, but by the house spotlights. Fred glanced up as the horses cantered round, then returned to hosing the timbers. The Cartwrights' pickup was gone, and the dirt of the yard had been well raked over. Lashing the horses to the rail, I headed over, perplexed by my continued freedom.

"I thought you were calling the police?"

"I did."

"So what happened to the bodies, the truck, etc.?"

"They dealt with it."

"And?"

"And nothing."

Without another word he dropped the hose — leaving it to spray vaguely at the timbers — turned and walked back into the house.

Chapter 42

The next morning, Fred acted as though nothing had happened, and even though I wanted to know what deal he'd struck with the sheriff, I decided not to push it. The following days were surreal; the town was either unusually friendly or strangely cautious around me. More than once I got free food at the diner and extra-friendly service in some stores, but I also caught uneasy stares from townsfolk I didn't know so well. It may have been my imagination, but then again, Facebook had nothing on the small-town grapevine — it's safe to say they were all talking about me.

I stayed only another week before deciding to move on and continue my trip. I'm not usually an emotional guy, but I'd formed a bond with the old fella. Not quite family, but certainly a close friendship. It wasn't until I was stuck in an I-5 traffic jam near the centre of Seattle that I found the note he'd somehow slipped into my pocket.

Fred's note read:

"Hey Kid,
You are hopefully well into your travels, well too far to turn back anyway. We've had some good times over the past few months and one that's best forgotten. Trust me when I say it's

been dealt with, but as much as I, and the rest of the town, will miss you, it is best if you never come back.

I'm going to take your advice and get on the internet, to advertise the gun range as well as the dude ranch experience you were talking about. I'll send you my email address.

Take it easy and keep your head down,

Fred

PS When you need to leave the country, go to the crossing at Willow Creek any Thursday morning. Ask for Bo. He is expecting you."

The last bit puzzled me for a few minutes until it dawned on me. My visa only had a six-month validity, and that was already past, meaning serious problems when I came to leave the country. True to his word, Fred had obviously arranged for me to leave under the radar. Sure enough, when I arrived at the checkpoint three months later, the officer on duty looked at my passport and smiled. It was the sort of smile that said, 'So you thought you could sneak your passport past some country bumpkin, well guess who's the loser now.'

"I've been expecting you," he said.

"Yeah, I was hoping you'd say that," I replied, very much relieved.

"You've got some good friends. Ordinarily, I'd detain you for questioning, but one favour deserves another of equal magnitude."

I looked at him questioningly, but he just stamped my passport and added, "You're free to go. Enjoy your visit to Canada."

I drove away from the checkpoint without really understanding why things had just occurred the way they had. I stayed in Canada for about two days before flying home. As beautiful a country as it is, I simply no longer had the bottle for the life of constantly looking over my shoulder for the authorities. It wasn't until I was in the air that I finally felt that the past few months were in my past. There and then I vowed to keep them there at all costs.

Chapter 43

I woke up the next morning to the sound of my biker friends packing up. The Northwest's infamous inclement weather was bearing down on us again, so they'd decided to move on, heading for Moab, Utah.

"Maybe I'll catch up with you guys in Moab," I said hopefully.

"For sure, man. It's the best riding around, period. We'll be in one of the town's motels."

"I'll do my best. Take it easy — but ride hard."

"Is there any other way?" He smiled. "Be safe, dude."

With that, I rode out of the campground to pick up groceries. My previous night's reminiscing returned as I followed the trail into town. I know what you're thinking: what am I doing in an Oregon campground when I clearly have good friends a few hundred miles further north?

Apart from being told never to return, Fred had passed away a few years ago. I still remember where I was when I heard the news. I'd just come home from another monotonous day at the office to find my new spaniel puppy had left me a present in the kitchen. After cleaning it up, I sank into the sofa with the post — bills and junk mail, mostly.

The airmail envelope caught my eye, and I immediately recognised the stamp as American. Tearing it open, I expected Fred's handwriting. Instead, I found a formally headed letter from a Seattle solicitor, inviting — or rather ordering — me to a will reading for a Mr Frederick Lowell.

It was an odd way to find out Fred had died, and it hit me harder than I'd expected. I didn't go to work for a few days and basically ignored Amelia, whom I'd just started dating. In the end, I booked a last-minute ticket to Seattle and flew out.

I'd imagined a crowd of people in the solicitor's office, but it was just me. Old age had finally caught up with him. He'd died about a month earlier, but because of his remote lifestyle, he hadn't been found for weeks. What came next stunned me and changed my life.

"To put it simply, Mr Miller, Mr Lowell has left you everything. You are now the owner of his entire estate," the lawyer said.

"Oh," I replied, nodding. I suppose it wasn't too unexpected, given I was the only one there.

"There is something else. He made some arrangements for his estate. They just need your approval."

I stayed silent, so he continued.

"To start with, the shooting range. He arranged for Bert Hankel to buy a 50% share."

I remembered reading in one of Fred's sporadic emails that Bert had taken over the hardware store a few years ago and was doing well.

"He and his partners will handle all the running. You'd be a silent partner, sharing in the profits — which I believe are comfortable. The price is $50,000."

I was surprised it was so much. Turns out the range had become very popular. Fred had been right — the urge to prove you were a better shot than your neighbour clearly carried bragging rights in Montana. The addition of a close-quarters combat range had helped, too, drawing in younger crowds — mainly gamers wanting to live out their Call of Duty fantasies.

"Where do I sign?" I asked.

A piece of paper was pushed across, I scrawled my name, and slid it back.

"Secondly, there's the issue of the house and adjoining land. This is a little more complicated. I'm not sure if you're aware, but the land has value beyond simple agricultural use. It was discovered — quite how, I don't know — that there are deposits of various precious and semi-precious metals."

That was a shock. I recalled Fred mentioning it the day we met, but I'd dismissed it as nonsense.

"It's believed some of the deposits are substantial, and after a closed-bid auction, the highest offer was sixty," the lawyer continued.

"Sixty what?" I asked, disappointed. With all the build-up, I'd expected a semi decent figure.

"Sixty million."

My heart stopped — or maybe it was just a lack of oxygen to the brain — but I suddenly felt dizzy and nearly fell off my chair.

"We're talking dollars, right?"

"Absolutely. About £40 million, I believe — with a couple of million in change."

I didn't know what to say. I just stared at the lawyer who, sensing my bewilderment, let the silence hang before speaking again.

"There is one decision you need to make. By accepting the mining company's offer, the town will become an industrial site overnight. You are, in effect, responsible for the town's future."

Well, if that wasn't the very definition of a catch-22, I don't know what was. One minute I had millions, the next I was deciding between my future and that of a town I owed my life and freedom to.

"So basically, if I give the go-ahead, every investor, entrepreneur, and a bunch of conmen and scumbags from a thousand-mile radius will descend on the town?" I asked.

"That's about right. Fortunately for you, Mr Lowell foresaw this dilemma and canvassed the townsfolk's opinion six months ago."

"And…?" I asked.

"Simply put, the town is all for it. Aside from a few older residents who like their peace, everyone else can't wait. Let's be realistic. Small-town America is under threat everywhere. Most towns have plateaued, and this one is no different. It needs this to start a new chapter — or else it will slowly vanish, probably not even making a footnote in the history books. There are ways you can influence things to preserve continuity, if that's what's on your mind."

He made it sound like I was forging a new way of life for them. No doubt he had a cut from the deal, so it was in his interest to talk me into it. Needless to say, my mind was already made up. The only question was what I'd spend the money on. I'd long wanted out of my job and dreamed of doing something with cars. £40 million would open a lot of doors.

In the end, I accepted the deal and invested half the money on shares in the mining company, ensuring I had some oversight on how the town developed, as the lawyer had suggested, with the bonus of sharing in the profits for years to come. The dividends would provide a steady income, while I could invest the rest in something I was truly passionate about. One such project was the creation of a charitable trust within the town, to support the older generations who might get left behind as the town grew and developed. On returning home, I quit my job, and after a few months of living the high life, I decided being my own boss was the way forward. Within a year, I had said goodbye to a large chunk of my remaining fortune with the purchase and refit of the riverside warehouse that was now the museum. I became a workaholic as I strived to become recognised as perhaps the most influential independent dealer within the UK/Europe. My lifestyle and stature grew from there, and everything was great until Jessica walked into my life.

Chapter 44

While wheeling my shallow "I'm a single guy" trolley around the supermarket, I bumped into a police officer. So I wasn't overly surprised to see a patrol car parked outside. As I stopped to adjust my backpack (the cans of Spam were digging into my back), I found myself next to it, looking through the driver's window. Looking back at me was a picture of myself, surrounded by several lines of text I couldn't quite make out. The only legible words were wanted and reward. Suitably panicked, I rode out of the car park and headed straight for the campground.

On arriving back, I switched my phone on and was instantly bombarded with countless text and voicemail notifications.

"Hey Eli, your face is all over the media. What's the deal? Call me, dude."

Jonny's message confirmed things had worsened considerably since leaving the city. All of Cisco was obviously looking for me. The only conclusion that made sense was that someone had implicated me in Steve's and Eva's deaths. I didn't understand — Isaiah was still alive; surely he would have set them straight.

Following this were messages from Amelia and Lucas, and then, to my surprise, one from Isaiah.

"Eli, you need to get over here. I don't quite get it, but they reckon you're involved in all this. Call me, ASAP."

Something in his voice didn't sound right. It lacked the usual mellow, chilled tone I knew, and there was something deeper I couldn't figure out. The message ended and the automated answering service began running through my options.

The revelation that I was now a wanted fugitive, facing a double-murder charge, floored me. How on earth had that happened? How had Isaiah not convinced them I was one of the good guys? Surely CCTV would show me helping, not as an aggressor? Too many questions, zero answers.

Then I remembered: after we found the bug in the house, Isaiah had said he was going to see Holtzman and Jessica. If he'd really done that, the FBI would know the team was compromised. So why was I being hunted? What if he hadn't gone to them and nobody else knew about the bug? That left just me and him, which would explain why he'd told me to lay low for a week, giving him the chance to spin a version of events that kept the spotlight firmly off himself. What if he'd shifted the spotlight onto Holtzman, especially after the heist fiasco? But then why had I been allowed to walk away from the café attack? Surely it wasn't just because I was late? If Isaiah had arranged the attack for the agreed time, my tardiness would explain why I hadn't ended up with a bullet in the head. At this point, I was tumbling down a rabbit hole of paranoia. What I did know was this: he and I were the only ones to walk away, and now I was the one being hunted. Every twist and turn, the spotlight always seemed to miss Isaiah. I'd have to be very cautious about contacting him again.

I hadn't noticed whether the cruiser's info had stated dead or alive, but with bounty hunters and every law enforcement officer wanting my skin, I doubted anyone would mind if I was "accidentally" shot in the head.

The dreary drone of the answering machine brought me back to reality, and I decided to give Isaiah a call. The prospect didn't really fill me with joy, and I walked to the side of the campground's river to sit and prepare myself. As I watched several birds fight over a fish one of them had just caught, I felt a peace descend over me, and I began to formulate a plan of attack.

I hit the speed dial button and waited. It only took two or three rings before it was answered

"Eli?" Isaiah's voice came through.

Just a lucky guess, I hope.

"Hi Isaiah, I just picked up your message, and I'm slightly concerned," I said, trying to hide my anxiety.

That was when I first heard the clicking noises followed by some faint whispering in the background. Isaiah seemed a little distracted as well; things just didn't feel right.

"Yeah, I'm err... not too sure what's going on. I explained what happened and understandably they want to hear your side of things. They just want to speak with you. Where are you? I can bring you in."

There was more line distortion and I heard "fifteen seconds" in the background. My alarm bells were going off like a world war 2 air raid siren..

"You dirty fuck," I shouted before thumbing the red end call button. I started to get the shakes again. My one supposed ally in all of this had just sold me down the proverbial river, another nail in his coffin as far as I was concerned. My suspicion was that my phone was being tapped to get my location, and as I pondered the brief call, people were probably already on their way.

Things couldn't get much worse — unless Amelia called to confess she used to be a man. (Note to self: set up a doctor's appointment, because clearly my luck is on a losing streak.) I briefly considered running straight into the river and letting it carry me off to the Pacific and a merciful end to it all.

Then it hit me — my phone was still on. Channelling my best Dan Marino impression, I hurled it twenty metres into the river, nearly decapitating a duck in the process. I know nothing about mobile phone tracking, but having watched enough Bruce Willis and Will Smith films, I was reasonably sure it worked by triangulation. If they'd needed another fifteen seconds to finish the trace, then all they knew was that I was on the Oregon coast — probably not much more. This was a comforting thought, but only slightly.

Thankfully, my favourite action hero John McClane came to my rescue. Suicide was out — it required more guts than I had. That left two options: pack Vaseline and brace for prison life (which I doubt is high on anyone's to-do list), or go on a one-man, winner-takes-all crusade to take down the bad guys.

The more I thought about it, the more I fancied my chances. All I needed was a confession — probably from Jameson — that he'd ordered the killings or that Isaiah was working for him and that I'd had nothing to do with it. Which meant going to Cisco... not exactly at the top of my to-do list.

Despite everything my brain seemed to be functioning surprisingly well, but I hit a stumbling block: I couldn't exactly walk up to Jameson and demand an explanation. That would most likely land me in prison with no bargaining power. Strangely, my instincts pointed to Seattle — or maybe I just convinced myself they did.

The two agents assassinated in their car, the ones whose deaths had kicked off my nightmare, had been killed at the docks in Seattle. They were there for a reason, and if by some chance I could find out what it was, I would have my leverage. A very long shot, admittedly, but it was still something, and right now something was better than the other options: male rape in prison or the gamble that reincarnation was a real thing. The only thing was I couldn't risk coming back as one of those baboons with the hideous anus.

With renewed vigour and a plan forming in my head, I headed back to the camp as quickly as possible. I didn't bother with the tent etc.; if the police found my spot, it might convince them that I was still around. I grabbed any clothes that were lying around, took my bike apart, and headed for the shower block.

As I finished my hurried and somewhat tepid shower, I almost made my first mistake: shaving. With my picture apparently everywhere, my appearance would have to change. Fortunately, I was on the West Coast of America where everything goes without even a second glance most of the time. I only had a few days of growth, but give it a few more days and I could start to pass as an established member of the hipster community.

To complete the look, I'd need to make a detour to Portland. I needed clothes younger and edgier than what I had. Portland — arguably the most European city in America — was perfect. A quick stop at Old Navy and I would look the epitome of trendiness... at least in the eyes of a twenty-something hipster.

The drive to Seattle was a good five hours, and with it being 2 p.m. when I set off, I didn't expect to stop till gone

8 p.m. that night, factoring in typical rush hour delays. As I drove, I pondered what lay ahead and came up against my second problem: where to stay?

Upmarket city centre hotels were the most attractive option but no doubt an obvious and expensive choice, meaning they were out. Then there were the out-of-town motels. The out-of-town motels were slightly less conspicuous, but they posed the risk of the desk clerk, who nearly always had a TV on and begrudged any interruptions. The chance of one of them putting my face to the news reports in about five seconds flat was worryingly high.

That left me with one choice, somewhat inspired if I do say so myself. The Seattle youth hostel. Centrally located, full of tourists who didn't watch much TV, and the last place you'd expect to find a multi-millionaire fugitive.

Chapter 45

I slept surprisingly well, considering a mixture of drunk Europeans and loud Americans (what other kind are there, I hear you ask) had invaded my dorm partway through the night. I made it to the hostel by nine and, after hiding the car in an underground garage, I charmed my way into a bed. Apparently, I was supposed to have a hostel membership card or something.

As I looked out of the kitchen window onto Pike Street below, the Washington weather, as predicted, had certainly arrived. Gone were the sunshine and cerulean skies of Oregon, replaced by thick grey clouds, drizzle and a stiff breeze. The best way to describe Seattle is as a smaller version of San Francisco. It, too, has hills to challenge any cyclist, and it sits on the edge of the Pacific. However, it's noticeably more conservative than San Francisco, which is both good and bad.

After chatting with a few German and Swedish travellers, I headed out on some errands. First stop was for weather-appropriate clothing — I was in the Pacific Northwest, after all. Then I headed to the Pacific Place shopping centre for a few essentials: a decent digital camera, a laptop and some brown-tinted contact lenses. I still had some cash left over, but it wasn't going to last much longer at this rate. It wouldn't be long before I needed to use the credit card, despite the risks that came with that.

I had decided on the drive up that I needed contact lenses — another of my self-proclaimed inspired ideas. As I have quite striking blue eyes, a new brown shade would help alter my appearance a little more. I also figured the contacts would diminish that eye recognition humans seem to have. Plenty of times I've approached someone I didn't recognise, but their eyes told me they knew me. I don't know the biology of it, but it's definitely a thing, and anything I could do to prevent that happening now was worth doing.

Wrapped up in my waterproofs, looking decidedly touristy, I headed down towards the ports on my trusty bike. Now, if you've ever been to Seattle, you'll know the port is one of the biggest in the US, and there was every chance I was wasting my time. However, I had one slight advantage: a semi-photographic memory. Unfortunately for me, it wasn't 100%; otherwise I'd be robbing both the rich and the poor under the guise of being a lawyer. I can remember things I see to a fairly accurate level — good enough to walk around a city and not get lost. Having seen several pictures of the docks while at Quantico, I fancied my chances. I was always optimistic when it came to my memory.

I was soon cycling on a busy quayside, which surprised me because I'd expected it to be quiet. I almost got crushed by two forklifts and then knocked into the water by another. As I slowed to take in the scenery, I took the opportunity to get my bearings and do some mental recognition. After the incidents with the forklifts, the final straw was grazing my arm on a container as I swerved to avoid yet another collision. With blood trickling down my arm, I pulled up outside a warehouse that was full of crates but seemed to lack anyone doing any actual work. I ducked inside to get a few minutes' shelter from the rain and to see how badly I'd injured my arm. My waterproof now had a small chunk missing and, as I looked out of the doorway, I noticed it hanging on the side of the container. On the plus side, I would live — it was only a flesh wound.

Now seemed like as good a time as any to take some pictures. I wasn't snapping anything in particular, just everything from people to boats to containers. With shots of my current location stored in the camera's memory, I wandered deeper into the warehouse. All I could see were wooden containers labelled "Alden Matzoh." I was just about to have a look into one crate when a voice echoed from deep inside the warehouse.

"Hey, what do you think you're doing?"

"Oh, hi," I said, spinning to face the voice. "I was just trying to get out of the rain."

"I think the roof will do that just fine. No need to get inside the box as well."

I didn't really have a clever comeback, so I just stood there as my comfort level quickly dissipated. The guy was about 5'10" but must have weighed 250+ pounds — most of it solid muscle. His neck was as wide as his head and his tattoo covered forearms weren't far off the size of my thighs — and he was coming towards me at quite a rate. I was about to jump on my bike and try to make a getaway when his next comment caught me off guard.

"Isn't that the new Nikon?" he asked, pointing at my camera.

"Yeah," I replied, somewhat relieved. "Here, have a look," I offered, hoping to appease any bad blood between us.

After a few minutes of playing with it, he handed it back.

"That is one fly camera. Each to their own, but you've a weird idea of what makes a good photo."

"Oh, you mean the dockside pics? They're for a piece I'm working on."

"Oh, right. You a journo or something? 'Cause we need as much press as we can get down here. This place is slowly going down the can; we need serious investment before it's too late."

From somewhere deep in my brain, an idea surfaced, and I went with it.

"I, err… write books about unsolved crimes and mysteries."

"Shouldn't you be in Dallas or Roswell, then? Why Seattle?"

"Normally, yeah," I said with what I hoped was a genuine chuckle, "but I heard about a couple of murders down here on the dockside. It sounded pretty weird, so I thought I'd check it out and get a few background photos — you know, the usual."

"Yeah, I know what you're talking about. Happened just outside, a few alleys down, I think. There was a whole lot of fuss about it — never seen so much PD per square metre. Had the area shut down for a whole damn week."

"So I hear. That's one of the reasons I'm here."

"There's nothing there now, but turn left out of the door, and I think it's the second alley."

Thanking the guy, I headed back out into the weather to test just how waterproof my new camera was. I took a few shots up and down the alley and then did my best to take some casual photos of the surrounding warehouses. I even stopped for a few minutes and watched the large cranes organise the containers into something akin to a game of

Tetris. It's amazing how I ended up in the right place — I guess the subconscious just takes over sometimes.

Everything was running smoothly until I turned to head back to the dockside and found myself confronted by several burly blokes in hard hats, one of whom was my camera friend from earlier. I seem to have developed a habit of attracting unwelcome, threatening company. My ribs were still a little sore from the biking accidents a few days back, so the last thing I needed was more pain.

"Hi, guys. How are we today?"

There was no response, but their movement towards me signalled their intent — one my health insurance wouldn't be happy about. My Spidey sense told me to run — or, in my case, jump on my bike and pedal like Lance Armstrong. I took a running start and jumped on like a cyclo-cross pro, wobbling slightly at first as I got my balance. A quick glance over my shoulder told me the advancing thugs were within a few metres of dragging me off again. Firmly in the saddle, I stomped on the pedals and thankfully began to put some distance between us.

As I reached one of the dockside's main roads, a black Lincoln Navigator suddenly blocked my path. Sensing this wasn't an encouraging turn of events, I grabbed the brakes and shifted my weight to help the rear wheel slide out. Stomping on the pedals again, I powered through an open side door into a warehouse on my left. This one also contained crates similar to those in the neighbouring warehouse. With my focus on getting away, I struggled to focus on the text stamped on the crates, but I'm pretty sure I saw the same Alden Matzoh branding as before.

I slowly weaved between the stacks before seeing the large entrance ahead. It felt like déjà vu as the Lincoln once again blocked my path. As I slowed to a halt, I heard voices behind me and got the distinct feeling I was trapped. I turned, searching for an alternative way out, as the rear window of the car slid down, revealing an unwelcome sight: a gun barrel — and a long one at that.

Things suddenly became considerably more serious than being chased by a few goons. I clicked up a few gears to build acceleration and headed for the nearest stack of boxes, weaving the bike to limit the shooter's chances of a clean shot. I never heard the report — probably suppressed — but I, or rather my bike, sure knew about it. The rear jumped as a round struck somewhere. Luckily it hit the seatpost; otherwise, the frame would have exploded, taking me with it. As it was, I no longer had a saddle — just a hazardous-looking shredded tube of carbon my arse wouldn't appreciate meeting.

As I reached the cover of a row of crates, splinters and pungent dust burst into the air. Bits of timber peppered my head; my eyes began to sting as I rode through the cloud. Further into the warehouse, boxes started collapsing, and, looking back, I saw footballs, basketballs and other sports kit tumbling everywhere. As I tried to ride away from the chaos, the green glow of a fire-exit sign caught my eye. Suddenly there were footsteps close behind; one of my pursuers had somehow got very close. I'd obviously eased up too much.

I sped up and headed straight for the fire door. As I neared it, I flung my weight back, naturally lifting the front wheel to smash the release bar. The door sprang open, and I burst into relative freedom. All my efforts were now focused on getting the hell out. A few times I thought I heard the Lincoln behind me, but I didn't dare look back — I just concentrated on reaching downtown.

By the time I got back to the hostel the rain had, at least, stopped. Despite that — and my new expensive waterproofs — my clothes were still pretty damp. Why, in this age of high-tech everything, can't they make a waterproof jacket that actually keeps water out? Locking the bike, I examined the damage and was dismayed. I was very lucky to still be walking. Another five or six inches higher and I'd have had a bullet in my lumbar spine. The bike wasn't a write-off, but I'd definitely need a new seatpost.

With someone clearly hunting me, I decided to keep my head down and figured I'd review my photographic handiwork after a shower. I'd rattled the right cages, but it was unsettling that the bad guys — who I assumed were part of Jameson's crew — knew I was in the city. I didn't get far with the pictures, apart from identifying a few boats that might belong to this Alden Matzoh group. It was at least a starting point. Judging by the vast amount of warehouse space they needed, Alden Matzoh was not insignificant. It surely couldn't be a coincidence that someone had murdered the two FBI agents outside those exact warehouses where I'd just escaped with my life. Obviously, it was circumstantial, and I'm pretty sure the FBI would have looked at this angle, but I couldn't shake the feeling I was on to something.

As it was, it felt that Seattle had nothing else to offer me. Next stop, San Francisco.

Chapter 46

I didn't leave town until around midday, keeping a low profile at the hostel. The events of the previous day were still bothering me. I couldn't understand why people were so concerned that I'd seen a shipment of sporting paraphernalia. If anything, it only confirmed my suspicion that something was going on in that warehouse. I was also puzzled how Jameson's crew had found me so quickly when it seemed that the FBI couldn't.

Both questions nagged at me for most of the drive back to San Francisco. As I once again passed familiar place names, I wondered whether returning had been such a good idea after all. I imagined the double murder would be old news by now, so hopefully my picture wouldn't still be plastered everywhere. I assumed the cops, of course, still had it — as well as a description of my car. The last thing I needed — and the way my luck was going I fully expected it — was for a rookie cop, keen to make a name for himself, to spot my car outside Dunkin' Donuts and light up the police band with my location.

As it was, I managed to avoid all the police cruisers, though a few state troopers did come tearing past at one point. It took serious restraint not to bury the throttle and assume they were after me. My journey ended at the St Regis hotel, one of the pricier city-centre options, where I opted for underground valet parking. That way, only two people knew where my car was, and the valet had 200 reasons to keep his mouth shut. Although I was going to have to use a credit card at this hotel, I had brought along a very obscure business card that wasn't directly linked to me. It was a risk, but one that I figured probably balanced in my favour.

As I waited for the bellboy to bring up my luggage, I quickly leafed through the Chronicle to find a short column about every effort being made to apprehend the individuals responsible for the shootout. The usual media line stated they had nothing, but then they were hardly about to advertise it if they were closing in on me. What I didn't find was a report about the bike crash I'd read about several days ago. This prompted me to use the room phone to give Jonny a quick call and ask for another favour. Given I'd thrown my mobile in the river at the campground, it took me a few tries to get the correct combination of numbers before I finally stopped bothering the random people that did answer.

Although I'd sworn off involving Jonny, it was clear now I had nobody else. After the call with Isaiah, he was my only option. After a few brief pleasantries, I explained about both the heist and the bike "accidents." He reckoned he knew some people who could help, but he'd need time.

With the call out of the way, I settled in, ordered room service, hung the "Do Not Disturb" sign, and lounged in front of the TV with a bottle of whisky from the minibar. Unfortunately, I spent the evening reflecting on the life choices that had led me here. Jessica's threat to my business had spurred me on, even though I probably could have survived it. True, the possibility of my Montana past being revealed was also part of it, but I was convinced nobody knew the truth. A protective streak in me had been used against me, and that realisation stung. No doubt fuelled by the whisky, I drifted off at some unknown time and woke up to headlines I couldn't have predicted in a month of Sundays.

Chapter 47

For once, it wasn't my face all over the morning news, but that of Edwin Jameson. According to NBC, CNN, Fox, and every other channel, the SFPD had raided his home overnight after fresh evidence surfaced. While his arrest was "allegedly" for organising the killings, the networks had all managed to find commentators accusing him of everything from running a red light to being a mafia kingpin. If they'd wanted to, I'm sure they could have pinned JFK's assassination on him and made it stick. My name was still mentioned as someone wanted for questioning, but no pictures were shown. Several channels suggested, according to sources deep within the FBI, that I was in Canada or Mexico by now. If only they knew.

This was certainly an interesting turn of events, though not particularly helpful to my current quest. I watched the coverage in the vain hope of learning something new, but prime-time ended with the story regurgitated, wording tweaked but content unchanged. The only fresh detail was that Jameson would have a bail hearing the following day. It was only a bail application, and likely to be refused, but it dawned on me that this was the opportunity I needed. No longer did I have to worry about finding him — the SFPD had solved that by locking him in the city jail. All I needed now was a plan to get to him.

Pretending to be his lawyer was too far-fetched — the guards would know exactly who his legal team was. I considered posing as a journalist, but that required a press ID, and Jameson was unlikely to talk to a journo anyway. The idea came to me while I was pounding away on the hotel treadmill. It brought a smile to my face despite the danger. I had a lot to gain if it worked, and not much to lose if it didn't.

The plan didn't need much preparation; it was going to rely mostly on good fortune — the worst kind of plan, but it was all I had. I spent most of the day at the hotel, though I did venture out briefly for fresh air. Market Street was heaving — it was peak tourist season, and San Francisco's constantly mild climate was a big draw, adding to the crowds. I avoided the really crowded areas to minimise the chances of recognition, but I couldn't resist spending some time around the Giants' stadium, taking in the sea air.

I didn't sleep too well that night, as my mind couldn't rest. I was constantly running through what would happen the next day, as well as what had transpired over the past few weeks. Every time, I seemed to come back to thoughts of Eva and Steve. The nerves were already beginning to build, but I had made the decision to not walk into the Pacific, and I owed it to myself to conquer my fears and cowardice and see this through to the end. I didn't, after all, have a better plan.

Chapter 48

I woke up feeling like crap, and as I brushed my teeth, I realised I also looked like crap. My four hours of sleep had not been kind — I could have stood in for Uncle Fester. I looked rough, but perhaps that might help, considering I was about to walk into an environment that could quickly turn hostile if I was recognised. I dressed casually in jeans and a T-shirt that looked like it had lived at the bottom of a gym bag for a few months. Combined with my almost-beard, unstyled hair and chestnut-brown eyes, I looked so different I might have struggled to recognise myself. I left all identifying possessions behind; the last thing I needed was my true identity being revealed. As I passed the reception desk, I left my room card too.

Despite the relatively early hour — 7:30 a.m. — the streets were busy. Groups of homeless people occupied street corners, while the morning rush consisted of cars charging towards the next series of red lights, with clusters of pedestrians patiently waiting to cross. I'm not sure why, but I love the morning smell of an unfamiliar city. Despite the noises being the same, the polluted air being the same, and the clusters of similarly constructed high-rises being the same, the city still held a refreshing, novel atmosphere — one I never got from London.

The courthouse was a decent walk from the hotel, and by the time I arrived I'd worked up a bit of a sweat — a combination of the sun and the hills. It was 8:15 a.m.. I knew the court was open, but had no idea what time Jameson's hearing was. After meandering through corridors for a while, checking each chamber's itinerary, I eventually found what I was looking for: his bail hearing was at 10:30 a.m.. That gave me a couple of hours to kill which, as I headed downstairs to the café, I realised wasn't a bad thing.

There were already about 15–20 reporters and cameramen spread around the tables. In years gone by, I could imagine a thick haze of tobacco smoke hovering near the ceiling. As it was, there were just cameras, microphones and notepads scattered across the floor while the chatter of coffee drinkers bounced off the walls. Grabbing a bottle of water, I settled near a trio of reporters busy gossiping about Jameson.

"Case of the year, I'm telling you."

"You got that right. Heavyweight socialite, friends with the mayor, sketchy details of the case — it's got controversy written all over it."

"Yeah, well, I reckon he's going down. I've been talking with some friends in low places, and the word is he's guilty as sin. By all accounts, his money's come from guns and drugs, not the big ventures he'd have us believe."

"That doesn't mean shit. If the DA doesn't get his finger out of his arse, he'll walk. My guess is he carries too much weight, and they'll bottle it."

"It's going to be O.J. all over again. He's probably got pics of the mayor shagging a hooker."

"Not to mention what he'll have on Judge Roosen."

All three chuckled, clearly sharing an inside joke. I tuned them out until I heard something that interested me.

"I hear that freelance guy who sometimes works for Fox has some dirt on this guy. Been investigating him for years — since his wife was killed. Some drug war or something. This is going to be his pay dirt; the info that guy's got is probably enough to bring Jameson down on its own."

"Who? You mean Pete Owens?"

"Yeah, that's the guy."

"I'm pretty sure I remember that story. Gunned down in a drive-by. People in Jameson's operation were linked, but nothing stuck."

A bell chimed in the distance. Like wolves descending on prey, the reporters grabbed their gear and headed out, presumably to the front steps. I checked my watch: 9:50. As the case was clearly generating a lot of media attention, I decided to get up to the courtroom now, otherwise I wouldn't see anything other than closed doors.

Outside, there was already a small crowd. I learned the media were assigned their own gallery, so at least I stood a chance of a seat. As minutes passed, more people arrived — it was turning into a tourist attraction. The previous hearing finished and, before the lawyers had left the bench, the crowd spilled in, almost fighting for the front rows. With all the hoopla, I'd been distracted from my worries, but as I sat on a bench at the rear I began to focus again on what I was doing. What sort of sane man walks into a courthouse in the city where he's wanted for questioning in a double murder?

As the bench filled with the last few people, I started to feel increasingly uncomfortable. Had I walked into a trap? Were they expecting me, and any minute now I'd be in handcuffs? I looked around and almost got up — until I saw who was next to me. My brain screamed conspiracy as I found myself looking at Isabella Jameson in profile. She sensed me looking and gave me a scowl. I forced a half-smile and quickly looked away. She didn't immediately recognise me. Given she'd been closer than this when we danced on the boat, I took it as a good omen that my disguise was decent. My eyes darted around for other familiar faces. I expected to see Holtzman — after all, this was the culmination of his grand plan. As hard as I looked, I couldn't find him. What I did find was direct eye contact with several police officers strategically placed around the room. I was way outside my comfort zone; normally I'd give up, but the option vanished as the rear doors closed firmly. Jameson appeared from a side door and was shortly followed by the judge.

"All stand. The Honourable Judge Roosen is now in session."

Judging by the journalists' chatter, I doubted the "honourable" bit. Late forties, reasonably tall, well groomed. A little young, I thought, to be presiding over something this big. After leaving us standing for a beat, he instructed us to sit.

"Before we start, I want to make it abundantly clear that I am aware how important this trial is to the city. However, any interruptions will not be tolerated."

That was clearly aimed at us, the public.

"And any showboating and/or grandstanding" — now to the legal teams — "will be recognised as contempt of my court, and you can be sure I will deal with it accordingly. Am I clear?"

Silence. He continued.

"So, we have a bail application for a Mr Edwin Jameson?"

"That's right, Your Honour," replied the chief prosecutor.

"And the charge?"

"That he paid for and orchestrated the double murder of FBI agents Weinhart and Fuentes."

"And how is the defendant pleading?" the judge asked, turning to the defence.

"Not guilty," came the authoritarian reply. "And I would like to take this opportunity — "

"Save it for the trial, counsellor."

After a pause, he went on.

"So, let's hear it. Why should the State grant this man his freedom with such horrific charges against him?"

"Your Honour, Mr Jameson is a respected, upstanding member of the community. He poses no threat to fellow citizens."

"Yeah — just to officers of the law," someone shouted.

An almighty crack of the gavel silenced the laughter.

"I warned you at the outset about your conduct. One more interruption and I'll clear the court. Now, counsellor, proceed."

"Sir, the defendant has lived in the Bay Area for years, donates large sums to inner-city charities, and is a notable philanthropist and close friend of the mayor. Simply put, he is a man with a demonstrably kind and loving nature who has always abided by the law — never even picking up a parking ticket."

The judge nodded.

"I accept these points and that Mr Jameson is a pillar of society; however, being a friend of our mayor doesn't fundamentally make him trustworthy."

Laughter again, and a smile from the judge. Strict rules, I thought — mostly so he could be the centre of attention.

"And the prosecution's view?"

"Your Honour, Mr Jameson's philanthropy is without question, nor is his incredible wealth. However, these charges are extremely serious. We believe that should bail be granted and the accused's passport be confiscated he still has enough resources at his disposal to disappear if he so chose. It is because of this flight risk that the People request that bail be denied."

As the District Attorney sat down, the judge leafed through some papers, and the court waited for several minutes in anticipation of the verdict.

"Bail is denied," spoke the judge.

"Objection," responded the defence almost immediately.

Glaring at the defence table, the judge replied, "My decision is final. Bailiff, over to you."

The gavel fell and the room exploded into noise. People were already heading for the doors. As I turned towards Isabella, she was almost out, dabbing at her face — probably catching a tear — before the media scrum grabbed a front-page shot. I thought about going after her, but I had something more important to do: talk to Jameson. The corridors outside were packed, cameras rolling, spotlights burning, and lawyers on both sides spouting meaningless lines about "concrete cases". Typical bullshit — one side knew it would lose. Why not admit it and save everyone the money? But then you only have to look at O.J. to see literally anyone could get off.

I headed for the adjoining courtroom. I had no idea what case it was; I only knew it was in session — that was what mattered. The door creaked as I opened it, and I staggered slightly as I made my way down the centre aisle, letting out a belch as I approached the front. The judge stopped mid-sentence and peered over his glasses at me. His hard stare offered a stern warning and spoke just as loudly as any words could have. I headed for the bench at the front, on which sat the only other 5 people in the viewing area. I perched on the end, making the others already there scoot down, and with it causing a purposeful commotion. With the disruption apparently over, the judge continued his regurgitation of several state laws. I wasn't paying attention; now all I had to do was simply wait for the right moment to crop up so I could put my plan into action.

"So, bearing in mind everything I have just stated, I see no reason why the motion can't be granted," the judge concluded.

This was it — now or never.

"That's bullshit," I shouted, in my best, slightly slurred Irish accent.

Everyone looked at me. I stood, to make it clear who'd spoken.

"Excuse me?" the judge said.

"I said it's bullshit. How can you just let a killer get away with it?" I pointed at an old guy in front, who stared back, bemused.

"Look, sonny," the judge said, "I'm not sure what you're on about, but you're interrupting my court, and I don't take kindly to that. Any more and I'll have you arrested for contempt."

"Have me arrested? Oh yeah, I hear you like men shackled up."

A few sniggers from those beside me — maybe I'd hit a nerve.

"Right, that's it. Clyde, arrest this idiot."

Clyde, the bailiff, strode towards me with worrying purpose. He looked ready for a fight, so I simply held out my wrists and waited for the cuffs. He looked disappointed, but stayed professional as he led me away to the cells. I gave the judge a cheeky smile, which seemed to infuriate him further. So far, part one was going to plan. Nobody had shouted, "That's Eli Miller," and Clyde's wand found nothing that might identify me. As we passed the cells, I realised getting arrested was the easy bit — the next part relied on pure luck. I tried to improve the odds by chatting to Clyde.

"That Edwin Jameson — he's a real piece of work."

Clyde gave me a sideways glance but kept quiet.

"Killing those two cops was wrong. Fucking coward."

This time Clyde grunted in approval. I was on the right track.

"These rich pricks think they can get away with anything. Give me a few minutes alone with that guy and I'll show him how useless all that money is in here."

We stopped, did a 180, and headed back the way we'd come. Outside a cell, another officer buzzed the lock, and Clyde kicked the door open.

"Got a visitor for you, Mr Jameson."

In the corner, Jameson sat on a bed. No one else was in the cell, though I could see other prisoners through the adjoining bars.

"Don't let me down, Irish," Clyde muttered, undoing the cuffs and pushing me in. The door slammed, the electronic lock buzzed. Jameson didn't really look at me — I sensed fear. No longer the party host he'd been on his yacht, he was hunched over and doing his best to appear insignificant and not worth bothering with. I gave it a few minutes, then sat beside him on the bed. Amazing. A god somewhere was smiling. A big slice of luck, a bit of determination and some giant balls — and somehow my plan to get arrested and end up in a cell with Jameson had worked.

"So, I see things haven't been going too well for you since we last met."

He looked at me, bewildered.

"I thought you were Irish?" he said, not waiting for an answer. "And I don't think we've met. You don't look like someone who mingles in my circles."

I smiled at the irony. Change the clothes, add a beard, and apparently I was a different person. I'd hoped dropping the Irish accent would be enough; clearly I needed to explain.

"If you say so. I seem to remember your yacht being fairly plush, and your daughter being very pleasant. We spent some cherished moments dancing."

He sized me up, his brain searching for a match between my face and a name. After a brief pause, he spoke, still trying to rationalise.

"Your accent's British, but you don't look anything like the only Brit I've spent time with recently."

"Looks can be deceiving," I said, gently removing one of my contacts.

"Now I'm confused," he said, getting up and pacing the eight-foot length of the cell. "Eli Miller is sitting in my cell, in some sort of disguise, apparently arrested for something or other. From what you told me that night, I probably have you to thank for all this. Although my contacts in the UK confirmed your story to the letter, so why exactly ARE you in my cell? Hopefully this isn't your idea of breaking me out. Don't tell me… you're now working for the FBI and they need my confession to actually stand any chance of keeping me in here? Do you think I'm going to admit all, just because you danced with my daughter?"

"I guess you don't watch the news very often. I'm here with a very different agenda."

"I have too much going on in my life to sit and watch the telly."

"Well, as it happens, I'm also wanted in connection with the murder of Steve and Eva."

"I'm guessing you mean the two I am accused of killing?"

"Yeah, that's right."

"And you have voluntarily got yourself arrested — albeit for something else? You really are insane. Isabella is normally such a good judge of men. She clearly misjudged you."

"Correct on all counts, but it was the only way for me to get to you."

"And what is it you think I'm going to do for you?"

"Clear my name."

His laugh was sharp, short and cutting.

"Okay… and what is it you think I can tell you that will help? Has it not occurred to you that I'm also innocent? After all, they want you for the same crime, yet you're here telling me you had nothing to do with it either."

That really got me mad.

"Damn it, they were my friends. You killed my friends, you bastard. I ought to beat the fuck out of you right now."

"Yeah… and that's going to help you how?"

"Maybe not at all, but having watched them both die at your orders, it'll help quash the helpless feeling I have each night while I'm trying to go to sleep."

"Look, let's get one thing straight. I didn't kill your friends, and I definitely didn't order someone else to do the job."

"And I guess you know nothing about the guys who died near your warehouse in Seattle?"

"What guys? What warehouse?"

"Oh, come on. It was their deaths that got me involved in this to begin with."

"Let me ask you something, Eli. What makes you so convinced I'm guilty?"

"Who else would want all four of us dead? You, Jurgen and Isabella were the only ones who knew about the FBI connections. Two days later a hit team's out on the streets trying to kill us all. What other conclusion would you like me to come to? Add to that the two dead agents in Seattle who were also investigating you. I've seen the files the FBI has on you, and let me tell you — it's a rainforest, pal."

"Ah, the FBI. The truth, the whole truth and nothing but the truth, huh? Ever considered they got it wrong?"

"Possibly. But then how do you explain the two goons from your club in our house on the day of the attack?"

"That, I'll admit to. I sent them to check your place out. I was about to arrange a slightly less-than-legal business deal with you and your friends. I was potentially exposing myself to a lot of risk."

"Sure — and remove the listening devices you had them plant."

He stopped pacing and looked at me.

"Now you've lost me. What listening devices?"

"Oh, come on — we found one in the kitchen area."

"You're a long way off the mark with your 'facts'. You've met Randy and Maurice. Do you really think they've the intelligence to plant and monitor a listening device?"

He had a point. Neither of them had given me the vibe that they even had a high-school diploma.

"They're simply muscle — nothing more. Not particularly loyal either. I heard they didn't turn up to work for a few days."

It was my turn to smile, despite how confused I felt.

"I think I had something to do with that. Let's just say we ran into each other, they lost their clothes, and ended up stuck on either side of a door. Perhaps they rethought their life choices after that."

"Right, whatever. So I'm guessing your friends at the Bureau found them and used their own 'lawful' blackmail to get them to rat me out?"

"Maybe so. So let me ask you — if you didn't plant the bugs, who did?"

"Not something I know the answer to, but I'm sure if you give it some thought you can find someone more guilty than me to accuse. There is actually an answer staring you in the face."

I really wasn't sure what to believe. Everything I'd been told at the Academy said this guy was lying through his arse. But sitting in a cell with him, I wasn't so sure. His answers were perfectly plausible; in fact, he'd practically convinced me on the bug issue. There was no way his two bouncers knew what to do with tech that complicated. If that was true, he had no reason to try to kill us. And as he said, my story had checked out to the letter, so my credibility with him was pretty good. Logically, if he wanted to work with us, why would he want us dead? As I processed it all, the next logical answer was an inside man — and that could only be one person. Isaiah.

We sat in silence for another ten minutes before Jameson broke it.

"So, what exactly is the FBI investigating me for?"

I was too deep in my own thoughts to think clearly and answered without much caution.

"Drug smuggling and gun-running."

"No wonder they're putting all this effort in. Shame it's not me they really want."

"How do you mean?"

"Well, it appears our beloved FBI has miscalculated. I'm a legitimate businessman. The people I do business with may not be, but there's nothing linking me to illegal guns or drugs. Admittedly, I compromised my morals many years ago to get some capital behind me. But for the last five to ten years — me, my business, my family — we've all been legit."

"So when I met you last week, it was quite clear I was proposing joining you in the drug-trafficking business, and you seemed only too willing to take us on."

"This is true. However, what you fail to understand, and what I purposely omitted, is that I act as a middleman for someone else. And before you ask — I don't know who. I simply rent out my freighters to them and occasionally direct some business their way."

"So basically, you're a pimp for drug dealers."

"You put it crudely, but accurately enough, I guess."

"And you get, what, 40%? That's the going rate for pimps?"

"No — more like 10%. But that's plenty when you're dealing in the figures I do."

"So let me get this straight. You want me to believe that while you have questionable morals, you're actually squeaky clean."

"Squeaky clean? No. A dirty white is perhaps more accurate. I've invested everything I've made over the years in property and software. That's where my fortune comes from. Before I incriminate myself any further, consider this: in all my years in this city I've not once been arrested, not once been questioned, not once been accused of a crime. If they really had anything on me, do you think the mayor, civic leaders and the governor of California would be close personal friends of mine? Don't you think their advisers would have warned them off?"

He had strong arguments — so strong I was starting to believe him; though it wouldn't be the first time high-profile politicians had cosied up to criminals. Which meant I was most likely wasting my time in this cell and not getting much from the meeting. We didn't speak again, and it wasn't long before Clyde returned to take Jameson away and leave me on my own to contemplate the conversation.

"One thing before you go?" I asked.

"Go on."

"Do you know anything about a company called Alden Matzoh?"

"No. Never heard of it. You should speak to my daughter; she's the business brain in my empire."

I just nodded, while internally the disappointment slowly seeped into every part of my body.

I spent the rest of the day in the cell, sharing it with a mixture of unsavoury characters. Eventually the door opened and Clyde led me out and back up to the courtroom where I'd been arrested that morning. Declining representation, the judge got on with it — apparently he had a round of golf to play.

"So, what do you have to say for yourself, Mr...?"

"It's O'Hanlen. Fergal O'Hanlen, sir," I said, slipping back into the Irish accent and picking the most Irish name I could think of.

"Well, Mr O'Hanlen, I don't take kindly to interruptions, nor to the insinuations you made about me. I hope you've a good explanation."

"Well, Your Honour, it's my Irish nature. I'm naturally outspoken, and I'd heard what that Jameson character was accused of, and I couldn't help expressing my view. When I thought you'd let him off, well…"

"Let me stop you there. The trial you interrupted was not Mr Jameson's, but a divorce hearing for a couple from Oakland. I believe Mr Jameson's bail hearing was next door with Judge Roosen."

"Oh… I'm such an eejit. Please forgive me, Your Honour." I had to grovel — the last thing I needed was a night in a cell that smelt like it had been freshened with urine-scented spray.

"An easy mistake to make. But tell me one thing before I rule. Why do you hate Mr Jameson so much? From what I understand, he's a respectable member of the community."

Awkward, given I was beginning to think something similar.

"Well, you see, my closest friend was killed in a drug war back home. Ever since, I've carried a hatred for drug dealers, which — from what I hear — is what Mr Jameson is."

"I sympathise, sonny, but we have laws and processes for a reason. You can't walk into a courtroom and shout whatever you like, no matter how valid your reasons."

"Yes, sir. My time in the cells has made me realise that. I'm truly sorry, Your Honour. I'll have to learn to control my feelings — but it's my Irish blood."

"Tell me about it. My wife is Irish, and she has a distressing lack of self-restraint," the judge smiled. "You seem genuine and remorseful. I think a day in the cells is enough to make you think twice next time, so you're free to go."

A wave of relief spread over me.

"Thank you, Your Honour. I won't forget the grace you've shown me today."

I felt like a tool kissing his arse like that, but it was necessary if I was to walk out a free man. I turned and left before he changed his mind. I caught a taxi back to my hotel, let the doorman pay the fare, and headed up to my room. I spent half an hour under the shower trying to scrub the smell of the cells off me, then ordered a huge pizza and some beers to replenish my depleted energy levels.

Chapter 49

The following morning was a very confusing time for me. This time yesterday I was expecting to have uncovered the truth and be halfway to clearing my name. Instead, I now felt further away than before. Unsurprisingly, the more I thought about it, the more unsettled I felt, and as midday approached I found myself seeking solace in a burger, fries and a chocolate shake. As I travelled to the lobby, the previously unnoticed lift music almost set me off into a rage. I mean — Engelbert Humperdinck. For the love of God. A piece of classical music would have been a much more appropriate choice for a hotel like this.

As I stepped into the lobby, I glanced right and caught the silhouette of a lady getting into the express lift. I'd already taken two steps the other way — by which point the doors had closed — before my brain registered that she was someone I knew. My gut told me I wasn't mistaken, but the logical part of my brain suggested it was highly unlikely to be who I thought. Either way, I decided to wait and see what floor she stopped at. The lift carried on past my 15th floor and finally stopped at 29. I only knew it was close to the top — maybe even the penthouse. I dashed to reception to satisfy my curiosity.

"Can I help you, Mr Michaels?" asked the receptionist.

I was still looking back at the lift area and it didn't immediately occur to me she was talking to me.

"Oh — yeah. Hi, Lori."

She smiled back. It was one of those trained smiles, not the sort I was accustomed to receiving from a lady I'd been flirting with. I guess the beard didn't suit me.

"I was wondering — I could swear I just saw a friend of mine getting into one of the lif… elevators. I just wanted to check if it really was her."

I purposely switched to calling them elevators at this point. The number of blank looks I'd had over the years from Americans when I'd referred to lifts had taught me that adapting my language to the local dialect sometimes made things flow more smoothly.

"Okay… do you have a name for me?"

"Oh, right — that would help. Miss Jameson. Miss Isabella Jameson."

She tapped a few keys and waited.

"Your eyes must be deceiving you, Mr Michaels. There is nobody by that name staying here."

"Oh… okay. Errr, thanks, Lori," I mumbled, barely able to believe I'd been wrong — despite the logical part of my brain telling me as much.

"No problem," she smiled. "Have a good day."

I stepped away, still convinced it had been her. I reached the main entrance and, still not quite able to believe I was wrong, figured I'd try my luck with the valet. Hopefully my generous tips had bought me access to his knowledge about the hotel's comings and goings.

"Hey, Eric."

"What's up, Mr Michaels? Going to do some sightseeing?"

338

"Yeah — Alcatraz. But I was hoping you could help me with something first."

"Sure, name it."

"A woman just came in..."

"That was no woman. She's a lady through and through. First-rate lady. Bit out of your league, though. No offence."

"None taken," I laughed. "You know her?"

"Only to look at. Beautiful curves, if you get my drift. You've seen the rest."

"But she's staying here, right?"

"Oh yeah. Checked in a few days ago. Tips as big as you."

I smiled, thanked him, and slipped him a twenty. I headed straight back in to see Lori.

"Hello, Mr Michaels," came her slightly weary reply — probably already knowing what I was about to ask.

"Lori, I've been thinking and I'm convinced it was my friend. Maybe she's staying under a different name. Her elevator stopped at 29, if that's any help."

"Floor 29 only has four rooms so, as I'm sure you can imagine, I'm aware of exactly who you're asking about. She is a valued customer of the hotel and I simply can't give you her details."

"I understand, but she really would appreciate seeing me."

"No doubt, Mr Michaels," she replied as cordially as possible, "but I simply can't help you with this. You could always just call her, given that she's such a good friend."

This time her smile — and the sarcastic tone — said, "Checkmate." She was right: I didn't have a plausible answer for that suggestion.

"I understand. Thanks anyway."

I forgot all about my previous plans and headed back to the lifts. Unsurprisingly, the express button just flashed red when I swiped my room card over it. Plan B was to use one of the "common people's" lifts and travel as far as I could, which turned out to be floor 20. Once out of the lift I followed the signs for the stairwell and started my ascent. I once ran up ten floors after betting a friend I was faster than the lift. Not only did I lose, I almost collapsed from oxygen starvation when I finally made it. With this in mind, I started the climb at a more sedate pace, careful with my breathing — despite being overwhelmed with anxiety at potentially talking to Isabella. By the time I reached the door to 29, my quads were burning and my lungs were definitely not enjoying the hot, humid air of the stairwell.

Chapter 50

I stepped through the door and into a different world compared with the rest of the hotel. There were no long corridors flanked by multiple doors leading to countless cookie-cutter rooms — just a large foyer decked out in marble and what looked like solid oak and mahogany. Four doors: two in front, one on either side. It wouldn't take much to knock on each before I found the right one. The only problem with my plan was that annoying guests on the 29th floor could quickly lead to me being forcibly removed by security.

Outside one room was the remains of room service — too much food for Isabella alone — so that left three. Someone had left a pair of brogues to be polished outside another, leaving me with two. My chances had halved, so I picked the door to my left and knocked.

No answer.

I tried the last door — nothing.

I was about to turn and leave when I heard faint footsteps.

"Yes?" came the surprisingly soft response from the large, casually dressed man, most likely a distant relative of the vikings, who had opened the door.

"Hi," I said, forcing my tone to sound friendly.

I paused, waiting for a response. Nothing. So I decided to end the awkwardness myself.

"I'm expected."

"Not by me you're not. Which means nobody here is expecting you."

Maybe I had it wrong, but I figured there was no harm in pushing a bit more. Worst case: I got told to fuck off.

"Look, pal, Miss Jameson is expecting me."

He looked a little surprised. That pause told me all I needed: I was at the right door.

"There's nobody here by that name. Now get lost."

"I'll tell you what, I'll let that one go. Now, tell Isabella that Eli Miller would like to see her — regarding her father."

He shut the door in my face. I wasn't sure what that meant, so I took a seat in the lobby, keeping up a confident façade, hoping that waiting was the right approach. Several minutes passed before the door opened again. The same guy stood there, staring.

"You coming, or what?" he asked at last.

I stretched, got up slowly and ambled past him without the faintest acknowledgement — he was the hired help. Given the Jameson family's status, I figured I should act like a pompous arsehole, letting him know the shit on my shoe was more important.

The hallway led to a large, lavishly decorated communal area. Ultra-thin TVs, leather sofas, ebony cabinets and carpets so deep it was like walking on a cloud — you can picture the rest. Sitting in one of the many chairs was Isabella. She glanced up from her newspaper and looked at me, puzzled.

"I'm sorry, but you must be mistaken. I know you're not Eli, so please leave before I have you removed."

I heard soft footsteps behind me.

"Isabella, it's me. I've had a small makeover since we last met."

My voice, although slightly desperate, seemed to convince her a little.

"Is that really you under all that hair?"

"Yep. Remember, we danced the night away on your dad's yacht. Under the watchful eyes of a friend of mine."

"Yeah, I remember," she said, pausing as memories resurfaced. "What are you doing here?"

"I need to speak with you."

"What — so you can indict me on some bullshit charges as well? Forget it."

She was visibly upset, beginning to snarl — not a good look for such a pretty woman.

"Myles, please escort Mr Miller out."

As I felt heavy hands on my shoulders, I played the only card I had left.

"Your father was much more accommodating with his time."

She glared at me, then waved Myles off.

"Go on."

"I spoke with him yesterday."

"Not possible. He's in jail."

"I know. So was I."

I explained everything that had happened the day before. By the time I finished, I was sitting comfortably on the sofa, with an intrigued Isabella by my side.

"So let me get this straight. The FBI think you're working for them, but now they've put out an all-points bulletin for your arrest. Meanwhile, you've been trying to clear your name to the extent of getting yourself arrested just to speak with Dad."

"You got it in one."

"That's one of the most absurd stories I've heard in a long time. So, what is it you think I can help you with?"

"Help me get out from under this thing."

"And what do I gain?"

"I think it may be possible to prove your dad is innocent."

"Now you have my attention."

"Well, he told me he acts as a middleman — recommends groups like the one I "represented" to a third party who handles all the illegal stuff."

"Mmm. Until the other night, I'd have said that was inaccurate. After you left, Dad and I had a long chat and it appears he is involved in some bad stuff — stuff he'd kept from me. It was the first I'd heard of it."

My sceptical face must have shown, because she looked almost shocked that I hadn't immediately believed her.

"The way you were conducting business on the boat the other night looked like a woman who knew exactly what she was involved in."

"That was business, pure and simple. A negotiation needed to be done, so I took control. The whats, whys and wherefores could be dealt with afterwards. You, of all people, should know the importance of negotiating from a position of strength."

She had a point. If true, it also showed just how shrewd she was — not to mention her ability to analyse and resolve a situation quickly. Before I could reply, she pressed on.

"Sure, I knew he had contacts in customs and helped clients dodge import taxes. But honestly, that's all I know. I still doubt he's told me the full story, and I'm starting to realise my dad might not be as clean as I'd like to believe."

She was either playing this beautifully or was genuinely clueless. Her tone leaned me towards the latter. Or maybe I was just falling for the spell of a beautiful, manipulative woman.

"Now, I hope you're about to tell me your fleet of container ships is involved?"

"Not really — or at least not as far as I know. We lease several ships, but not for illegal activity. All that stuff is above board. As I said, it's really only the occasional tax-avoidance scheme that my dad helps out with."

"Shit. I thought I was onto something."

I explained what had happened in Seattle.

"Matzoh... rings a bell. Give me a minute."

She pulled a laptop from under the sofa, tapped a few keys, then spun it towards me.

"Alden Matzoh is a company we deal with. Not much info — import/export stuff via our fleet. I've never even met the guy. All correspondence is via email. They make sizeable, regular payments. What's weird is that there are absolutely no details about what we're billing them for."

"Are you sure there's nothing else?"

"Nope. I know all of Dad's questionable dealings, and I'm pretty sure this isn't one of them."

She paused.

"Thinking about it, ages ago I did meet a representative from this Alden Matzoh company. He came out to one of Dad's parties on the yacht. I didn't really speak to him much, more of a quick introduction. Can't say I remember much about him. He was a pretty nondescript guy, middle aged, a bit out of shape. Other than being a little sleazy, he wasn't very memorable."

Well, I'd not made much progress, but at least there was a clear link between the Alden Matzoh Corporation and

Jameson. I didn't know if that meant anything, but I guess it was something to work with. Disappointingly, her description of the only known employee of Alden Matzoh described practically every middle-aged man in America, and effectively made that avenue a dead end. Not wanting to appear ungrateful for her time, and hopefully her honesty, I did my best to hide my disappointment.

"Well, I guess it's something. Thanks."

"Is it enough to get my dad out of jail?"

"I don't think so," I said after a pause. "But if I can find out who this guy is, then I'm fairly confident it'll give us leverage."

I needed time to think. I got up, and Isabella rose too.

"Perhaps... you'd like to stay a while? Seems like we could both do with unwinding."

"Another time," I lied, hopefully convincingly.

The last thing I needed was to piss off one of the few allies I had left.

"I need time to get my head straight."

Without waiting for a reply — or seeing the disappointment on her face — I turned and headed for the door. To my relief, the lift going down didn't need a passkey, so I rode it straight to the lobby. Eric had me in a taxi less than thirty seconds later, and before long I was back on the ferry to Alcatraz. It seemed I just couldn't get enough of prisons right now.

Chapter 51

I wandered and pondered for the next few days, hoping for inspiration that simply wouldn't come. I was painfully aware that I had absolutely nothing — just the name of an import/export business that didn't exist online and the vaguest description of its owner. About as useful as being told life sucks, which was already apparent.

I'd discovered a fantastic coffee house that doubled as a cigar shop. It had become my regular spot over the past two days — so much so that I'd even started smoking again. It was pretty much the only thing I could enjoy. The reality of trying to go home, knowing my passport would likely trigger a SWAT team at the check-in desk, had been gnawing at me.

With my car far too recognisable, I was left with buses, the metro or taxis. Cash was tight, so taxis were out, leaving even fewer options. On top of it all, I had no motivation to enjoy anything. My future felt like it had one destination: twenty-five to life.

A radio broadcast, struggling to compete with the daily café hubbub, convinced me to waste the afternoon watching the 49ers. They'd been playing decent football in recent years, so it wouldn't be a total waste. At least it would take my mind off things.

The game was good, with the usual grandstand finish in the 4th quarter. The journey back involved an hour-long ride on the BART Green Line. Surrounded by fans, I managed to block out the noise and concoct a plausible strategy for the following day. Although I'd wanted an early night, I decided to take advantage of being across the bay to see Jonny. I wasn't sure what to expect, but I hoped he might have dug up something on the heist.

I changed trains at West Oakland, taking the Red Line to Downtown Berkeley. Being game day, cabs were plentiful, and I was soon heading into the hills. I didn't know Jonny's exact address, so I had to rely on memory to direct the driver. Once we'd passed the house, I gave it another 200 metres before telling him to pull over. That way I hoped Jonny wouldn't be automatically flagged as involved if the driver recognised me. I waited until the tail lights disappeared, then spun round and headed back.

After a short walk and a quick shoulder check to make sure I wasn't being tailed, I knocked gently, stepped back and waited. The door yanked open and there was Jonny — beer in one hand, fat cigar in the other. He just stared. I couldn't tell if he was surprised or annoyed to see me. Either way, waiting to find out wasn't on my agenda.

"You got one of those for me?" I asked casually, pointing to the beer as I stepped forward, signalling my intention to not wait for an invitation.

"In the kitchen," he muttered, stepping aside, running a hand through his hair before closing the door softly.

I perched on a barstool, cracked open a Bud, and waited for Jonny to join me. It didn't take long before he ambled in and stood opposite, eyes fixed on me, not looking overly pleased.

"Dude, this is not cool. Don't get me wrong — I'm happy to see you in one piece. But you're still hot property in this city. Phone calls and secret meetings are one thing, but coming to my house? Even I don't have the juice to handle this."

I took a couple of swigs, sighed deep and slow.

"I know. I know. What can I say? I'm sorry. I'm in up to my neck and there's no way out right now. I needed to see a friendly face — it's lonely out there."

"And I don't suppose this visit has anything to do with our call the other day?"

"Well... I can hardly say it wasn't on the agenda, but — "

He held up his hand, set his bottle firmly on the counter, and strode round the bar. For a moment, I thought I was about to catch a right hook. I braced, recoiling slightly, ready for the blow. Instead, he wrapped his arms around my shoulders and pulled me in close. The hug lasted just long enough for me to know it was genuine.

"Sorry, man."

"No way. This is all on me, mate. No apology needed."

"Let's just call it what it is — a shitty stick. And you've been left holding it."

"I'm not going to disagree," I said, and we clinked beers almost in sync.

"Look, make yourself comfortable. I've got a call to make. I need to speak with a buddy. Crystal's out for the evening, staying with friends, so put whatever you want on the box, okay?"

Without waiting for a reply, he grabbed his phone and disappeared into another room, out of earshot of the TV. He was gone ten, maybe fifteen minutes. In that time I'd opened another beer, raided the snacks, and started watching Top Gun: Maverick. Jonny eventually snuck back in and dropped onto the sofa beside mine, snatching the crisps without a word. I figured I'd give him time before pushing for info.

I tried to get into the film — it wasn't as bad as I'd expected for a sequel — but something was niggling me. My gut had been working overtime these past weeks, and I'd been learning to trust it. I looked over at Jonny, chomping through a bag of Lays, eyes on the screen. Pretty normal, except I'd never known him to watch more than five minutes of a film. That set alarm bells ringing.

The longer it went on, the more suspicious I became. I was just about to test the waters with a question when the doorbell rang.

Jonny shot up so quickly I'm positive that he knew the bell was about to go, like he'd been waiting for it. As he disappeared to the front of the house I couldn't help but get up and prepare myself for the worst. At the very least I knew something unexpected was about to happen. I strained to hear the voices but all I got was silence, until the sound of returning footsteps could be heard. Only it was more than one pair, if anything it sounded like three. Once again I listened. Once again there was no talking. If these were Jonny's friends there was no way it would be this quiet. There would be all kinds of jovial banter going on. Had he screwed me over? But how and why?

The first question was answered almost immediately as Jonny walked in with two other guys. Both were dressed in dark coloured pants and light coloured shirts with the top buttons undone and their ties loosened. My eyes were immediately drawn not to their faces but to their belts where I saw that each had a holstered pistol and, more concerningly, both had golden SFPD badges glinting in the room lights.

Chapter 52

O h shit, Jonny had truly fucked me. My instinct was to run, but that would only get me shot, so I stood still, gripping the barstool in front of me. I locked eyes with Jonny, who didn't look particularly apologetic.

"Eli, it's not what you think," he blurted, clearly reading the anger and shock on my face. "These guys are friends, I promise."

"They're fucking cops, Jonny. Remember thirty minutes ago when we agreed I was in a whole heap of trouble? Well, these guys are right up there on the list of people I don't need to be seeing right now."

"I didn't have a choice, OK. I… "

"Hey, you two," one of them cut in, firm. "We haven't come out here to listen to you bicker like two old women at the launderette. Park it until we've had a chance to chat with Mr Miller."

"I ain't saying shit to you," I replied, staring unblinking at both of them.

"Fine by me," said the quieter one. "You think we don't have a heap of other work? You don't want to talk, then put these on and we'll go earn ourselves a pat on the back and a medal from the mayor."

He reached not for his pistol but behind his back for a set of handcuffs, placed them on the worktop and, with a firm shove, slid them towards me. This was not how I'd seen the evening going. I stood in silence, trying to conjure a plan that didn't end with me in shackles. Jonny's voice interrupted before I made any headway.

"Eli," he pleaded, "you need to give these guys a chance. They're IA."

Internal Affairs. Suddenly, a little less threatening — and a lot more interesting. I wasn't about to treat them like old friends, but at least there was an opportunity. I just needed to play it right.

"You know who Internal Affairs are, right?" asked the first cop.

"Yeah. You guys are the cops' cops."

"Exactly. So I'm sure you can connect the dots and figure out we've got legitimate concerns about the info you asked Jonny to get you."

"OK. So what do you know?"

"Come on, Mr Miller. We're not about to tell you details of an active IA case without first hearing what you have for us."

I looked at them both for a good thirty seconds, then decided I had nothing to lose and everything to gain. I explained the whole thing — well, what they needed to know. It took about fifteen minutes, with pauses for questions and clarifications.

"So let me sum this up, because that's some crazy-ass story," said Detective Stewart — the one who'd cut Jonny and me off earlier. "The FBI asked you and three of their own agents — two of whom were gunned down in the street a couple of weeks ago — to carry out a jewellery-store heist and help them resolve a long-running, high-profile case. Just before you committed these multiple felonies, four other guys on motorbikes carried out the exact same job, right in front of you. SFPD killed two at the scene, and now you're telling us the other two were killed in a fake hit-and-run in Northern California last week."

"That's about the size of it," I said with a resigned sigh, taking a swig to moisten my very dry mouth.

"And on top of that, Edwin Jameson — currently in jail for murdering the agents — is somehow connected, but denies involvement in any recent events. He is, however, claiming high-level protection within law enforcement and that there's another layer above him."

I nodded.

The two officers spoke quietly for several minutes, as if I wasn't there. I sensed disagreement and that I might be about to get screwed over for the umpteenth time that evening. I took the bull by the horns and cut in.

"So?"

"So what?" asked Stewart, clearly irritated.

"So what's the deal? I've told you my end. What do you know? What's the big picture?"

Stewart stared impassively; his partner, Dawson, was more fidgety. They clearly disagreed on what came next.

"Well…"

"Dawson, I'm warning you," Stewart snapped. "If you say anything, you'll be on traffic duty before sunrise."

Dawson looked conflicted.

"Ah, fuck it. He deserves to know," he said, first at his partner, then at me. "Since the robbery, we've heard unusual chatter from officers on the street. You were told there was no ID on the two killed at the scene — well, that hasn't officially changed. We ran prints, DNA, tattoos — the whole nine yards — through every database in North America. Nothing. The thing is, they've both got jailhouse tats, and several officers swear they knew them. Kind of weird the computer says they're first-timers, wouldn't you say?"

That was a step in the right direction. I kept quiet and let him run with it.

"That's when we got involved. That kind of thing doesn't happen by accident. The accident up north crossed our desk a few days ago — by pure luck. A state trooper at the scene had witnessed the heist while holidaying in the city and recognised the bikes as similar colours. What do you think we found?"

"Nothing?" I asked, hopeful.

"Exactly. Almost a carbon copy. The two dead guys were as clean as a nun's browser history — but covered in prison tats. We've been showing their pics around and, guess what? Several of the city's most beloved degenerates recognise them — and know their names. What's more, our intel suggests they all served time in the same prison. Four guys, all career criminals, suddenly looking like boy scouts? Absolutely no way. That's no coincidence. Someone's been turning them into ghosts on purpose."

"So you reckon there's a dirty cop?"

"Hell yes — maybe more than one. And from what you've told us, sounds like the FBI's up to its neck too," Stewart said, now clearly on board with airing this out.

I wasn't about to disagree. Holtzman felt like the prime suspect now that I knew national databases had been touched. If Steve were alive, he'd have been high on the list, but it's hard to make a case against a dead man. And Isaiah... that phone call where he'd all but sold me out still didn't sit right. Maybe there was a side to him I didn't know. Let's face it, I'd only known him six weeks. Time to capitalise on the moment — and their suspicion that there was a traitor to unmask.

"Well, I don't think I can give you names, but I might be able to do the next best thing."

"Go on," Stewart said.

"Things started going sideways when the robbery went down, but it snowballed when Steve found a bug in our house. He said it was 'super high-tech' — the kind government agencies might use. I'd bet if you searched the house you'd find more. Might lead you somewhere."

"Could be a start," Dawson nodded.

"And if you speak to Jonny, he'll give you the details of the guy who looked over my car. I'm pretty sure he can give you something that might help narrow it down."

"Why don't you just give us the name of your case officer?" asked Dawson. "Seems like they're either working for Jameson or pulling the strings."

I didn't disagree — but I wasn't going to drop Jessica in it. So far she was practically the only person I didn't suspect. Also, the last thing I needed was the wrong person being tipped off and going to ground. Regardless of promises, their priority wouldn't be clearing my name. They wanted crooked cops — even better if the FBI got embarrassed. If I ended up in jail in the meantime, so be it.

"No can do. Sorry."

"In case you forgot, you're not exactly negotiating from a position of strength."

"Maybe not. But I think I've given you enough to know I'm not involved the way it's being spun."

"Maybe," Dawson said, "but you're still wanted by pretty much every agency in the city."

"Exactly. Nobody's working this from the angle of me being innocent, so I still need a way out — even if I have to do the hard yards myself. What I don't need is you two asking the wrong people the right questions — tipping them off and letting them get ahead of what's coming."

"And what exactly is coming?" Stewart asked, wary.

"Justice," I said, meaning every syllable.

"Can't argue with that," he said after a beat. "As long as you're not planning any felonies along the way."

I gave him my best butter-wouldn't-melt face and decided to end it before he changed his mind.

"So, we have a deal?"

"Just so we're all clear," Stewart said. "If anything you've told us tonight turns out even one per cent untrue, I'll drive you to the bridge and personally throw you off. Understand?"

"Loud and clear," I said, deciding not to joke about police brutality.

"OK, then give us the address of the house. We'll get the rest from Jonny. If you find anything else, you tell us five seconds later. OK?"

"Got it."

"And don't forget where you're staying," added Dawson coyly. "In case we need to speak to you again."

I gave them the Hyde Street address. There wasn't a hope I'd tell them where I was actually staying, so I named a guesthouse I'd seen in Sea Cliff. I just had to hope they were focused enough on the IA angle not to immediately check. Things were heading roughly where I wanted — albeit with an added variable I'd hoped to avoid. I kept quiet and let them quiz Jonny a little longer.

"Mr Miller, we're heading off. Need a lift into town?"

Though Stewart phrased it like a question, it felt like an order.

"I'll drop him back, Don," Jonny said before I could answer.

Stewart glanced at Jonny, held his gaze a second, then nodded and turned on his heel, Dawson right behind him. They moved with purpose — like men who had the bit between their teeth and were ready to arrest some of their own.

Jonny and I didn't speak for a minute. I broke the silence.

"I need to get out of here."

"On it, pal," he said, snatching car keys from a shelf and heading for the garage.

There was no sign of SFPD as we pulled onto the road but I still kept half an eye on the mirrors as we headed to West Oakland BART. I could tell Jonny was building up to something, so I gave him space.

"Heh, man, I'm really sorry about what went down back at the house."

I held up a hand to stop him. I'd moved past the initial anger and accepted Jonny wouldn't have done it without reason.

"I got you involved. I should be apologising for showing up out of the blue. You're the only friendly face I know in the city."

"Maybe. But you need to understand — when I reached out to Stewart after your call, he was at my place about thirty minutes later. The questions you asked triggered alarm bells in IA. I basically wasn't given a choice. If they found out I'd been in touch with you again, I'd be arrested immediately — and they made it clear I wouldn't be farting without them knowing. If there's one thing I know about this city, it's that you don't get on the wrong side of the cops."

"Don't sweat it, OK? I put you between a rock and a hard place. You made the right choice. End of."

Another word didn't pass between us during the final ten minutes of the journey. As we pulled up at the station, a question struck me.

"Those guns you left me — are they clean? Any link back to you?"

"Nope. No connection at all."

"Good. Last thing you need is the ATF on your arse. Listen, this is it as far as I'm concerned. You won't be seeing or hearing from me again. You've done more than enough, and this thing is close to blowing up. You don't need to be anywhere near it when it does."

"Eli… "

"No, Jonny. You're done."

I stuck out my right hand; he clasped it and shook firmly — accepting he'd done his bit for me. I unbuckled and cracked the door.

"There is one more thing you can do for me."

"Name it."

"If I don't make it out the other side of this, give them hell for me."

"Done deal."

I nodded my head in respect and acknowledgement of this before getting out and disappeared up to the platform.

Chapter 53

Despite the drama of the previous evening — and at least two SFPD officers knowing I was in the city — I slept well and woke feeling refreshed and invigorated. Once again, I headed to the courthouse. Despite taking a taxi this time, it still took me fifteen–twenty minutes, and I was a little stressed I'd be too late. Once I'd been dropped off, I went straight for coffee rather than the courtrooms. My luck was in: still chatting away was a group of reporters, a few I recognised from last time. With no big cases today, the media circus was nowhere to be seen — these were clearly the daily court reporters. I got a coffee, sat, and waited. One by one they grabbed their gear and headed upstairs, leaving one guy on his own. Perfect — he was one I'd eavesdropped on the other day. I wandered over.

"Hey there. Mind if I sit here?"

"There are plenty of other tables, but help yourself. I'm going in a minute."

"Thanks." I paused. "Listen, weren't you covering the Jameson case the other day?"

"Yeah. What of it?"

"Just wondering."

His journalist senses had obviously kicked in; he was now giving me his full attention.

"You got something for me?" he asked, lowering his voice.

"Maybe — but I need something in return."

"How much?" he shot back. "Bear in mind anything over $500 and my editor needs to authorise it, and he's a skinflint."

"Is he Scottish?" I asked — then realised the joke would be lost on him. "Never mind. I'm after more than a payday."

That was obviously a new one on him.

"Go on."

"Peter Owens. I want a meeting."

He sat back slowly without breaking eye contact.

"Why?" he said at last. He'd made the connection immediately: a stranger asking about an investigative reporter tied to the city's biggest case in years.

"Because I have some info that may interest him."

"And what do I get out of it?" he asked after a beat.

"How about the first interview with Edwin Jameson when he's acquitted?"

"Don't you mean if?"

"No — I mean when."

He had a lot to think about and paused again.

"OK. Give me a number."

"I'm staying at the St Regis — room 1527. The name is Michaels."

"I'll see what I can do. No promises."

Before I could thank him, he'd left the table and headed upstairs, camera dangling and satchel over his shoulder. With things in motion, all I could do was sit in my hotel room, cross my fingers, and wait.

I spent the rest of the day in my room, patiently waiting for the phone to ring. It never did. I called down countless times to ask Lori if there were any messages — so many that she started answering with, "No, Mr Michaels, no messages yet."

TV became boring despite the avalanche of channels, and I finally nodded off sometime around eleven — still in my clothes, of course.

I woke to the faint sound of a ringing phone. It took a moment to realise it was real, not a dream. I fumbled in the dark across the bedside cabinet before finally finding it.

"Hello," I said, semi-comatose.

No answer. I was about to ask again when I realised the receiver was on my ear and I was talking into the earpiece. I spun it round and tried again.

"Hello?"

"Room 1527?"

"Yeah."

"Mr Michaels, then?"

"Yeah. Don't you know what time it is? What do you want?"

"It's more about what you want from me."

That got my attention, but sleep fought for it too.

"There's a cab outside. Get in and go to Candlestick Park."

"Why?" I asked — but the line was already dead.

Well, this was what I'd been waiting for. With renewed energy, I sprang out of bed and splashed water on my face. I looked like hell and could have used an IV drip of pure caffeine, but I was awake enough to function. While I waited what felt like an eternity by the lift, I chewed gum — nothing worse than bed-breath. As promised, a taxi idled outside the doors.

"Mr Michaels?" the driver asked.

"Yep," I said, closing the door behind me.

"Where to?"

"I thought you knew," I said. He shook his head. "Candlestick, please."

"You know the 49ers aren't there anymore?" he said, no doubt pegging me as an out-of-towner from the accent.

"I know," I nodded, then settled back, signalling I'd had enough chat.

It was roughly a ten-minute drive at this time of night; the interstates and roads were quiet. We arrived at the stadium complex in silence.

"Any particular part?"

"Don't really know. Let's just drive around and see if we find anyone."

"Sure thing — it's your dollar."

We drove for several minutes, but nothing obvious was happening. We reached a security fence and a booth with a guard. He stepped out and waved us down.

"Morning, guys. A little early for a meeting, isn't it?"

"I know, Joe," the driver said, "but my fare says Candlestick, so that's where I go."

The guard shone a torch into the back, looked hard at me, then walked off. It was a little disconcerting; security guards in the States consider themselves cops — many of them are armed. I watched him return — his gun still firmly buttoned in its holster. He came straight to my window, which slid down — presumably the driver hit the switch. This was all a little too orchestrated for my liking but what choice did I have.

"Mr Michaels, I've got this for you," he said, handing me an envelope.

A bit surprised and still foggy with sleep, I hesitated before thinking to ask where he'd got it. By the time I'd thought of the question he was almost back in his booth. I tore open the envelope. A small handwritten note fell out — but nothing else.

> *'Even when they're asleep, it still stinks. I hope you haven't been at the whiskey, for your sake.'*

Not really in the same league as the Da Vinci Code, but cryptic enough for me at 3:30 in the morning. I read it to the taxi driver.

"You aren't a proper tourist, are you?" He laughed.

Without another word, he spun the car around, and we were soon back on the interstate.

"So, where are we going?"

"See if you can figure it out. Whoever wrote that note is definitely a local."

That, at least, was encouraging. We almost completely retraced our steps, passing my hotel on the way to our destination. We came to a stop in familiar surroundings — Fisherman's Wharf.

"You need to go down there," the driver pointed.

It was a gangway that led to the waterside. It was surprising to still see a few people around — that was at least reassuring.

"You want me to wait?"

"Err... no, it's okay."

"I handed him a hundred and headed down the gangway. Fisherman's Wharf is a popular tourist area where ferries depart for Bay crossings and trips to Alcatraz. As I walked, a stiff sea breeze jolted me awake, carrying a smell I recognised immediately. The best way to describe it is like a neglected toilet block, only fifty times worse. I instantly understood the riddle in the message and certainly was thankful I hadn't been drinking whiskey — otherwise, it might have come back up. I had been sent to visit the Bay area's sea lions.

As I approached the viewing platform, it was clear no one else was there. Most of the sea lions were asleep, though I could hear a few splashing around in the water. Thankfully, the rest were mostly quiet. I waited for ten minutes, the cold slowly wearing down my resolve. Finally, just as I was beginning to get cold, I decided to take a stroll to get the blood flowing again. I had barely taken three steps when I noticed an envelope flapping in the wind, attached to the railing."

'Thanks for coming, but I don't think so.'

Well, that really pissed me off. Someone had got me out of bed and wasted an hour of my time for absolutely nothing. As I reached the road again, my annoyance grew when I realised there would be no taxis at this time of the morning. Nor would the trams be running, which meant I'd be walking back to the hotel. This guy had really pissed me off — getting me up in the middle of the night was simply not funny. My walk back was fairly uneventful. I passed several groups of homeless people, which in most other cities would have meant problems. The San Franciscan homeless, however, verged on the respectful, happily moving out of your way, smiling at you, and never begging for food or money. It was down to an unofficial city law: bother the tourists, and you'll be bunking with Billy Bob in the state pen faster than a fat kid can eat a cake.

As I finally got back to the hotel, my normally polite English nature had deserted me; I completely ignored the doorman's greeting and headed straight for the lifts. As I pushed my keycard into the slot and waited for the light to turn green, a wave of tiredness swept over me. I didn't even flip the light switch when I entered — just launched myself, fully clothed, onto the king-sized bed.

Sleep was beginning to swallow my consciousness when the quietest of sounds brought me back. I couldn't place it; I only knew it was alien to the room, and it was coming from behind me. I didn't move — more to the point, I didn't dare move. I focused on the sound while trying to filter out the air con and the hum of the TV, which was on standby. After about thirty seconds, I figured it out: someone was breathing. Oh shit. Someone was in the room — sitting in the corner, by the sound of it.

Who?

Why?

And what the hell was I going to do about it?

It could only mean trouble. I stayed still for about a minute, half waiting for my guest to make a move, half trying to come up with a plan. The decision was taken out of my hands.

"I hope you're not asleep, Mr Miller?"

I didn't answer immediately. After a brief pause, I snapped the light on and spun towards the voice. A middle-aged man sat there — neither tall nor short, fairly unremarkable in every way. He could easily have matched the description Isabella had given me a few days ago. One thing was clear: he'd spent more time in sports bars than in a gym. Casually dressed, hair in a messy attempt at a side parting, and geeky tortoiseshell-rimmed glasses halfway down his nose.

My eyes dropped to his hands — empty, as was his lap. The absence of an obvious weapon didn't mean he wasn't armed, but my prospects of not being murdered in my bed had just improved.

"Who the hell are you? And what are you doing in my room?"

"I would have thought you could figure those questions out for yourself."

"The elusive Peter Owens?" I asked after a moment's thought.

He answered with a slow nod.

"Well, you are a prize prick. All you had to do was knock on my door. No need to send me on a midnight tour of the city and then scare the shit out of me by hiding in my room."

"Well, if you're going to be like that, I'll leave you to get back to sleep," he said, starting to rise.

I flew off the bed and blocked his path.

"To hell you will. I want to hear what you've got to say for yourself. Look at it from my point of view: you get me up and send me on a wild goose chase in the middle of the night. I'm a little tired and, obviously, cranky — so bear with me."

He stood for a few seconds, then reached for the bottle of water on the cabinet and sat back down.

"So, Mr Miller — it is Miller and not Michaels, right?"

"Yes, you're correct — it's Miller. Being a journalist, I'm sure you understand me using another name. I hardly think you'd knowingly meet with one of the country's most wanted."

"You're right — hence the little taxi trip. I'm sorry about that, but I needed time to check you out, make sure you didn't have any impure plans for me."

"And how could you be sure I wasn't carrying anything?"

"The way you launched yourself on that bed was a pretty definite sign. I also had the taxi driver check you out — they have a sixth sense for recognising trouble."

"Fair enough."

Silence descended briefly before my uninvited guest continued.

"While I've been waiting for you to return, I've been considering exactly what I can help you with. From where I sit, you're involved in the murder of those FBI agents — which means you're involved with Edwin Jameson, since he's been arrested for said murders. With my life dedicated to the demise of said drug baron, we appear to be on opposite sides."

"Quite the contrary. I've spoken with Jameson over the last few days, and I think we can help each other."

"And what help can you offer me?"

"The truth about your wife's killer."

He stared, anger in his eyes.

"What makes you think it's not Jameson?" he snapped, matching the anger and hurt etched on his face.

"I'm not saying it isn't. However, I'm fairly certain he's innocent of the FBI killings — even though they're undoubtedly linked to drugs. You have background on Jameson's business dealings; I have more information on the current situation than you can shake a stick at. I'm pretty sure we could resolve both our problems if we combined forces."

"And let me guess — you want to clear your name?"

I nodded. He sat in silence for a few minutes, eyes fixed on me.

"I think you're talking crap," he said at last, "but I'm interested to hear what you think you have. If there's one thing I've learnt, it's that a story can never have enough background."

"Right then — let's get started. Where's your stuff?"

"Do you know what time it is?"

"Only too well — thanks to you."

He chuckled, then continued.

"No. You get some sleep and fill up on breakfast. I'll send a car for you around noon."

My face must have screamed mistrust.

"Don't worry — no city tours this time, I promise," he said, placing his hand on his chest — but not over his heart.

With that, he sprang from the chair and left. Despite the exhaustion, excitement kept me awake a little longer. I finally felt like I was getting somewhere. I eventually drifted off — still with the lingering fear that somebody was hiding in the wardrobe, ready to pounce and end it all.

Chapter 54

I slept late — unsurprisingly — and consequently found myself in a hurry. Room service arrived while I was in the shower, and I ate eagerly while getting dressed and simultaneously trying to watch the news. As I finished my toast, Lori called to say a car was waiting for me. With half a piece of toast in my mouth, I hurried to the foyer and was surprised to see the same driver from the night before.

"Uh, uh — no way. He really expects me to get into your cab again?"

"There's no need for distrust this morning, Mr Michaels. Mr Owens has told me where to go, so you can just sit back and relax. It's a quick journey."

I studied him briefly and realised it was irrelevant whether I trusted him or not. If I wanted to see Peter Owens again, I simply had to get into the taxi and hope that neither he nor Peter Owens were messing with me. We drove in silence and, to my relief, it appeared he'd been true to his word. About ten minutes later, we pulled up to a beachside condo.

"3325. That one," he said, pointing at about ten o'clock.

I handed him a twenty.

"Don't worry, Mr Owens has already taken care of it."

"It's not for the fare," I said, pushing the twenty closer.

Without a word, he took the money and slipped it into a small wallet by his seat. As I got out, he nodded in gratitude and tore off, barely allowing me time to make sure the door was fully closed. The house was only a short distance away and within thirty seconds I was knocking. It wasn't a big place, but worth a few bob (that's English slang for money, in case you're wondering) just for the view. I peered through the front window as I waited. To put it simply, it was a mess: papers strewn everywhere, open books scattered across the floor, and what looked like piles of pictures. The door finally opened and an unchanged — possibly even more dishevelled — Peter Owens stood there.

"Don't worry, I wasn't followed," I said as I stepped inside.

"I know, Terrell wouldn't have let that happen."

"Oh," I replied, slightly surprised. "You've your own personal taxi service, do you?"

"Let's just say we have similar beliefs."

I nodded as I walked down the hallway toward the kitchen.

"Make yourself at home," he said, slightly sarcastically, as he watched me pull up a bar stool and perch at the breakfast bar. He brought me a glass of orange juice, grabbed an apple, and sat opposite.

"Tell me again how you think I can help you?"

"Basically, I think you have information I need."

"Information you need to clear your name?"

"Something like that."

"And what do I get out of it?"

"Well, if I'm right, I can find the guy you've been after for the last few years."

"I don't see how that benefits me. I already know who that guy is, and I'll have my day in court — pretty soon, actually — so I hardly need you or your help."

I shared my reasons for believing he was focusing on the wrong people: my intuition about Matzoh, my meeting with Jameson and Isabella, the info I'd got from the IA officers, and the entire journey I'd been on with the FBI so far.

"Still doesn't mean shit — all circumstantial. Although I'll admit it sounds pretty fishy."

"And I suppose you've ironclad proof that Jameson is the crime boss you make him out to be?"

"Hell, I've got pictures, transcripts, testimony, rumours. I've got the lot."

"Yeah? So how come he's been walking around a free man for so long?"

"Look, man, don't fuck with me. I've been working to get him for years. His time is almost up, and I can finally get on with my life."

"I'm not trying to stop you moving on; I just think there's more to it. I've been on the inside, I've spoken to him myself, I've seen the FBI files, and I'm positive there's another figure lurking just behind the scenes."

I omitted the part about Isaiah; I still wasn't one hundred per cent convinced I'd got that bit right. He sat in silence, staring intently.

"Let me put it this way — what have you got to lose?"

"Nothing," he said at last.

With that, he slipped off the bar stool and headed towards the front room.

"You coming, or what?" he shouted from halfway down the hall.

I picked my way through to the study and found a chair in the corner. Once seated, the onslaught of paper began. With each ring binder came an explanation and follow-up questions, and with each photo, a request for clarity. The sun had set long ago, and we kept reading and talking into the early hours.

"I've got to stop," I said at about 2 a.m. "My bladder is about five mls away from exploding and I'm so tired I'd struggle to aim it straight."

"Yeah, me too. We can carry on in the morning."

"If you don't mind, I'll get my own taxi."

"Don't be silly — I've a spare room. You can stay."

"Thanks. You sure?"

He didn't answer — just disappeared. Our relationship had grown noticeably less strained as the day passed. It was probably because I could provide answers to some of his long-held questions and suspicions. Under less stressful circumstances, we might even have been friends. After what felt like a marathon-length pee, I found my bed on the second attempt and crashed out.

Upsettingly, I woke early. One of those mornings where, no matter how long you lie there, you just know sleep isn't coming back. My brain was in overdrive, thinking about all the potential information waiting for me downstairs. The previous afternoon and evening had been a little disappointing: no information on Matzoh, nor any real insight into who Jameson's less-than-legitimate clients and friends might be. There was however a shit ton of information about Jameson but it didn't seem to add up to much of anything. I pulled on yesterday's clothes and headed to the kitchen for some orange juice to wash away that early morning stale taste. Still swirling it round my mouth, I took a quick tour downstairs — more to see whether Peter was up than to snoop. A couple of minutes later I was back in the study, Peter presumably still in the land of nod.

From the large gable-end window, the morning looked spectacular: bright sun, vivid blue sky with only wispy high-level clouds, and hardly a ripple on the Pacific — just small waves lapping at the beach. Surprisingly, the beach wasn't empty despite the early hour: dog walkers, power walkers, joggers, a cyclist, even the odd sunbather starting early. When you've a resource like that on your doorstep, I guess you use it.

I turned back to the room and the mountain of papers. My small early morning energy reserves quickly dissipated as I stared at the seemingly never ending piles in front of me. I still hadn't gotten over the overload from the previous evening, and with my eyes and head still feeling pretty heavy, I decided to head for a shower in the hope it would freshen me physically and mentally. As I tried to step over one of several bundles of papers, my left foot caught a small pile of photos that were keeping the door open. It was tempting to carry on heading to the shower, but considering the friendship Peter had offered, I figured it would be rude not to clear up the mess I'd created. My back cracked as I bent and reached to place my glass to one side.

The pictures were all of people — some had names on the back, others didn't. I didn't recognise any until my poorly stacked pile predictably collapsed again just as I was about to finish restacking it. Staring up at me was a face I wasn't expecting to see — a very familiar one. The picture looked quite a few years old, judging by the style of clothing. I flipped it over, hoping for confirmation. No joy — it seemed Peter didn't have a clue who it was. I just had to hope I wasn't imagining it, but it certainly tied in with the description Isabella had given. The picture alone wasn't proof, but it added another dimension to where this was heading. The big question now was why did Peter Owens have the picture in the first place?

I was already forming some interesting — and damning — conclusions. Before anything else, I needed to confirm one very important thing — one that would answer nearly every question I had. I rifled quickly through the remaining photos, but found nothing useful. I sat for a while with the photo in my hand, weighing my next move. There was no option but to head back to the hotel; I just wanted to make sure I'd considered all possibilities before doing anything rash. Convinced there was no better plan, I jumped up, scribbled a quick note, left it on the stairs, and practically ran out.

Although it was still early — well, 8 a.m. is early to me — the sun had obviously been up for a while as it was already warm. I looked up and down the beach road for a taxi — no luck. I soon wished I'd kept up with my regular exercise; the jog to the main road hurt. Fortunately, I managed to wave down a cab, and it wasn't long before we were pulling up outside the St Regis.

"Hard night, Mr Michaels?" Eric called as I jumped out.

"You could say that," I replied, passing without even a smile.

"Hey, Eric, could you pay the cab for me? I'm caught a bit short," I shouted over my shoulder.

"Sure thing."

"Thanks," I said, stopping to give him a quick grateful smile before continuing on.

I didn't even stop to say good morning to Lori, who I noticed looking my way. There'd be other times for apologies. Thankfully, the lifts were all on the ground floor, and I jumped in and punched 20. The journey seemed to take ages, made worse by the theories and possibilities whirling in my head. I felt the lift slow and mentally prepared for the nine-storey hike. This time I took the stairs with considerably more vigour. By the time I reached the foyer of floor 29, I was breathing hard and had worked up a sweat. After a moment to catch my breath and wipe my face, I carried on.

Fortunately there was no guessing game this time. I banged on the right door until it opened. It shouldn't have been a surprise, but still was: it wasn't Isabella who opened — it was Myles. I could hardly push past him.

"Good morning," I said politely, hoping to get off on the right foot. "Could I see Isabella, please?"

"You're in luck, pal; she just got up. Grab a spot on the couch and I'll fetch her."

Myles was surprisingly pleasant this time. I'm guessing he'd been told to treat me as a friend if I showed up. I didn't have to wait long; Isabella joined me quickly. Dressed only in a towelling robe and without make-up, she still managed to look better than most women in full party mode.

"So, tell me you have some good news?"

"Potentially," I said.

I reached into the back right pocket of my jeans, pulled the picture I'd taken from Peter Owens' house, and slid it across in one motion.

"Do you know who this man is?"

She looked for no longer than five seconds.

"His name, no. But that's him. That's the guy who spoke to Dad about some shipping business. A few years ago — before my time, really. I wasn't part of those conversations, but I remember him coming out on the yacht. He represents that Matzoh company you were asking about. I'm sure of it."

"How sure?"

"As sure as I can be."

"Thank you, Isabella," I said, leaning across to kiss her cheek.

"So what does this mean? Are you going to get Dad out of jail?"

"I can't say for sure, but I'm almost positive he's innocent now. I just need a little help from a few friends to prove it."

"Tell me — or do I not want to know?"

I told her everything that had happened in the last twenty-four hours and how I believed it linked with my recent adventures. It was midday by the time we'd finished, so we chose to have lunch in the hotel restaurant before going our separate ways. As we headed for the door, I spotted a small bag of white powder on a dresser. I paused, detoured, and picked it up. I knew what it was — that wasn't why I'd been drawn to it. Isabella saw.

"Have some if you want. I can get more. I've been using it to get through the days lately."

"Thanks, but it's not my thing," I said, opening the bag and bringing it to my nose — careful not to inhale. The familiar odour hit immediately, and another piece of the puzzle fell into place. And like dominos falling I was hit by a sledgehammer of a realisation that linked the man in the photo to Alden Matzoh.

"You fucking dope," I muttered quietly

"Did you say something," inquired Isabella

"It's nothing, I just realised how dumb I've been.

She looked at me curiously but didn't ask further.

Lunch was nice. It was the first time I'd truly relaxed in at least a week and a half. Partly the company — but mainly because I now knew what was going on.

"So what next?"

"I'm not too sure," I said. "I know what I have to do and where it needs to be done, but I haven't figured out the actual doing phase."

"Well, if you need anything, let me know. I'm not leaving town until my father's released, so you know where I'll be."

The rest of lunch was business-free. We reminisced about our childhoods, and I even found myself laughing at times. It was about 5 p.m. when we finally headed back to our rooms — Isabella with renewed hope, and me with more burdens on my mind.

Chapter 55

My sleep was erratic. I couldn't even manage two consecutive hours until it was time to get up — at which point I slept until about midday. My investigations had led me to another of my uncomfortable situations. In my mind there was some clarity about what I needed to do. The sticking point was how well I was going to implement it. If I were a betting man, I'd say I wouldn't even make it to my destination. If I got arrested — which was the biggest risk I could see — it would be all over. It would seem like I was fabricating stories to save myself, rendering everything I'd discovered useless. I guessed that was a risk I'd have to take. I ordered a light snack on room service while I slowly got dressed and prepared myself for what I hoped would be the conclusion of my time on the FBI's most-wanted list.

Thirty minutes later, as I exited the lifts, I decided a little additional security wasn't a bad thing, so I took a brief detour to see Lori at the front desk.

"Hi, Mr Michaels. I see you've joined the world of male grooming," she joked, as I was now clean-shaven and looking more like my normal self.

"Well, somebody once told me I looked better without facial hair," I replied with a flirtatious smile.

"What can I do for you?" she said, clearly still immune to my charm.

"I was hoping to settle my bill, please."

"Of course. Will you be staying tonight, or are you leaving now?" she asked as she clicked her mouse, tapped a few keys, and grabbed the paper the printer produced.

"I hope to be here tonight. I just want to settle up in case I... err... get caught up with something," I said, scribbling my signature and pushing the form back.

"Oh?" she asked, a little quizzically.

"Let's just say that if I'm not here in the morning, you know what to do."

I'm not sure how seriously she took me as I didn't exactly have the James Bond flair of Connery or Moore. I paid with one of my personal credit cards. I'd had enough of hiding. It was time to go on the offensive. With the bill paid, I headed for the foyer and was grateful to see Eric still on duty.

"Afternoon, Mr Michaels. Looking very sharp today. You might even have a chance with Lori now," he said with a grin.

I was about to protest my innocence but figured there was no point — she was pretty hot and only a gay guy wouldn't be interested.

"Maybe, Eric, maybe. Tell me — where do you keep the cars?"

"In the garage, round the back and under the hotel. You want me to get you the Shelby?"

"No, it's alright. I've a few things to sort out with her. Just point me in the right direction."

He pointed me round the corner and explained where to take a left to reach the underground garage. As I was about to walk off, I slid a hand into my trouser pocket and found some cash.

"Hey, Eric — I almost forgot. Thanks for earlier."

After handing him a couple of folded hundreds, I turned away. Over-generous, sure — but he wouldn't forget me in a hurry, which was exactly what I needed. I'd taken a few steps before Eric finally responded.

"Thanks a lot. Anything you need, Mr Michaels — I'm your man."

I simply waved a hand dismissively and kept walking. The garage was larger than I expected, so it took a while to find my car. I'd dressed in the one suit I'd picked up from the house on Hyde Street before my Seattle adventure — the same suit I'd bought in DC for my first day at the Hoover Building. Karma and omens had never held much sway with me, but right now I'd take anything that hinted I might be successful, no matter how tenuous.

The heat and humidity underground quickly became oppressive, so I slung my jacket in the passenger seat. Opening the boot, I took out the first of several items I needed. The bulletproof vest had to be against the skin, so I quickly peeled off my already damp white shirt and cinched the Velcro straps tight. Next, after putting the shirt back on, I threaded on the shoulder holster and clipped the belt holster at the base of my spine. Ejecting both magazines, I fully loaded them — plus the spares — reloaded both pistols and re-holstered them. Although it was likely to be overkill, I slid the spare magazines into the pouch under my right arm. There was every chance I'd lose both guns within the first couple of minutes; but if you don't try, you'll never know. Unzipping the bag a little more, I checked the APC10 — still there, still fully loaded, waiting to be used in anger again. I had no intention of using it today; there was, however, comfort in knowing it was there if I suddenly needed more firepower.

The car started first time, the V8's note rebounding off the concrete with a deep, resonant boom. I crawled up the ramp, listening to the engine through the open window. Level with the edge of the building, I stopped and waited. I didn't have to wait long. The Chevy Impala I was expecting pulled up at the front of the hotel. Out jumped two smartly dressed guys who completely ignored Eric's attempt at small talk and pretty much sprinted through the main doors into the lobby. I was surprised they'd arrived so quickly — it showed I was still hot property. I inched forward until I could see Eric, blipped the throttle to get his attention, and beckoned him over.

"Eric — remember how you said you're my man?"

"Sure, Mr Michaels. What do you need?"

"In about two minutes, you're going to be asked if you know me and where I went."

"OK," he said slowly, brain catching up. "And you want me to deny all knowledge?"

"Not quite all knowledge. Just tell them I went out on foot."

"No probs. Get in a bit of trouble last night?"

"Something like that. Just don't let me down, OK."

With that, I reversed back to my corner and waited. I used the pause to put another plan into action. I grabbed my phone from the passenger seat, flicked through contacts and hit dial. It was answered within three rings.

"Do you know who this is?" I asked.

"I can guess," came the Italian-accented American. "My cousin's friend?"

"Yep. Listen — you should have something of mine?"

"I do. Did as Matteo told me. You need it back?"

"Not yet. But I need a favour."

"Go on," the voice said, dubiously.

"You buried it underground, right?"

"Yep — and I even covered the engine with foil."

"Perfect. And nobody's been sniffing around it?"

"Nah, man — not even the Pope could find that car."

"Good. So I need you to go for a drive. Anywhere you like, but make sure you head out of the city. Just don't stop. Keep driving."

"I can manage that. When?"

"In about fifteen minutes. You need to know you're going to catch some heat for this. You will get pulled over, OK. If that happens, do it by the book. There's a good chance of trigger-happy cops. Don't give them a reason to open fire — and stay in busy areas. The more witnesses, the better."

"I got you. And then what?"

"I'll take care of you. They've no reason to hold you, but you'll get a hard time. I'll call in a few days to collect the car. If you don't hear from me, it's yours. We good?"

"We're good."

I thumbed end and looked back towards the front of the hotel. Sure enough — and true to form — the suits reappeared on cue and, on the way to their car, accosted Eric. I watched, dismayed, as they flashed badges and saw Eric's confidence drain. I thought he was going to let me down; I selected first, anticipating a quick getaway. Fortunately, he kept his cool. At no point did he point in my direction. The feds jumped in their car and rejoined the afternoon traffic. I pulled out, gave a worried-looking Eric a grateful wave, and merged about six cars back.

Let the game of cat and mouse begin. For now, I was the cat — though I expected that to change imminently.

Chapter 56

The traffic-light gods were on my side — I didn't have to stop for a red — once which made it pretty easy to follow the Impala. I must admit, I was a little concerned about being spotted, driving a car as unique as the Mustang but as far as I could tell they hadn't clocked me; at least, I couldn't detect any sudden change in their driving that suggested they had. Soon enough, we arrived exactly where I'd hoped to end up. By paying with my everyday personal credit card at the hotel, I knew the FBI would be alerted that I was back on the grid — especially after the media had reported how desperate they were to find me. As expected, the two agents who showed up at the hotel promptly gave me a guided tour back to their command centre — a location I would otherwise have spent the next week searching for. The FBI doesn't exactly list its covert ops centres in the Yellow Pages.

I parked on the corner of a side street adjacent to the building and watched as the Impala headed down into the underground parking. There was no way I could guess the PIN code for the barrier, nor was there any chance I was simply going to walk through the front door and announce my arrival. Admittedly, my plans for the day had overlooked this small but important detail.

Ten minutes passed without anything happening. Then all hell seemed to break loose. I heard a warning alarm —

an alert to pedestrians that the main garage doors were opening. A couple of uniformed security personnel appeared on the pavement, arms extended to stop both traffic and pedestrians. Then, without warning, various saloons and SUVs began to spill out onto the street. At first, I worried I'd been spotted, but they didn't stop — they tore off down the road with lights flashing and sirens blaring. I assumed the BMW was back on the grid and they were going hunting. This worked in my favour: the fewer agents left in the building, the better. It didn't resolve my actual problem — I still needed a way in, and with all the agents chasing what they thought was me in the BMW, nobody was coming back to the building anytime soon.

Before I could come up with a solution, the passenger door was yanked open. I'd obviously been so preoccupied with the street that I'd completely forgotten to keep an eye on my surroundings. I began to reach for the gun under my left arm, but paused as my brain registered who had dropped into the seat. The clunk of the door closing brought me out of my shock. I just sat there, staring at my passenger, struggling to process what my eyes were seeing.

"Hi, how are you? Nice to see you. It's been a minute — these are some of the normal greetings you could use. Pick one; they all work."

"How about 'Hi, Eli. Sorry you thought I was dead.' That's a much better opener," I replied, a mixture of anger and confusion in my voice.

"Fair."

"Fair? Is that the best you can offer? I saw you get shot. I saw you lying dead in the street. I've seen you in my dreams every night. For fuck's sake, Eva, do you have any idea how much I've been haunted by you?"

The slightly cocky look on her face almost instantaneously disappeared, replaced by genuine sorrow.

"I'm sorry, Eli. I genuinely am. I never meant for that to happen. You have to believe me."

"A text, an email, a phone call — hell, a bloody carrier pigeon would have done the job. Instead, you let me think you were dead — that I might have been responsible for your death. Do you have any idea what that's like?"

"What was I supposed to do? I didn't know what had happened. Your name was all over the news. I had to assume you were involved in all this."

My brain was working at a thousand miles an hour, barely registering what she was saying. The suggestion I was involved was ridiculous but I had a much more pressing issue to deal with.

"Wait, does this mean Steve is alive too?"

"No, unfortunately not. I checked on him — he's definitely dead," she replied somberly.

"So why aren't you? I saw you get shot."

"Body armour. I had it on under my shirt. I got hit in the chest by three rounds. It knocked me off my feet and I smacked my head on the pavement — knocked me clean out. I probably looked dead, but I was just unconscious."

"But why has the FBI been telling everyone both you and Steve are dead?"

"When I came to, I saw you and Isaiah getting in the car and driving off. Then the black SUV tore off in the other direction. Steve was lying in the road — obviously dead — and I could hear sirens approaching. I had to make a split-second decision. As I looked around, I noticed the waitress lying on the floor. She was a Hispanic woman, similar build to me. She'd been shot in the face. I decided to put my ID in her pocket and disappear — knowing it wouldn't buy me much time, but a few days was better than nothing. I needed time to figure out what to do."

I pondered all this as she spoke. As far-fetched as it seemed, it was at least plausible.

"And I suppose you've been busy investigating since then?"

"Not quite. We'll get to that, though. First, tell me what you've been up to."

I decided I had nothing to lose at this point. Maybe she was on my side; maybe she wasn't. At this point, it didn't really matter. So I gave her the condensed version of my past few weeks.

"And then you got in the car, and here we are."

"So you really think it's Holtzman that's behind all this?"

"I genuinely don't see another good explanation. Literally everything points to him as the guy pulling all the strings. I mean, give me a better explanation?"

There was silence for a few minutes as Eva processed the information I'd just shared, and the conclusions I'd come to. While she did, I was feeling pretty good about myself when a question suddenly popped into my head.

"How exactly did you know to find me here?"

Eva smiled at this.

"I kind of figured you'd screw up eventually. I've been monitoring the surveillance channels, just waiting for them to find you. I have to say, you've done a pretty good job staying off the radar this long. I gave you a couple of days at best."

"Thanks for the vote of confidence," I smiled back. "But you do know I did it on purpose — letting them know where I was?"

"Not at first, I didn't. But when I saw where you were going, I began to realise you're smarter than I thought. Not

386

sure how you did it, but the BMW touch was especially good."

"Thanks," I said, feeling a little pride soften my anger towards her.

"What I don't get is what your plan is from here. You know they aren't going to just let you walk in there, right?"

"Yeah, I know. I was just going to wing it — maybe try and tailgate someone into the garage."

"I can probably help with that," she said, fishing in her jacket pocket and producing her FBI ID card. "There's something else you need to know, though. You asked earlier what I'd been up to since Steve was killed. To be honest, I've been laying low — very low."

"Didn't you want to get to the bottom of all this?"

"The thing is, I already knew the answer. I told you I saw the black SUV driving off after I came to, right? Well, I also saw the driver."

"Who was it?" I asked, interrupting when it would have been quicker to keep my mouth shut.

"Danny."

"You've got to be shitting me," I said, relaxing back into the seat. "Are you absolutely sure? Are you trying to tell me that innocent southern boy was all an act?"

"One thousand per cent. What I've been doing while you've been working your arse off is looking into him a bit more. Turns out he's been Holtzman's boy for some time. And before that, he was an army sniper. It's probably not a giant leap to assume it was Danny who shot the agents in Seattle."

"And who shot at me when I was up there last week, too."

"Yep — most likely."

387

"Now I'm even more convinced Holtzman is at the heart of this."

"Yep — I'm pretty sure I agree. I can't see Danny doing this without Holtzman at the very least knowing what's going on."

"Well, things just got a whole lot more complicated — but at least we know who we can trust. What about Isaiah? Whose side is he on?"

"If I had to bet, I'd say he's one of the good guys, but I'm not sure I'd bet my life on it right now — especially after everything you've been saying about him."

I paused again. It was good to finally have an ally in all this, and I certainly wasn't disappointed it was Eva.

"If you're coming in there with me, you may well be," I said, nodding towards the FBI building.

"Dare I ask what the plan is?"

"To be honest, I've never been one for planning. With you on board: best case, we go in there, kick their arses, then arrest anyone and everyone involved. Worst case, it'll be body bags. I'm not really seeing a middle ground."

"Jeez — don't sugar-coat it," she replied with a smile.

"Never was much of a salesman. The way I see it, those pricks need to go down. We owe Steve that, if nothing else."

"And I, for one, need to give Danny some payback. Might even just shoot him in the nuts for the hell of it."

I laughed at the image — it had the right symbolism, and to be honest, I'd do it if she didn't.

"So...?" I asked.

She replied after a short pause.

"Screw it — I'm in."

"Just don't get shot again, OK? I'm not sure I could cope with going through that again."

She gave me a look of mock disapproval.

"Drive the fuckin' car already, before I change my mind and shoot you instead."

"Yes, ma'am," I said with a grin, dipping the clutch, selecting first, and swinging the car across the road towards the down-ramp of the garage.

I pulled up to the barrier and scanned Eva's ID at the security post. There was a slim chance her ID had been revoked, but I figured the FBI would be about as organised as most other government bureaucracies. Thankfully, the green light on the post lit immediately, and the security measures began to retract from their defensive positions. Twenty seconds later, we were heading down the spiral driveway — driving into the heart of a beast. Pulling off at the first available level, I was glad to see several empty spaces. I guess the FBI had sent people home for good behaviour — or else the notorious American work ethic wasn't all that true after all.

Having parked, we lingered in a shadowy corner near the car for a few minutes, in case a silent alarm had gone off and we needed a quick getaway. To my relief, a horde of FBI agents didn't descend on us. While that was good, I was slightly concerned things were going so smoothly. It made me wonder whether they were simply waiting for me to come to them rather than risk a shootout.

We made our way to the stairwell, keeping an eye out for security cameras. The car park had more than its fair share, so an eagle-eyed guard had probably already spotted one of us. Nevertheless, I did my best to act naturally. We reached the stairwell, knowing full well there would be cameras on most levels. We were officially at the point of no return, so we headed straight up to the next floor. Fortunately, our exit put us on the non-public side of the front desk, although there was still an electronically operated barrier to pass through, manned by a guard. Not ideal — and I was suddenly glad to have Eva with me.

The guard took the briefest look at me and then didn't — more likely, couldn't — take his eyes off Eva as we walked towards him.

"Can I help you?" he asked, basically ignoring me.

"I think you probably can, Bryan," Eva replied, catching his name badge from twenty metres away. "We're just heading to see Dean Holtzman. We have some updates for him about the case he's working."

"That explains it. I don't recognise either of you — guessed you must be from out of town."

"You got that right," I said.

A puzzled look spread across his face. I wasn't sure why at first, then the penny dropped. I'd been here so long I'd almost forgotten how bizarre my accent sounded — especially inside an FBI building.

"The accent, right?" I added with a smile.

"Yeah — just not what I was expecting."

"I get it all the time. We've been flown in from D.C. — come to help Mr Holtzman find that English guy that's running around."

"Good for you. It's about time we caught that bastard — the more help, the better. Although I think it might have been a wasted trip. Most of his guys just tore out of here like they had a rocket up their collective arses."

"Well, that would be frustrating — if you know what I mean. I take it Mr Holtzman is still in the building?"

"He sure is. You'll find him in the crisis suite up on eight."

"Oh, good. I was a little worried he might have been playing golf or something."

"Not Mr Holtzman — well, not recently anyway. He's pretty much been living here."

"Perfect. Which way to the lifts… I mean, elevators?"

"First off, I need to see your ID or warrant card before I can let you through."

"Sure," I said, beginning to wish I'd left Eva to do all the talking. I started searching my pockets, praying for divine intervention. Eva, clearly realising this could go sideways, stepped in and distracted Bryan with some grade-A flirting. To be honest, when a woman as beautiful as Eva starts talking, you'd be hard-pressed not to be drawn in. Barring some Irish luck — which doesn't tend to run in my family — I was screwed.

As I reached into the inside pocket of my jacket, one of my guns momentarily visible, my fingers touched a piece of plastic. If it was what I thought it was, then my grandmother must have been shagging an Irishman on the side. Much to my relief, it was my original pass from the Hoover Building. I held it out for Bryan, who was too distracted by Eva to look closely. I assume he recognised the emblem on the pass, because had he looked any closer, I'm pretty sure he would have noticed the name. I decided to leave things to Eva — she was on a roll. She wrapped it up quickly, but Bryan wasn't done trying to be helpful to his new crush.

"I'll phone Mr Holtzman's office and get Danny to come and show you up. What's your name again?" he asked, looking at me.

"Don't worry. We don't need to drag Danny out of the crisis meeting. I wouldn't mind a wander to get my bearings anyway. We've been sitting on a plane for four hours — the exercise will do us good."

He paused, clearly torn between Eva and his protocols.

"I shouldn't really, but I guess I can make an exception for you," he said, eyes fixed on Eva. "Follow the signs for the staff area once you get off the elevator. You'll past his office. The crisis suite will be right there."

"Thanks. And don't worry — it's just between me and you," Eva said, gently touching his forearm.

Heck, I was only observing this and felt slightly weak at the knees. He let us through the barriers, and we headed for the lifts.

"You are an absolute heartbreaker," I murmured, with a cheeky smile.

"Gotta use what God's given me," she shrugged.

"Remind me never to trust a security guard again."

Eva laughed as we boarded the waiting lift. The ride to the eighth floor was fast and uneventful. I clipped my D.C. pass to my jacket, just to avoid getting stopped or attracting suspicious looks. As the doors opened, we were faced with a small group of men and women, and I feared the worst. My hand almost instinctively went inside my jacket for my gun — then I noticed none of them were holding weapons or riot shields, just briefcases and satchels. I relaxed and pretended to itch my armpit. The eighth floor was surprisingly empty; I guess it was the domain of the head-honchos, and given it was Friday, they clearly weren't at work.

Chapter 57

Leading off to the left and right were signposted corridors, and we quickly found we needed the left one for the staff area. The rest of the signs read like a list of serious crimes which, technically, is exactly what they were. Sandwiched between "grand theft auto" and "anti-terrorism" was the restaurant area. We quietly headed down the not-so-narrow left-hand corridor — not surprising, considering the size of some Americans. It wasn't long before we arrived at the staff restaurant area, and as I looked around, I could see Holtzman's name on a door, with what must have been the crisis room next to it.

I indicated it to Eva and was about to walk over when the handle began to move. We both ducked behind a low seating area as Holtzman's voice boomed through the partially opened doorway. A few seconds later, the door opened fully and the two agents from the hotel exited, looking very dejected. Having felt the force of Holtzman's tirade, it was easy to understand why they looked so glum — especially since both they and I knew the situation was out of their hands. I looked on as the door to the meeting room slowly closed. Still in the room were four faces I recognised. Holtzman and Danny I expected; Jessica and Isaiah I didn't. This complicated things quite a lot. We obviously knew which side of the fence Holtzman and Danny sat on. I had my doubts about Isaiah, but I hadn't even contemplated Jessica being involved in this. In fact, if you'd asked me thirty minutes ago, I'd have bet a serious amount of money that she had nothing to do with it. Other than Holtzman wanting to sleep with her I couldn't think of another plausible reason why she'd be there if she wasn't somehow caught up in all this.

I quickly scanned the restaurant area and spied the toilets. I signalled to Eva where I was going before we both quickly and quietly scurried over to the men's room.

"Too much coffee for breakfast?" Eva asked with a smile.

"Ha ha," I replied with an unimpressed smile as I took my jacket off. "I figured on a little security. It always pays to have a plan B."

At this, I unclipped the belt holster and spare magazines, then hung them on the back of the first cubicle door. I still had one gun in a shoulder holster. It's not like I was going to have an extended firefight in the crisis room where I needed a spare gun and loads of ammo. At least this way, I had an element of surprise if it all went to shit, and it gave me somewhere to retreat to if it came to that. I think Eva twigged what I was doing as she briefly walked out — I guess she went into the ladies' room.

"There is still time to back out," offered Eva on her return.

"And do what?" I asked.

"Hand ourselves in? Let the system work it out?"

"What, and hope that justice will prevail? No offence, but do you know how many innocent people there have been on death row?"

She just nodded in response, having obviously come to a similar conclusion. We looked each other squarely in the eye for about ten seconds. This moment didn't need words — I think we both knew how the other felt.

"Shall we?" I finally asked.

"Age before beauty," she said, extending her hand towards the door. I slowly opened it, checked that the coast was clear, and took out my Sig Sauer as I stepped out, heading towards the now-closed crisis room door. As I reached it, I stopped, took a deep breath and firmly knocked. I looked over my shoulder to see that Eva had positioned herself off to one side. We briefly made eye contact one last time. Although I could hear my heart beating, it wasn't loud enough to drown out the voice from the other side of the door.

"YES," shouted Holtzman.

I was about to reach for the doorknob when I felt Eva's hand on my shoulder. Immediately getting the message, I stepped to the hinge side of the door and started a rhythmic knocking.

"What the fuck is wrong with you people?" boomed Holtzman from inside the room. "Whoever you are, stop thumping on the door and get your arse in here."

We didn't move; I just carried on with my irritating knocking. I heard a chair scrape and footsteps head towards the door. I brought the Sig up and aimed it at the door jamb, approximately head height. I was hoping it would be Holtzman who came to the door, but I figured he was probably orchestrating things from the comfort of his chair. As predicted, it was Danny's face that appeared. He clearly wasn't expecting to see me. If I'd had time to fully appreciate just how shocked he looked, I'd be feeling pretty good about myself right now. As it was, this momentary surprise needed to be capitalised on.

"What's up, Danny?" I said as I thrust the door back into his body, knocking him backwards and onto his arse.

I looked to my right to see Holtzman beginning to get out of his chair. Jessica was reeling back with a look of part astonishment, part horror on her face, while Isaiah sat opposite her impassively, like he was waiting for a train. I stepped up to Danny, who was still on his back, stood on his right arm and pointed my gun at his face. I looked over my shoulder to see Eva making a beeline for Holtzman, her gun aimed at the middle of his chest. Holtzman clearly made a quick calculation that this was not a situation he was on top of, as I watched him slowly lower himself back into his chair.

"Don't do anything stupid," I said to Danny. "I'd hate to shoot before giving you the chance to entertain us with your bullshit excuses for being involved in all this."

He looked like he was about to say something, then thought better of it and just relaxed. For the first time, that innocent puppy-dog look had disappeared, replaced by something far more vengeful.

"You won't be needing this," I said, leaning down, reaching inside his coat and removing his gun. As I began to straighten, my eye caught sight of an ankle holster, so I emptied that too.

"You three too," Eva commanded coldly.

I stepped off Danny's arm, took a few steps back towards the door and pushed it closed. Danny slowly got himself up, rubbing his right arm, and returned to a seat next to Jessica — but to Holtzman's right. Several guns had appeared on the glass table, although it was clear that Jessica hadn't coughed up hers. I looked at her expectantly and she shook her head.

"I don't carry a gun," she said meekly.

I tilted my head in a questioning manner.

"Honestly," she said in a somewhat appealing tone, desperate to be believed.

She just stared at me. I thought for a moment, decided to believe her, then scooped up the rubbish bin, dumped Danny's guns into it and swept the ones on the table in too. I placed the bin in the corner of the room, as far from the table as possible, and then walked to the end of the table, opposite Holtzman. He was still staring at Eva, clearly not understanding what he was seeing.

"Surprise," she said sarcastically. "Bet you didn't expect to see me again."

"So… who exactly is in the morgue?" asked Holtzman, quizzical after a slight pause.

"I don't know — some waitress. I guess you got lazy with the forensics."

"But how?"

"After that prick shot me," she replied, momentarily pointing her gun at Danny. "I hit my head and knocked myself out. He obviously figured I was dead, so when I came round, I decided that putting my ID in the dead waitress's pocket was my only move."

"I'm happy to give it another go," said Danny with a sneer.

"Any time, you arrogant fuck."

"Perhaps you two can go at it a little later," I said, interrupting before it got out of hand. Everybody's attention turned towards me, and Eva moved into the corner behind Holtzman, leaning against the wall and relaxing her gun hand down to her side.

"How exactly did you two manage to get in here?" asked Holtzman.

"Nothing like the charm of a beautiful woman."

"That fat fuck Bryan, I presume?" asked Holtzman.

I just nodded as Holtzman shook his head in resignation.

"So what's the play here? You've broken into the FBI's West Coast HQ for what? To clear your name, catch the bad guys, and send everyone to prison?"

"So you've seen Die Hard then." I said in a cold, dead pan tone.

"Real life really is nothing like the movies, but whatever — your funeral."

"What exactly do you think is going on?" asked Jessica earnestly.

"Oh, come on, Jessica. Don't treat me like an idiot. You did that already by getting me involved in all this shit."

She looked genuinely confused and mildly offended.

"I... I... err... don't know what you mean," she stammered defensively.

"Don't worry, you're not the main event. I'm here for that prick," I said, indicating Holtzman, "and his boyfriend."

Jessica clearly didn't understand what I was on about, but Holtzman snorted, and Danny just stared at me before raising his middle finger.

"So, let's hear it then. What's this theory you've concocted that's going to result in me, a multi-decorated senior FBI agent, going to prison — and you somehow walking into the sunset?"

"If you ignore, just for a second, that Eva not only saw Danny in the street the day Steve was killed, but also saw him get in the assailant's car and drive away, I think I can spin a pretty believable story that, at the very least, raises some doubts about my involvement and gets you some time under the interrogation lamp."

"Pah," said Holtzman, waving me away and relaxing back in his chair. "Nothing to do with me. Sounds like you've got Danny dead to rights."

"Straight under the bus at the first opportunity," I said, looking at Danny, who was no longer looking at me, but straight at Holtzman.

"Still doesn't look good for you, though, does it? Your personal aide involved in the execution of a fellow agent."

"Maybe, maybe not. Either way, I come out of this relatively untouched."

"Maybe, maybe not," I said, smiling as I mimicked him.

"I've never really understood, right from the start, why I was involved in all this. It was completely unnecessary — other than you needing someone to deflect onto and blame when this all went wrong. It's taken me a while, but that was the plan all along, wasn't it? How else to throw the attention off you? Blame the foreigner. That way, you get a bit of heat for a few weeks — poor judgement and all that — but then you're golden again, back to working away in the background."

"I have no idea what you're talking about," said Holtzman, still looking relaxed.

I reached inside my jacket, replaced the gun in the shoulder holster, and took out the photo I'd taken from Peter Owen's house. With a flick of the wrist, I launched it into the centre of the table. It stopped roughly in front of Isaiah, who picked it up and studied the image. He handed it to Jessica, whose face showed both surprise and recognition, then passed it to Danny, who looked at it for the briefest moment before handing it to his boss.

"You got my good side," he said, pausing — undoubtedly trying to figure out where the photo had been taken.

"Except, as I'm sure you know, that photo is at least eight years old. Which means I didn't take it."

"So who did?"

"It's really not relevant to my story, so let's just say a friend, who will happily testify to where and when it was taken."

Holtzman waved for me to continue — but with a little less enthusiasm than before.

"Anyway, I showed it to another friend, who is relevant..."

"And who would that be?" asked Holtzman, mildly annoyed I wasn't making it easy.

"Isabella Jameson. You do know her, right?"

"We may have crossed paths before — wouldn't say I know her, though."

"If you're going to lie, at least keep it as close to the truth as possible — it makes it slightly more believable. Not that it really matters. Turns out Isabella recognised you straight away — and not for being an FBI agent."

Holtzman sat in silence, perhaps slowly realising his world was about to unravel.

"She told me the man in the picture was the head guy at a company called Alden Matzoh. Before you say it, I know it's not illegal to be involved with a private company — but Isabella tells me she and her dad are sometimes middlemen for people looking to do less-than-legal business. Turns out they have nothing to do with drugs and guns other than maybe connecting people."

"And you believed her?" Holtzman asked, derisively.

"Actually, I do — because guess what I've found out about Alden Matzoh? Absolutely nothing," I said after a pause. "It's like they don't exist, which is strange for a company that imports sporting goods. You see, after you tried to kill me, I went on a little adventure. I accidentally found myself in the Alden Matzoh warehouse — full of footballs, basketball hoops, tennis rackets. Kind of odd that they have no public face when you think about it. What's also odd is that while I was there, somebody else tried to kill me but I think you already know about that."

I said this last sentence while looking squarely at Danny. I had no idea if it had been him or not, but I was swinging for the fences, so why not? Danny didn't flinch; he just sat there, motionless. Perhaps he was trying to figure out if he had a way out of this mess — who knows. I took his lack of reaction as confirmation and ploughed on.

"Seems a little excessive for a company selling sporting goods, wouldn't you say? More like a company with something to hide."

"So? Still not seeing what this has to do with me?"

"Unfortunately for you, Danny isn't quite as good a shot as he needed to be. A couple of his rounds hit the merchandise. One thing you probably haven't considered is that, in the social circles I mix in, Class-A drugs are quite common. Never really seen the point myself, but I definitely know what that stuff smells like. As I was making my escape, I smelt something I couldn't place at the time, but now know it was cocaine."

This revelation seemed to knock the wind out of Holtzman's bluster — he sank ever so slightly into his chair.

"And to add a couple more nails in your coffin, this warehouse where Alden Matzoh holds its stock just happens to be right next to the spot where those two agents were killed earlier this year. Not close by — right bloody next to it. How that didn't get investigated was either complete incompetence or corruption — and I'm pretty sure I know which."

Eva already knew this, so I didn't pay much attention to her face, but Jessica looked stunned, struggling to get her head around the new reality I was suggesting. Isaiah still hadn't moved. He continued to sit there impassively — clearly listening, but his face was blank of any emotion or reaction. Danny and Holtzman both looked a little stressed, probably trying to figure out where the holes in my theory were and how they could exploit them to get out of this mess.

"And just to top it off. Alden Matzoh. Really? It took me a little while to see it, but it doesn't take a genius to spot the similarity to Dean Holtzman. Are you really that egotistical that you couldn't come up with another name that didn't point straight at you?"

"Worked for 15 years," he said so softly it was barely audible.

That was tantamount to a confession, and I was pretty sure I was on to a winner. I was about to start with some questions — and a few more accusations — when the door to the room suddenly opened. In walked the two guys who'd been at my hotel earlier. The one in front had his jacket over his right arm and a box of doughnuts in his left. His colleague, a couple of steps behind, had his hands full with two trays of coffee. The guy at the front saw me and, in a split second, was reaching for his gun. I went for mine — but got my hands caught up in my jacket and almost immediately realised this was a contest I was destined to lose. I slowed my movement and raised my hands.

"Don't move, dickhead," he screamed, over and over.

Chapter 58

I just stood still, holding his eye contact to make sure he knew he had my full attention. Almost simultaneously — and I have to give it to the old guy — Holtzman stood and sent his chair flying towards Eva. She wasn't expecting it, her attention drawn to the door, and couldn't move her gun hand in time. Her hand was forced into the wall, the gun dislodged and thudded to the carpet. Holtzman's nimbleness surprised me again as he sprang towards her and, in one seamless motion, scooped up the gun. The shouting stopped and Holtzman began to wave the weapon at Eva, directing her to join me at the other end of the table. The coffee duo deposited the cups on the table and stood vaguely behind us, thankfully with their guns re-holstered. I noticed that Danny had gone to the bin, retrieved his weapons and handed the others their respective guns. Holtzman had repositioned himself at the far end, seated and wearing the smuggest grin imaginable.

"Thanks for doing my job for me. It was becoming an issue that we couldn't find you, but now we can shut this whole thing down and move on."

"And how exactly do you plan on explaining Eva being here?"

"I'm sure we can figure something out," said Danny.

"Like you did with those agents in Seattle — and with Steve?"

"Steve was a prick. I actually quite enjoyed that one," he said, smiling.

I shook my head in disbelief and, for the first time, caught the slightest reaction from Isaiah: the barest twitch of his right foot and a purposeful deep inhalation. I figured I needed to draw this out a little longer and turned my focus back to Holtzman.

"So tell me, Dean — how did I do?"

He looked at me for a few moments, deciding what to do, then his ego got the better of him.

"Credit where it's due. I think you missed your calling. You'd have made a pretty good agent — although I think it was more luck than investigative skill."

"Every investigation needs some luck," I said. "What I don't really understand is why you've been gunning for Jameson. When I spoke to him the other day, he pretty much told me you two had some kind of partnership going on."

"You spoke with him?" Holtzman asked, puzzled.

"Yep — proper little jailhouse canary, that one," I said smugly.

"You were in jail with him?" he asked, incredulous.

"I think you'll find Eli is surprisingly resourceful," said Eva, with a touch of pride.

Holtzman just shook his head, not quite believing it.

"You were about to tell us how you and Jameson ran this whole thing," I prompted, eager to get him talking again — and to give Isaiah a bit more time to decide which side he was on.

"He is — or was — an important part of the organisation. I've worked with Jameson since the early years. His operation does more than he probably told you. He put me in touch with my South American suppliers at the beginning, but it goes much deeper than that. We attach a watertight container to the hull of his container ships and fill it with whatever contraband we like. Typically powder, sometimes pills. The container has a GPS chip pre-programmed with coordinates. When the ship is within five miles of the drop, the capsule automatically disengages its magnetic connection and sinks. It then sends out a highly encrypted signal telling us exactly where it is."

"And don't tell me — you send a few Navy SEALs down to collect it?" I asked.

"Ha ha," Holtzman said, sarcastically. "No — what happens is we sail out and collect it. I say 'we' — obviously not me. Do you remember Jurgen, who you met on the boat?"

I nodded. He was on a roll now — keen to brag, to show us how clever he was. Who was I to interrupt?

"Jurgen's a whizz with electronics. He developed the tech that makes this work. He's also an experienced diver — match made in heaven for us. Once we arrive at the coordinates, Jurgen sends down a submersible drone with a cable attached. The drone triggers several CO_2 canisters which inflate the underwater lift bags. We then use the drone and cable to bring the cargo to the boat."

I was impressed. Slick, low risk on the surface — and clearly effective, or I wouldn't be standing here. I didn't want to stroke his ego too much, but I needed him talking.

"Sounds very… creative. But all it takes is a random Coast Guard boat passing by and seeing what's going on."

"What you probably don't know is that Jameson's boat has an internal dive pool. From the outside it just looks like the yacht's moored."

"So that's how Jameson fits into all this — he supplies the boat?"

"Ah, yes — Jameson. I 'rent' his yacht for a day or two under the guise of a corporate event. The money's clean, and his accountant daughter does whatever she does to limit his tax liability. That's his cut."

"And Alden Matzoh?"

"I'll agree — that was a naïve decision. But it no longer really matters. It's a legit sporting-goods distribution company for North America. As you found, we pack some merchandise with our other products and off it goes to our sales team."

He made it sound like any other business — which, in some ways, it was. Overlooking the misery and death he was fuelling was part of being a major drug importer.

"I don't get it. Jameson seems integral. Without him the logistics fall apart. Why have you been trying to get rid of him?"

"Money."

He didn't elaborate, so I kept quiet. Sure enough, he filled the blanks.

"Jameson's become increasingly belligerent: upping his cut, reducing access to the yacht and scaling back use of his freighters. I think it's his daughter. I always got the impression she didn't know about the drugs and Jameson was trying to distance himself for her sake. It was only a matter of time before the relationship broke down, leaving me exposed. I couldn't have that. So I hatched a plan to get rid of him. The deaths of the agents in Seattle were regrettable but necessary — the only way I could bring in an outsider."

"Why exactly… " I began.

"Because the chance of failure was almost guaranteed," Isaiah offered, out of the blue. "The FBI had been trying to break this up for some time. The agents' deaths brought an ultimatum: either shut it down or scale it back. Your involvement was supposed to buy us breathing room — and ideally end with Jameson on the run in South America, or dead. There'd be a professional cost to Dean and me, but that wouldn't matter in the long run. If all else failed, we had plans for Jameson to have an 'accident' once the focus moved on. Voilà — problem solved."

Had Isaiah just confessed to being neck-deep in this? I'd had my suspicions after the phone call, but hearing him speak so openly still shocked me. It made sense of his team-lead role — ultimate control. There were a thousand questions about how and when he'd betrayed us, but one rose to the top.

"I guess we have you to thank for the jewellery-shop fiasco?"

"No — that was Steve," Danny said smugly.

"Steve? Fuck off. No way was he dirty," I snapped, my brain stuttering at the claim.

"The computer logs would disagree."

I looked at Danny with a mix of confusion and distrust. I couldn't process it. Rather than ask more, I let his smugness get the better of him.

"Can't sell you on that? If tech ever did search the system all they would find was Steve's access details assigned to deletion of the profiles belonging to 4 career criminals. What they wouldn't find was the fact that Steve had shown me how to do it, but unbeknownst to him I was using a key logger the whole time. All I needed to do was log on when he wasn't around and start deleting stuff at will, virtually and in reality. A quick call to some local bangers and it was all set. Nobody was going to miss those clowns. We did society a favour."

I'm not sure why I needed to keep asking questions, I guess my curiosity was getting the better of me and it was kind of nice to be filling in some blanks, and having my ego stroked to hear that I'd got a few things right.

"I don't get it. Why not tip off the police and leave us to do the heist? If we were killed, it would've saved you a job."

"Self-preservation. Isaiah is one of us. We weren't willing to risk something happening to him," Holtzman said.

It made a kind of sense. Speaking of self-preservation, I needed to find out why I'd been drawn into all this.

"So why me? Why not just pick someone else?"

"Well, we didn't want someone from the security services, they would have been too unpredictable from a professional point of view," replied Holtzman.

"And it was all going to plan until you went all rouge and came up with your new plan for getting to Jameson," offered Isaiah indifferently.

"What can I say? For once I'm glad I managed to fuck up the plans."

"And that's exactly why I chose you," Holtzman jumped in, eager to be centre stage again. "Always a smart-arse. Love knocking people like you down a peg. I'd never heard of you till last year. I was flying to the UK, reading the inflight magazine, and saw an article about you and your business. Reminded me of all the over-privileged pricks at college. Your life seemed too perfect, and I decided there and then to screw it up. When I found out about your time in Montana, I knew it was a done deal. Nothing personal, you understand."

"Sounds about as personal as it gets," I said, disbelieving.

"What exactly happened in Montana? We never could find out."

My heart pulled in two directions. He didn't know — which meant the FBI didn't know. Good. But the whole reason I was here was because they'd played on that fear.

"Go fuck your mother," I said angrily, taking a step towards the table.

Holtzman laughed. Out of the corner of my eye, I saw Isaiah twitch again. I didn't understand his game — but I was too focused on the conversation to dwell on it.

"And what about this tosser?" I said, pointing at Danny.

"Ex-Ranger. Sniper. Dishonourable discharge after Afghanistan where he 'accidentally' shot some locals. I needed someone with no morals; he needed a job. Perfect fit. I got him into the agency and on my staff. He's watched my back ever since — and apparently got you hook, line and sinker."

I thumped the glass table in anger — not truly pissed off, but trying to create a distraction. As the table reverberated, Isaiah suddenly moved. He knocked his coffee cup towards Jessica. She instinctively pushed back from the table to avoid the hot liquid. It was as if it happened in slow motion: Isaiah gripped the table, planted both feet, biceps tensing. I guessed what was coming — even if it made no sense. I lunged forward, grabbed the nearest coffee and flung it at Holtzman's face. A split second later the table catapulted into the air, crashing down on Danny as he tried to escape the inevitable. Holtzman got his hands up a shade too late; the coffee scalded his face and he began to scream.

Behind me, Eva launched her left shoulder into one of the men behind us, leaving me to pivot on my right foot, load through my quads and drive my weight into the remaining target who still hadn't reacted. He smacked into the wall and crumpled. Both Eva and I stayed upright and, with a quick glance around, realised it wasn't over. Danny was fighting the table off; Holtzman was wiping coffee from his red face. Eva and Isaiah were already moving for the door, so I followed.

As I reached the door two loud bangs, followed by wood splintering right next to my head, had me diving for the floor. I scrambled up in time to see Eva heading for the ladies and Isaiah going the opposite direction. The way I figured it, there was only one route out of this — and that route needed a gun. I sprinted for the gents as two more shots rang out — wild, probably fired on the move. As I reached the door, another shot cracked; this time my right flank exploded in pain. I was catapulted through the door and slid across the tiles.

Chapter 59

Regardless of the fact I was wearing body armour, blood was seeping onto my shirt and the floor. My desire to live overcame the pain and the shock, so I forced myself to my feet and into the first cubicle to reacquire my spare gun and ammo. I pulled the slide back and briefly touched my side to find a ragged hole in my shirt and blood still oozing out. There was nothing I could do about that now; survival was my number-one priority. I took off my suit jacket and crawled under the row of sinks, putting myself out of sight from anyone entering. The only sound I could hear, other than my rapid breathing, was the drip, drip of my blood onto the tiled floor. Almost immediately the door flew open and the coffee duo cautiously stepped in, guns sweeping the room in high and low arcs. The more forward of the two silently indicated towards the cubicles, all with closed doors. They would only need to take two steps before they'd see me, so I needed to act fast. Hyper-aware that the human eye is drawn to movement, I quickly put my gun round the end of the sink unit, roughly in the direction of the door, and pulled the trigger twice. The noise was deafening but nevertheless a hefty thud followed almost within seconds. To my surprise, which is ridiculous given I knew there were two shooters, a further two shots rang out, though they were considerably more distant than mine. Again, a heavy thud followed, and I peered out to see two bodies on the tiles: one bleeding from two chest wounds, the other missing the back of his head. Due to the way they'd fallen, the door was wedged open and I could see Eva standing in the doorway to the ladies', smoking gun in hand and that 'don't-mess-with-me' look plastered on her face. I mouthed a thank you — she returned a weak smile — and I began to extract myself from my position.

As I stood, I saw Eva's face switch to shock, presumably at the sight of my bleeding. Then she disappeared, just before I threw myself against the wall as several more shots rang out. I couldn't place the direction of the shooter, as the sound reverberated off every surface. I was pretty sure Eva had managed to take evasive action before getting shot, but I was back in survival mode and didn't have time to give it more thought. I wasn't sure if they — I assumed Holtzman and Danny — knew I was in the toilet block. It would have been logical enough to assume Eva had killed the other guys, so I leant up against the wall and waited as quietly as possible. I must have given it two minutes and hadn't heard a sound, so decided to risk a quick look. Quite why I thought this was a good idea I don't know; it was the most illogical move — but hindsight is twenty-twenty. Keeping tight to the wall, I placed no more than half my body through the doorway and scanned the large communal area, matching my eye movements with my gun sight. Nothing: just tables, chairs and a few vending machines. I checked behind me — nobody there either. Just a long corridor with offices on either side. It took me back to my days at the shooting range in Montana and the urban-warfare simulator I'd built. Although that was a long time ago, the familiarity of what I had to do de-stressed me a little. The corridor behind me was an absolute no-no: too many hiding spots, too many angles to cover. I gave it another thirty seconds and, when nothing developed, I plotted a route to maximise cover. I grabbed a gun from one of the dead guys, tucked it in my waistband, and then slowly zig-zagged my way between the furniture, concrete posts and random pods.

I made it back to the crisis room, which at first glance appeared empty. I was about to move on when I caught the slightest movement out of the corner of my eye. I found Jessica sprawled on the floor, bleeding from the head. I hurried over; she was unconscious. I checked her pulse — found one — and noticed her breathing was laboured. She clearly needed help, but that would have to wait.

I wasn't sure what the play was. I was a wanted felon running around an FBI facility with a gun while simultaneously being hunted by a drug kingpin and his personal hitman. And now I was faced with the dilemma of putting all that on hold to try to save someone who may have been integral to getting me into this mess.

Thankfully, I didn't need to think any further: a high-pitched feminine scream suddenly cut through my thoughts. It could only be Eva. Without a second thought, despite feeling light-headed and a little wobbly on my legs, I took off down the corridor towards the lobby where the lifts were. As I rounded the corner I found Danny in the middle of the lobby. Eva was on her knees in front of him, bleeding from the mouth and nose. Danny was in the process of drawing the pistol from his belt holster — his intention of executing Eva all too clear.

"Oi, fucknut," I shouted.

At this point I thought I was ready for anything. My Sig was raised with the intention to shoot, and Danny was squarely in the sights. Unfortunately for me, Danny was as skilled as an ex-Army Ranger should be. The speed and fluidity of his movement made it hard for my brain to register what my eyes were seeing. He adjusted his body, bringing his gun up not only in my direction but directly at me. The most impressive thing was that he didn't even look — he never took his eyes off Eva. It was like one of those no-look passes you see LeBron James pull off. My brain was already in the process of firing, so I didn't have time — or the mental capacity — to react. We both fired at the same time. At almost precisely the same moment, I became aware of several gunshots from behind me. What followed was the strangest sensation, like there was too much stimulus for my brain to process at once. It was as if I'd been punched in the chest by Mike Tyson while simultaneously kicked twice in the back by a donkey. My chest felt like it was being crushed from both directions, my body unsure whether to fall forwards or backwards. After what felt like an eternity, I lurched forwards and landed face down. Amidst the sensory chaos I somehow caught a glimpse of Danny collapsing forwards onto Eva, a large bloodstain spreading across his shirt. If nothing else, at least I'd got the fucker.

The pain was so bad I couldn't comprehend it. The idea of trying to move was out of the question and I couldn't even get my head around what had just happened. I sensed someone approaching, mainly due to the small amount of light flickering and changing. I felt something kick at my right hand and then something wedge under my pelvis. In what felt like an out-of-body experience, my senses completely scrambled, I suddenly found my world spinning and somehow I was on my back, first staring at the ceiling and then at the weirdly placid face of Dean

Holtzman. I tried to speak but had no idea if anything came out. I'm guessing not, as Holtzman started talking.

"Shame you tore past the offices so quickly. I was waiting to pick you off as you tried to play hero and rescue Eva."

"At least I got your boy."

"Minor inconvenience," he replied dismissively. "Don't really like shooting a man in the back, but you didn't leave me much choice. Lucky for you that body armour works. Unfortunately, the next bullet will be going straight in here," he said, tapping the barrel of his snub-nose revolver on my forehead.

"Feel free to put... one in your own... head," I managed to stammer — surprisingly breathless.

"You know, I'm actually going to enjoy this. You've been nothing but a pain in the arse since day one. One less pretentious, jumped-up little shit like you in the world is never a bad thing."

"I've just got... one last... question?"

He looked at me expectantly — maybe hoping for one last chance to show how smart he was.

"Is... your arse jealous... of the amount of shit... that comes out of your... mouth?"

I grinned as best I could. He didn't see the funny side. He brought the gun up and aimed at my face. I closed my eyes and pictured Amelia. There was no way this prick would occupy my last thoughts — though I half hoped there was an afterlife where I could come back and kick his butt over and over. A sudden wave of pain from my side sent my chest and back into unbearable spasms. I'd never really thought about the physics of being shot in the head, but I assumed you'd never hear the shot. Turns out you do — or, in my case, it was two shots I heard before everything went black.

Chapter 60

I came to, surrounded by machines making all kinds of beeping and hissing sounds. My pain levels were surprisingly muted, which meant I couldn't really pinpoint what hurt — until I tried to sit up and found it was pretty much everything. As I adjusted to the bright lights in the room, I began to focus on the faces around me. I was pleased to see two friendly faces: Peter Owens and Amelia. Both smiled back at me as I stopped struggling to sit up, prompting Amelia to grab the controller for the electrically operated bed and bring me up into a semi-recumbent position. It was at this point that I saw both Isaiah and Eva standing in the corner. I eyed them suspiciously.

"She can stay, but he needs to leave right now," I said as forcefully as possible, only to hear a weak, raspy voice.

"Settle down, darling. You need to rest," said Amelia from the foot of the bed.

"I think you'll find that you owe your life to him," added Peter Owens.

I had to pause for a minute as my memory of the events in the FBI building slowly returned to my consciousness.

"I doubt that very much," I finally said with as much conviction as I could manage. "I don't remember him doing anything to help us when we needed it," I continued — while, almost simultaneously, starting to recall him flipping the table that allowed us to escape. Perhaps I needed to slow down and get a little more clarity before I continued down this path.

Eva, ever the voice of reason, decided it was time to set the record straight.

"Eli, Isaiah has been working inside Holtzman's organisation for some time. The Bureau had its suspicions about Holtzman for a while, and he was inserted to work undercover. I know you think he sold you out, but I promise you he didn't. I've seen the paperwork — he's legit, the real deal. Everything that was said in the crisis room was recorded by Isaiah. We got all the evidence we needed to convict them."

At this moment in time I didn't have the mental awareness to challenge what Eva was telling me. Given I implicitly trusted her, I was just going to have to take it at face value that she knew what she was talking about.

"Needed? You make it sound like it's not going to happen. Hell, don't tell me the FBI is trying to save face on this one."

Despite feeling pretty groggy, the idea that Holtzman might be getting away with it was enough to sharpen my senses — and my sense of morality.

"No. Holtzman died last night."

Well, that wasn't what I was expecting. I wasn't quite sure how I felt about that little bombshell. He deserved it for being a grade-A arsehole, but I equally felt disappointed that I wasn't going to get to visit him in San Quentin penitentiary.

"Last night? How long have I been out? And, more to the point, how did he die? Please don't tell me he topped himself."

"You've been in an induced coma for four days," said Isaiah as he stepped forward. "And Holtzman died

417

because he had a gun to your head, and your English wit and sarcasm has begun to grow on me. It was either you or him which, on reflection, isn't a choice I'd wish on anyone. I guess time will tell if I did the right thing."

"So I guess that makes us even then?" I asked with a smile, appreciating his sarcasm.

"I guess so," he replied, smiling back.

"At least you've got an IOU from me," said Eva with a smile.

I tried to sit up a little, but the movement caused considerable pain in my back.

"You were very lucky," said Eva, stepping forward to help Amelia move me up the bed. "The bullet in your flank just missed your kidney; otherwise, you would have bled out."

"So why have I been in a coma for four days?"

"Unfortunately, despite your body armour, the bullets Holtzman shot you with fractured your ribs, which caused a pneumothorax and a cardiac tamponade."

"A what?"

"One of your lungs collapsed, and your heart began to fill with blood," said Isaiah, dumbing down the medical stuff for me. "After I shot Holtzman, he collapsed on top of you. By the time I pulled him off, you were covered in blood and unconscious. For a minute I thought you were dead, given how much blood you had on you, but unfortunately you still had a pulse," he grinned, knowing I'd appreciate his newly found sarcastic side.

"Thankfully, Bryan — the security guard we met — somehow heard the shooting and had already got the EMTs heading in our direction. Probably saved your life," said Eva with an ironic grin.

"I take it all back. Someone buy that man a thank-you cake," I said with a chuckle that really hurt.

Eva smiled; everyone else just looked at me with a bemused expression that I translated to mean, "It's OK, it's just the anaesthetic wearing off."

I lay there, staring out of the window for a few minutes, when I suddenly remembered Jessica.

"What happened to Jessica? She was unconscious in the crisis room last time I saw her."

"She's fine," said Isaiah. "She's a few rooms down. Looks like Holtzman pistol-whipped her. She had a small bleed on the brain, but she's going to be fine."

"And was she involved in any of this?"

"Too early to say, to be honest. My gut says she wasn't, and currently there's no evidence to suggest she was. We still haven't had the chance to debrief her yet, so who knows."

I nodded in understanding before moving on to another important question.

"What about my cars?"

"You and your bloody cars," said Amelia, as everyone laughed.

The visitors stayed for another fifteen minutes before finally leaving me and Amelia alone.

"Eli, what have you been up to?"

"Not much," I replied in my typically understated manner.

Epilogue

I remained in hospital for two and a half weeks. During that time, I received visits from several high-ranking FBI officials, the San Francisco mayor, several news crews, and the Jameson family. When I saw on TV a few days earlier that Jameson had been let out of prison, I wondered if he would visit. I was a little surprised to hear he was a free man. After everything Holtzman had revealed, and the fact Isaiah had recorded it all, it seemed inevitable he would have some prison time coming his way. At least he was no longer on trial for double murder.

Despite all the media interest, there was surprisingly little official news from the FBI. It would clearly be a terribly damaging revelation for the Bureau if the full details of Holtzman's activities ever got out. No doubt the lawyers were throwing the "national security" line at anyone who dug too deep or asked the wrong questions.

Sure enough, Jameson, along with Isabella, arrived a few days before I was discharged. Both of them appeared a lot more humble than the last time I'd seen them together. I think the trials of the past few weeks had opened their eyes to a world where they weren't calling the shots. After chatting for ten minutes or so, I learnt that Edwin had struck a deal with the FBI to avoid a costly and embarrassing trial. In exchange for full disclosure of his activities with Holtzman, he had accepted a sentence of life in prison, suspended for twenty years, that basically covered any crime. I wasn't sure how I felt about this. On one hand, it seemed very lenient; on the other, he was revealing the inner workings of one of North America's largest drug-importation rings. The impact was likely to be massive and, I suppose, deserved some kind of reward. There were apparently still some financial repercussions coming his way as well, but I'm sure Isabella could deal with those. From my point of view, I wouldn't be keeping in close contact with them, despite the fact Isabella and Amelia appeared to be getting on like old friends. I was, however, gifted an IOU for basically any favour I'd ever need. I guess getting someone off a double-murder charge had its value.

There were multiple media requests for interviews — which the FBI blocked — and I frequently came across my picture in newspapers and online. I even had a few visits from some Hollywood types seemingly desperate to make a film about how I had single-handedly brought an end to one of the largest drug rings in the country. For the few weeks I was in hospital, I became a local hero, receiving fan mail and some preferential treatment from the nurses.

I tried to get in to see Jessica on several occasions however every time either the doctors or her guards found a reason why now wasn't suitable. I would just have to wait for the official report to find out exactly what her involvement had been.

By the time I was discharged, I couldn't wait to get home. The Feds had booked us first-class seats and promised to arrange shipment for the Shelby as soon as possible. I'd decided to leave the BMW in the States — more specifically with Matteo's cousin — as a form of compensation. After all the drama following the shootout, and the fact I was unconscious for several days, it turns out the FBI had temporarily forgotten about him, meaning he spent a few more days locked up than he should have. I'm sure he could have sued them for something, but I figured a free high-value car would go some way to easing his pain.

Amazingly, I slept on the flight, and as we touched down I woke feeling refreshed. Although Amelia was keen to get me home, I had a hankering to go see Lucas, Abi and the gang down at the museum.

As my phone reconnected, it began to ping and vibrate with far too many messages to read. No doubt there would be more media requests now I was out of the FBI's clutches. Our bags were waiting on the other side of customs and airport staff escorted us out to the concourse and on to the waiting taxis just outside Departures.

"Mr Miller?" asked a young man who had been standing off to the side.

"Who wants to know?"

"If you and your wife would like to follow me, some of my associates would like to have a chat with you. You can leave your bags; my colleague will deal with them," he added, slipping his MI5 credentials back into the inside pocket of his jacket.

THE END

Printed in Dunstable, United Kingdom